one
red
thread

ERNIE WOOD

TYRUS
BOOKS

Copyright © 2014 by Ernie Wood.

Published by
TYRUS BOOKS
an imprint of F+W Media, Inc.
10151 Carver Road, Suite 200
Blue Ash, OH 45242. U.S.A.
www.tyrusbooks.com

ISBN 10: 1-4405-8273-4
ISBN 13: 978-1-4405-8273-8
eISBN 10: 1-4405-8274-2
eISBN 13: 978-1-4405-8274-5

Printed in the United States of America.

10 9 8 7 6 5 4 3 2 1

Library of Congress Cataloging-in-Publication Data

Wood, Ernie,
    One red thread / Ernie Wood.
        pages cm
    ISBN 978-1-4405-8273-8 (hardcover) -- ISBN 1-4405-8273-4 (hardcover) -- ISBN 978-1-
4405-8274-5 (ebook) -- ISBN 1-4405-8274-2 (ebook)
    1. Architects--Fiction. 2. Time travel--Fiction. I. Title.
    PS3623.O62395O54 2014
    813'.6--dc23
                                        2014021989

Cover image © Shutterstock/Joyce Vincent.

This book is available at quantity discounts for bulk purchases.
For information, please call 1-800-289-0963.

For Ruth, Laura, and Emily

Past, present, and future

PROLOGUE

That was the last time I'd ever open the door without making damn sure who was on the other side. But I was woolgathering, thinking about one thing and not the thing before me, when I happened to be walking by. Someone rang the bell, and I turned the knob. Just like we all do. It was an automatic gesture, an innocent gesture, I'd like to think. But it was not a wise gesture.

I looked the old man on the porch up and down as he gave his three-word introduction: "I've been waiting."

The guy was about ninety years old, plainly dressed with a tie but no jacket. Big brogan shoes. For sure, not one of the formal and wary bankers or the rumpled and assertive builders I'm used to seeing in my work as an architect. So in the way I always do, wondering and examining and trying to make order out of things, I stood there searching for another pigeonhole to put him into. I should have been slamming the door, but I stood there gaping and waiting, wordlessly anticipating more from him or an a-ha from myself.

"Mr. McBride." He addressed me, a man not quite half his age, as if I were the senior person, the man in charge, though we both knew that was him.

"Mr. Eddy McBride, I've been watching." He pulled open the screen door. A-ha. Now I knew him. When I was a boy, he'd been the yard man. Long dead, I'd thought.

Back then, this house belonged to my great aunts. The yard man lived outside town, down by the river, and every spring he'd bring his mule to plow the garden. He seemed very old, graying like the whiskers on his mule, deeply wrinkled and burned by the sun, and when he came I always followed. I walked the furrows behind him in my bare feet, breaking the clods that the plow left whole.

"Eddy McBride," he'd called me. "Walter Lee," I'd called him back. There was a touch of protectiveness and a lot of hurt pride in the way he insisted on whole names. Walter Lee, I came to believe, needed his name, and he needed the family that went with it. He needed something no one could take away. But that was just me reading between the lines. Walter Lee never talked about himself. He never asked for anything. Not until now.

"Eddy McBride," the old man repeated. He took hold of my forearm. "Are you ready?"

"Let go of me." I stiffened and pulled against his grip, testing his resolve and making sure I had more strength than a ninety-year-old.

But mostly I was staring the old man in the eye. I was wondering what parts of our shared story he was dredging up. And how in the hell he could still be alive. After all these years.

"It's almost time," he declared.

I was pulling away harder now. Whatever he wanted, I could tell it was nothing good.

"You have to try."

I was still trying to pry loose when Walter Lee paused in his ordering me about and opened his claw. Thinking I was ready to follow, I supposed. Until I realized he was putting me in my place.

Unexpectedly freed, I fell backward, waving my arms at nothing to break my fall and landing hard against the model of a never-built house I'd once been proud to have designed. The balsa wood went flat with barely the sound of a snap.

I sat on the floor, glaring at the old man.

In the open doorway, Walter Lee was backlit against the bright sun outside. It was the kind of image a film might use to portray a ghost, all washed out and white and fuzzy, kind of cheesy and amateurish, if you want to know the truth. But if ghostly was his intention, it was working. I squinted to see him better, but I just couldn't hold my focus.

Walter Lee was real, I was certain of that, but it was as if I could look through him. My eyes kept going to the world behind, which seemed extraordinarily clear considering it was only background. I could have counted the leaves on the big pecan tree twenty yards out in the yard.

"It's your turn," he said.

PART I

*Whatever is has already been,
and what will be has been before*

one

I never was an Eagle Scout, but I'd always tried to be a good scout. That's what people called me when I was a boy and that's how I still liked to think of myself back when all this began. Trustworthy and honest. Good scout. Give me some facts to learn or a job to do and I'd be all over it. I'd study, I'd investigate, and I'd ponder. Then I'd ponder some more. I'd do whatever it took to get the job done, and I'd do the work honestly. Along the way, I'd hope to find a semblance of truth.

Ah, the truth. The truth and I have always had an uncomfortable relationship, but it's not the shortfalls and deceptions you might think. If anything, I have too much, too many truths. I can't resist trying to make sense of how the world works. Find some meaning. And I can't keep my sticky fingers out of the trouble that my searching sometimes brings. Unintended consequences. Not so good for a scout.

Years ago, when we first met, Sheila said truthfulness was what she found appealing in me. After we were married, when she had to live with my pondering and ruminating, she wasn't so sure.

"You're getting ahead of yourself," she'd warn.

"Anticipating my options," I'd counter, as I thought and projected some more.

At that point she'd usually throw something. Okay, it would be something soft or small, a pillow or a magazine. Sheila wouldn't really be angry. At least I don't think so. She just wanted me to stop. The strings of observations I floated could be more than she could stand.

I have to admit, Sheila was often right. I could be a driver barreling into the night so fast I couldn't stop in the distance my headlights illuminated. But I do believe I saw more than most people did. Sure, what I illuminated could be just tiny glimpses, but they could also be full-blown stories. I didn't know how they were connected or what they meant. But I did know where I'd started. I did know family history. And I did have this nagging, ongoing sense that history was directing me from somewhere behind, taking me wherever I was headed.

Examples? You want examples? Sure. Here are a couple of the stories I knew at the beginning. You, all of us, let's sit. Right here on the porch. You listen. You ponder for yourself. I'll be thinking about how the pieces of life go together.

You'll probably see me unconsciously trailing my fingertips along the contours of my nose, the break and the crook I earned about a year after the old man showed up. That's one result of my found truths and missed meanings. Good scout. That's a laugh. But then, the scout's code doesn't say anything about wisdom, does it?

I heard this one told.

It was many decades ago, before dams were built to control flooding on the river that runs through the city, and the rain was falling hard. On a sidewalk downtown, a crowd of mostly men stood ankle-deep, but out in the center of the wide street the water was knee-high and rising. People in the crowd were waving their arms and arguing. "Strong man maybe coulda made it across an hour ago," one of them was saying. "But a tiny woman like that? What in the world possessed her?"

A stout rope had been thrown across the avenue, stretched taut and firmly tied to lampposts. At the center of the flood was a woman, on her knees, clinging. She tried to stand. She fell. A man stepped off the curb, one hand on the rope. The water was moving fast, and he, too, went down. A police officer pulled him back to the sidewalk.

And then, almost out of nowhere, there was my great grandfather. Old Jacob, he was called. Old Jacob, the Confederate veteran. The story goes that this was his sixty-fifth birthday, that he was fastidiously clad in the neatly pressed white suit he always wore, and that he moved with the assurance of a soldier in uniform. He was unstrapping the harness that held a horse to its delivery wagon. He was leading the horse from its traces. He was climbing a bench in front of a café and swinging one leg over the animal's back.

Old man and delivery horse were moving forward, and the crowd of younger onlookers parted without a word.

The flood rippled white with every step, but Old Jacob guided the horse slowly and surely. The horse never lost footing as the pair made their way to the stranded woman who, seeing her rescuer coming, stood shakily, still holding the rope in one hand, stretching for help with the other. In one smooth motion, Old Jacob grabbed the woman's outstretched arm and lifted her to the horse's back. She lay in front of him. She did not try to sit. And when she finally slid to the ground at the sidewalk, the woman was crying from fear, from relief, and with joy.

The police officer rushed to wrap the woman in a blanket, but she did not want to leave the horse. She kept one hand on the animal's neck. She covered her face with the other.

"Look," said Old Jacob. "Even your watch is all right." My great grandfather leaned his head back to better focus as he cradled in his fingertips a small, brooch-style pendant watch she wore pinned to her blouse. "It's still working fine," he said, now leaning his ear closer. "I can hear it ticking."

I lived this one.

"Now listen," my father was saying. We were wandering aimlessly around the grounds of the big Victorian house that my great grandfather, the same Old Jacob, had built and where my great aunts and uncle, Eleanor and Lillian and Hugh, still lived. Daddy stopped at the garden and gave a tug at one of last year's corn stalks. He turned to look behind and sighed. "Boy, are you listening?"

"Yessir." I trotted to catch up.

"No, you're not." My father waited for shame to sink in.

I nodded. A squirrel had caught my attention. He was chattering in the big pecan tree Old Jacob had planted decades before. I squinted and scanned the branches.

My father pulled the dry and spindly remains of corn up by the roots. "Doesn't matter."

No, I didn't imagine it mattered either, but even as an eight-year-old boy I wanted it to. I generally had no clue what Daddy was talking about, but I watched in earnest this time as he pointed across the yard with the knobby bottom of the corn, its dead roots still clinging to a clod of earth. The stalk bent at the middle and the heavy clod end sagged, a divining rod of sorts, but my father wasn't looking for magic. He flung the dried stick as hard as he could, end over end, and as far as he could. It landed just shy of the aunts' compost heap.

"Dead things." It was then that my father pulled the pistol from his pocket.

I was a statue.

Daddy held the pistol straight out, arm's length, sighting along the barrel and aiming at the compost. He shot. Perfect center on a rotting cabbage head.

"I knew what to do with a gun when I was your age," he said, taking a bead on a badly bruised apple but lowering the pistol without shooting. "I also knew what not to do. 'Don't shoot toward the house.' That's what every-one always said."

And with that, he swung toward the house. "Unless, of course, that's what you want to hit."

I heard the pistol pop and pop pop again. I heard glass breaking. And the world was silent.

One parlor window was completely without glass.

Yeah, that one. The window right behind you.

It was all broken out, and inside, the mirror over the fireplace bore an off-center spider web shatter. The bottom half of a vase stood alone. And a McBride family icon, our baseball autographed by Babe Ruth, was gone.

The ball had jumped from its display stand on the mantle, caromed off the wall behind, and taken a high hop when it hit the brick hearth. It came to a lazy rest in the middle of the carpet. I couldn't believe my eyes. He'd shot it! Daddy'd shot the Babe Ruth baseball! I rushed inside and picked it up.

Well, by now all of us here, we've seen that ball a million times. It's almost like the bullet hole is supposed to be there. But that hole was entirely new and it was very frightening to me that day, punctuating the autograph in the middle of Babe Ruth's name, right there at the front end of the R. That tiny blackened circle stared straight at me. I felt as if the pistol were pointed between my eyes.

And when I turned back toward the shattered window with a boy's mil-lion questions—all pointing at the one big "Why?"—I saw my father leaving. And that frightened me, too. Out in the yard, I saw him drop the pistol in the grass. I saw him pass through the quiet shade of the pecan tree. I saw him keep going, a man with a purpose, across the lawn, down the driveway, and to the bus stop at the corner.

I never saw him again.

Life seldom takes the path we think it will, does it? Logic would take us in a straight line, from birth to youth to old age to death. Then it would repeat, generation after generation. But what really happens, I know *I* can't make sense of it. How do you explain a family's descent from heroism to vandalism—hell, to vandalizing your own family legacy—and then this disappearance? Who knows?

Was my father just naturally nuts? Or had something driven him there?

The cat I used to have operated under a similar set of unknown rules. Ike was a little yellow tabby who'd jump and run for no apparent reason. He'd leap straight into the air, pound like a racehorse across the parquet floor in the parlor, round the turn at the front hall, and bound up the stairs. A few minutes later, he'd be quietly nosing around his food bowl in the kitchen.

It's a mystery what Ike felt, but I'm sure it was something. Maybe a flea just took a bite and Ike just took off. Or maybe Ike heard some sound I couldn't hear or sensed some energy I couldn't know. Maybe Ike saw something coming, something from the back or the side, something out of the corner of his eye, in his peripheral vision.

I needed to know what Ike knew and what everyone else, Old Jacob and my father and the rest of them, knew. I thought that maybe if I could honestly examine every detail and understand every connection, maybe then I could chart the path of events. One history, one present, one surefire future. All I needed was the something that Ike saw. The only question was where I should look for it—and what direction it would make me run when it bit.

Backward. For a while, looking and running where the McBrides had come from, chasing family mysteries and my own compulsions, these were my only choices. Assuming I had any choices at all. And for a while it worked. Until it stopped working. Truths, you know, can have disastrous outcomes.

When I ran into history, I met people and I witnessed events and I did see connections. I was one of those connections.

What was it like, people used to ask. What was it like visiting the past? I had my stock answers. "I get wet when it rains." That was my favorite. What I meant was that the past is real. It's still out there.

Old Jacob and my family, they were all out there, and they were almost waiting for my arrival. For me, for Sheila, for a childhood friend named Libby. For Tim, who was our business partner at the time. Tim, who punched me and broke my nose. Those of us in the present, we were sometimes delighted, occasionally enlightened, too much frightened, regularly pissed off, often hurt—and strangely united by what I discovered.

But I'm getting ahead of myself.

two

Time passed. A little more than thirty years since my father shot our baseball. A little more than twenty years back from where we sit today. By then I was living in the Victorian house myself

It was a July day. I was out in my garden, in the same spot where my great aunts had had theirs. And I was worried about my cucumber vines. They were getting awfully leggy, wandering around in the dirt and drooping their tiny fruits dangerously close to the ground. So I did something I hoped no one would see.

I dragged over an old set of steps I'd recently torn off the back porch and replaced, and I dropped them in the corner of the garden. The idea was to make a trellis. It was an embarrassingly ugly trellis. It was a horrible thing for an architect to even consider. Or maybe it was good. Maybe it was funky sculpture. Outsider art. One of Duchamp's "readymades." Could have been an heir to his bicycle wheel. Or just a quick, easy fix. Either way, when the cukes were big and the vines were leafy . . . .

But you know, that was me, always overthinking. I just needed to drop the damn steps. There was no cosmic meaning, no significant truth in an upside down flight of ratty old steps.

Except that the cosmos really did have meaning, its truths really were significant, and it all really was coming my way. In only a few minutes, a shiny new Land Rover would pull into the driveway and bump into the potholed space beside my faded old pickup truck. And a tall woman of about my age would stand on my front porch, just as the old man had done. Only she'd be a lot more appealing. "This is wonderful," she'd say, "really wonderful."

Now over the years I've looked back on that day often, and I've always wondered how old Walter Lee knew this was going to happen. You know me. Always searching. I'll take just about any idea or fact or event and give it consideration. I've thought it could have been just a coincidence, but that was too easy. I've thought Walter Lee could have been psychic, but that was too weird. So what I finally decided was something much simpler. I decided Walter Lee must have been reading the society pages of the newspaper.

When he read she was coming back to town, I figured, he'd come straight-away to my front door. Planted the seed. And here we were, less than a week later. The opportunity Walter Lee had been waiting for had arrived. Long ago, Walter Lee had known me. He'd known Eddy the boy. And he knew just how I'd react as a man.

Mary Elizabeth Peacock, my greatest childhood pal and always just Libby Peacock to me, was peering into a window beside the front door. She knocked as expectantly as Walter Lee, then stepped back to the yard. She scanned the gables and dormers and chimneys that angled in all directions from the big Victorian house's roof. "Wonderful," she cried.

I was struggling to tie the last of my cucumber vines to the steps, hoping to finish before she could see what I was doing. No such luck. "Eddy!" she called. "And it's wonderful to see *you!*" Libby came with long strides across the lawn. She gave me a big familiar hug, but I knew she was eyeing my trellis over my shoulder as if it were some mess a little boy had made.

I hadn't seen Libby in years, though I'd heard a lot. She'd grown up, grad-uated from sorority to society, moved away, married money, divorced. The usual thing. But of course it was our childhood that mattered to me. And the two of us, we went way back. Back to when I was a baby.

It's a funny story, really.

Libby was four when I was born, and for some reason, maybe because she was an only child, she appointed herself my big sister. When I arrived home from the hospital, she'd sit quietly and watch my mother nurse me. She'd help with my baby baths. When I was sleeping she'd stand outside the nurs-ery and tell everyone to be quiet. Then one day, when I was still only four or five days old, she peeked over the top of my basinet and started screaming.

My mother called the doctor, moved the basinet and my little yellow self closer to the window, and took me for long sunny walks in the baby carriage. Newborn jaundice was not a big deal and it was easily cured. But Libby told everyone she'd saved my life.

Our parents would joke about it over drinks or at dinner. "Remember when Libby saved Eddy's life?" But Libby wouldn't let the story go. For years, she reminded me about what she'd done, or what she believed she'd done, and I was into the second grade before I figured out that it was all a stupid, childish misunderstanding.

By then, it was too late. And it was less funny.

Whatever Libby asked, I still felt I owed her a debt. Libby would tell her story about my turning yellow, and it would be impossible for me to tell her no. I was a teenager before I figured out I'd had it exactly backward. Libby may have acted like the boss, but she needed me more than I needed her. She was fighting life's pains and disappointments not by rescuing herself but by looking for another person to rescue. Libby needed to set things right, make the world the way she wanted it to be. And if it didn't all work out, well, she'd run. I remember those times. It could take hours to find her, but we always did. My debt may have been meaningless, but Libby was my friend and I had to help. A scout, after all, is loyal.

"Come on," Libby announced that day she showed up at the Victorian. "I've got some money I need to spend that used to belong to a certain cheating ex-husband." Then, turning before I had a chance to respond, she began crossing the lawn to the Land Rover. "Come on," she urged. "I'll show you what I'm thinking."

As we passed the oversized wind chime I'd hung from my great grandfather's pecan tree, Libby gave one of its steel tubes a shove. Colliding with its companions, it produced a deep-throated baritone. "Can you imagine the racket we'd have made with this when we were kids?" She elbowed me in the ribs. "Bring something to draw on."

I dutifully grabbed a sketchbook from the cab of my truck and climbed into the Land Rover beside her.

For a moment, I considered returning her elbow poke, but I thought better of it. Libby was acting like the rambunctious girl she'd once been, but I wondered who or what she was now. Underneath, people sometimes remain the same as they were as children. Other times, events tear and hurt, twist and reshape so deeply there's no way to stay the same.

In the architecture business, I was used to people who forged ahead. I was used to people on a roller-coaster ride through cities, relationships, and business ventures. Professionally, at least, I knew how to be comfortable with whatever ride Libby was on. I knew how to deal with people who thought they knew, or wanted others to think they knew, exactly what they wanted.

So for Libby, I'd be the boy from the old neighborhood when she needed me to be, and I'd be an accomplished architect when she needed that. Whichever, I'd do her bidding, and it wouldn't bother me. It was an odd balance of humility and ego, but there was some of each in me. Maybe it was a scout's balance. A scout is supposed to be kind, friendly, and helpful—and be damn cheerful about it, too—not just trustworthy and honest.

"Yeah," she said, still eyeing the wind chime and absently repeating herself, "like when we were kids." But that's as far as Libby went. Stopping at the foot of the driveway to wait for passing traffic, she looked up and down the street and wrinkled her forehead. Libby appeared as concerned with how much everything had changed as with how much it was the same.

Libby looked good, very good. Big-city stylish. Ready to impress on her arrival home. I may have been a small-city guy in chinos, running shoes, and a knit golf shirt—my carefully cultivated, slightly rumpled, casual-in-the-midst-of-hard-work, schlub-while-not-really-a-schlub, aging preppy persona—but the designer in me could spot her fashion sense a mile away.

Libby, though, Libby was more than stylish, and she sported even more than society demanded. There was a certain independence about her. Usually, this kind of character shows in the eyes, but I could see it in Libby's hair. At the time, we were in our early and mid-forties, but Libby's long blonde hair, several inches below shoulder-length, was graying almost to white. She was aging well, she knew it, and she wanted everyone to agree.

So to independence, add self-assurance. And this made me very happy.

Because if Libby was doing what I thought she was doing, offering me a design project, I felt pretty certain she would not be one to demand the hand-holding so many clients required. I could do without the social obligations and the role of personal confidant. I wanted to keep the dinners with her envious friends and the crying on the shoulder when painters screwed up a color to a minimum. I just wanted to do the work. I hoped Libby could cut out the bullshit the way Libby the boss of us kids had always done.

"Tell me where you've been," I said as the Land Rover crossed the river and headed through downtown.

"How long have you lived in the Victorian?" she replied. Libby took a turn around the courthouse.

"The aunts died," I answered, keenly aware that she had avoided my question. "Ten, fifteen years ago."

"Eleanor and Lillian? Eleanor and Lillian!" she cried. "I remember when we were little, going over there." Libby craned her neck at a street sign. She seemed a bit confused by the growth of trees in her absence, but she didn't offer our destination and I didn't ask.

"Eleanor and Lillian. My great aunts. The maiden ladies," I confirmed.

"What did your parents and those old ladies talk about anyway? Hours and hours, sitting in the parlor, drinking sweet tea, talking. Old family stories, I guess. And you and your brother. The two of you used to get into that porch hammock and screech like monkeys. I thought you were going to flip out and land on your heads for sure."

I shook my head and held my tongue. I could tell now where Libby and the Land Rover were headed, and it was not making me happy. We were still blocks away, but there was nowhere else we could be going, not in this part of town, except the scene of our childhood. But a scout doesn't say no. All I could do was wait, watch, and listen.

Libby was taking me back to where we'd started out so happy the way children do, and back to where we'd ended up so hurt in ways children never expect. Back to where our families fell apart and no one understood why.

Libby and I arrived at the street we'd once shared, with its 1920s bungalows, big shady trees, and, in Libby's and my day, plenty of families. Old houses and young children, that's what everyone had. Libby wanted to know if it looked familiar. "You know," I said, looking away, staring blankly out the Land Rover's window, "I never come to the old neighborhood anymore."

Years ago, I'd decided that the best way to come to terms with the events that occurred here was to cut myself off from this place. For all my success in business, for all the houses and stores and schools and offices my architecture practice had designed, I'd disengaged from this chunk of my hometown. The city still had only a few hundred thousand people, but it had grown big enough that I could successfully avoid the old neighborhood and any people I'd known growing up.

I had no family left here. My father had disappeared the day he shot the Babe Ruth baseball. My mother had moved to Florida as soon as I went away to college. That family descent I mentioned, the one from heroism to vandalism to escape, the one that nearly destroyed the family itself, well, maybe it was complete. Aside from me, the McBrides were gone, as far as the present-day world was concerned.

But Libby was in high spirits, and she gave me a you-know-what-this-is-going-to-be-about elbow poke as we pulled to a stop in front of a shuttered building.

It was the old florist shop and greenhouse, once proudly fancy and Mediterranean and tropical in its style, the one Libby's father used to run. A happy fellow and grand fixture in the neighborhood, never a stranger to anyone he met, he'd suddenly gone quiet when we were children, retreated into himself, and died when I was still in high school and Libby was away at college. Drowned, if you want the details. Some said it was an accident, others a suicide. Her mom had long since remarried.

Libby was well beyond family grief. At least that's what I assumed. She didn't say a word about her dad, but unknown to me until just now, the shop had been hers for years.

I was sad, as both a friend and an architect, to see how Libby had neglected the place while she was off living her other life. Big chunks of stucco had rotted and fallen away. The frames of the metal casement windows were rusted. Here and there the shop's tile roof was missing pieces. I was sure it leaked.

But Libby was happy. She had an idea.

Libby wanted to renovate the shop and the greenhouse. She wanted a classy townhouse, a showstopper. "This space . . ." Libby was saying as she opened a padlock on the front door. "You ought to be able to make something really special."

It looked like Libby was still out to rescue things, and that was probably good, but I remained quiet. I was waiting and watching and listening, pondering and examining and turning possibilities over and around in my thoughts. I couldn't say no. But there was a lot to consider here.

You know the saying, right? The one about an unaddressed subject being an elephant in the room. No matter how hard you try to ignore it, you simply can't. It's too damn big. It's always in the way. Well, that was certainly true here in the florist shop and here in the old neighborhood. Libby may have had definite ideas about the new townhouse she wanted, but as she and I walked the empty building, I had my own ideas, and they were called bad memories. Libby and I definitely had an elephant in there. It was wide and tall, big-assed huge and virtually impossible to get around.

three

The next thing I knew, we were in a rooftop pub downtown drinking beer. I introduced my old friend to Sheila and Tim, and the three of them looked all of a piece, Sheila and Tim coming directly from the office where we were partners and owners of the practice, and Libby in her big-city style. I was the odd man out in my garden-grubbing chinos, but that was okay. You could be whoever you wanted here, sitting at a picnic table under a family of green awnings. The roof was an ideal place to rest from the world and a grand place to consider what life should be.

Tim and I took long pulls on our beers. Sheila simply wet her lips with foam, then set her glass on the table. Libby stared at the awning underbellies as if she'd seen the light. ("Wonderful!") As if she'd just then decided this city was the place she loved most and aimless talk was how she wanted to spend her days. ("So wonderful!")

"Now tell us," Tim jumped in. He was gently cradling his already empty glass, fingers of both hands interlaced around it, as he ventured an introduction to Libby. Tim was one of those gentle giant types. He stood six foot four and he'd had a time in the basketball limelight when we were in college together. Then suddenly, in mid-career, he'd dropped out of the program for the more bohemian life of architecture. Ever since, it had been as if Tim were trying to make himself smaller and retreat into his own quiet background place, a bench warmer, as it were, rather than his formerly soaring, high-scoring, flamboyantly long-haired, forward-playing self.

"Tell us where you've been." His request was the most gentle of suggestions. "Tell us the real Libby."

"And the real Tim." Libby delivered her most self-assured smile.

I caught a little gleam in their eyes. Tim, a bachelor all these years, was flirting. It was a shy, tentative, middle-aged flirt, but a flirt nonetheless. Libby was fully receptive in an unmistakable happy-to-be-home and happy-to-have-met-you way. And that was fine. Fine that Tim and Libby were off in their own world. After the place Libby had taken me, I was somewhere else, too. I was only lightly aware of their conversation.

Tim was painting a portrait of his Deep South childhood. "There were always June bug skins stuck in the screen doors," he was saying. "Humidity so thick you could smell the houses rotting."

He signaled to the waiter for a couple more beers.

Libby, she was telling tales of our old neighborhood. In the front room of her parents' house, she knelt on the sofa they kept pushed up under the window, rested her chin on the sofa back, and waited for her dad to come down the street from the shop. "That was our evening routine," I heard her explain.

At the far end of the bar, the band was running its sound check.

I was hovering my pen over my open sketchbook.

And Sheila was giving me the evil eye. I knew what she was thinking. From years of experience and my uneasy preoccupation there at the pub, she knew I'd been revisiting and worrying about some very unhappy times.

I lowered pen to paper, a nervous architect drawing what he knew too well.

My bedroom was on the second floor, in the front with a dormer window, and my parents' room was across the hall. The pen worked slowly across the page. Below my bedroom was the dining room. The living room was under my parents' room. The back porch . . . .

I wadded up the sketch.

The back porch was where my older brother, Stan, and I had so often played. I always remembered—though I don't know why—one scorching summer day when the back steps were too hot for bare feet. I must have been about three and Stan about seven. He put on our father's galoshes and flapped like a big-footed clown down to the above-ground swimming pool my parents had squeezed into our tiny backyard. Stan was the ingenious one.

Stan was the one who figured out all the Army insignia so the kids in the neighborhood would have the right patches on their shirts when we played war. He was the one who hit home runs when we had a baseball game in someone's front yard. And when he did, he never slung his bat carelessly as he ran to first base, never endangered any of the other players. He was the boy the young Girl Scouts hoped would answer our door when they came peddling cookies. Stan was the clever one, the considerate one, the popular one.

I stared blankly at the table before me. It was carved with initials and dates, even complete sentences and a joke or two, but I didn't see any of that. None of this could drag me away from the memory.

Stan was dead; he had been for more than thirty years. I thought I'd pretty well put this behind me, but with Libby's return to town, now I couldn't stop thinking about him.

A week into the seventh grade, twelve-year-old Stan jumped off the school bus and was killed by a hit-and-run driver. Libby and I were still on the bus, still in our seats. I was eight and she was also twelve. Her birthday, in fact, was only six weeks behind my brother's. The two of them were usually inseparable.

But on this day, Libby and I must have had some kind of after-school activities. Maybe I was going to a friend's house; maybe she had a piano lesson. I really don't remember why we weren't getting off with Stan, but I wished to God we had. Maybe we could have saved my brother.

So the bus had stopped—lights flashing, everything legal about it—on the same street Libby and I had visited earlier that day.

From where the bus stood, the McBride and Peacock houses were a few doors down in one direction. The florist shop was a few doors down in the other.

And no one, not Libby or me or the bus driver or any of the other kids, no one saw Stan bolt for home. No one saw the car run him down and keep going. As soon as the bus driver opened the door, he'd turned away to tell some misbehaving kids to be quiet. There were no mothers waiting for their children that day, no mailmen on their rounds, no yard men trimming shrubs. It should have been a normal day. But the car didn't even slow down.

Now, on the pub's rooftop, I took a sip of beer and forced a swallow to keep from crying. When I looked up, I saw that Libby had unwadded my sketch and was carefully spreading it flat on the table.

"I'm sorry," she said, looking at the floorplan. How many times, I wondered, had she been in my house? Shit, every day, when we were little. Playing with Stan and me. Then she looked up, her eyes meeting mine. "I think about him, too," she said.

"I thought I could . . ." I began. "We were all very young. So much time has passed, I should be used to it now."

Beside Libby, Tim shrank into his background place and reached for Sheila's untouched beer.

"And you still want to do this?" Sheila asked. She was incredulous. "You still want to live there?" Libby and Tim and I all turned in her direction.

Sheila had a talent for this, for nailing what everyone else was thinking but was unwilling to say.

"The shop is what I have," replied Libby. "Now I can make this place right." Sheila, avoiding my eyes as much as Libby had sought them, stared at her lap. I knew Sheila was intensely unhappy at the talk of my brother, but Sheila was Sheila. She may have had strong opinions, but she also knew when to avoid making a scene.

Libby turned back toward me. "They never found the driver, did they?"

"No, they didn't," I managed to say. The police had looked. I have to assume they tried in a diligent and professional manner. I suppose they did whatever they could, as much as they knew how. But they never found the driver and they never found the car. Into thin air. Gone. All they found was the dead boy.

"I always wanted something like your family," Libby said, taking a different angle but not leaving the topic completely. She must have had second thoughts about bringing up Stan, though I could tell she didn't really want to talk about anything else.

"You had it," I replied. "Yours was just different."

"Yeah," she agreed. Libby let her thoughts float somewhere above us. She didn't need to say more, not for me. I knew about her family, how Stan's death seemed to affect the Peacocks as much as the McBrides. Mr. Peacock had taken me under his wing like I was his own after my father shot at the family homestead and disappeared. I guess Daddy was angered by some McBride family responsibility he felt for the death of his first-born son. But a sadness also infected the Peacock household. I knew Libby was thinking about all of this.

"Daddy's gone and so, in her own way, is Mother," Libby finally said, "but I think family is really what's bringing me back here."

Well, yes and no. It pulls and it repulses. For me, family was a bittersweet thing I usually thought I could handle, sometimes discovered I couldn't, but always knew I should understand better. I could stay out of the old neighborhood all I wanted, but like Libby, I had to admit that family was what had been keeping me in this city. I could never leave the place where my brother had died, especially while the mystery of his death remained.

"You have to try," old Walter Lee had said, and it was looking more and more like he'd been right. I'd known for years that sooner or later the mystery of Stan's death would return and that I'd have no way to avoid it. Maybe I'd even solve it. The old man was a prophet, I suppose. A guide of some sort. Or was he a hypnotist?

Hell, Walter Lee was a pusher. He'd waited patiently until he'd found my gateway drug, which turned out to be Libby. Follow the leader. Hide and seek. When we were kids, Libby'd always been the one to organize games. Mother, May I? We'd all be in and out of backyards, kids ducking under fresh washing hung on clotheslines, roller-skating up and down and around the block. Then up and down and around again.

So that day at the pub I resumed sketching.

I could tell myself it was for the professional opportunity that Libby's job presented, or the obligation to cheer an old friend who'd hit a rough patch in her life. I could claim it was a way to rescue an architectural artifact for the present and the future, just as Libby would want it. I could convince myself, on an academic sort of level, that I wanted to know more about my family story. The one thing I did not want to admit was that I was failing, and failing very rapidly, at maintaining the equilibrium and distance from my painful childhood that I'd tried so hard over the years to maintain.

I was being pulled hard by everything that had come before, by the family and friends I'd avoided for so long. Maybe I did need to make amends, to leave something good at the site of my brother's horrible death. Damn. The past was there. Right in front of the shop was where my brother died, where the car dragged his body and where he came to rest. And now that I'd returned to the scene, I was there to stay. Painful and difficult as this wrestling match with the elephant of Stan's death was sure to be, I couldn't say no.

I handed Libby a quick sketch of the greenhouse. "Work in progress," I apologized.

"But I like it."

I immediately started another. "I think I can do something with that old place," I said. Sad history or no sad history, I thought. Obligation to Libby or no obligation. This was where I needed and wanted to be.

Libby, the girl from down the street, Libby, my old pal, reached across the table and punched me in the arm. "So wonderful!" Her punch glanced off lightly, hardly hurting the muscle but lifting the spirit big time.

Sheila glowered.

"I don't think you should take this job," Sheila said later as we prepared for bed. Buttoning my pajamas, I turned, deflating quickly and suddenly on the defensive. Sheila was already in her nightgown, sitting on the edge of the mattress and aggressively rubbing lotion on her legs.

"No?" I asked.

"No." Sheila squirted more lotion onto her palm. Ike the cat, who'd been sitting beside her, jumped to the floor. Ike never liked that splurchy sound. "Too much history," Sheila explained. "Too much something."

"Something," I mumbled. "Not much of a reason."

Since the pub, I'd been thinking about my brother, about Libby when we were young, about all those old things, of course. But Libby'd got my mind going in two directions, into the past and into the future simultaneously, so I'd also been trying hard to leave the past and convince myself of the good part, of opportunities for the future. That's where Sheila always put her attention. "You should have relaxed," I told Sheila. "Finished that beer."

"The firm has other jobs. Bigger jobs that will pay a lot more money and cause a lot fewer headaches." Sheila put the cap back on the lotion. "And I can't."

"You haven't seen this place." I was really trying now. Trying to make this my new focus. "Libby is bringing us something that's very, very cool. This one's not about the money. This is something that can make our name." I paused to let the conversation catch up with my racing thoughts. And to let my thoughts catch up with the conversation. "What do you mean 'can't'?"

We did it all the time, this ignoring what had just happened, changing the topic, pretending there was no disagreement even while we were still arguing. Sheila'd begin with her "I've-heard-it-all-before-and-I-don't-want-to-hear-it-again" attitude and I'd launch my "I'll-understand-what-I'm-thinking-after-I-take-the-time-to-talk-it-through" response. We'd both be so assured we were right (isn't everyone, when an argument begins?), but it wouldn't be long before we'd reach a point, as we had at the pub, when we'd start pulling our punches. Finally, we'd quit the confrontation altogether.

It's hard to imagine two approaches that were more incompatible. Sheila would narrow her focus, and I'd feel hemmed in. I'd turn up some new thing to ponder, and that would drive Sheila bonkers. I could see how my ever-expanding discussions would annoy a person who wanted to wrap things up and move on, but at least the places our arguments went were usually the truth. I don't believe we lied to each other. And that was important.

Our indirect, punch-pulling style of sparring had kept the peace for years, but of course, it never really solved anything. We always wound up doing what we damn well wanted to do or believing what we damn well wanted to believe. But that's so often the human condition. Listening but not changing. Was avoiding a lie enough if we never agreed on the truth? Were we really as okay with each other as we thought?

I repeated: "What do you mean 'can't'?"

So Sheila and I sparred for a minute or two more. This time it was about whether or not she'd tell. Of course I wanted to know. I always did. She finally gave in.

"I can't drink," she said, "because I'm pregnant."

The hairs stood up on the back of my neck and my eyes went straight to her belly. Was she kidding? After all these years? I could feel the blood rising to my face. Now my scalp was tingling. It was tingling wildly.

Sheila was of middling to average height, five foot five, with the slim build of the runner she'd been for years. Now all I could think of was the image of her carrying a bowling ball out in front the way some very in-shape and athletic women do. (Tim, after a couple of drinks, would note when we announced our news that while pregnancy changed some women's bodies entirely, he expected Sheila would look like "a string with a knot.")

The prospect of carrying a baby/ball/knot did finally solidify Sheila's long-time status as our nurturing earth mother, the one who took care. Even if earth mothers—at least in the eyes of children—usually are a bit softer and a lot taller. Sheila'd be a great mom, though on that night, uncharacteristic of observant me, I just couldn't articulate how. Not yet. I had to peel myself off the ceiling first.

"We need to be thinking about the future." Sheila matter-of-factly turned away and turned out the light. Punctuation added. Discussion over. No visible belly to ponder, though on my part there was scalp tingling to spare.

Changing the subject always worked. I guess this was how we wound up pregnant. Sheila wanted a baby. I didn't disagree; I just wasn't sure. We never really tried to have one. We just quit trying not to, if you know what I mean. And here we were, forty and pregnant. There wasn't much more to say on the topic other than to cheer. "Huzzah! "Wowie-zowie!" Or perhaps a polite "Well done!"

But nothing more coherent. Nothing more specific. Not until the fact sank in deeper.

Sheila must have already thought the pregnancy through, because when she did speak she was still on her other topic, still sparring in the dark, over there on her side of the bed. "You reject this job," she said. I could hear her pulling the sheet up over her shoulders. "And we can move our practice and our lives ahead. You accept this job, and it's something we'll be dealing with for a long time."

I just lay there, tingling and worrying, already aiming toward what we both knew would be an exciting new life (wowie-zowie!) and knowing we should avoid what Sheila was warning could be a horrible mistake.

Maybe five minutes passed.

Sheila again: "And I don't want to hear any more about car accidents and dead children."

four

The storm that blew through the city that evening began with no rain, just wind. It was a wind so strong it woke me. I opened my eyes in the darkened room, and the stoutest and oldest limbs in the tree outside our window were swinging wildly.

When the rain did come, it started slowly, making hard, individual pings on our roof. The rain speeded, slowed, speeded up again. Now it had an even pattern. Now the sound was coming in waves.

When lightning struck, it was so close the shock wave set off a neighbor's car alarm. Somewhere outside a dog began to bark. Here in the house, Ike ran. I wrapped an arm around Sheila, gently and carefully, right at her small and not-yet-showing pregnant belly, ready for what would happen next.

Then, surprisingly, I fell back asleep. The noise of the rain had reached a steady state, one prolonged musical note, as if the storm were one giant raindrop enveloping the world. I slept and I dreamed that damn dream. No car accidents and dead children. This was another thing that had been scaring me for years.

___

In my dream, there is a flood gauge, a white painted post at the intersection of creek bank and roadside, and it measures the water running over the road at one foot deep. Through the rain, fifteen or twenty yards downstream, I can see a swept-away car of some indeterminate year and model. It is stuck on a shallow sand bar. It rocks gently from side to side in the rising water.

The driver is waving his arms through his open window. Signaling for help. He leans farther through the window and looks uncertainly to the front and back. Look up! He does, and he spots low-hanging branches.

Now the man sits like a window washer. His legs are still inside, but from buttocks to head he is outside. Maybe he is reaching for the branches. Maybe he is signaling again for help. Most likely, he is in a panic.

I look at the flood gauge. Water up another foot.

The car shifts slightly, and the driver searches the roof for a handhold. There is none.

The car shifts again, turns clockwise from its tentative mooring, and begins a slow float.

The man is still halfway out the window, clinging precariously to the smooth roof, when the car heaves and slowly, sickeningly slowly, begins to roll.

And I'm surprised. Now the man appears calm. He sits up straight, looks across the water at me. He raises his right hand to his brow and delivers a salute.

Then, as the car continues its roll, he disappears under the waves.

Upside down, the car pauses, its tires pointing toward the sky, its belly exposed. A wave of muddy water washes over the vehicle. The car resumes its roll. Passenger side up. Roof. Driver's side. The man is gone. The car floats another twenty yards downstream, bumps the base of a cypress tree, and rocks back to an upright position. Water pours from the empty driver's window.

———————

I woke to bright sun and no wife. No cat either. Sheila was up early and off to work. Efficient, I hoped, not still distant, not put out by my behavior the previous evening, my reappearing feelings about my family and my dead brother. Ike was out. Just out, I assumed, the way cats so often are. In the kitchen, Sheila had left only a little juice, but the coffee carafe was full. Pregers! She must have been off coffee as well as booze. Baby on the way! "Sheila, pregnant Sheila," I chanted. "Sheila Bedelia!" I added that old Irish name. It means "strength." Mother of my child, that's her.

As for myself, I needed to be a little childlike and playful that morning. I needed something to push away the drowning man.

"Ikey-doo!" I called. I'd be feeling more playful if I could find the cat. I needed someone to talk to and Ike made a good audience. He didn't talk back or give me disapproving looks like Sheila. But Ike had disappeared more completely than Sheila ever did. I leaned close to the window and scanned the length of the porch, then looked out to the yard and up into the trees. Ike usually stayed pretty close to the house, mostly where we could see him, on the porch or by the garden. He must have been really spooked by the storm. So I went searching. "Ikey-doo!"

Looking for Ike was really a very pleasant task. I always enjoyed walking the property that surrounded this old house, the full two acres of it. Hell of a big lot for the city, a place where I could just walk, look, listen, ponder, and lose myself. It was something I'd done for years.

When I was a boy and my aunts, Eleanor and Lillian, lived here, I'd visit often and roam the land freely. I'd crack open nuts from the pecan tree. I'd climb up and down the dry creek bed at the side of the property, and I'd slip and slide in the mud there after rains. This particular day, after the night's rain, I needed to be careful about mud. But it had been great fun for an eight- or nine- or ten-year-old. This land was also a place for contemplation. I'd sit quietly at the grave of my family's long-ago dog—"Gene, a faithful friend"— who died in 1931. And this land was where I seriously began to draw.

I drew whatever caught my eye. Birds, snakes, a neighbor's dog, they all found their way into my sketchbooks. And there was something about the aunts' vegetable garden, that large patch where I later planted my own garden, that I found fascinating. I examined every detail. My eye followed the intricate way the tomato plants twined together. I committed the patterns to memory and recreated them with my pencil. I paid attention. Scout's attention.

Just like I was paying attention on my search for Ike. (Well, I confess, my mind did jump to other topics. I pictured Eddy the Scout helping Sheila the Pregnant Lady across the street. Pregnant! Imagine that! But wandering in my thoughts was usual for me.)

I'd already looked inside the old carriage house at the head of the drive-way, under the Victorian's porch, in our neatly trimmed shrubbery, and in our weedy back lot when I emerged from the stand of trees that bordered the now running creek.

Like the mornings after so many storms, when the rain has washed the air clean, the world seemed different that day. Sounds were clearer. I could hear the voice of each little singing bird. Smells were sharper. The rising perfume of honeysuckle was everywhere. And the air was crisper. I could feel the tini-est shifts in movement, density, and pressure. The air touched me firmly, a hand placed at my back or on my face.

For sure, this day was something new.

Then there was a clang of metal on metal and a clicking of something ratcheted, and what I saw was something old.

I saw the man I'd dreamed about the night before. It was Libby's father, her long-dead father. He was steadying an extension ladder while a teenage boy climbed toward the roof of the porch that wrapped the house's first story.

Strangest thing, this daydream, this woolgathering, this new place for paying attention. I remembered this tiny bit of my younger days well. But what I was seeing was as real as if I'd been standing there again, returned to the day it actually happened.

It was during my early high-school years. I was sixteen, and as I climbed, I was telling our neighbor, pontificating really, about old houses. Budding architect and budding obsessive observer, I was. I pulled a hammer from my tool belt and eyed the damaged gutter. I'd wondered for the longest time how those big dents got there, and I'd long felt compelled to repair them.

"Dents aren't so important. They don't stop the water," Mr. Peacock was saying, looking up from where he steadied the ladder's foot.

"Dents stop leaves," my teenage self corrected, looking side to side along the roofline. "And leaves stop the water. It's a chain reaction."

The boy extracted ten or twelve nails and the damaged section sagged. "I've got to fix this damage, " the boy said, wrenching the old gutter free and dropping it carefully so it wouldn't hit the neighbor. "I've got to make this old house better than it was."

Without another word, Mr. Peacock raised his hand and gave a salute. Then he handed up a length of new gutter.

I remained at the tree line, separated from the scene by my aunts' garden, pondering the pair of salutes I'd witnessed, one from the bottom of a ladder and the other from the door of a floating car. And I felt again the bond that Mr. Peacock and I had shared after my brother died and my father left.

On my part, the bond had eased the double-barreled brother and father loss that defined my growing up. My neighbor's presence had given a lonely boy the guidance to move on to whatever professional and personal success I'd achieved. Architecture practice, marriage, and now an impending child. But on his part, our bond seemed only to intensify some sadness and some very deep regret. Some pain that wouldn't let go or go away. Even at sixteen, I sensed that in helping me, my neighbor not only felt his own pain but somehow magically and tragically transferred the weight of my hurt to his own shoulders.

Once, Mr. Peacock had been a teasing jokester, a dapper gent with a pencil moustache, a man always on stage. Whenever Stan and I went over to the greenhouse—that exotic, thick, humidity-sweet, misty jungle that was a favorite playground for all the neighbor kids—he'd issue a booming "Hello, girls!" We'd feign outrage. "We're not girls!" As proof, we'd rub our hands vigorously across the burr of our crew-cut heads.

The profound sadness that later overcame Mr. Peacock wiped away the joking. "Oh. I'm sorry!" Mr. Peacock used to correct himself when we were little. "Boys!" Stan and I would grin with vindication. But those days were gone with the rest of childhood. The day Mr. Peacock had helped me with the gutter was one of many times he tried to substitute some kind of wisdom and some kind of presence for jokes that weren't so funny anymore. Now the neighbor man and whatever wisdom he was trying to impart to a boy had been gone for years as well.

On the ladder at the Victorian house, teenage Eddy took a new section of gutter offered up by Mr. Peacock, raised it straight in the air, then tipped it toward his own brow in a salute to the man. He looked like a giant robot with an unbending arm, like something from a science-fiction film a boy his age would have liked. It was a sweet little scene—until thunder rolled in the distance. The boy raised the metal half pipe higher, as high as his arms could reach, and waggled it back and forth in the rising wind. Showing off, stretching for humor amid danger, defying the gods the way immortal teenagers always do.

"You shouldn't do that," said the man.

Thunder rolled closer, and though the boy really hadn't had time to respond, hadn't had time to lower the dangerous metal even if he'd wanted, Mr. Peacock began shouting as if the boy had disobeyed. "Stop it!"

The boy looked down, frozen, still holding the gutter high.

"Get down, Eddy, get down! Hurry!" Mr. Peacock shook the ladder and shook it hard. "Get down!" The top end of the gutter began to wave in wild circles. "Get down!"

And under Mr. Peacock's breath: "Oh, God." A simple little prayer. Or a gasp of hopeless desperation.

Then the thunder rolled again, and this time it was farther away, skirting the boy, the man, the old house, and the city. The boy now seemed unsure what all the fuss was about, but he complied with the man's order. He regained control of the waving gutter, set it down at the edge of the roof, and descended.

All's well that ends well, I suppose, but what I'd just witnessed was the sort of adolescent stupidity that lives forever in memory. Courting thunderstorm danger and upsetting a man who was only trying to help. It's so damn embarrassing. Over by the edge of the garden, my adult self looked away, searching for some relief from the teenage dopiness that none of us want to admit to but that all of us, or the boys among us at least, regularly committed.

That was when I heard a rustling under the trellis, under the old steps. It was Ike. He'd found a safe little kitty house. "Ikey!" I cried. "My friend!" I scooped the yellow tabby into my arms.

And when I looked back to the big house, the man and the boy were gone. Ike and I stood alone among the tomatoes and cucumbers. I stared at the gutter, the one I recalled making new. It was undented, but it needed painting. Time and the elements take their toll.

Time, however, does not always take a toll on memory. My dopey teenage behavior was one of those seemingly meaningless events that have a larger life than they deserve. It wasn't like I'd fallen off the ladder and broken my arm, and it wasn't like I'd physically hurt Mr. Peacock, dropping the gutter on him or anything like that. There wasn't anything about this day that should make what I'd seen or what I remembered so clear.

But if I was honest with myself, I know that dopey and irresponsible behavior is always a cover-up. For some fact we don't want to face, some act we don't want to admit, some self we don't want to be, or in my case some pain we don't want to bear. And I'm afraid that doesn't always change when we're adults, even when we try hard to be honest, even when we want to be a good scout. The most trivial event, I began thinking that day, could be much clearer and much more present than we want it to be. Because it can cover something that's much deeper, something that's not trivial at all.

I'd simply stepped from the trees and there it was, waiting for me. In ambush. Asking me to discover the meaning and fears behind the event I was seeing. I'll be honest with you, it was rattling. But even from this one experience, obsessive observer that I was, I knew it would be addictive. And impossible to avoid.

The past had come at me the way a dream does, like my dream the night before. You know the kind, a dream you've had so many times that it seems real. Maybe it is. Mr. Peacock's drowning was one of those stories that everyone in a family or a neighborhood or even a city knows—or thinks they know. No one had seen Mr. Peacock die, but everyone had a version of the story, a personal image of how it happened and how it should be told—to others but especially to one's self.

In all likelihood, my story of Mr. Peacock's death wasn't true in the way that my teenage behavior was true, but so what? Over the years it had become true for me. True like the June bugs in Tim's childhood screen doors, the ones I'd heard him talking about at the pub. Maybe one June bug stuck, maybe hundreds stuck, but there was only a single way Tim remembered it. I suppose Libby's return home was, in addition to a reminder about my brother, a suggestion that I re-experience my version of her father's story. And that I think about what was true. For both events.

I was in mid-reverie at mid-garden—mid-pondering the way I tend to do—when Ike jumped from my arms. The cat disappeared among the tomato plants, appeared again on the far side of the garden, and scooted across the lawn. He leapt up the porch steps all at once and came to a halt beside the front door. He turned and looked in my direction. He seemed almost about to salute, just as Mr. Peacock had done in my dream.

I remained where I was, staring Ike in the eye. Eventually, I followed, but I took a less direct route. I skirted the perimeter of the garden, adding an extra loop for good measure. I wanted a bit more time for observing and for thinking. For diving deeper, for discovering some meaning, for getting all I could out of what I'd just experienced.

And maybe I did. For just an instant, I saw different men. Through the kitchen window I saw someone chipping at a block of ice. In the driveway, a young man wearing some kind of white uniform was walking up from the street. Across the lawn, a hired man gathering his tools at the close of work paused and stared my way as if waiting to see what I'd do next. Was that Walter Lee?

These may have been real events, real memories, or real made-up stories. The episode on the ladder may have been a vision I'd have only once, a vision that would return again and again to haunt me, or a vision that was the first in a long chain. It may have been just something I stumbled upon at random, something that was part of a recurring pattern that had yet to reveal itself, or something I could visit at will. I just needed to observe the world closely, to tune in to whatever it was I'd tuned into that day, right? Or maybe not. Because everything I'd seen that day disappeared so quickly. I probably wasn't ready for other options. I still had Mr. Peacock on my mind.

Then, only a month after we fixed the gutter, my neighbor drowned. I always wondered about his timing. Was Mr. Peacock's death the end of a story or just the end of a chapter? Was he wrapping up affairs? I worried that it was my fault, that he'd been waiting for some sign from me. Waiting, I suppose, to see that I'd grown enough, that I could get on with the job of living, that I could stand alone after my brother's death.

But now the wind was picking up and the sky was looking like rain again. Now that time was gone.

I'd had an interesting and insightful memory, but it was time to go, time to forge ahead, time to get to work. I slowly climbed the steps, heavy with thoughts of long ago, and followed Ike into the house.

five

After my brother was killed, my parents did what any progressive parents of their time would have done. They sent me to a head shrinker, a psychologist. Then they retreated into their own misery and pretty much forgot about me. Since we learn from our parents, I suppose their behavior put me on the path to familial inattention. So I apologize for all of my family, for running down my own path and ignoring where others needed to go. But my doctor, he did have an influence that, for a while at least, seemed positive. By the time he finished with me, my head was shrunk, probably not fixed, but maybe understood. At least in part.

I spent a lot of time in that doctor's office, talking or not talking, listening or . . . well, I really was listening. And you know the one thing that sticks with me after all these years? It's not something he told me about the accident or my brother, though of course we spent a lot of time on those. It's not something he told me about my parents or our neighbors. It's something he told me about myself. The doctor said he could clearly see that I was observing too much, thinking and worrying too deeply, understanding too well what was going on.

Understanding too well? Maybe later. But at the beginning, that was a laugh. I was eight damn years old.

In the first months after the accident, I spent a lot of time thinking and talking about Stan as if he were still alive. How would he react to those lima beans Mom was planning for dinner? Not so well. Stan hated the damn things. Was he going to have so much homework that I'd be stuck washing the dishes? Probably. But even if he didn't, he'd still try for the exemption.

That kind of thing.

Next, I began thinking about what might have been. Whether Stan would have become captain of the high-school baseball team, which I knew was his ambition. Or class president, which I'd never heard him discuss but which was supposed to be the kind of thing the best kids did. I wondered what his first car would be like. Fast, no doubt. What his steady girlfriend would be like. Not so fast, or at least that's what he'd have told everyone.

I never wondered, though, about what Stan would have been or what he would have done after high school. I never wondered about Stan's college or his job or his kids or anything else that might have come after he'd grown up and left me. The Stan I thought about was always somehow with me.

And then he wasn't with me.

Because as I got to know my friends in a deeper, adult kind of way, and as I got to know myself in a complete, analytic kind of a way, I realized I hadn't really known my brother and that I barely remembered him at all.

When he died, I was a young kid and he was only a slightly older kid. We'd never discussed the careers I later avoided speculating about. We'd never discussed important things like the Vietnam War or crazy things like disco music or the merits of Pabst Blue Ribbon beer.

Hell, we'd barely discussed girls. There was a point toward the end when we did talk about Libby, but Stan spent all his time hinting and suggesting, and he seemed to be talking around what he really meant. He acted like he was embarrassed to be talking about Libby at all. When we did talk, I didn't get it. I was still little. She was my pal.

By the time I was sixteen, my talks with the doctor had wandered far from my brother's death, and I was feeling pretty normal. I didn't think I was exhibiting behavior that was any different from the itchy restlessness every teenage boy goes through. Aside, I mean, from waving an occasional gutter pipe in the air during an occasional thunderstorm. The doctor told me, however, that he wasn't worried about that. He told me I'd done a good job of putting my brother's death behind me.

Whether that good job was a good idea, however, may have deserved some more exploration. I still felt like I should have known and remembered Stan better. Problem was, talking about Stan was painful. I just didn't want to do it anymore.

My defense, other than trying for normal, was to look in another direction. And this was when I began to be somewhat obsessive about noticing what was around me, about observing and pondering people and places and events. As my memories of Stan slipped farther into the past, I was coming to realize the whole world was just as transient as my brother had been. But if I paid attention, I thought, maybe it wouldn't it be too late to capture and hold onto it.

So I was glad when the doctor, all on his own, moved from discussing Stan to discussing my observing. A quick pivot: Stan to me. Gee, as the boys Stan and Eddy would have said, my shrink and I really had left my dead brother behind.

I felt some guilt about that, but my shrink was excited. He told me he could help turn these tendencies to my advantage. What was I, his lab rat? But I didn't care. I was, as the saying goes, much obliged. I was happy with this new direction he was taking me—or the new direction he was letting me go.

The doctor would talk abstractly about how much I saw, and I'd sit staring at the specific details of his face, casually noticing how much he needed a shave. I'd be staring intently across his bony shoulder and his faded plaid shirt, out the window, and into the clear light bathing the filling station across the street. The comings and goings of cars and the pumping of gas were extraordinarily interesting to me in those teenage years.

"You're a creative person," the shrink would be saying. "We've seen that in the drawings you've done and the interest you've taken in old houses. And, of course, it's natural for a creative person to be observant." He'd turn a page in his notebook. He may have been observant, too, but he seemed to need some prompting. I wondered if that would happen to me with age. "Now, an observant person doesn't just see things and let them go. An observant person remembers, and an observant person makes connections."

I remember him saying this because at just about that time I'd usually be making the connection between my sketchbooks and the filling station, wishing I were outside drawing pictures of people with their cars. Cars and art and psychology and faded old shirts. One thing I was learning in these sessions was how my brain could be in more than one place at a time.

So he'd tell me I was paying extraordinary attention to details that most people process quickly and then put aside. Information they don't need so they forget it.

And I'd turn from the window and stare more closely at the stubble on his chin, following it up the jaw line, rounding the corner, sliding down his neck nearly to his collar.

He'd go on about how I had this wonderful gift for amassing information I could use creatively. Or how I had a paralyzing condition brought on by too much information. Or maybe a tremendous distraction that could make it hard for me to prioritize what was important.

"We'll need to work on this," he'd say. "I believe you have an obligation to use these talents."

I'd give him a blank stare. At that point, it had been a couple of years since we'd moved on from Stan, and I was getting tired of this whole analysis business. To my mind, I'd already worked on my observations. That job was complete. And as for an obligation, that was something I could do without. I rather enjoyed these abilities I'd developed, and I wanted to leave it at that.

Of course I'd been sad when Stan died. Of course I felt guilty for surviving. Of course I wished I could have saved him. Those were all the standard issues. I hadn't really needed a shrink to explore any of that. And if I'd ever dared to raise any other questions, like who was driving that damn car anyway, I have no doubt I would have been slapped with another five or six years of therapy. He'd tell me that playing the blame game would only backfire and hurt me some more. He'd say justice was something I could never really achieve. He'd say I needed to find a way to live my life that would suit my needs, not my brother's. Well, maybe that last one was right. But to hell with the rest. I could see these things for myself. I was observant, you know.

So I kept my obligation to attending our sessions until I went away to college, and I kept my sanity by looking at whatever was there in the world in front of me. I moved on to building up the architecture career I wanted, marrying the woman I loved, and maintaining the big Victorian house I'd inherited. I made damn sure to stay out of the old neighborhood.

And then all my resolve fell apart.

Because then there was Libby, standing at my door, as bright and shiny as she'd always been, dragging me back to where she wanted to be. Libby was trying to rescue that place and put it right. As if nothing had happened there. As if I couldn't—and she knew I couldn't—say no to what she wanted. Because when it came to Libby, I did feel an obligation.

"What's up with all this?" Sheila asked. I looked at her belly, thinking: What's up with you? Then I turned back to what I was doing. She'd found me on the floor in the empty apartment over our old carriage house, attempting to solve a mystery.

I spread a pair of scissors and carefully sliced the tape on a cardboard box. Bits of my younger self were inside, but in the present Sheila was waiting for a response. It was no mystery what had brought her here. It was almost noon and I was still not at work.

We all worked together in those days. McBride, LeFevre & McBride, Architects. All proudly up there on the office door showing off our wares with the whole architect schtick: our hundred-year-old building with walls the cool white of exposed limestone, floors the warm strength of heart pine. In the reception area Tim had installed Old South antiques. Charleston, Savannah, Mobile, New Orleans. And I'd hung my drawings of buildings under construction. Think: Depression-era Thomas Hart Benton. Noble workers. It was a good decision, I'll tell you, this mixing of renovated building, antiques, and art. At McBride, LeFevre & McBride, otherwise known as Eddy, Tim & Sheila, we were successful, ambitious, visionary—all the things mid-career professionals were supposed to be.

Me, I was the designer, crazy about all buildings but especially the old ones. I drew new iterations as fast as I could, bringing the past into the present and the future. I just wanted to do the work. That was my mantra. I felt that way about Libby's greenhouse. I felt it on every job.

Tim was the steady one. He had an MBA on top of his architecture degree, and we trusted him with the business side of things. He was good at keeping clients happy. He was a genteel, well-mannered southerner. He'd settled down considerably since his younger days.

Sheila was our future. She was a landscape architect by training, but landscape work was slow and she'd taken to marketing. Like any good landscape and marketing person, Sheila liked to plant and grow for the future. She liked to nurture.

I stole another glance at her belly and sneaked a little smile. Nurturing.

But Sheila wasn't smiling that day and she wasn't interested in nurturing me. I'd been wrong when I assumed there was no lingering emotion from our bedtime discussion. Sheila didn't appreciate my truancy, but what really angered her was my disregard of her explicit request to turn down Libby's job. She feared I was about to dig too deeply into the florist shop project and ignore our current work. She didn't have a clue how deeply I'd already reached and how far I'd already dug into her other fear, her deeper fear, the events that surrounded and followed childhood death.

Then there was the fear that was bothering me—the possibility that the long-dead Mr. Peacock may have reappeared. That what I'd seen wasn't just something I remembered. How in the world had that happened?

Ike's jump and run had brought me back to the present, but I remained unsure what I'd seen. Memory or reality? The answer was still beyond my grasp. But here with my box of keepsakes, I was intent on finding out. The first thing I needed to know was whether my vision of Mr. Peacock had arrived entirely on its own—or whether it had been prompted by something I'd done or seen, something I'd heard or thought, something that brought the past before me.

I opened the box. Somewhere in there, under my catcher's mitt and other remnants of childhood, I hoped I'd find evidence that would shed light on my experience.

"I'm looking for something," I said.

"Tell me what I don't know."

I already had the catcher's mitt out on the floor. "No, I'm really looking for something." I reached into the box and pulled out a pressed flower, a faded lily. Once a bright yellow, I believe, but its color was nearly gone. I cradled it in my hand, smelled for long-ago scent, and tucked the fragile thing into my shirt pocket for safe keeping.

"What was that?" Sheila asked.

"Something," I murmured.

Sheila waited.

"Something from when I was a boy."

I reached into the box again and removed a bundle of elementary school report cards, lovingly tied with a blue ribbon by my mother. Under the report cards, flat on the bottom where they wouldn't suffer wrinkles, lay my sketchbooks.

I flipped the pages. Here were my careful renderings of tomato plants, with their complex patterns of deep black and shades of gray. Here were the looming towers of the Victorian house, the pecan tree heavy with nuts, and a man waving and gesturing, planting and pruning, swinging a hoe. Mr. Peacock. Helping out his friends. A relationship still to ponder. But not now. I set the sketchbooks aside and peered into the box.

At the box's very bottom, where they'd settled after sliding through the cracks and crevasses of other memories, lay three nails, bent remnants of that ordinary day when Mr. Peacock and I replaced the gutter.

"Something." Sheila was growing impatient.

I imagined her toe tapping in the doorway, but I sat quietly, facing the other direction. I wasn't being evasive. I simply wasn't ready to put my experience into words. I certainly didn't have a meaning to assign to it yet.

"This is not the Eddy I know," Sheila said. "Eddy always says what's on his mind. Come on." She waited. "Tell it."

No, I was thinking an explanation wasn't necessary. The man, the boy, and the ladder did seem like a memory. In fact, the sketchbooks almost guaranteed it. Years earlier I'd observed Mr. Peacock closely. And the nails. I'd apparently kept them so I wouldn't forget my early architectural accomplishment, my neighbor's kindness, whatever had been important to me at the time. That's what it was, then. It was a memory. But I felt uneasy, like I still might not have found the truth.

"Eddy," Sheila said, "don't do this."

I felt more uneasy with the suspicion that Sheila might have known something, too. "Don't?" I asked, bouncing the nails up and down on my palm. They jangled and I closed my fingers tightly around them. "Don't look at this old stuff?"

"Don't look," she cautioned. "That's exactly what I mean. Would you read someone else's diary? Secrets someone left lying around? You might discover things you're better off not knowing."

I picked up one of my sketchbooks and pointed it at her. "But it's mine."

Sheila sighed as if she were tired, not angry. "Eddy," she said, "I know you better than you know yourself. You take every little thing and give it more attention than it deserves. You move everything you think up to the surface and then you obsess about it. But all that visibility is dangerous."

I took up the scissors and played nervously, snapping them open and shut. I set them on the floor beside the box.

"I know you," Sheila continued. "You'll learn things you shouldn't learn and you'll do things you shouldn't do and we'll all get hurt. You're Eddy. It's what you do." Sheila paused and I could have sworn I saw a tear in her eye. "But just this once," she said, "this one time, don't do it."

And she left me.

I tried to stay calm as I placed the sketchbooks on the floor to one side and the nails and my other memories back into the box. I'd forgotten the dried flower in my pocket.

Alone, it was my turn to sigh. I didn't want to get into a lying and cheating game. I didn't even want to get into a secrecy game. But on that day I started something.

Our indirect sparring had always been a twisted "Gift of the Magi." You know. That story by O. Henry. Sheila and I gave what we thought the other wanted in the way of openness or information. Neither of us was hurting the other, but we had to hurt ourselves and we had to hurt our relationship to do it. Gifts are hard to give when the motive creates tension. Even harder if the tension is below the surface, out of sight.

That day in the carriage house I put a big dent in our relationship. And Sheila had been right. This time, it wasn't below the surface. It was right where we'd see it, where I'd constantly feel it. When I decided to take Libby's greenhouse job, then not to tell Sheila that I'd seen the man who once made that greenhouse his life, who appeared in my drawings, who helped as I pulled those nails, I put a dent in my usually honest, aspiring good scout heart. It was a little dent that hurt like hell. And it immediately began to deepen.

Sheila had left quickly, as if she were frightened by what might happen next. Well, I'd be Eddy. She was right about that. What I hadn't realized was how frightening that might be. All these years, she'd been quietly watching my behavior while I'd been assuming that my pondering and my thinking happened only on the inside of my head. I should have been listening more closely to my wife.

More than once Sheila had warned me about becoming my father. He'd fed on tragedy and sorrow, maybe on regret and guilt, who knew? It had poisoned him. Made him crazy. And he'd turned on his family.

I needed to take care with my own thoughts and memories, she'd said. Her timing was perfect, right when I was beginning to feel guilt again about moving on and ignoring my brother. But I knew what she'd meant. Now that she was about to be a mother, Sheila was most frightened for the baby. If she had to choose, she'd move on, too. If her fears turned out to be true, whatever they were exactly, she may not be able to save me at all.

I closed the lid and gave the box a vigorous shove toward the closet. It slid in a sluggish way. It seemed not to know its destination. Then it stopped short, stuck, kind of like my much-prized honesty, in the middle of the floor.

six

A dream, a memory, my keepsakes in a box—despite Sheila's warnings I thought these would be the end of my visions. What I overlooked was the way one vision opens to others, just the way memories daisy chain in a never-ending, looping, branching tale. It's easy, you know, to overlook how much is out there, especially how much came before. But in a world of observations and details and connections, perhaps even a world with a few meanings and truths, an awful lot can appear awful quickly once you start looking. Unexpected things already had appeared. And then there were more.

I was descending the steps from apartment to yard along the outside of the carriage house when the scent of flowers met me with a force I hadn't felt in years. Day lilies, pungent and strong.

Now, when the subject was Libby, I may have felt I couldn't say no. But pondering what I'd seen since, brief and lightly engaging as those events had been, I was beginning to think what I really should be saying was yes to this opportunity. Maybe I was operating against my own best interests, but I was beginning to wonder what I'd been afraid of. Libby's appearance had brought back my brother's memory. I'd survived. And the rest of what I'd seen was fascinating stuff. Maybe enlightening stuff. And it was right here at the house. How could I refuse?

So as the scent of lilies hung in the air, I decided to give chase.

I walked to the garden and sniffed closer. I raised a bloom and the dust of pollen came off in my hands. This was it. Yes it was. But the big scent was coming from another direction.

I inhaled and dutifully followed.

Across the lawn. Up the porch steps.

Then as soon as I opened the Victorian's front door I got the snootful I was expecting. But I also got an eyeful that took me by total surprise.

Lilies surrounded a casket in front of the fireplace.

I took another very deep breath. I needed to bring myself as close to this time and place as I could. I needed my senses if I was going to discover what this was all about.

What I'd dreamed and seen were my neighbor's final days. Mr. Peacock and I fixed the gutter. He drowned. What I was seeing now was the next logical step. A funeral here, in a more formal setting than his own small house and with a family that had become so important to him, was just as real.

Everyone else was already sitting, and I sank into the chair beside an elderly woman in black. This time, I planned to stay a while.

The room was dim, its curtains drawn to create a solemn mood, and between the semi-darkness and the mesh of the old woman's veil all I could see of her face was that it was thin and very white. Her lipstick was very red. So were her eyes.

"Lord . . ." began the priest at the front of the gathering.

From my chair, I strained to see the deceased. It was all I could do to keep from standing for a better view. I was working hard to tamp down my excitement.

". . . you consoled Martha and Mary in their distress; draw near to us who mourn, and dry the tears of those who weep."

"Hear us, Lord," the people answered.

Priest again: "You weep at the grave of Lazarus, your friend; comfort us in our sorrow."

I leaned forward in my seat. Amid the gloom, I was nearly ecstatic.

People again: "Hear us, Lord."

And then, as if he knew I was hanging on every word, as if he knew I was an observing and pondering outsider stepping for the first time fully into a scene of past and departed lives, the priest seemed to be speaking directly to me: "You raised the dead to life," he said. "Give to your brother Hugh eternal life."

I jerked to attention. Well, I'll be damned. Hugh? This wasn't Mr. Peacock's funeral after all.

There are some things in every family that no one understands. I'm talking about things other than the good luck and the bad, the unexpected fortunes and illnesses and short-term, one-off events that strike every household. I'm thinking about long-running stories with faraway origins, stories embedded in the family consciousness. The McBride family certainly had one of those stories. Its name was Great Uncle Hugh.

I remembered Hugh. He was a quiet man, simple and innocent as a child with the family but a mysterious specter about town. I was eight when he

died, and even before the funeral I met a barrage of playground specula-
tion about the old man's death. According to one story, he'd walked out the
front door and disappeared, only to be found later dead in a ditch. Another
claimed he'd stepped behind the clothes hanging in his closet and put a bullet in his head. In this version, his body lay among his shoes and piled-up
dirty shirts for days.

You know how kids are. They were letting their imaginations run, trying
to be as gruesome as possible. I tried to argue them down. "That's not right!"
But no one believed me.

The family, of course, was more respectful. As far back as I could remember, whenever anyone spoke of Hugh, it was only in whispers and hints. He
may not have shot himself in the end, but he'd suffered something cata-
strophic when he was young. No one ever told that complete tale. And if
I asked for more, I was shushed. Hugh, I was regularly reminded, was a
delicate soul, and I was not to disturb my great uncle or anything about him.

As a boy myself, I wondered long and hard about Hugh when he was my
age. That's the thing. Being a kid often means dealing with the gruesome,
though it could also mean sympathetically wondering about other kids.

But the only evidence I had was the Hugh I saw before me, and all I
could gather was that he came and went. He worked some kind of job downtown, but at home he remained alone as much as he could. On weekends,
he worked by himself in the garden. The only excitement I ever witnessed
or even heard about was the day he cut the head off a snake with his shovel.

Killing that snake hadn't been necessary, but it may have been an honest
mistake. It was a corn snake, and, yes, it was a frighteningly long five feet,
and, yes, it looked a lot like a copperhead. But it was one of the good snakes
that keep down the rodent population without hurting people. It wasn't poi-
sonous. And now it was dead.

No one criticized Hugh as he stood in the garden, quietly alone after what
he'd done. Everyone always gave Hugh latitude and the benefit of the doubt.
But I saw him crying as he looked down on the lonely head and the lifeless
body in the dirt. Hugh spent the longest time just looking and crying. When
he finally dropped his shovel, it fell straight and neat into one of the plowed
rows, as if he'd wanted it that way, as if this action wasn't a mistake. Then he
turned quickly, crossed the yard, and entered the house. He cried all the way.

Killing a good snake was sad, it was bad, I knew that, but like I said, that was all the excitement I could ever find in Hugh's story. Every time I was up at the big Victorian house, I'd watch him from a distance, across the yard or down at the other end of the porch. Hugh was such a mystery. I never knew what to say to him, so I said very little. I'd go out and fetch him when one of the aunts asked me to, and take him a glass of water on a hot day in the garden. "Thank you," he would say. Always the same response. Always respectful in his own meek and far-off way. I'd linger, kicking a clod of dirt here and there, waiting for a little more insight or for something to happen. But it never did. Or I never saw it. I was only a boy.

"Edward," the old lady at the funeral whispered in a voice rough with tears. "I know this is hard, but you sit here by me. And you be good."

Instantly when she spoke, I recognized her as Hugh's sister, my great aunt Eleanor. She gently reached across her lap and twined the fingers of her gloved hand with my fingers. But how did she know me? She couldn't have recognized me as a man. She was treating me like a boy. She squeezed my fingers gently.

The priest began his eulogy, though he didn't have much to say about a man who kept to himself. There was some story about Hugh's fascination with the mother-of-pearl inlays of some accordion. That, I'd never heard. "Hugh was always there at parties," the priest was saying. "He was always quietly watching." But that. Yes, that was Hugh.

After the ceremony, Aunt Eleanor put her hand into the crook of my arm and began steering toward the foyer. I couldn't stop looking around. The house with its furnishings was at once so different from the one I lived in and so familiar in my childhood memory. "No one ever knew," she said, leaning against me as we walked, "what poor Hugh was thinking. But all these years, it was like he was just waiting, waiting to die."

"Ma'am?" I hadn't addressed anyone so formally in years, but it seemed like the right thing to do. "And how was that?"

By then we'd been joined by Great Aunt Lillian. "You know," she frowned. "It was last week."

I stared at the ceiling. That playground story about suicide said blood had dripped through from Hugh's closet.

"No," I whispered. "No, I don't think I do."

"Sister," scolded Eleanor. "It's not a mystery."

"No," replied Lillian, "but he knows this." Both women turned my way. "You were there."

I wracked my brain. My childhood didn't yield up whatever there was to remember about Hugh as easily as my teenage years yielded up embarrassment over my behavior with the gutter. Everything I recalled about Uncle Hugh was fuzzy. The man's entire life, at least to an observer who'd been only a boy, seemed, well, vague. Uncle Hugh was a presence that simply hovered. Somewhere above me. Seen though a mist. Through a kind of sickbed grogginess.

And that was it. A week earlier, I'd been sick in bed, sleepy and groggy in our house across town.

"My God," I whispered. "The measles. He caught the measles and he died."

"He caught the measles and he caught pneumonia," corrected Lillian. "He coughed himself to death."

"Hugh tried to help," said Eleanor, her voice quavering. "He always tried to help." She removed a carefully folded tissue from the sleeve of her dress, where she kept it against the inside of her wrist. She dabbed her eyes, left, right, left again, and returned the tissue to its hiding place.

"I remember," I said, watching as the men from the funeral home navigated the casket toward the front door. "Uncle Hugh sat on the side of my bed and he fed me soup. I was propped up with a pile of pillows in a dark room and he was leaning over me."

"Hugh never did anything to hurt anyone," said Lillian, "and look what happened to him."

"Sister," interrupted Eleanor. "You stop that. It's not the boy's fault."

"No, it's not the boy's fault, but you just think what happened to our little brother. He was the child of our father's old age. When Hugh came there was so much hope, and all of it was stolen. Now people are saying he caught that pneumonia on purpose."

My adult ears pricked up. On purpose? Were they all killing themselves? Mr. Peacock and Uncle Hugh both?

Aunt Eleanor was aghast. "Don't even think that!"

Both deaths could have been my fault. That's what I was thinking.

"Well," said Lillian, "they are saying it. They are saying he wanted to die. But our brother didn't die only last week. The boy we knew died fifty years ago, the day he went out with that crowd of men. The day the boy we loved came home and he wasn't himself anymore. That's when our brother really died."

The maiden aunts put their arms around one another and cried for their brother, but for the longest time no one stepped forward to console them. Uncle Hugh's funeral had been awkward enough, memorializing a man who had been dead to most people even while he lived. The only one who made the gesture was a boy. He seemed to understand. The boy put his arms around the women and wept with them.

Eleanor pulled the boy closer. "Poor thing," she said.

My childhood self had arrived.

I wanted to say something about arriving before the kid. Hey, look at me! For ten or twenty minutes, I'd been a participant at the funeral. This, unlike the time I'd seen myself on the ladder with Mr. Peacock, was definitely no memory. I'd seen and talked to my aunts. Long-gone aunts.

But I could tell they wouldn't see me now. They'd see me as the boy. Or they'd see me as both the adult and the boy, all in one. They'd see me the way our former selves and the people we later become blend over the years and live together.

Lillian stroked the boy's hair. "Poor child."

I took a step backward, my adult self now back to being an observer. That's what I should have been doing—closely watching. And that's what I should have been seeing—other people and their pain. What was I thinking instead? Hey, look at me! Still that teenager. What an idiot.

The aunts each held one of the boy's hands, and with her free hand, Lillian plucked a yellow lily from the spray on the casket's lid. She passed the flower to the boy, who raised it to his nose. The blossom was slightly damp. I could see the droplets of water. It was cut and dying but still alive.

"You wear this now," said Eleanor, taking back the lily after the boy had sufficiently considered it, stripping away the leaves and pushing the stem through the buttonhole in the boy's lapel. She reached behind the fold and tugged so only the bloom showed. "And when you get home tonight," she said, "you put this flower between the pages of a book. You press this flower, and you'll keep a piece of this day for the future."

From where I stood, shunted off to the side of our family drama, I raised my hand to my shirt pocket and felt the pressed flower inside.

In the quick space of a day, I'd gone from a dream of Mr. Peacock's drowning that I knew was a dream, to the image of my teenage self emerging from sorrow that I thought may have been a memory, to the aunts speaking to me at Uncle Hugh's funeral, which I knew was the true past. Whatever the cause: suggested by Walter Lee's knock at my door, triggered by my neighborhood visit with Libby, or made real by my obsessive observing. Whatever the vision: repressed memories, false memories, or the plain, honest truth. But you know me. I'd always go for observation and truth. There's less to worry about there. At least I believe there is.

Lillian straightened the boy's tie, paused, and looked up at her sister. "And with Stanley not six months in the ground."

Well, that shows what I know. I'd observed the scene, and worry had returned.

This trio of deaths, Mr. Peacock, Uncle Hugh, and my brother, Stan, may have set the stage, loaded the gun—you pick the metaphor—for what I could learn about family in the present, but the boy Eddy was stuck at his brother's accident. Nothing could equal the horror of that. The aunts still held his hands, trying to keep him in the full family story, but my childhood self was sleepwalking through old tales of their generation.

Eleanor was weeping again for her own dead brother.

Lillian adjusted the funereal flower once more in the boy's little suit jacket.

Across the room, only one person remained sitting in the parlor, a man reading a hymnal, swaying and rocking as if he were an Orthodox Jew davening, but I knew he wasn't, not here with the priest. The music had long since stopped, and now he seemed to be reading lyrics as poetry or making music in his head or something.

"You remember fifty years ago," said Lillian, and Eleanor cried harder. "You remember Alexander Lee, poor soul, the way he died that day."

Eleanor nodded yes and blew her nose on the tissue.

"You remember that other man, the grocer. I wish none of us had ever laid eyes on that one."

Now Eleanor shook her head side to side, as if wishing this grocer man out of existence.

I felt like a child again, eavesdropping as my parents visited the aunts. Little bits and facts and dates, a few distant names, shorthand spoken like everyone knew what these details meant. But I'd never heard this story. I knew nothing of these people.

"That was a black day for the McBride family," said Lillian. "I'll never forget the way Hugh came home and slammed that door, how he wouldn't come out of his room."

Here it was. The sad and painful story that had made the entire McBride family something fragile.

"And how much he had changed when he did come out," sniffed Eleanor. Any composure she'd managed earlier was now long gone. This time she let her tears fall freely as she began methodically shredding her tissue and dropping the pieces to the floor. They gathered around her feet like down from a sad little molting bird. "He was so full of life before that day. He was never the same after."

Across the room, the lone man slowly closed his hymnal. He set the book on the seat beside him, smoothed a thick shock of snow-white hair, placed his fedora on his head, and turned my way. I didn't know who Alexander Lee was, but I recognized this man. This was the old doorbell ringer, commander, pleader, order issuer. I knew this man. This was Walter Lee.

Names like that were too close to be a coincidence. There had to be a connection. But at this point, I couldn't tell what it was. I'd never seen this Alexander Lee, and aside from that day at my front door, my only encounter with Walter Lee in years had been in my memory, or whatever it was, that day I watched my teenage self on the ladder. And that encounter had been at a distance. Now he was fully present, come up from an earlier time or down from today, but he wasn't offering any clues, not about his own presence and not about the aunts' meaning.

Was the old bastard following me? I guess that was what he was doing. On the other hand, I could have been following him. Except I'd thought all along that I'd been following Libby. Or maybe it was both.

It could be that behind the scenes Walter Lee was steering me in some direction of his own design. I pondered that, and the more I thought, the more I leaned toward . . . hell, at this point it could be any of these options. What I did know was that Walter Lee was an old man and he'd been back here in this time and place before. I had to assume he knew what he was doing and that he knew where he was going.

Maybe the reason I'd been able to avoid the past all these years was because I'd convinced myself it was gone. I'd thought I couldn't do anything about it. Now it was looking like the past wasn't gone at all. And who knew what I could do.

Across the room, Walter Lee stood without taking his eyes off me. He raised his hand to the brim of his hat. Made an adjustment. Lowered his fingers to his brow. And gave me a little salute. As if to say, "Welcome."

Welcome to what? Hugh's coffin had been wheeled away, the flowers had been packed into the hearse for the gravesite, and my maiden aunts were following, taking my boyhood self with them. I was left alone.

Now if you'd asked me that day, I'd have admitted that following Walter Lee into the past, if that's what I'd been doing, was questionable at best. Dangerous at worst. But I pondered for only a second. I stared across the room at Walter Lee just as I'd stared at Ike across the garden that day I saw the past that first time, and I gave the old yard man a nod in return.

seven

McBride, LeFevre & McBride was busy that summer, and not just with small jobs like the florist shop. We had an office building and a school in the early stages of development. Our hot job was a theater that was supposed to bring new life to old downtown. But the shop renovation was the one that demanded my attention. It was a favor for a friend, a gift to the old neighborhood, maybe even a gesture to art. It was an obligation, but it was an obligation of the good kind, because it was also a labor of love. And we all know what happens with labors of love. Time and attention, swallowed up. One gulp. Gone. All my other jobs appeared through the lens of this one.

I'd go to the theater site, and I'd look around for details. The building was going to be built where the city's minor-league ballpark used to be, so I'd look for inspiration among the weeds. If anyone at the office asked, I'd say I was looking for design ideas, that I needed to be on the ground to properly imagine future black-tie operas and champagne intermissions. But I was more honest with myself. Threading my way between patches of weeds that flowered yellow and around spiky others that reached knee-high, I knew damn well that what I wanted to see were remnants of the past. I was looking for Cracker Jack and beer and loudmouth razzing of any opposing player with the misfortune to come too close. I was trying to find a way to make the past appear again.

I'd wander around looking for home plate and the pitcher's mound. An announcer would start up in my head. "Runners at second and third, two outs." The tall weeds would wave in the breeze and I'd pick up the closest thing I could find to a baseball-size rock. "Batter's got an even count now, two and two . . . ." I'd throw toward the plate. "Caught him looking at a breaking ball!"

But it was all in my head, and that's where it stayed. Every architect or painter or poet knows, or should know, that creation is not about forcing the muse to sing. It's about tracking her down on the crowded street of observation, about gathering in as many ideas as you can while you're following her curious path. That's when you're ready to hear the song. You can't ever tell the muse to sing, but when you're ready to listen she'll be there. The trick is in knowing when you're ready.

And though I'd already seen the past, even joined in on events, I guess I just wasn't ready. Or the place I was standing wasn't where the past remained. Or the era I was trying to visit wasn't in sync with what I was feeling. Maybe I needed Walter Lee for guidance, if that's what the old man's role really was.

Instead, events were like the pair of skinny dogs, strays from the look of them, who appeared in the outfield one day, trotting, stopping occasionally for a sniff in the dirt, one of them taking a quick roll on his back. One time, the past had appeared all on its own. One time, I'd made it happen. But it was still as random as those dogs.

Besides, there was this omen. Coming out of my reverie ("Caught him looking at a breaking ball!"), I'd squinted into the low morning sun and seen that the outfield was alone in its weeds. While I'd been worrying about what I had or hadn't seen, those dogs were gone. They must have decided there was something better to smell or a more appealing place to wriggle in the dirt.

It was time for me to do the same.

For the next eight weeks, I threw myself into Libby's work, into plotting and planning to build on what had come before rather than simply observing it, into making the future happen and watching where that would take me.

Day after day, Libby and I walked the empty shell of her father's shop, reworked sketches at my office, brainstormed in coffee shops. And everywhere, we pondered details. It didn't matter whether we were coming, going, or at the site, whether we were together or home alone. The project interrupted the books we were reading, worked its way into the dinners we were cooking, brought us to a full stop on the errands we were running. More than once, I pulled my truck over to the curb to record ideas before they vanished.

Libby wrote furiously in a notepad and passed her ideas to me. I drew nonstop on any blank space I could find, from formal sketchbook to grocery sack to the white backgrounds of magazine ads.

Then, in a remarkably short sequence, the plans were finished, transferred to computer, ready for permitting by the city, ready to go out to contractors for bids, ready to break ground. And one day Libby and I found ourselves standing in front of the florist shop, watching. The sun had yet to crest the tops of the neighborhood's ancient shade trees, but work on the building had already begun.

First thing, workers unbolted the shop's display cases from the floor, freeing them from the role they'd filled for a generation. The men carried the cases to the curb, where Libby couldn't take her eyes off them. A person who did not know the cases' history would have thought they were trash. To Libby, who had seen them every day of her childhood, they were lonely and sad. They stood empty, with dirty glass cracked in a half-dozen places.

Morning dog walkers stayed on the other side of the street, happy, I was sure, that this long-vacant eyesore was finally being repaired but wary, I knew from experience, about any work here at all. How long and how loud would this disruption be, this chaos of trucks and men, this mess of building materials lying about? But Libby and I weren't worrying about the neighbors.

Libby had to turn away from the discarded display cases to keep from crying. I put an arm around her.

"Just as long as the job goes smoothly," she said, a little girl trying to be brave.

"It won't," I replied. "There'll be pipes in the wall or something we don't know about." Now Libby really was crying. Why do I say things like that? Why this insistence on the truth?

But there were no surprise pipes, not yet at least, and Libby cheered up. It wasn't long before workmen were knocking down a wall that had been added to make a storage room. No one minded losing that ancient piece. And at midday Tim arrived with barbecue sandwiches.

I dropped the tailgate of my truck, and the three of us sat swinging our dangling legs the way children do. Tim sat close to Libby. I suspected it was our client and not the barbecue that had been his motivation in coming. All was well.

But, of course, I put my foot in it again. "I've been thinking about your dad," I ventured. Libby let her sandwich rest on her lap. Lunch stopped. I immediately regretted what I'd said. But how was I to know her father's death was a sensitive subject after so many years?

Libby was looking at the sky. "Mackerel sky," she said, nostalgic and suddenly sad.

Neither Tim nor I knew what she was talking about.

"You see how the clouds look like fish scales?" Libby asked, her eyes still on the distance. "It's called a mackerel sky. It's supposed to mean a change in the weather." Libby took a bite of her sandwich, but the bite was small and tentative, and she continued her story. "Daddy was in the Navy, you know, during World War II, and he knew a lot about the sky and the weather."

Libby took another small bite and waited.

"I remember," I said. I had to let Libby know that I was listening and that maybe I even understood. But mostly I was searching for some bland and noncommittal statement. I didn't want to say anything that could make matters worse.

"I think that's when he started to die," she continued, making matters worse all on her own. "Back during or right after the war. My father covered it up for years, but his death was long and slow and painful. He didn't die that one night at the river."

As a boy, I'd thought it would be great fun to grow up to be Mr. Peacock. Now I wondered if my neighbor might have been trying too hard to be cheery, if maybe there was something in his life that he wanted to forget or hide. I didn't have any proof, but I'd learned over the years that there's always a reason why people force a good time.

If I'd been the adult I am now, I would have noticed the changes that came over Mr. Peacock after Stan died. The man was never cheery again. He acted as if Stan had been his son, not just his neighbor. Mr. Peacock sat behind the shop counter, on an old folding chair. He sold his flowers, but he didn't work very hard at it. He just waited for customers to come. He seemed very sad, very blue. Everyone saw it. To one extent or another, everyone who lived in the neighborhood, even the children, we all knew his mood. It was as if something had happened that he had anticipated, something that he had feared.

Libby had said it. She said virtually the same thing that day about her father that Aunt Lillian had said about Uncle Hugh at the funeral: "Our brother didn't die only last week. The boy we knew died fifty years ago." And so I sat there on the tailgate pondering all our deaths. It could be that everyone who lives to adulthood dies one hit at a time. Only children like Stan die suddenly. It wouldn't be long, however, before I'd begin to wonder if that was true, if even very old events, including events from before we are born, pound on even the youngest of us.

I was sinking deeper into gloom when Libby unexpectedly perked up. Maybe remembering her father had been cathartic. She could have simply decided to forge ahead. Or she could have been forcing cheeriness. Like her father used to do. "This place will be happier now," she said. Then she placed two fingers into her mouth the way I'd seen her do so many times when we were children and issued a shrill and piercing whistle.

"I haven't felt like I could do that for years." Libby smiled broadly. "Not in public anyway." Before I could reply, she jumped from the tailgate like a child leaping from a swing and walked over to the worker she'd been signaling.

While Libby and Tim and I had been eating, a removal company had taken the shop's cabinets from the curb and had deposited a big, green dumpster in their place. The workers were now throwing old two-by-fours, drywall, and window frames over its tall sides. A small pile of rubbish on the ground nearby had caught Libby's eye.

"Where did you find this?" she asked the man. Libby squatted on her heels for a closer look.

The worker said it had been behind one of the cabinets. Said he thought somebody might want it.

"Well, thank you," said Libby. "Thank you very much."

The cache was a time capsule of sorts. A couple of old calendars sent by insurance agents. A never-paid phone bill. A package of dried-up Chesterfield cigarettes. A scorched doll.

"Oh," said Libby, turning meek.

I joined Libby at the curb. "What's that?"

The doll's once-long, once-blonde hair, which the young Libby had brushed and braided by the hour, was blackened stubble. The doll's flawless skin, to which Libby had applied real makeup stolen from her mother, was blistered.

"So this is where it went." Libby was speaking to herself.

"What?"

"I went away to camp one summer and my mom cleaned out my room. She gave all my little kid stuff to Goodwill."

Libby kicked the calendars, the cigarettes, and the phone bill into a pile. "There's too much history here," she said.

I begged to disagree. "It's trash."

"It's trash," Libby repeated. Then she turned to the worker, businesslike. "You can throw all this stuff away."

All but the doll. That, Libby quickly stuffed into her purse. "Stan," she said, then repeated herself by way of nervous, almost apologetic explanation. "Stan went down to Goodwill and bought this one back. He bought it just for me." Libby still had her hand inside her purse, still on the doll. "Before any of this happened."

I considered making some wise-ass remark about Stan and Libby both rescuing the doll, about their saving its life. Maybe I'd give Libby a poke in the ribs and we'd laugh at our childhood selves. Well, they'd saved the doll, and that was the truth. But for once that day, I thought first before I said or did anything more. To Libby these memories were serious stuff.

eight

When lunch was over and Libby and Tim were gone, I remained behind, sitting quietly on my truck's tailgate. I should have been heading back to the office myself, but I begged off with some excuse about checking on the workmen's progress. What I really wanted was time alone. I'd reconnected with the neighborhood in the weeks we'd worked on the shop design, but I wanted to sink in and know this place still more.

It was hot, one of those steamy August days without a hint of a breeze. I closed my eyes and listened to the cicadas singing loudly in trees or bushes or wherever a person would never see them. Then I slipped from the tailgate and took a turn down to the street corner. Big, spreading oaks sheltered the sidewalks. The shade ran together almost endlessly.

On each side of the street, yards were carefully manicured. Grass was neatly clipped and edged; flowerbeds were cleanly weeded. Peering between the houses, I could see swing sets in the backyards. In front of one house, a spinning lawn sprinkler threw water across the grass. Water pistols, swim goggles, and the lump of a wet towel lay nearby. It hadn't been long since children were dancing and cooling themselves in the spray.

There was a serene order here. The 1920s-era houses weren't new, but all were freshly painted and well maintained. Friendly and welcoming. Front entries stood open behind screen doors decorated with palm trees or flamingos in their metal frames. Very nice. Very trusting and guileless.

That's me, guileless, truthful Eddy. I'm a product of this place and this time.

Me and the cicadas, always the cicadas, same pitch, same volume, same background to all the summers I'd ever known.

I'd barely noticed them at first; they were so expected. But I found that if I listened closely, I could bring them from background to foreground.

Okay, amp it up.

I could move the cicadas to the surface, right to the very top of what I was sensing.

Now dial it back.

And when the cicada volume returned to where it was supposed to be, I recognized the earlier time and place.

The dumpster and my truck were gone. The shop was open for business. A sky-blue Cadillac, its white convertible top up, was parked at the curb. It looked to be brand new.

A woman emerged from the shop with an armful of purple irises, crossed the street, and disappeared around the same corner I'd just visited.

Now came Mr. Peacock. Same pencil-thin moustache, but younger, eight or ten years younger than the Mr. Peacock who'd helped me fix the gutter at the Victorian house. His hair was jet black. He must have been only in his mid- to late thirties.

I hung back in silence, half hidden behind a tree. What I'd missed at the ballpark was the real-world focus and attention I managed now. Dreaming up radio announcers, trying to bring events out of my head, wasn't the answer. Events were right here, right around me. I'd found them in the scent of flowers at Uncle Hugh's funeral. I'd found them in the sound of cicadas here in the neighborhood.

The past was waiting to be seen. I really could make this happen.

Now, at Libby's family shop, at the scene of my brother's accident, I was compelled to make it happen.

Mr. Peacock let the screen door slam and walked around the shop to the back. Less than a minute later, he returned, pushing a power lawn mower and carrying a metal gasoline can. It was a typical suburban scene. A little yard work, a little lawn mowing, and the world would be right.

Yet I had this nagging feeling that things weren't as right or as simple as they appeared. They weren't nearly as right as the day Mr. Peacock helped me with the gutter.

For one thing, Mr. Peacock never mowed his own lawn. He had this stiff back, a war injury, and he always hired me for the job.

Mr. Peacock pushed the mower down the middle of the front walkway, and when he met the street he set the gas can at the curb, beside the Cadillac. He rolled his sleeves tightly above the elbows and loosened his tie, tucking the ends between two shirt buttons, military-style. He gave the cord a yank and the little motor started. I looked around. There were no children playing, no sprinkler dancers. There was only one other yard worker, a man in overalls pulling weeds a half-dozen houses away. He stood and looked silently my way. The putt-putting of Mr. Peacock's mower was the only sound on the block.

Mr. Peacock started his slow, methodical work. He began at one side of the yard and pushed his machine front to back, back to front, circling bushes and trees in the middle of the lawn, keeping meticulously parallel lines. This was exactly how I mowed the lawn. Employer must have been watching yard boy. But the scene wasn't quite right. The grass was still short. It wouldn't need cutting for at least another week.

Front to back. Back to front. Mr. Peacock stopped at the sidewalk to light a cigarette. He put his lighter and the pack of remaining smokes into a front pocket of his baggy, pleated trousers. I thought my former neighbor appeared distracted, only halfway paying attention. Funny thing, too. I noticed that Mr. Peacock wasn't so stiff. It was as if he were on a mission, focused on something or somewhere else so intently that his war injury didn't seem to exist.

I think I was right about that distraction and that somewhere focus. For as Mr. Peacock turned the mower at the sidewalk to have another go at the lawn, one of the front wheels clipped the gas can, sending it tumbling off the curb and clanking into the gutter. The can must have been full, and the cap must have been loose. Gasoline spilled out and ran across the asphalt under the Cadillac. Mr. Peacock ignored it.

Front to back. Back to front. Mr. Peacock continued mowing as the gasoline spread. Almost finished now, with only a small strip remaining down the far side of the yard, he stopped one more time. Mr. Peacock took a long, slow drag on his nearly finished cigarette and, half turning toward the street, flicked the butt into the air. It sailed high, then landed in the gutter. Flames leapt under the car.

Mr. Peacock pushed the mower one more length of the lawn, carefully finishing the last ribbon of grass. He shut off the machine and returned it to the storage building. He emerged and entered the greenhouse through the front door. He never looked at the spreading fire or his shiny new convertible.

What the hell?

At first, there were only small flames. The blue heat seemed gentle as it quickly spread, wandering its way under the vehicle, looking here and there for venues and opportunities. Grease on the undercarriage was easy fuel. So were the tires. Black smoke and the smell of burning rubber rose from the once gleaming whitewalls. The convertible top followed, leaving only a metal skeleton suspended over the car's interior.

Overhead, a huge cloud of black smoke was curling into the blue morning sky.

At first in the distance, then closer and closer, came the wail of fire engines. Meanwhile, up and down the block, neighbors began to appear on their front porches. One of the women, probably home with a young child at this time of day, must have called in the alarm, but none ventured close to the burning Cadillac.

"Step back, sir," a voice behind me commanded, and I turned to see a man in a long, yellow coat and tall, rubber boots, carrying a big canister-style fire extinguisher in each hand, climbing down from the truck.

I'd thought I was just watching, that I was outside this drama. It was only then that I realized how close I'd been standing to the burning car. The heat had blasted my entire left side, from face and neck to the skin on my arm.

"We'll take care of this." The firemen aimed their extinguishers at the car and let fly with foam. A few blobs of white floated toward me. I remembered the car's gasoline tank and moved away quickly, but there was no explosion. Just flames, now smothered.

The car, of course, was ruined, a total loss save whatever items may have been in the glove box, in the trunk, or maybe under the seats. People let all sorts of things rattle around in their cars, forgotten for the longest time. Why, just the other day I'd discovered in my truck a long-misplaced fountain pen, once my favorite for sketching, its ink a hardened cake of royal blue.

It wasn't long before the charred Cadillac stopped smoking, much to the disappointment of the neighborhood children. I'm sure they would have liked the excitement to go on longer. At their age, I certainly would have. Now, I felt relief. Firemen were hosing down the street, washing away debris. They were stowing their equipment in the truck. They were gone.

Up and down the street, screen doors were slamming. The neighbor women and their children were returning to lunch-making or floor-scrubbing or TV cartoon-watching. The street was quiet again and I was alone again.

Until I chanced to look one more time at the florist shop. There, in the doorway, slightly out of focus behind the insect screen, stood a twelve-year-old Libby Peacock. She was quietly crying, hugging herself with arms crossed. She stepped from one foot to the other. She lifted one hand and with its heel smeared the wet away from her eyes, down onto her cheek. She stared directly at me. Then she turned and ran, disappearing deep into the greenhouse.

I felt like a cheater and a sneaker-arounder. Not the guy who's stepping out on his wife with another woman. That's never happened between Sheila and me. But there I was, an hour after the car fire, standing in the office elevator, getting ready for a world-class confrontation—or world-class avoidance. I had no idea what direction that would go, but I was so excited I was tingling all over.

Sure I was tingling. My skin was red, like a sunburn.

I raised my right arm to my face and pressed my sleeve against my nose. Smoke. Burned rubber and gasoline smoke. Dirty smoke. Disaster smoke. I took another deep breath before lowering that arm and turning my attention to the other.

I gingerly rubbed my left forearm. Then I let my fingers explore the left side of my neck. I stroked my cheek slowly. The skin was tender. It hurt. I couldn't get enough of the sensation.

I stared at my reflection in the chrome elevator door. I saw a man who looked like he'd been driving with his arm resting too long in a rolled-down car window. "Damn," I whispered as the doors slid open. I crossed the elevator lobby and automatically reached for the office door handle. There, I stopped. I couldn't keep my eyes off my arm. I couldn't stop smelling the smoke.

I pulled open the door and paused above the threshold. "Damn," I said, to no one in particular.

The office receptionist asked if I was coming in or not.

"Damn," was all I could say.

When I'd encountered Mr. Peacock at the ladder, I'd simply watched. At Uncle Hugh's funeral, I'd talked with the aunts, though the real participant turned out to be Eddy the boy, not myself as a man.

I'd been thinking about what I'd learned years ago with the shrink. Those first two encounters with the past had proven that my attention could certainly be in two places at one time. One brain, here in the present, but two or more thoughts, perceptions, insights, who knew where. Now it looked like the body could share that experience. I ran my fingers across my arm. I'd not only been to the past but it had physically affected me.

"Damn." I floated into the office only lightly noticing the receptionist's curious stare.

I didn't really have a choice, you know. Libby, in her mission to save her father's shop, may not have realized what she was doing, but she'd pulled and obliged me. Walter Lee, after first only suggesting the path, now appeared to be guiding me. My own insistence on truth had captured me, and the mystery of my brother's death had returned to haunt me.

But I also have to say: Once I'd had my first experience in the past, I couldn't wait for the next. I'd had a false start at the ball field, but it looked like I had this business down now. I'd gone deeper each time.

I touched my skin. I was bringing back proof.

Problem was, I was looking only at myself. Big mistake, I'm sure, but that's what I was doing. I should have been paying better attention to what I'd seen, to what Mr. Peacock had been destroying, and I should have been thinking about why.

"Damn." I continued on by the men's room and an opportunity to scrub clean. I closed my office door behind me.

Sheila had told me not to take the work I'd taken, and she'd warned me not to see what I was seeing.

But . . . "Damn!"

Couldn't I have it both ways? As much as my examining and pondering and truth-seeking had always consumed me, as much as Libby's presence now was taking me back into our shared lives—with whatever truths that might reveal and whatever consequences that might bring—Sheila also had a powerful hold. Sheila was always there to reel me in. Sometimes she acted as much like my parent as my wife.

And I knew exactly how Sheila would react.

She'd see the burn on my skin and she'd put her hand gently on my arm. She'd smell the dirty disaster and she'd ask what had happened. I'd tell her this was a positive thing and she'd instantly recognize the lie. Sheila may not have seen the places and times I'd visited, but she would see through me.

She'd make a good mom, that's for sure.

Maybe a bit forceful, however. A bit determined, a bit of a wanting-to-know-what-she-wanted-to-know kind of mom. And that did worry me.

Hand on my arm, Sheila would want to turn her light touch into a tight squeeze. She'd want to grab my reddened flesh hard and teach me a lesson.

Then she wouldn't. The two of us would stand in silence, not knowing how angry or truthful to be. We'd stare until one of us blinked, literally or metaphorically, it didn't matter. Then we'd simply walk away, in opposite directions.

Remind me, please, of why I'd come to the office.

I simply couldn't remember, aside from the fact that work was what I did and where I was expected to be. Or because there were supposed to be people in this place I could lean on. But those connections weren't working. When Sheila acted like a parent, or when I feared she was about to act like a parent, the best plan I could come up with was to stay away. Otherwise, even a tiny confrontation would turn into the big nasty I'd just imagined. My brain always did that to me.

Already it was time to escape.

I opened my office door and stepped into the hall.

"I'm here, you know." Sheila called as I turned back toward the exit.

I kept walking.

"Eddy?"

I walked faster and caught the elevator on just the right cycle, its doors already open, complicit in my escape.

"Eddy!"

Sheila sometimes complained that I didn't pay attention to her, but she was wrong. I thought about her all the time, just not the way she expected. Conjecture, that was a lot of it. I imagined how things might go with her, and if that conjecture turned out bad I imagined my options for turning my attention elsewhere. I was always looking for ways to avoid hurting her, hurting myself, and hurting our relationship.

But in reality, I'd hurt Sheila, and I'd hurt her some more. I wasn't proud of it, but that was me. In those days, I didn't seem to have much choice.

nine

When I arrived home, I found Tim stalking the cat. I asked him what he was doing and he pointed toward a black-leather portfolio on the porch steps. Hell, I'd thought he was avoiding work like I was. That really would have surprised me. But Tim was as diligent as ever.

After decades off, since his student days, really, Tim had started making pictures again. "Every architectural firm needs a photographer," was how he put it. "Can't take our work to the clients, can we?"

"Hardly," I'd replied, but I didn't think Tim's resurgent interest was really about photography. Sheila was out chasing commissions. I was out wrangling contractors. And now that Libby had arrived, catching his eye and disrupting his businesslike routine, Tim was going stir-crazy in the office. Libby was interested in style. Tim had this flair for pictures. He just needed to practice first on the cat.

Truth be told, Tim should have done this earlier. He had a way of looking. For Tim, architecture was sometimes the star, but mostly, buildings were his backdrops, the stage sets where life happened.

Tim's real subjects were the people in and around buildings. People gave the architecture life and they gave it motion. Tim's photos captured tiny moments, as all photos do, but they showed much more, as the best ones do. His pictures hinted at why people came to the buildings and what they were doing there. Maybe even where they'd come from or where they were going next.

"You know how I'd shoot this place?" Tim asked.

"This house?"

"Your house." Tim pulled a well-worn Leica from one of his bags—the camera must have been fifty years old—and he began walking across the yard and down the side of the house. Tim had been here hundreds, thousands of times, but he was acting like it was all new. He was acting like he didn't know where the porch would take him.

"Yeaaaaah," he said, drawing out the word as if he had found what he was looking for. "I'd photograph your cat."

I walked down the porch, following Tim's progress in a parallel line. At the end of the house, far down on the side, I could see Ike, the yellow tabby. He was perched on the railing, surveying his domain in the morning sun.

"A cat . . ." Tim said as he stalked not only Ike but the proper architectural details, the proper photographic angle, and, as it turned out, the proper pondering of our lives. For years, he'd been listening to me. My ramblings appeared to have rubbed off. "A cat isn't like a person. A person would put the house in a specific point in time."

Tim stepped back from the house to make a quick picture that took in the entire porch. His Leica was the rangefinder style with one fixed lens. It forced him to be in the exact place he needed for the shot. The camera saw what the eye saw—and the eye saw what the camera saw.

"But your cat," Tim was saying, as he drew closer. "Your cat looks like your parents' cat." He took another step forward. "Or your grandparents' cat."

Ike was keeping an eye on the photographer now. I had to admit I was transfixed, too. Tim had no idea what I'd been seeing in earlier times, including what I'd seen right here at the house, only a few feet from where he was standing, but he was speaking directly to my experience.

"A cat," Tim said, "can be a reincarnation or a symbol. These little guys . . . ." He held his breath as he drew still closer to Ike. "These guys always seem so damn serene, but there's something else in there. Something . . . ."

Suddenly, but not unexpectedly, Ike jumped from the railing and ran into the garden. He'd had enough of this intruder. It was time to hide among the tomato plants.

". . . something powerful." Tim let his camera hang from its strap as he turned back toward me. "Now, let's talk about Libby."

"I thought you came here to harass my cat," I said. It would be just like Tim to show up for two purposes. Like the lunch he'd brought to Libby and me at the florist shop, the one that hadn't really been about lunch at all.

"Your cat's fine. He's home. He's settled. He's happy. Libby should be so lucky."

I tried to recall that first day of construction. Sure, Libby'd been a little weepy when demolition began. She'd pulled into a shell when I tactlessly asked about her father. But I wouldn't say she was unhappy. Disoriented maybe, but that wouldn't be so unusual amid the chaos of change. And eventually she'd come around. She did seem glad to have her doll back.

"You didn't notice?" asked Tim. He shook his head. "No, you wouldn't. If you were photographing this house . . . no, you'd draw it; that's the difference. You'd take days, examining every turn of the porch details and every angle of the sun. People and cats would come and go and you wouldn't be able to fit them into your picture because you'd be so focused on what you wanted to focus on."

I couldn't argue. I needed to spend more time on the people. But it was like I'd told Libby at the shop: You never knew what you were going to find. There was always something in places, an event from the past, a desire in the present. Looking closely at people could be frightening. God forbid I'd get a glimpse into some life-changing future.

"She needs a place to live."

I exhaled with relief. The logistics of life. This we could fix. Not what had already happened. Not the pains of our youth and not Stan's death that Libby and I shared.

"You have a place," Tim said. "You can let her stay in the apartment over your carriage house. There's no one using it. You and Sheila can watch over her."

I had, in fact, guessed that the hotel where Libby had been staying was probably costing a fortune, but I hadn't noticed that she needed watching. What did I know? Maybe Tim had already learned something about Libby that I'd never known or that I'd known and forgotten. I found myself nodding in agreement.

Tim clapped me on the back. Criticism over. Guilt nailed down. Campaign successful. That hadn't taken long.

Tim did have a talent for getting his way. He could charm a decision out of the most reluctant client, do it in a way that made the client think the decision was all his, and arrange for a check to be written on the spot. That's what made him a great business partner. Tim always elicited cooperation.

Tim pretended he hadn't done anything. He raised his camera and aimed it at Ike, who was peering out from behind a drooping tomato plant. "Click," Tim said, loudly and with gusto, without actually snapping the shutter. The cat skulked backward, finished for the day with people.

Tim may have thought he'd won when he finagled Libby's move into our carriage-house apartment, but I knew that Libby's arrival would help me as much as it would help her. I might have to do a selling job on Sheila. She still seemed uncertain about my friend. But of course. No problem. I'd keep an eye on Libby. And in the process, I'd learn what she knew.

I raised my fingertips to my reddened cheek. Libby was sure to have some insights into the day her father set fire to his brand new car. And maybe more. Her father had sunk into depression. He'd drowned in the river. My brother was dead.

I should have been ashamed of myself. Tim wanted to keep Libby safe. I wanted to scarf up information. Letting my old friend have the apartment wasn't about her at all, was it? It was about me. I understood selfishness. And that's the truth.

It was only a couple of hours later that Libby arrived, bumping her wheeled suitcase across the lawn. I was sitting on the apartment steps that went up on the outside of the carriage house, a six-pack of beer between my feet, expecting her. I held out a bottle at arm's length and Libby left the suitcase where it was, halfway from the driveway. She joined me in the late-afternoon shade.

"Too hot for moving day," I said.

"You're red already," she replied, taking a swallow and then pressing the cold bottle against my scorched arm.

At once, I saw both the playful adult Libby trying to recapture our common youth with a "Really wonderful!" on my porch and the twelve-year-old Libby wiping tears from her eyes at the florist shop.

My plan was to let Libby speak. This was the first time we'd been together since I'd seen her father burn his car. More important, it was the first time since Libby the girl had seen me standing close to the fire. I wondered if she'd act differently now. I wondered if she and I shared some new knowledge, if we had a new bond.

The event I'd seen had had an influence on me. Now I was wondering whether I'd had an influence on the event. How deep had I really gone?

I opened another beer. I drank. And when I set the bottle down I didn't say a word for a minute or so. I didn't want to influence Libby.

Fat chance of that. I couldn't contain myself.

"Do you remember the day your father's Cadillac caught fire?"

Libby froze, beer bottle still on my arm. She narrowed her eyes. "I saw it."

"Tell me."

She stepped back. "I was in the greenhouse," Libby began, looking across the distance from the Victorian's hilltop toward our old neighborhood. Then she turned back. "Why do you ask?"

I bumbled an answer about what I remembered. Something about our work together at the shop and our many recent visits there. She seemed to buy the explanation and she continued.

"It was a weekday, I remember, and I was home sick from school. The shop wasn't very busy; most of the customers came in on the weekend. I wasn't all that sick; I probably just had a little cold, so Daddy asked me to water the plants in the greenhouse. I got out the hose and started making a real mess, like I always did. Water was running all over, but it didn't matter. The greenhouse had a drain in the floor. It was fun. I loved it when he asked me to do that job.

"Daddy was outside. I could hear the lawn mower, but I really wasn't paying attention. The splashing water was making a lot of noise. Then Daddy came back in. He walked over to the counter, sat down in his chair, and lit a cigarette. I remember he said, 'It's done,' but he wasn't talking to me. He just said it. At first, I thought he meant that he was done mowing the lawn, but then I smelled smoke. It was a really strange smell, and I ran to the front door.

"I turned around and stared at Daddy. He looked like he was crying. I'd never seen my father cry before. I'd never seen any man cry."

Okay. Inside the greenhouse was easy.

"What did you see outside?" I asked.

"Our car," said Libby, "our beautiful new car was on fire. I remember staring at the smoke coming up from the grille. I thought it looked like a man, maybe a clown with a cigarette letting smoke out though some crazy, big, toothy grin. There was a huge cloud of black smoke going up. There were a bunch of puffy white clouds in the sky, and the smoke just rose and rose and covered them up."

I asked her about people.

"Firemen were jumping off their truck and squirting foam at the car. There were a lot of moms and their kids standing on the sidewalk down the street watching."

I asked if she remembered who was there.

"Not really. They didn't come very close. I was standing inside the screen door, and I was crying. I was crying really hard, so the whole thing was kind of blurry. I remember the fire and the smoke, but I wasn't paying much attention to peoples' faces."

I was relieved.

"Except one."

Uh-oh.

"There was one person," she said slowly as if she'd found a new insight, something she'd noticed for the first time.

Oh, shit.

"He was standing on the sidewalk, close to the car, watching it burn."

Had I entered her memory?

"Eddy," whispered Libby.

Had I changed this piece of history?

"It was you."

Had a new history taken over from the old? It sure looked that way. I was about to jump out of my skin.

"But that doesn't make sense."

No, I don't suppose it did, not if you hadn't studied it hard. I had some theories about what was going on. They were still pretty much preliminary, but maybe I could test one on Libby. Send up a trial balloon, run it up the flagpole, as they say.

Back at Hugh's funeral, when my aunts spoke to me, I'd wondered what they saw. They addressed me as Edward, just as they had years ago. Did they see me as a boy? Certainly they couldn't have recognized me as a man. They'd never known that version of me. Libby had a different view. She'd known both boy and man, so I needed to know which she'd seen. "Are you sure it was me?" "How old was I?" "What did I look like?" "What was I wearing?" "What was . . . ."

"Shit, Eddy, it was just you." Libby set her welcome-home beer on the bottom step. "How can I explain it more clearly?"

I'd been blunt and I'd been clumsy. That damn searching-for-the-truth thing, I'm afraid. Libby quite obviously wanted to send the discussion somewhere else, but I could see that she couldn't. The pondering and questioning and worrying bug had bitten her, too.

"If it was you," she said, and I could tell she was growing more confused the more deeply she got into this, "you'd have been a kid. But I remember wondering why this guy wasn't at work. And why he didn't have on a tie. When do you ever wear a tie?"

Libby stared hard at me as if she were searching for a tie. I shrugged.

"I remember," she said, going more slowly now, speaking in a way that made me feel like I was looking in a mirror, seeing my own pondering behavior. "I remember very distinctly what we used to call Saturday clothes, chinos, like maybe for a game of golf."

And then Libby brightened. "So it must have been your father. It probably was. I'm sure it was him."

I felt myself physically deflate. My shoulders slumped. I'd been there! I'd brought back evidence, the red skin on my arm, the odor of smoke that still rose faintly from my shirt. That adult, he was me! And Libby had almost had it. She'd almost seen me, but then her overthinking (sounds familiar, huh?) turned the man beside the burning car into my father.

From my seat on the steps, I looked down at my own chinos, then up at Libby. "Okay," I allowed. Best to give up, hide my disappointment, I supposed. "Just something I was thinking about. You know how I am."

I had the wisdom not to take this any further, not to explain a theory I'd been nurturing that Libby or the aunts or anyone else in the past who saw me was seeing some kind of essence, maybe my soul, maybe something that was unchanging. That would explain what the aunts saw in me at the funeral. It wasn't the adult Eddy or the child Eddy; it was just Eddy. Until the point where the actual child showed up, the one who lived in their era, my age and physical condition had been irrelevant. Age and physical condition are not what a person is about. That much was apparent when they looked at me. Relationships and connections and influences, that's what we were; that's what we are.

So I told Libby thank you for the memory and tried to make a joke about it. There was a song called "Thanks for the Memory" wasn't there? Yes. Frank Sinatra. Bob Hope. It was a well-known song. But Libby didn't think my joke was very funny, given the sad events she'd just recalled. She seemed more than a little pissed off at my digging and probing, and she was now a lot ready to leave.

This kind of conflict was exactly what I'd been trying to avoid with Sheila. Now I'd created it with Libby. And she seemed to know. Libby seemed to know that this wasn't one little event I was remembering and asking about. She seemed to know that it had the potential for being something big, though the exact character of that something was a prediction none of us could make. Not yet.

Libby squeezed by me and sadly climbed the stairs. She climbed like she was carrying a weight, maybe the weight of loneliness or regret or anger, probably the weight of relationships. Her heavy suitcase still stood on the lawn, left behind like some test for me, a test of whether I would encourage her to stay or not, a test of whether I was willing to give support or whether I just wanted to take.

This was a no-brainer. I knew I shouldn't have been so wrapped up in what I'd seen in another time that I'd mistreated my friend in the present. I grabbed the suitcase by the handle and followed quickly, up to the second story.

The apartment door was open and through the screen I could hear Libby inside, muttering. "Thanks for the memory . . . ." She sounded like she was close, probably in one of the living room's old, overstuffed chairs. In the early evening, she had not turned on the lights and the room was dark. I couldn't see her, though I could imagine Libby sitting, legs curled underneath her.

But imagination was as far as I could or should go, and I left the suitcase on the landing. There were probably some things that were best for me not to know, Libby's mental state being one of them. I wasn't so heartless that I'd prod and poke to learn more, and I wasn't so clueless that I'd dismiss her pain with a "Yeah, sure, whatever." When it came to Libby, I'd keep to myself for a while. But in other areas, I knew I'd go ahead with the prodding and the poking, even if doing so wasn't such wise idea.

To myself, at least, I had to admit: There was something pulling at me, but there was also something that made me want to run full tilt, chasing after it. Hours after seeing Mr. Peacock torch his car, I was still jumping out of my skin with excitement. There was still a lot I needed to figure out.

ten

At first, there was only the nightlight on the far wall, but it put out enough light that I could see the bedroom around me, Sheila asleep beside me. She lay on her side, facing away, a prelude to the future of her pregnancy when lying on her back, lying where I could see her, would be awkward. She'd once had long hair that spread over the pillow. I used to love looking at that. But she'd cut it off, and now she slept with a smaller halo.

I lay on my back, staring at the ceiling. I was pondering my theory of what I looked like when I visited the past, whether I was a soul or an essence or some other self. You know how nighttime pondering goes. Wake up in the dark and the inside of your head is the entire universe. I'd been making astounding progress with all sorts of theories, I thought, until the daylight revealed Sheila. Then there was the cat.

Ike had decided that the gap just above my pillow at the base of the head-board was a comfortable little nest. He, too, was awake. I knew this because he was purring, right into my ear.

I'd always been the princess and the pea. Every creak of the house, every itch on my skin, every twist in my pajamas, every irregularity in the mattress, I felt them all. Every night was like a night in an unfamiliar bed, like it'd be a good long time before I'd be comfortable where I was. But I never seemed to find that place.

I waited in the shadows until the birds outside began to sing. Then I quietly moved to the bedroom window seat. I raised the sash. The outdoors and the room were bright now. Sheila opened her eyes, ran her fingers through her hair, sat up, and took a drink of water from the glass on her nightstand. I gave her a little wave, but she didn't see me. Sheila pulled on her robe and left the room. I heard her in the bathroom, throwing up.

I turned back to the window. Had the birds ever been so loud? It sounded like they were yelling, screaming, hollering. Maybe I was just noticing more than usual. I stared at the trees, looking for feathers among the leaves, but they were hard to find.

Sheila returned. "I'm beginning to understand," I suggested from my place on the window seat.

"I'm feeling great," she replied, flopping back onto the bed. "Thank you for asking."

Three or four days had passed since I'd seen the car fire, since I'd sneaked and run to avoid Sheila's displeasure. A long, hot shower and clothes dropped straight into the laundry had erased the smoke. Red arm and face and neck I could explain away as the usual consequences of summer. It seemed to work. I'd expected to see daggers flying out of Sheila's eyes, like a pissed-off character in an old comic book, but she hadn't raised even the first question. Of course, if I'd been paying attention, I'd have understood that Sheila was too busy feeling crappy in her pregnancy to notice I was worrying about something I alone had seen. The birds continued their racket and I sat spotlighted in a beam of morning sunlight. Now I had ideas to float, suggestions about how all this business could be happening. I had truths to discover about what it all meant.

I also had punches to pull in explaining this to Sheila.

I turned her way. As the warm summer air had flowed into the room, she'd pushed the sheets to the foot of the bed.

"Look at him," I said, nodding at Ike, who was sitting up straight now, a porcelain cat, symmetrical, with eyes like saucers. His face rotated around, around, around in counterclockwise circles. "I don't know what he's seeing, but he's seeing something. Some tiny, little bug."

Sheila sat up, swatted at the air, and fell back to her pillow. Ike looked around, confused. Nothing to watch now. He rolled over, and Sheila began scratching his belly. "No bug," she announced.

"There's something out there," I said, opening another window. I looked down at the gutter edging the porch roof below. "You know how the air is always clean after a storm and everything smells different? How there are sounds and smells and there's a light breeze you usually don't notice?"

"It didn't rain last night," Sheila said. She ran her fingers the length of the cat's tail.

I stood and crossed to the last closed window in the room. Raising the sash, I could feel the slight breeze, barely enough to move the curtains but definitely there.

"Let's leave all the windows open," I said. "Let's see what happens."

"What happens," said Sheila, "is the house gets hotter than hell. It's August."

I now crossed the room to the thermostat and turned the air conditioning to "Off." I unplugged the clock on Sheila's dresser. "Let's see what happens if we totally open up to all the sounds and smells and moving air that are out there."

"Let's see what happens," said Sheila rising from the bed, "if I go downstairs and make some breakfast." She threw a light dressing gown around her shoulders and turned toward the door. She either wasn't noticing what was going on, not picking up on the topics I was so gingerly dancing around, or trying hard not to notice. One thing for sure: She didn't want to talk any more than Libby did.

But I had this gut feeling that Sheila knew. She knew, I could feel it, what I'd been planning to say. She wanted, I knew for a fact, to say something critical, something nasty, something to make me give up this foolishness.

"Save me," Sheila said from halfway down the stairs, trailing eye-rolling sarcasm behind her.

And so she left me, standing in the morning sunbeams, thinking out loud, dropping hints, suggesting visions that I wasn't entirely ready to reveal, but needing to clarify what I was slowly understanding about how I'd seen the past.

I turned back to the window and took a deep breath. "After all these years, still out there." I looked down at Ike. "Did you see it?"

I'd be a professor with a one-student class. And it was okay if that student was a cat. My Socratic musings were mostly aimed at myself anyway.

"It's like when I was in bed," I began, "awake, before the sun came up. Above the nightlight there was this bright spot on the wall. It was amazingly bright."

I walked over to the nightlight and switched it off, then on, then off. I switched it back on and left it. Ike lay on his back, his stomach waiting for more scratching.

"Now that the sun's up, that little light is hard to see, but it's still on, and it's still putting out the same amount of light it did in the dark." I turned toward Ike. "I'm thinking the past is like that. The present is so bright we can't see anything else, but the past is still out there."

I spun quickly, flipping the window curtain with my hand.

"Damn!"

Ike startled, bounded off the bed, and followed Sheila downstairs.

"Turn off the TV!" I called down the stairwell, smiling with the thought that Ike, not Sheila, might be the one to heed my instructions. I pulled on an old pair of chino pants and hung a faded green golf shirt on the bathroom doorknob. I took a quick shave. "Turn off the radio!" I called as I emerged, drying my face with a towel.

Pulling the shirt roughly over my head, stretching it but not caring, I clattered down the stairs. I was entirely in the present now. My analysis seemed right. Long-ago events were riding on sounds, smells, and moving air. The present simply overpowers our ability to see them.

Until we look in just the right way, at the right time, in the right place.

In the parlor and the kitchen, I pulled televisions away from walls and unscrewed cables. In the living room, I not only unplugged the stereo from its power, I disconnected each component. CD player, speakers, amplifier, all stood mute. There would be no distractions in this house, not if Eddy McBride could help it.

I rushed from room to room, raising windows from the bottom and lowering them from the top. I swung open the transom windows over the old house's interior doors so air would flow freely across the ceiling.

In my mind, the house would prepare itself all day, capturing sounds, smells, and hot—very hot, I had to admit—summer air. By evening, enough time would have passed to swap out all remnants of morning. And I'd see what the old Victorian held.

I was ecstatic.

I grabbed a cup of coffee. No time for breakfast.

I gave Sheila a peck on the cheek. This entire time, she'd been quietly reading the morning paper at the dining room table.

She wasn't excited at all.

I passed Ike, seated on the porch railing. Who knew what he was thinking?

Ike's eyes were wide again, but his pupils had narrowed to slits against the morning sun. Not a blank stare. He was intent and absorbed the way cats sometimes are, but I didn't think there was a bug this time. It was as if the cat could see the air itself, as if the atmosphere were something solid, a flowing connective tissue between animals and people and trees and houses. Between past and present, perhaps. It was as if all the pieces of experience were out there together, as if what usually seemed invisible, the space between, was always full of life.

Damn, I wished I were a cat.

But a cat can't drive a truck, and my truck was what I needed now. I climbed in and gunned it down the driveway.

"You always go to the place where you start." My mind was taking off in all sorts of directions and I was talking to myself as I drove my old Ford pickup. With its V8 power and its 1964 aesthetic, its original paint a tone called "Caribbean turquoise" and its current greenish hue like the patina on a courthouse dome, it seemed just the thing to take on a quest back in time.

"That's right," I said as I drove. "That's where you go. You go where you start."

I drove by the weedy old ballpark without stopping. Babe Ruth had swung his bat at this place. The energy from his swing was out there, I was sure of it, still bouncing around inside the atmosphere. But aside from showing me the origin of the autographed baseball on my mantel, that place didn't hold the history I wanted. I needed another place, other sounds and smells and other currents in the invisible air.

Soon to be visible, if I had this thing figured right.

It was as if tiny remnants of long-ago events were traveling across time, much the way light travels billions of miles and thousands of years from stars. When we look into the sky we're seeing what it used to be, not what's there now. Same here on Earth. I just needed to put myself in the place where those remnants were landing.

I pulled the truck to a stop in front of the florist shop and its greenhouse, slammed the door hard to make sure it was tight, but didn't bother to lock it. I left the windows down. This was my old neighborhood. No one ever locked doors here. Life was simple; life was good. That's the way it used to be. That's what I was looking to see again. This seeing-the-past business had started off on a happy enough note, with Mr. Peacock and myself fixing the house. Uncle Hugh's funeral and Mr. Peacock's torching his car hadn't been much fun, but I had high hopes I could get back on track with the good times.

Ever since I'd seen the burning Cadillac, in fact, I'd been daydreaming about one of those good times, resurrecting over and over again the day Mr. Peacock brought his new car home. Mr. Peacock was a bit of a showoff, but his antics ("Hello, girls!") were something that everyone counted on and looked forward to. He bought a new car every year, and to Libby and me and my brother Stan, to our entire neighborhood for that matter, the day of its arrival was as significant as Christmas or Thanksgiving, the first or last day of school. It was our own special day.

In those times, the trees were small, houses well tended, and sidewalks flat. No buckling yet from gnarled roots, in great shape for roller-skating, an invitation for children to run fast and be free.

The world was as new as a 1959 Cadillac. With its white-wall tires and fender skirts, its soaring tailfins, its dropped convertible top, and its white vinyl interior gleaming in the sun, the car seemed like an arrow poised to fly through the air. Its sky-blue paint made it look like it was part of the ether.

"Oh, wow!" I found myself whispering as I leaned my elbows on the hood of my old truck and stared off down the street. "A convertible." I was ready for the past to appear.

I remembered a lot about that day, a lot of little pieces.

I remembered children and dogs running, housewives stepping briskly down their front walks, neighbor men showing up with pruning shears and paint brushes still in their hands. They'd been that excited, too excited even to put down their tools before joining the crowd.

I remembered exclamations and questions arriving in a flood. "Can we go for a ride?" "Show us how the top goes." "How's this big battleship gonna fit in that little ol' garage?" "Oh, wow!"

I remembered Mr. Peacock grinning behind the wheel. I remembered watching him put the car in park, turn off the ignition, swing his right arm over the back of the passenger's seat, lean way back, and grin some more.

A girl pushed through the crowd. "Oh, Daddy! Let's go now!" I remembered Libby. I remembered the boy who came running, tearing full speed across the street. It was Stan. And I remembered Mr. Peacock sitting upright fast and holding out his hand like a traffic cop. My brother stopped a good ten feet short of the shiny new Cadillac. Everyone respected the man with a new car.

In a flash, Libby and Stan were in the back seat. Mr. Peacock was waving at his wife. "Come on, honey!" She paused to clip a loose strand of hair back from her face with a bobby pin before easing into the front seat beside her husband. Mr. Peacock turned the key and we all listened to the engine with admiring pleasure, listened knowingly to highly advertised and high-price quality, before the car glided smoothly, oh so smoothly, away from the curb.

I remembered all that because on that day I'd been standing just to the side, watching. Probably, I'd have missed the spectacle if I'd been a part of it.

I'd have missed the car's triumphant return, too, as it rounded the corner at the opposite end of the block and slowly showed off to the neighbors again. Stan and Libby were standing in back waving like celebrities in a parade. "Hey, Eddy," they called when they saw me sitting on the steps of the house next door. "Eddyyyyyyyyyyy!"

I carefully closed a tablet of drawing paper, stood, and tucked a pencil behind my ear. Then, I started running. Enough with the observing. I was ready to join the action. Cadillac lust!

But observation always won with me, even when I was a boy. Halfway to the street, a little out of control in my haste and excitement, I stumbled and dropped my tablet. It skidded across the sidewalk and I pulled up short, retrieving my sketched record of the day and smoothing wrinkled pages. Excitement gone. Worry on my face, I'm sure.

"Oh, Eddy," moaned Stan. "C'mon! Hurry up!"

"Eddyyyyyyyyyyy!" pleaded Libby.

I remember the pair leaning over the side of the car, gesturing as if they were urging a runner to the finish line. "C'mon!" urged Stan, flopping almost completely over the top of the side panel, his arms dangling halfway to the ground, exasperated.

"That's right, son," said Mr. Peacock, giving the rearview mirror a twist and adjusting his tie. "This train's not gonna wait all day."

eleven

I'd stood in the street for only a few minutes, anxiously ready and waiting to rejoin my memories, to see Mr. Peacock and his Cadillac once again, but in those minutes the wind had picked up and trash, old forgotten and discarded stuff, suddenly seemed to be everywhere.

I'd been looking for something good, but now I put my foot down hard on something less desirable, pinning a plastic bag, a jellyfish kind of amorphous thing, to the pavement. I grabbed a snap-on, fountain-style soft-drink lid that was rolling on its edge. Here, in the old neighborhood, it reminded me of the childhood tale of the johnnycake. Can't catch me! But I did. A step or three later, I was in the yard, with a more annoying story to deal with. Overnight, someone had stuffed an old sofa into the dumpster.

I picked up one of its cushions, once apparently nicely flocked, now ripped and stained, that lay on the ground. Like a player at a carnival midway, I tossed it toward the green container's side door, and just like every toss in my youth, when I'd always been inept at midway games, the cushion missed. It rattled the loose door in its frame with a muffled clang and bounced back into the dirt.

But dull and muffled as it was, that clang resonated. And in the wind, I thought I heard it again.

I stared beyond the dumpster, down the street, but no one was there. I could hear workmen hammering somewhere at the back of the shop, but workmen weren't what I was after. Where was that Cadillac? Where were the running and laughing children and the envious neighbors? I was ready, damn it. Why wasn't the past ready for me?

The dull clang was gone, but I remained staring at that green door. Green door, green door. I thought about the sofa and the rest of the crap behind the door—to which I added the plastic bag and the soda lid—and it came to me then, that old, mysterious, semi-hipster tune. Something, something. I couldn't really remember the lyrics, but it was a story about some kind of speakeasy, people behind the door having a good time while the singer's stuck outside.

And then there was a saxophone in the distance playing that same song. It played smoothly, stopped, then started again. Two or three times, it resumed at the same point in the music. Then it picked up a few bars later and noodled freely. Then it played the whole tune straight through, without stopping.

I began slowly walking down the sidewalk, attentively following that saxophone from the florist shop down toward the house where I'd lived.

The sound was sweet, and when it was over, I found myself standing alone in my old front yard, applauding. I didn't know where in the cosmos the sound of the dirty, old sofa cushion hitting the dumpster door might have gone and whether or not I'd ever hear it again, but this music was something that I could listen to, something I should be able to ride back to where I wanted to be—the day that Mr. Peacock's Cadillac arrived.

Years ago, I knew this saxophone and this music. A man in the house behind us practiced beside an open window, always alone, always single-minded, almost ascetic in his devotion. Then when he'd mastered his material, he'd call his friends. They'd jam and drink beer in the backyard. He was a good musician, and the people in the neighborhood generally enjoyed the free, live entertainment. It was a far step above our scratchy phonographs and tinny radios.

Those were the nights. My brother Stan and I would be in our beds on either side of our window. The streetlamp outside would cast just enough illumination that we could make hand-puppet shadows dance on the far wall. We'd whisper and laugh until what seemed to be impossibly late, though I'm sure now it wasn't even midnight. Downstairs on the porch I could sometimes hear my parents, together with Mr. and Mrs. Peacock, drinking their favorite highballs and making their laughter dance to the music like our wall shadows. Stan always fell asleep at about this time, but even though I was younger I was never tired. I was fascinated with adult rituals and with listening to every note the saxophone and its mates played.

Finally, in the wee hours, when the musicians' beer and jazz refused to stop, someone in the neighborhood would call the police to complain, the music would reluctantly end, and I'd drift off to the silence.

That musician's house behind ours had been silent for years, but that green-door tune came back clearly. I wished I could remember the lyrics as well as I could remember those long-ago nights eavesdropping on music.

But hold on. What I was hearing was not something I was remembering. I looked around. Down the street, my truck was gone and the greenhouse was advertising fresh flowers. The trees in all the front yards were small again. I'd ridden that music into a complete and familiar world.

From the house behind, the saxophone player in his open window stared down at me and gave a slow, military-style salute, holding his hand at his brow for the longest time before snapping it away and stepping back into the darkened house. Walter Lee. Damn him.

Because suddenly I knew not only the place where I stood and the people who inhabited it, but I knew the time. I knew it to the day, but I wished I didn't. It was not the time I wanted or expected, not by the longest shot imaginable. I rushed to the curb, hoping for some help, searching for a way out, but finding neither.

It was then that I saw the yellow school bus. It was about a block away, coming in my direction.

And from the other direction, a speeding car.

I tried to curse but no sounds came. No words were bad enough for what was about to happen.

The bus lurched closer, swaying with its load as the driver turned a corner, springs creaking and brakes squealing. The bus windows were down and I could hear that the kids inside were loud and boisterous. One threw a football and dozens of hands went up to catch it. "Sit down!" the driver yelled. No one did. The tall, grim man stared up at the rearview mirror, which was trained on the passengers. His eyes were off the road, off any approaching or following traffic as the ball sailed nearly the entire length of the bus, bouncing off the rear window this time. "I know who threw that!" he called. "Sit down or I'll put every one of you out. You can all walk home." The bus was slowing for one of its regular stops.

The car came faster, its body the blur of speed, its chrome a flash in the sun. Tailfins sliced air. The motor purred with big-cat power. Avoiding occasional other vehicles that were parked, the car took its half of the street out of the middle. Had there been a stripe dividing lanes, the car would have been perfectly centered over it, wheels equidistant from the line, riding it like some futuristic monorail. The car inched to the right, as if the driver knew where the vehicle should be. Then it returned to the center, as if unsure of its path. And it kept coming.

When the yellow bus stopped, red lights at the roofline began to flash. Black lettering on each said: "Stop." A metal arm swung out from the side. In larger red lettering, it said the same: "Stop."

I alone was paying attention.

Now, it is a common belief that time seems to stop when an accident is about to happen. Speeding cars move slowly, coasting as if they've shifted down gears. Running children bound forward in slow motion, floating on air and instinct toward a destination they are not watching. This was not what I experienced. To me, the inevitable accident kept its pace. What changed were all the details that surrounded the accident. As the accident played out in the background, I saw details more clearly than I'd seen anything before.

I felt like the person in a crowded restaurant who cannot keep his attention on one conversation. A snippet of gossip coming from my left, the punch line of a joke from behind, these could make the auditory experience overwhelming. Now it was swirling visions of my entire childhood—black-and-white pictures on the television, lime-green Tupperware on kitchen counters, and muddy soft-drink bottles, a returnable gold mine at two cents each, found under bushes.

I did not imagine or remember these things. I saw them all around me on lawns and porches, through open front doors and kitchen windows. I thought about crossing to the neighbor's yard and lifting one of the concrete ducks that waddled across the grass. It would surprise me, as the ducks always had when I was a boy, with its solid weight. I eyed the bicycle leaning against a neighbor's garage. If I mounted it and rode away, the playing cards pinned to the frame would flap against the wheels' spokes and delight me with their motorcycle sound. The details of childhood made being here richly real. And they made it inescapable.

The car approached without slowing.

Twelve-year-old Stan hopped off the bus and ran into the street without looking.

The car swerved back into its lane to pass the bus.

It hit the boy squarely with the center of its gaping maw of a grille.

My brother gave a little gasp before bouncing off the chrome and disappearing under the streak of passing blue. Where had he gone? I saw only the wide hulk of the car still coming my way. When I finally understood, I wished I hadn't seen at all.

The car had snagged Stan on its undercarriage and dragged him fifty yards, unseen, before spitting him out behind. Oh, God. Let him be unconscious. Let him be already dead. Stan's body was scraped and bloody, his arms and back twisted at shocking angles. Broken. His clothing had been shredded by the pavement. One of his shoes remained at the point of impact. The other landed directly in front of me.

I felt my whole body snap and jerk. I knew the sensation, and it always frightened me. It was the same feeling that snapped me awake when I dreamed I'd missed the bottom step in a flight of stairs. I felt I was falling a short distance in an even shorter time. Then I looked around. I stood in front of the florist shop, dumpster behind me in the yard, pickup truck to my side at the curb.

"No," I said aloud, but I was not sure what I was rejecting, whether stepping into the past or returning to the present.

"NO," I shouted, and this time I knew why. Stan again lay in front of me, but I could not look down. Not yet. I stared after the car. Now I saw. It was a Cadillac. "No," I whispered. I needed to identify the driver, but as the vehicle receded, all I could see was linen white. The convertible top was up.

Down the street in the opposite direction, the school bus pulled away from the curb. The captured football sat on the driver's lap. The man grinned, certain he had brought order to the world. The student passengers punched each other, scattered books, stole jackets. Chaos was their favorite diversion. My brother had disappeared quickly and landed far away. No one had seen the events outside.

Stan and I were alone together now, a boy and a man, each shattered in his own way. No birds sang. I noticed the quiet. No neighbors came. I was not ready for comfort anyway. Minutes passed before I could take myself to my brother's side, where a puddle of blood swelled, red on its blacktop background, trickling toward the gutter. I reached out my hand toward Stan.

A saxophone played again in the back neighbor's house, and like the music my right hand hovered in mid-air. Five digits spread wide cast a spidery shadow across my dead brother's face, gently shielding the afternoon sun. I lowered my hand, but the shadow was the only touch I could give his body. I pressed my palm flat and full into the puddle in the street. I left it there for a long time, In my mind, the singer was still trying unsuccessfully to get into the speakeasy. But I'd made it into my family story. I looked over my shoulder, hating the musician I once loved to hear, wishing he would stop but knowing he wouldn't. That damn song had been my dead brother's favorite. Walter Lee, the old bastard, was guiding me into this hell. On my front porch that day, he'd challenged me to discover my past, to learn the truth. Whatever his game was, it looked like he'd won.

twelve

In the late summer afternoon, I was shivering. Just as surely as if it had been winter, my hands were shaking and my teeth were chattering and I couldn't stop. I climbed into the refuge of my truck, rolled up the windows, and sat waiting for the closed-in summertime heat to do its job. I still had Stan's blood all over my right palm. Blood was smeared on the truck's upholstery, and it dripped when I rested my hand on the gear stick. I should've driven, escaped, but I sat. My brother's death was something too horrible and too compelling to stop watching. I shivered again as I stared, almost without blinking, at the drips.

I'd thought I had this thing figured out, this business about energy and sounds and smells riding in on some kind of waves. It was science. All I had to do was pay attention. Then I'd land comfortably in the happy day I wanted to see, a time I wanted to live again. To hell with that. There was a lot more to this business than simple waves of energy. Understanding how I was seeing wasn't telling me what I really needed to know. I needed the reason why.

I watched a drop of blood gather itself at the tip of my pinkie finger, slowly pull away, and stain the floor. What I'd seen was real. It was not some family tradition repeated until the story became something everyone took for true, and it was not some weird recovered memory that I was finally allowing myself to see. As an eight-year-old, I hadn't been at the scene of the accident. I'd been on the bus. I didn't have anything to remember. Not until I'd stepped into this time and place. Not until Walter Lee and his music took me there.

The sun had set by the time I pulled into the Victorian's driveway. I used my clean left hand to depress the door handle and shoved the door open with my shoulder. I held my bloodied right hand in the air, a salute or a symbol or simply a way to avoid dripping even more as I walked straight to the garden hose at the side of the house.

There, behind the shrubbery, I squatted on my heels and washed. Red water puddled. A few dried leaves, curved like bowls, caught and held the watery blood and the bloody water. Others floated like little boats, moving gently where the mixture would take them. But the blood thinned as the water ran, and when I turned off the hose, water and blood soaked quickly into the earth.

What in God's name? I dried my hands under my armpits. I stared at the spot where my brother's blood had disappeared.

What in God's name? Not ready to stand, I shuffled from side to side, duck-like. I had no plans to go into the house, not yet. I plopped onto a dry spot of earth and sat, wondering how long I could avoid Sheila and wondering how long it would be before I could let go of these new visions, this Stan that had returned after so many years. I held my head between my knees. Behind my eyes, the Cadillac still bore down on my brother.

What in God's name? And in a rush I knew.

The events I was seeing were not random. There was a pattern. Damn.

There was a pattern that I hadn't been able to see until a few key events had played themselves out. Key points in my life. Lived backward. Last to first. It was an archaeological excavation, a peeling of an onion—or an opening of my keepsake box from the carriage house closet. Every event I saw, every artifact I moved out of the way, made it possible for me to look deeper, to see what had come before.

At the top, Mr. Peacock and the new gutter. It was a day like so many others: on the surface hardly memorable, but in reality a revealing snapshot of how a neighbor helped a lonely and devastated boy. Uncle Hugh's funeral. My brother had only recently died. Aunt Eleanor said so. I was a bystander, a boy grieving only for his brother, while the rest of the family reeled from cumulative tragedies I could not understand. The burning Cadillac. The hit-and-run vehicle gone. And now the accident itself. This was the event that snapped everything into perspective. It was the foundation of the others.

It was an event I couldn't skip. I couldn't go straight to the earlier arrival of the new car the way I'd wanted, juggling the sequence of events and calling them up the way I could juggle and call up memories. I first had to pass through the tragedy the Cadillac had brought.

Sheila probably had been right when she'd warned me not to get involved with Libby. My old friend's arrival had turned me toward a time and a place I should have avoided. But neither Sheila nor Libby knew about Walter Lee. I'd be damned if I was going to tell them. Now the old man was looking more and more like an influence I could not avoid.

And, of course, there was my Eddy nature. I was beginning to sense that there was some string, one red thread as the saying goes, that ran through all these events and tied them together. And that even if it turned out to be a not-so-hot idea—a terrible idea, a disastrous idea—I needed to see that hidden, unifying string. I was worrying that it was my fate to give that string a good hard tug until events unraveled.

Crouching in the bushes, I looked from my clean hands up to the night-time sky. For everyone's protection, for mine and Sheila's and Libby's and maybe even for Tim's, I had to keep the day of my brother's death inside. But I was home. It was too late to run out on Sheila tonight the way I'd run out on her at the office.

"Are you there?"

Sheila was suddenly at the porch railing, peering through the dark across the yard at the truck.

I wiped my hands on my shirt one more time and stood.

Sheila jumped back. "Oh, my God! What are you doing down there?"

"I was dirty. I got dirty down at the job site, down at the shop." It wasn't a lie, not really. I coiled the hose and hung it from its hook below where Sheila stood. "I didn't want to mess up the house."

"You'd better get inside. It's too dark to be washing out here." Behind her, across the threshold of the open kitchen door stood the little cat Ike. He stood as if he agreed, front paws on the dark porch side, rear paws on the lighted house side. Sheila scooped up Ike with one hand and in my mind's eye, I saw her put her other hand on her belly. It was still early in her pregnancy, but I wanted to see the future. At that moment, I was trying for the future, I really was. Then she re-entered the house and slammed the door. I stopped abruptly, only a few steps behind, bewildered as an animal at being shut out in the dark.

I loved Sheila, always had, whether she realized it or not. And I was grateful for the way she'd kindly overlooked my behavior when she found me washing in the shrubbery, or the way she'd blissfully missed the signs that something was going on. It was a perception and an imagination thing, I suppose. Sheila and I never looked quite the same way at the events we experienced, and we never took from them the same truths. She never made the mental leaps that I made. These were leaps—I'll be the first to admit it—that I made too often.

I think Sheila could have done it, but she refused to play. Sheila knew how to turn off external stimuli. Sometimes I wished I could do the same, though mostly I found her behavior disappointing. But that's the way our life was. Not every couple has everything in common. I suppose none really does.

In the parlor, Sheila turned a page in her book. She looked calm; yes, she did. Maybe I'd been overthinking her behavior. She may never have smelled the smoke on my clothes at the office. She may have thought that my washing in the shrubbery was simply to get rid of dirt just as I'd implied.

I gave a sigh and Sheila looked up. She smiled. "Don't you have anything to read?"

Oh, yes. I eased into a chair across the room and assured her that I did but that I just wanted to rest for a moment. The cat jumped into my lap. Yes, I'd pet him for a while.

No, Sheila was not hiding anything. No, she did not appear to be upset.

Yes, I needed my wife. Yes, I needed some understanding. I needed something to bring me down from the death I'd just seen and something to keep me grounded and sure that the world made sense.

I went to the kitchen and began slicing limes. I squeezed the juice over ice in a tall glass, added a couple of ounces of gin, then a couple of ounces more. I stopped just short of filling the glass with tonic. A splash more of gin for good measure. Yes, that would do it. Then I prepared a ginger ale for Sheila. As I handed her the glass I looked again at her belly. Only a couple of weeks in and nothing yet to show, but this looking was becoming a habit. It was as if I were waiting for bread to rise or water to boil. No, I couldn't fully imagine the future, at least not the way Sheila could.

Sheila had settled into the sofa with her book. I leaned over and gave her a quick kiss and she gave me a quick smile. Maybe I could make this evening into one of those ordinary times when our ships simply passed in the night. Ordinary was what I needed. After long days at work, we too often ate dinner, went to bed, got up, and did it all over again. If we wanted to live hand-in-hand and side-by-side in each other's company, we'd have to work at it. We'd work at it tomorrow, I thought.

Or not. Sheila still held her smile. It was a smug little "I-told-you-so" smile and she seemed to be waiting for me to respond. I concentrated on my gin. Then the music Sheila had put on the stereo changed tracks and I knew what her smile meant. The windows were closed. The air conditioning was humming. There was music. Sheila had put the house back to normal and put an end to my open-house experiment.

She'd won.

We'd work on our relationship tonight.

I set down my drink, took Sheila's hand, pulled her to standing, and without a word, we began moving across the room. The music was a waltz, a singer-songwriter, tinge-of-country, step-step-step waltz. Damn! We spun across the floor, navigating around armchairs and the coffee table as if the pieces of furniture were other couples on a dance floor. When we flung open the door and step-step-stepped out to the porch, Sheila began to laugh. I stared at the ceiling and managed a straight face. Or a parody of a guy with a straight face. This was wonderful. We spun around a pair of rocking chairs, into the dark at the porch's far end, and back again.

"Siblings," the shrink who treated me after my brother died once said, "can feel an almost mystical connection to each other. Losing the other is like losing part of one's self. You may think for a while that your brother is gone, but in reality you're likely to feel that something is missing for the rest of your life. You'll search for the missing part and make much of things that might have been."

Sheila supplied my missing part. "I love you," I said as we danced, but she didn't reply.

When being together worked, words were not necessary; Sheila and I seemed to know what the other was thinking. Communication came through our eyes, our fingertips, through smells and gestures, through the very heat and pull of gravity that a living body transmits to the universe around it. That night, Sheila and I danced and we laughed. We were almost together, but we were not completely one. There was, after all, something between us.

I'm sure Sheila had her reasons for not saying "I love you." For all my stream-of-consciousness talk, for all the baring I did of my soul, I could be horribly clumsy when thoughts and emotions really mattered. And all too often, I thought only of myself. As we spun across the porch, I glanced up at the carriage house and wondered if it was such a good idea to have Libby so close. But that's what I'd done. I'd put what was turning out to be my gateway into a very painful time right in our backyard.

I had not yet told Sheila what I'd seen. She had not told me why she was afraid of my seeing. Different reasons I'm sure, but the result was the same. Sheila and I both knew something was being held back. We each were secure in our private knowledge, but our feelings were not something we were ready to explain.

The music floated from the stereo through the door we'd left open behind us. It wriggled through the branches of the heavy pecan tree, and as the notes glided out into the neighborhood, they seemed to make the fireflies dance. On an especially clear evening like this, maybe the music even made the stars twinkle. Light years away, could stars hear the notes? All the music had to do was travel through blackness. But we'd never know for sure unless the stars sent the music back.

PART II

Zophar: "God is far above in Mystery."

Eliphaz: "God is far below in Mindlessness."

Bildad: "God is far within in History."

ARCHIBALD MacLEISH, "J.B."

thirteen

SHEILA

Let's hold on a minute. I believe I understand Eddy pretty well. I'd been living with him for years when this business of visiting another time started. I watched how he behaved and I listened to him as he thought out loud, in his typical Eddy way, while it was all going on. And now I'm sitting here listening to him tell his side of the story. We could all be around a campfire taking turns at telling ghost stories or around a conference table giving depositions. Except we're just here on our porch, here in our rocking chairs.

And that's okay. It's not like we haven't heard most of this before. Eddy's told his story. We've all told our stories. But until now, no one has asked us to tell them together. We've always told just a little bit here and a little bit there. Eddy and his brother and their shadow puppets on the wall. End of story. We've all pieced it together, each in our own minds. We all know what happened. Except we really have missed something. We've missed talking about, or at least we've missed understanding, what kind of impact all of this was having on each other.

So it's my turn. I'll begin by saying this.

It always surprised me when Eddy acted like he was the only one noticing things. Because he wasn't.

So there.

Just because I kept quiet back then, just because I didn't talk about every idea that popped into my head, didn't mean I wasn't seeing; it didn't mean I wasn't thinking, and it certainly didn't mean I wasn't feeling. It didn't mean I wasn't smart, and it didn't mean I wasn't imaginative. It just meant I wasn't Eddy.

I never wanted to dwell on every detail I noticed. As a matter of fact, there were plenty of details I never wanted to see. And there were certain details I never wanted to see again.

Now it's not that Eddy's observations were wrong. There was always something to what he saw and what he said. I know he prided himself on discovering truth, but I can tell you, Eddy's truths were selective. He directed his attention where he wanted it to go. He thought he was figuring things out because he was talking about them. If only he'd watched and listened to the people around him more—and I don't mean just me, as gratifying as that would have been— he'd have been surprised at how much truth he really could have learned.

That's the thing about Eddy. He tends not to notice that when something happens that's as big and deep as what we were about to go through, no one goes alone.

Let me give you an example. You heard what Eddy said about the day he waylaid Libby at the apartment steps and hounded her into talking about the day her father's car burned. Yes, his questions upset her. And yes, I know all about it. Because Libby told me. She didn't tell Eddy. He didn't ask.

Everything had started out so well. That first day at the pub, Tim had ventured a bit of flirting, and I think Libby was enjoying the attention after her divorce. And later, she was also excited about the work on her father's old shop. Eddy's design had turned out exactly the way everyone had hoped. Even I, as opposed to the project as I'd been at the beginning, had to admit he'd done a great job. But there was this subtext going on. A couple of months later, Eddy and Tim both told me, separately, that they'd been concerned about Libby's behavior the day construction began. They were confused about the way she'd spaced out over lunch and mumbled about mackerel sky and her father. But it was pretty obvious to me. Her father may have been dead for years, but she still missed him. She missed the way life used to be.

Libby was wrestling with a paradox. For all her bravado about turning the shop into some kind of architectural showplace, this project was hitting a little too close to home. Pun intended. She missed the old days in the old neighborhood, but every new day she spent there brought reminders of how painful the chain of events that occurred there had been. Then Eddy started dredging up the details about one link in that chain. His questions were just too much.

What would you do? What would I do? Libby ran.

She behaved exactly like our little cat Ike in the story Eddy told a while ago about Tim following him with the camera. Libby didn't like being stalked any more than the cat did.

I don't know where Eddy's brain was. He was seeing something, that's for sure, and he was acting distracted. Finally, after some prodding, he told me about his conversation with Libby, about how he'd so-called "remembered" her father's car fire. He said he wanted to find out what she remembered, too.

But he didn't seem to notice what was really going on. He knew she was upset, but he took a step back when it came to finding out more. I was the one who saw that there was no activity at the carriage house, no Libby only a day after she'd moved in.

Eddy didn't seem to notice either that I was the one who discovered what had happened to his friend. In a couple of days, he'd stand in the morning sunlight, lecturing the cat like a babbling fool, going on as if he were describing an experiment in a science lab. He'd entirely missed what was going on in the real world and what was happening to real people.

I did wonder why I was doing this, chasing down Libby. I told myself it was for Eddy. And for Tim. Our partner was falling hard for our client. Remember what Eddy called me: nurturing earth mother. Well, so be it. When real people were concerned, I could duck out of the office and take off on a quest, too, you know.

The workmen were gone by the time I arrived at the shop, but the day was long and the shop was still bright in the late afternoon sun. In the greenhouse, motes of floating construction dust made the sunbeams visible. This place was so bright it couldn't hold a mystery if it tried. I stopped just inside the front door. I knew exactly what I would find.

"I need to be awake," Libby announced as I turned the corner. She sat, posture perfect, on an old folding chair meditatively drinking coffee from a cardboard to-go cup. Her father, she told me, had presided over business from this very spot, and I could imagine what a young Libby would have looked like if the counters had still been in place. I'd have seen only the girl's head as she peeked from behind a fat cash register.

Libby took another swallow, then pointed with her chin at the wide-open room. "I wouldn't want to miss any of this."

Whatever "this" was. Everyone speaks in shorthand.

I wondered if she meant the eviscerated building. Or her vulnerability in the wide-open space. She'd told us she was happy with the work so far, but now she was acting like she regretted any progress she and Eddy had made. I wasn't about to ask. I just pulled up a second folding chair and sat.

The two of us remained in parallel silence for the longest time. At the top corner of the greenhouse, a couple of adult house finches came and went, also quietly. They mostly ignored the nest where they'd hatched their young, where months earlier there would have been incessant chirping, noisy, stressful, hungry crying.

"How's the baby? How are you feeling?" Libby asked.

"Tired."

And we returned to silence. Libby and I sat sharing womanly pregnancy thoughts, prompted, I suppose, by thoughts of cute baby birdies. But there was a strain between us. It was silent and dull, but it was present. Oh, was it ever present.

Libby broke the silence first. "That night at the pub. You didn't like me very much, did you?"

"I never said that."

"Am I right?"

"I didn't know you."

Libby nodded.

I tried to recover. "But I could sense that life was very difficult and very complicated for you."

Libby nodded.

"I just wondered whether that was what Eddy needed in a client."

"Or in a friend."

"A friend's another matter. You do what you have to do for friends."

"We never used to get birds in here," Libby said, staring at the high greenhouse corner. "Daddy took such good care of this place. He made sure none of the windows in the greenhouse were broken. If one even got a crack, he'd replace it right away."

Another finch stuck its head through a broken pane, hopped on the window frame for a second, and turned its back to us. Another hop and it flew away.

"All the tables," said Libby, "they used to be covered with flowers. People would buy flowers to take to the hospital or to celebrate anniversaries or for no reason at all." She set her cup of unfinished coffee on the floor, aligning it carefully with a front leg of her chair as if she were trying to create some order in the empty shell of a building. There was a scorched baby doll under the back of her chair, too. Libby had arranged it carefully in a sitting position, propped against the wall behind her. One more thing for me not to ask about, not until Libby was ready to tell. "People would buy just because they liked flowers. This place was very popular."

I stared across the shop, imagining rows of display tables overflowing with blooms. A greenhouse where plants crowded together to create a forest so thick it was difficult to penetrate. Years ago, these plants would have grown like Topsy. The greenhouse's beauty would have come spontaneously, not by design. I was sorry the old days were gone. I would have loved to see them.

"Now it's dead," said Libby. "But I'm glad you're here."

"I'm glad I found you." I was feeling empathy for Libby, too.

"I'm right here."

"Drinking coffee."

"Right here. Drinking and thinking. I don't run far."

"You still want to do this?"

"I don't have a choice." Libby was matter-of-fact now. "I owe it to myself, and to my father." She looked down and nudged the cardboard cup with her foot, tipping it slowly until its contents spilled onto the concrete floor. She seemed to be concentrating on the cup to avoid whatever she was thinking. Or concentrating on her thoughts and not realizing what she was doing with the cup. Probably a little of each. The coffee spread slowly under her chair, flowing almost to the doll's feet, then stopping of its own accord. "I owe it to other people, too," she said.

Libby seemed to have reached the point where even the most put-together person would break, or at least crack. She'd apparently been holding a lot in, suppressing her emotions and responsibilities, acting brave and being everyone's friend. "All that hail-girl-well-met crap" was how she put it. But her time had come. Her time when pain simply overflowed its container. A little shove and over she'd go, like her coffee.

"Chicks like us," Libby declared, "we've reached an age when we understand that things go away. When I was first separated, I thought a lot about my ex. For about three weeks. Now it's like all those years never happened."

"Makes us tough." I was thinking about my own experiences, with and before Eddy. Libby must have thought I'd appeared from nowhere, I talked about these things so infrequently. But I didn't want to go there. I wanted to get Libby straightened out.

I made a little elbow motion in her direction, something like the gestures I'd seen her make toward Eddy when they were bonding over their childhood, a gentle poke that would have hit her in the arm or maybe the ribs if we'd been sitting closer. Libby didn't appear to notice.

"Except some things don't go away. Some things come back." Libby paused as if she wanted to take another sip of coffee, as if she needed to punctuate her sentence, then apparently remembered that she'd already done away with the cup. "Stan was killed right out front, you know."

"Everyone sees bad things." I was serious again.

"And Eddy. I suppose I partly brought this on myself by coming home, but he didn't have to go connecting the dots. Stan's death is one of those things I can't forget. But I'd managed to pretty well block out the day our car burned."

Libby took another long pause. Her eyes were down, focusing on something far away in her mind's eye or unfocusing on the blank gray of the floor, I couldn't tell which. She looked like she really needed that coffee distraction now. She looked like she didn't want to go where she was going. But she had no choice. She looked up and locked her eyes with mine.

"I know I haven't been around much in the last few years, but I really did love my dad. And after he died, I was finally able to build him up in my mind almost to the point where he was the wonderful person he'd been when I was a little girl, before he got so sad. Before he . . . . Oh, I'll say it. Before he burned his car. Yeah, I know. I know he did it on purpose.

"So now I'm back where I started because Eddy made me remember that day. Shit, I'm back to thinking I should have been able to do something to keep all that crap from happening. And I'm back to thinking it was my father who killed Stan. Yeah, I think that, too. I think he burned his car either to cover up evidence or punish himself or somehow atone for doing a horrible thing. But I don't know any of that for sure. None of us does, do we?"

fourteen

EDDY

Sheila and I could be on such different tracks. Of course we'd started out together. We'd met when we were students. I was in architecture and she was in landscape architecture, but we kept bumping into each other in electives. City planning, design theory, that kind of thing. We were young and innocent, and just about anything in our chosen fields was new and attractive and absorbing. Or maybe it was simply because we were newly together. Maybe it was the two of us that were doing the attracting and the absorbing.

It had been years, though, since I'd been able to imagine the young woman I'd married. So much time had passed and changes had come so gradually that Sheila was always, well, she was always Sheila. To see her young, I would have had to go back to a photo album. Sometimes that past was what I wanted. Sometimes it wasn't. Sheila and all our years of incremental, cumulative, barely noticeable change did put me firmly in the present. And the present was what I needed after watching my brother die in the street outside the florist shop.

Oh, the florist shop. Now that meant Libby, and Libby meant something else entirely. There were such huge gaps in my connection to my childhood friend, all those years when she was living away, that it was easy to imagine Libby as I'd seen her before, as she'd been in high school, junior high, or the day her father torched his car. For better or worse, Libby took me straight back. With Libby, there had been no incremental change, so everything she did, every inflection of her voice, every facial expression, every tilt of her head or her hip brought back those days and a keen sense of the passage of time.

My relationships with these women, my wife and my old friend, were very different, but I'll tell you one thing that was the same for both. The last thing I wanted to do was hurt them. What worried and frightened me was the knowledge that I could hurt them so easily. I'd do it in an instant if I ignored their feelings, if I put all my attention instead into my good-scout pursuit of truth.

Freaking truth. I'd swallowed a lot of versions over the years. "Beauty is truth, truth beauty" if you want to get all Keatsian and academic about it. "Truth, justice, and the American way" if you want to go the popular-culture route. Of course, there was the Bible: ". . . and the truth shall make you free." But I was beginning to doubt that one. I hadn't wanted to see my brother die. I'd shown up at the old neighborhood looking for happy memories, and I'd been pulled into the saddest day my family knew.

Damn that Walter Lee, whatever his intent was, wherever he was leading me. It was looking more and more like I wasn't free at all, like searching for the truth was making me captive.

But then there'd been a tall drink of gin, a wistful dance with Sheila, a lingering look into the starry night, the inevitable escape into that pondering mind of mine. And I felt pretty normal. I had, after all, lived with my brother's death for thirty years. My shrink had urged closure. Eventually, he'd pronounced me cured.

But damn me, too. Damn me because my brother was dead and I should have remained sad. Damn me because right under my nose, my wife and my friend were angry and upset, and I'd missed their feelings by a mile.

Damn me because now I was treading the line between choice and no choice, free will and fate, curiosity and obligation. When Walter Lee didn't appear over the next several weeks, I turned willingly to wanting to see how these people I'd been seeing in time behaved, to watch their stories unfold, to know what they knew. While waiting alone in the present for Walter Lee's pull or my own obligation to step again into other times and places, I'd had this entirely selfish and not unpleasant thought. Traveling backward through time, once I'd reached the years before my birth, what bad things could happen? I'd begun picturing some kind of safe zone of family stories and nostalgia.

Remember those two stories I told at the beginning? It would be like that. My father shooting the baseball and leaving home had hurt. That story came out of my life. But earlier, Old Jacob's heroics at the flood made everyone feel good. No hurt in that story. And if there were, it couldn't be nearly as bad as what I'd already felt.

How could I leave Stan? Yeah, from the outside, that would seem difficult, insensitive even. But remember: Closure, I'd been taught, was the right thing to do. I shouldn't feel guilty. I'd moved on before. Besides, I still felt my obligations.

So when I once again felt Walter Lee's pull, I went. The old man must have known I'd needed some time to heal. But not so much that I'd lose momentum. He timed it right. Because when he pulled, I did see things. I did learn things. And this is what they were.

Summer had passed and it was getting to be that time of year when the days were still warm but the nights and early mornings were cool. I'd leave the house wearing a light jacket, hang it on the coat rack at work, and forget about it for the rest of the day. On the trip back home, sometimes I'd need the jacket, sometimes not. It all depended on whether the wind was kicking up. Like it was on one particular evening.

Walking from my truck to the house, I pulled my jacket tight around me, ducked my head against the blustering change-of-season weather, and aimed for the front door. Home was wonderfully familiar. I knew just where it was. And where I was. All I had to do was keep my head down and walk across the lawn.

And then I stopped. Mid-step. For a moment, a very short moment, the air had blown cold, wintertime cold. Maybe it was the on-again-off-again puffing that comes with a seasonal front's leading edge. I pulled at my loosely flapping jacket, but then the wind blew warm and I heard the sound of some other fabric, some other flapping, slapping against the porch, some snapping in the darkness. I raised my eyes. The porch was festooned with American flags, the eaves over the front steps hung with a hand-painted bed sheet that danced in the wind and proclaimed "Welcome Home!"

Not for me, I was sure. Would Sheila have done this? Ha.

I circled the house slowly. Inside, there were people, a lot of them, and the brightly lit rooms were smoky. Someone had opened windows for ventilation. Conversation and music—I recognized clarinetist Artie Shaw on the phonograph—floated out with the smoke. In fact, sound floated more freely than smoke. I could hear nearly every word that was said, while the air in the house never seemed to lose its haze.

Outside in the dark, I stood silently in the clear air. And I was invisible. As long as I kept my distance, I could move about and listen without being noticed.

It was like that party line we used to have, the phone connection we shared with the Peacock family when I was a boy. To us kids, to Stan and Libby and me, it was the most wonderful thing. Ordinary people had only their own conversations. But we had ours and we had other people's, too, and when we picked up the phone we never knew what we were going to get. It could be a dial tone, another person's secrets, or boring plans for grocery shopping. Sometimes we could lurk unnoticed. Sometimes our breathing or a noise in the room would give us away. That was the best part, the surprise of it all.

"I hung all the flags," came a voice from inside the house. It was proud, but with some hesitation. "I made the sign over the door. I took the sheet off my bed, and I found the paint in the carriage house. You needed a proper welcome, that's what I thought."

The speaker, I could see clearly, was my great uncle Hugh. He was wearing a white shirt with suspenders. He'd always been thin, I recalled, but the vertical lines made him appear dangerously skinny.

A man in a sailor's uniform with his back to the window clapped Hugh on the shoulder and raised a glass of beer. "Thank you, Hugh," he said, draining the glass all at one go, and when he finally came up for air, he continued. "I appreciate it. I really do." The sailor lit a cigarette. He reached for another bottle. And as he began to pour more beer into his glass, I recognized this speaker as well.

It was Mr. Peacock.

Now wasn't this interesting? Here I was, safely in the dark outside the house, safely in an era before I was born. Just as I'd hoped to be.

"We whipped their butts," proclaimed Hugh. "Yes, we did."

I'd just picked up the party line and I was listening. It was that simple, that innocent. Nothing was going to happen to me.

The party crowd floated in the background, moving one by one toward Mr. Peacock. "Alvin!" a woman proclaimed. She seemed a bit tipsy as she gave Mr. Peacock a big kiss. Her welcome struck me as the flipside of that famous magazine photo, the one with that sailor kissing a nurse in Times Square. I do believe it was the woman who became Mr. Peacock's wife, though on this night, after their kiss, she slipped quickly back into the crowd. Not unnoticed, but not a part of the sailor's life yet.

It was 1945. Maybe '46. This was wonderful, really wonderful!

Everyone wanted to talk with Mr. Peacock, to ask the same questions about his ship, about the war, about what he was going to do now that the fighting was over, and Seaman Alvin Peacock answered with the same politeness and deference he would have given his superior officer.

"It's good to be home," he said again and again. "It's good to be home."

"Your people are not from here," Hugh said to him.

The former sailor took short drag on his cigarette and a long pull on his beer. "This is home."

"It's not where you were from, before you came here."

"It's not where I was, but this is home."

It was evident that Hugh had somehow known Mr. Peacock before the war and that in some quiet, obsessive way had faithfully followed every movement of the sailor's ship. Hugh could not stop from recounting events. Seaman Alvin Peacock did not need to hear any of this, but he was polite. He took another swallow of beer. He looked to be feeling enough of a buzz that he didn't really care what anyone said to him.

"Nineteen forty-three," Hugh began. He rattled off the story quickly: a destroyer traveling from a shipyard in Texas to the north Pacific and anti-submarine patrols off the Aleutian Islands. Late 1944, reassigned to convoys between New Guinea and the Philippines. Early 1945, reassigned to combat operations off Okinawa. It was there that the Japanese Kamikaze had attacked. Three hours of futile damage control. The ship capsized and sank.

"You went over to starboard." Hugh was proud of the detail. "Tell."

"That's your job." As Mr. Peacock reached for another beer, he grabbed for his back with his free hand. He could not twist one way or the other, bend, or stand straight. He took a death grip on his bottle and inched toward a chair.

And now, perhaps brought into the story by his pain, the sailor began to tell after all. "When they pulled me out of the water . . ." Mr. Peacock sat with a thud, ". . . I fell on my face. I couldn't feel anything, not my feet, my legs, my back. I suppose that was a good thing."

"Two hundred eighty-two men in the water." Hugh was back with his statistics. "Nobody went down with the ship."

"Nobody went down with *this* ship." Mr. Peacock changed the emphasis. "An awful lot of boys went down with others." Even sitting, the former sailor was exhausted. Physically, emotionally, he needed to rest, and he needed to leave the war behind.

Hugh was filled with energy. It was a fidgety, youthful kind of energy and in many people it would have gone entirely undirected. In Hugh it was aimed at one place. "When do we begin?"

"Begin what?"

"You know."

"I swear, I don't know." Mr. Peacock lit another cigarette. "What?"

"You know. What you promised. Accordion lessons."

I jumped a little. The priest had told a story about an accordion at Hugh's funeral. Fingers running across mother-of-pearl inlays.

Mr. Peacock twisted in his chair, trying to make himself comfortable. He looked away from Hugh, across the room at something, anything.

"You said," continued Hugh, "that you'd teach me to play."

"Not now."

"Tomorrow?"

"Not ever." Mr. Peacock wriggled himself straighter and drank more beer. Then his glass was empty. "It's at the bottom of the Pacific Ocean."

Hugh exploded. "You had three hours," he cried. "Three hours. You could have got it into a boat. You could have got it home."

Former Seaman Alvin Peacock had no reply, but I knew what he was thinking. I'd overheard pieces of the story throughout my younger years, usually after our neighbor had downed a few too many drinks, but I'd never understood until now.

War was harder than anyone at home could imagine. The pain was sharper, the fear was deeper, and the confusion—well, goddamn the confusion. When his destroyer was steaming across the flat glass of the calm ocean, even when men were at battle stations taking incoming fire, orders and regulations and military discipline kept life in line and, everyone prayed, death at bay. But underneath, there was always doubt, a stabbing awareness that neither he nor anyone around him had any real control of events. A fear that no one would know what the hell to do or how to do it when the worst happened.

By the time he hit the water, Seaman Alvin Peacock was lost. Bobbing, surrounded by hundreds of his shipmates, he knew rescue would not take long. Other ships in the fleet were nearby. But from true sea level, his eyes only inches above the waves, the ocean stretched on forever.

Alvin Peacock gave no thought to the accordion. Not until hours after his rescue, lying in sick bay, did his mind turn to the instrument, and by then he no longer cared if he ever played again. It was part of happier days, suddenly and irrevocably gone.

"You had three hours." Hugh's face fell still farther, his expression still sadder. Hugh slowly backed into the crowd, bumping guests as his eyes remained on his sailor friend. He seemed unaware he was jostling arms and spilling drinks. "You had three hours," he murmured at the bottom of the stairs. Then Hugh turned, ran up like a child in a tantrum, and slammed his bedroom door behind him.

Former Seaman Alvin Peacock—a shattered version of the jaunty Mr. Peacock I'd known as a child, a man who I knew would rise like a phoenix, reinvent himself as the jolly florist, and then mysteriously sink, quite literally sink, again—sat quietly, shaking his head in disbelief.

The crowd around him quickly snapped back into its original configuration, as if Hugh had never parted it. The welcome-home occasion that had brought them together was likewise forgotten. The guests were absorbed in their own concerns, some big, some small, but all their own. The former sailor observed this as he sat alone in his corner, and I observed it from the darkened yard.

No one had come to talk to him for quite some time. He stood slowly, ignoring the pain in his back. "Balls," he cursed. No one else seemed to hear, but I recognized the old expression I'd often heard from men of his generation, just a hint of dirty but not dirty at all by today's standards. On his feet now, the former sailor grabbed the neck of his empty beer bottle, raised his arm over his head, and let the bottle fly, cartwheeling end over end toward the lowered top half of a living-room window.

I saw the bottle coming, directly toward my head.

I didn't know whether Mr. Peacock, Hugh, or any of the others at the party had seen me. I'd felt entirely safe outside in the dark. But I suspected I may have reached that edge where the unseen becomes the seen, and where the newly seen becomes a threat.

When the bottle hit the window screen, it stopped in mid-air. It hovered. It bounced. With my eyes trained on the bright room and its occupants, I'd never noticed the mesh barrier between inside and out. The middle ground had not been my concern, but now it was all-important. The bottle might rebound into the room. It might tear its way through and continue its flight. As it happened, the frame was only loosely fastened to the house, and the whole thing pulled free. The screen pitched outward onto the porch, bounced across one of the rocking chairs, and fell with a clatter at the base of the railing. The bottle went along for the ride, on a flying carpet.

As the screen came to rest, the bottle slid neatly under the porch railing, landed on the lawn, and rolled forward, stopping inches from my toes. I reached down and picked it up. "Welcome home," I said out loud. Then, suddenly aware that I might have betrayed myself, I retreated deeper into the darkness. I hoped no one had heard.

But in the yard in the dark I was not alone. I heard a rustle behind me.

I turned, tightening my grip the bottle's neck. I could break the brown glass and make a weapon, but the face I saw was smiling, it was not angry, and it was clear that a weapon would not be necessary. I dropped the bottle. Behind me stood Walter Lee.

How long had he been here? More important, why was he here? Without a word, he raised his right hand and snapped a quick military salute.

At first I thought his gesture was a tribute to Seaman Peacock or a greeting to Uncle Hugh. The old guy acted like he knew the whole story, start to end, and he seemed to be approving the way they'd played out this scene.

But before he lowered his hand, Walter Lee turned my way. Now his message was clearly approval for me as well. "So far, so good," he seemed to be saying. Then, when his salute was finished, he crooked his finger and wiggled a "follow me" motion.

It was as if Walter Lee had something else to show, some new family pieces for me to see, some larger message that he was leading up to and that I needed to understand. Walter Lee turned and took a step into the deeper darkness, but I was slow to respond.

I'd been paying too much attention to my own conjectures, I'm afraid, and not to what the yard man was trying to teach. And so for that night, at least, I lost him.

fifteen

SHEILA

It was one of those quiet days at the office when one work deadline has come and gone and the next is still in the distant future. The receptionist was away from her desk. The drafting area was empty of its dozen young architects. No impromptu group sketching, no chatter across the tops of cubicles, but I knew I'd find the person I wanted. Through the glass walls of the conference room, I could see Tim in a meeting. Clients, bankers—even on a slow day, Tim was always busy.

I caught his eye and pointed down the hall toward the executive offices. Tim nodded almost imperceptibly and looked discreetly at his watch. Then he gave up the pretense and rolled his eyes toward the ceiling. Crazy guy, pretending to be buttoned down. For both our benefits, I offered up a closed-lip smile.

Inside Tim's office I paced the floor. It had been some time since I'd met Libby in the greenhouse, but I was still worried about her. Maybe a talk with Tim would do the trick. That was me, always Sheila, always getting other peoples' takes on the story. Inside their heads, inside their hearts, visiting and listening, these were my yin to Eddy's observing-but-not-always-connecting yang.

I took a deep breath. Then another. It was beginning to look like this wasn't the best place for me to be. Tim's office was making me nervous. It was supposed to do the opposite, I realized that. Tim's office was supposed to be comfortable. Tim's office was supposed to be fun.

Businessman Tim worked hard at having an office that looked like he never worked at all. Cameras and camera equipment were always lying about, but it was the toys that caught everyone's eye. Tim had a huge collection of toys, mostly antique cars, and they overran the place. Like Christmas morning. Or locusts. Tim said he kept them because he loved their design. Visitors found them irresistible. I couldn't count the number of times I'd seen Eddy playing with those cars, rolling them back and forth across Tim's little conference table while the two men talked. I think Eddy loved those things, he always loved detailed little things, even more than Tim did. Assuming, of course, that Tim loved them at all.

Because you know what? To me Tim's office showed something other than fun. And what it showed depressed me. I'd thought for years that in spite of how focused Tim seemed to be on his work, the things he kept at hand betrayed how unsettled he really was. Cameras, toy cars, or, for God's sake, the electric keyboard he once kept beside his desk, ready for a few quick strides, a little stretching for the big man's long, restless fingers. Here was a man who was searching for a place to land. Even in his middle age, it seemed like Tim was still searching, and that made me sad.

There could be only one thing worse. Tim also could have been a man who was afraid of something. A man who needed distraction. Distraction with toys, with taking pictures, with music, with working hard, with whatever helped. Distraction, quite often as it turned out, with drink. And when I thought about what he might be avoiding—okay, I knew very well what he was avoiding, but it was something we never discussed, it was something we just danced around—I got shivers up and down my spine.

"Your husband hasn't been around much recently." Tim dropped a fat, three-ring binder from the meeting onto the table. He paused to punctuate his statement. "We've got a lot of work."

"I'm worried about him, Tim."

"He's not pulling his weight."

"No, I'm really worried about Eddy. Eddy the person, not Eddy the architect." I sat, exhausted, in one of Tim's guest chairs. "Clueless bastard."

Tim sat at the table, across from me. He picked up a toy car and carefully set it aside. No playing allowed.

I couldn't stop the tear that was running down my cheek, so I turned toward the window. But if I could show anyone how I felt, it should have been Tim. Tim would understand. "Heartless bastard," he said as he passed me a handkerchief.

I'd suspected something was up that first night at the pub with Eddy's childhood-home sketching and the memories he'd shared with Libby about his brother's death.

When Eddy went digging through boxes in the apartment closet, I knew it had started, and when he ran from me at the office, trailing the smell of smoke down the hall, just a few feet from where I was sitting now, I knew it wasn't good.

My suspicions grew stronger when I caught him washing up behind the shrubbery. And dancing on the porch was no help. Eddy wanted me to say, "I love you." I did love him. I still do. But what I really wanted to say was what I was telling Tim: "I know."

I knew what he'd been doing. And I knew that he hadn't stopped. But my knowing was one more thing, along with the hurt he'd caused in people he was supposed to care about, that detail-obsessed Eddy hadn't noticed.

How I knew was a bond that Tim and I shared. I was just hoping Eddy would stop his foolishness before I needed to reveal the secret. Or before I did something foolish myself.

I accepted Tim's hanky with one hand and with the other I shoved that big binder across the table and onto the floor. I put all my fury into it. Then I cried some more.

Remember when Eddy opened all the windows? I knew.

Five minutes after he left the house, I'd closed the windows, reconnected the cable, and switched on music. But using the house to tell Eddy, maybe even to try to stop him, was too subtle a hint. It didn't even register with Eddy. And that only made me angrier.

So I shoved a couple of smaller books, though this time I was so shaken that I couldn't even hit the floor. One landed in Tim's lap, and with the same even keel he'd shown when he'd moved aside the toy car, he set the book back where it belonged. Then he waited. None of what was frustrating and worrying me was Tim's fault; he knew that, and he knew that the crying and the shoving and the venting were necessary to relieve the way I felt.

"I'm not the boy who cried wolf," I said as I regained my composure. I paused. Then: "You know he's poking around in the goddamn past. You understand this shit."

"That was a long time ago," Tim replied.

"But you remember."

Tim sat stonefaced, as I gave my nose a hard blow, then a light blow, then I slowly and thoughtfully folded the handkerchief and stuffed it into my pocket. I was being as compulsive in my attention to nose blowing and handkerchief folding as Eddy would have been.

Finally, I looked up. I needed a break. I needed a delay. A pause to ready myself before this conversation began. One of those little side trips I always took into other people's lives, not mine. "How's Libby?"

Oh, Libby was great.

Tim either didn't know about the way Eddy had treated Libby, which I doubted, or he'd chosen to suppress his feelings for the protection of everyone concerned.

Libby, he told me, had been spending a lot of time at the shop, though with the work going well, he wasn't sure what she did there. Tim thought she was simply feeling the old place for what it was, sitting under a tree or in her car and just being.

She'd told him a story about this saxophone player who lived on the next block and how she'd always hated his noise.

But more significantly, when she returned home in the evenings, she said, there'd been this recurring dream. And that part did worry Tim.

There was a storm and a river and a late-model sedan twenty or thirty yards away. Lightning struck and Libby could see clearly. There was a man behind the wheel leaning out the window and waving his arms. There were sirens from a rescue crew off in the distance, but they never got any closer. There was rain that kept coming and a river that kept rising and a rescue that never came any closer.

"My God," I said. "What do you do?" I could say little more. I certainly couldn't reveal that Eddy had been having the same dream and that he'd been having it off and on for years. I was scared to death Eddy may have said something or done something that infected Libby.

"I listen," answered Tim. "I'm not Eddy."

"You know," I began, "that Eddy's going around asking Libby about things that happened a long time ago, things that are upsetting her."

Tim made no reply. He just reached for one of his toy cars. I could tell he was bottling up what he felt again, but he was bottling it up for me and I appreciated that. Tim was letting me go ahead with the story I felt was important. His story could wait. Tim wouldn't interrupt me with what he felt, not ever, not like someone else we knew.

"A couple of months ago," I said, "Eddy showed me this box full of report cards and sketchbooks and other stuff from when he was a kid. If I'd found the box on my own, I wouldn't have thought anything about it, but Eddy must have pulled it out for a reason. This kind of thing always matters to him. I feel like he's always looking in some kind of box these days, a box that's real or a box he's imagining, always pulling out more sketches and memories and things that happened a long time ago."

"Wait," Tim said, "until Eddy gets down to the X-ray glasses. You know, the ones they used to advertise in comic books. See through women's clothes."

No, Tim wouldn't interrupt me with what he felt, but when he wanted to avoid a subject he could be damn obnoxious.

"Be serious."

"I am serious." Tim pulled a comic off his shelf and started leafing through it. "I think there's one of those ads here."

"Look, Tim. Eddy is back in the past . . . ."

"And you know this how?"

"I know this. You know this. But you just want to joke. I thought I could count on an old friend."

I could tell Tim was embarrassed by his actions and that now he was as nervous as I was about Eddy. He was eyeing his desk, and I knew that if he'd been sitting there instead of at the conference table, he'd have pulled out the bottle of bourbon he kept in one of the drawers. Now, he just quickly put the comic aside. "No. Yes. I mean I get it. I really do. And I'm here. You can count on a friend."

"You of all people should understand how serious this is." I was growing exasperated, and I was afraid I was about to cry again. I didn't know which emotion would win, whether anger or despair. Or, assuming I had the choice, which emotion I should show.

"That was a long time ago." Tim paused. "I try not to think about it."

"We all do." I gave my nose another hard blow. "But he's poking around out there, and I couldn't be more worried."

"Snapshots," said Tim. "Little bits of time that are randomly out there."

"Well, maybe random for now." I picked up a camera from the desk, turned it over once, and set it back down. After my behavior shoving books, I didn't want to worry Tim about his equipment. He might fiddle with a comic or a car, but I wasn't here to play with his stuff. I was here with concerns about people, about all of us.

"What I'm worried about," I said, "is when he organizes those snapshots. What happens when they go into some kind of an album? What happens when they tell a story that makes sense? What the hell happens when these snapshots tell a story people have been trying to forget?"

sixteen

EDDY

From a sunny spot on the Victorian's front steps, Ike raised his head and looked at me. He was indifferent as I crossed the lawn from my truck. I was more effusive. "Hello, friend!" I dropped to one knee and faced the cat at eye level. I ran both hands the length of his back, and a fluff of fur rolled with them. I rubbed my hands together and the fluff floated across the porch steps.

I scratched Ike behind the ears. The cat's skull always felt so fragile and small for a creature who exuded such a large presence. Ike tilted his head back and closed his eyes. The cat was purring, and for a moment, a very brief moment, I was as absorbed in the sound as he was.

Until purring was swallowed by the step-pounding of heavy wingtip shoes. Lighter, sandal-flapping footsteps and a woman's laughter followed.

"Hello, friends!" boomed a man's voice. I looked up. Wingtips and Sandals had disappeared into a crowd that filled the porch.

People occupied the seats and perched delicately on the arms of the Victorian's rocking chairs. They leaned against the wall and the porch railing. A few feet away, a man inside was having an animated conversation through an open window with others on the porch. At the far end, people were filling highball glasses with crushed ice from a galvanized tub and pouring liquor. Somewhere in the crowd a radio was playing.

I stood slowly, took a couple of tentative steps toward the front door, and stopped at the edge of the crowd. "Here you go," a man said, putting a drink into my hand and disappearing. I took a sip. Gin with a fizzy, lemony mixer. Tom Collins. I hadn't tasted the drink in years, not since Stan and I used to steal sips from our parents' glasses. Tom Collins had been their favorite. I'd loved it, and I instantly loved being wherever in time I'd landed.

I looked and listened. The radio was playing Benny Goodman, Glenn Miller, the Dorsey Brothers. A half-dozen of the men were in uniform. The women wore dresses with belted waists and hems three or four inches below the knee. Their stockings had seams. This had to be earlier than anything I'd seen yet.

I finished my drink quickly and made my way through the crowd. I was carefully trying not to bump anyone, and I was avoiding speaking. The gin had given me the confidence to step into the heart of the party, but I was growing increasingly aware of what my presence might mean. Standing in the dark and looking through windows had been safe. But there'd also been that invitation, Walter Lee's finger crook. And I didn't know what following could mean. My presence might change the past, and if I did change something, then what?

Arriving at the tub of ice and the makeshift bar—liquor and mixers were lined up on the windowsill; the party was that easy and simple—I refilled my glass and paused. I thought about continuing along the porch. If I walked down the back steps, I could pass through the garden, disappear among the trees, and be gone, back to the present.

But hell, I was in that safe zone before my birth, and I figured the best thing to do was simply enjoy what I was seeing and hearing and learning. I just had to be careful. I backed up and stood as inconspicuously as I could, leaning against a porch column and scanning the crowd.

A couple of soldiers were roughhousing. One grabbed his friend's cap and landed in a headlock for his trouble. Both spilled their drinks. They headed to the bar for refills. A man and a woman took four or five steps of a fox trot, stopped, and kissed. Conversation buzzed around them, unnoticed by the dancers. Sheila and I weren't the first to dance on this porch.

Then a skinny man in a bow tie, also apart from the crowd, turned to me and spoke in a timid, barely audible voice. "Cigarette?" He extended a pack of Camels in my direction.

"Oh, uh," I stammered. It had been years since anyone had made such an offer. "No, thanks."

The man pulled an unfiltered cigarette from the pack and tamped it several times on the crystal of his watch, settling the tobacco. Turning toward the garden, he struck a match and raised it to the cigarette. He took a long inhale of smoke and, waving the match absent-mindedly in the breeze, contemplated the carriage house across the lawn and more guests walking up the driveway. In the time it took to smoke half the cigarette, he gave no further acknowledgment of my presence. I felt as if I'd disappeared. Then, speaking to anyone or no one, the man announced, "These things are always the same."

"Pardon me?" I was not sure whether I was a participant in the scene or I'd reverted to observer, whether the man was still seeing me or not.

"These parties," the man said, staring into the crowd but clearly aware of my presence. "Everyone just gets drunk. They forget what they're supposed to be celebrating."

"Yes?"

The man seemed surprised that I didn't know. "Birthday," he said. He took a final pull on his cigarette and dropped the butt into an empty highball glass. "This is the Confederate's birthday party. He would have been one hundred and one."

"I remember when he died." I was faking it hard.

"Just six years ago. 1936."

"It's good to keep celebrating."

The man nodded.

Now I recognized him. It was Hugh, my reclusive great uncle, maybe forty-five now if he'd been fifty that last time I'd seen him, the time I'd stood in the dark watching that other party. The deceased guest of honor would have been Hugh's father, the McBride family patriarch, Old Jacob. I looked around quickly. Who else was here? Using the pretext of another drink, I excused myself to look around. I left my half-full glass on the windowsill bar as I passed.

I circled the porch to the back of the house, opened the kitchen door, and entered. At the sink, a man was stabbing a large block of ice with an ice pick, trying to make chips the right size for highballs. I passed without a word. In the living room, the man at the window was still talking with his friends outside. Otherwise, the room was empty.

Empty to everyone but me. I knew there was important family history here. Not important in the grand scheme of things, I suppose, but damn important to me. I crossed to the mantel and lifted from its little display stand the baseball autographed by Babe Ruth and someone named Albert Cara, the famous and the unknown, one as immortal as you could get, the other forgotten, with an autograph that had all but completely faded years later when the ball came down to me—by the time it had gained a bullet hole.

Carefully, I rolled the family icon between my hands, tossed it lightly in the air, and set it back in place. I wondered how much the people on the porch really knew about my family. Or were they just here for the gin?

Hell, I wondered how much I really knew about my family. What could I learn here in 1942 that I'd never known before? Was Walter Lee here this time? I smiled in the dim room. Or maybe I was ready to teach myself. This business of seeing the past, it could really be quite wonderful when it wasn't so freaking horrible.

On the porch, a cheer went up from the crowd. Someone was playing the accordion. I crossed to the window and stood beside the man there. He kept talking with his friends. I craned to catch a glimpse of the musician. It was a sailor, in his blue winter uniform, though the day was warm. I left my window view and rejoined the party on the porch.

The song was an old one, a Gershwin tune, but it was a popular one, and every time the music came around to the chorus, cheers went up from the crowd and the party sang louder. Musician and singers went through the song three full times before anyone tired of it.

As the music finished, men pounded the sailor on the back and shook his hand. A woman squeezed in beside the accordion on his lap, put his cap on her head and kissed him full on the mouth. She waved to the crowd. Then the partiers returned to their friends.

That ballplayer Albert Cara wasn't the only one whose fame was fleeting. But I wanted to see. I squeezed through the crowd again, angling as best I could in the direction of the sailor. I had a suspicion. Glancing toward the porch railing, I saw Hugh standing where I'd left him. He, too, was intently watching the sailor.

"Hey, Swabby," called a voice from the crowd. "Here! Grab one of these."

The sailor turned and I knew him. It was Mr. Peacock, a very young Mr. Peacock, Alvin Peacock I suppose I should be calling him in his youth. He was no older than twenty or twenty-one, boyish in his build but with an early version of that pencil mustache I'd known so well. Then when the man behind him, the man carrying drinks in both hands, finally caught up, I recognized him, too. He was my father.

Against the railing, Hugh stood watching.

I could hear my father telling the sailor about the reason for the party, how Old Jacob had survived the Civil War and returned to build this house. "The thing my grandfather liked best was baseball," my father said, "but it's not the season. So we do this." My father drank from his Tom Collins.

And through the crowd, I could see Hugh approaching.

I heard my father telling more about how the house had stayed in the family even though there wasn't much family left. Hugh and his sisters still lived here. My father's father, their other brother and the only one who married, had moved across town to some more modern place, a place built in the teens or twenties. I loved it. Modern! From my perspective fifty years later, I couldn't help but smile at that kind of thing.

Hugh elbowed his way to my father's side where he whispered a question.

"He was sitting on the park bench reading the paper," my father replied. "That little park with the bandstand, the one down by the courthouse."

Hugh turned to the sailor. "You must be very brave," he said. "I never go there." No one seemed to hear, no one except me.

"He had this black suitcase beside him," my father was saying between sips, "and it turned out to be this accordion. We started talking. Tells me he's a gunner's mate on a destroyer with a long wait changing trains. Lonely sailor could use a party, I thought."

Hugh reached out a hand and tentatively, almost reverently, touched the accordion's mother-of-pearl inlays, its bands of shiny chrome, the buttons on one side of the bellows, and the black-and-white piano keys on the other. "Teach me to play," he asked the sailor.

"Sure, buddy," came the reply. "I can do that." Gunner's Mate Alvin Peacock, lonely sailor turned center of attention, was in a fine mood.

Hugh beamed.

"Except I'm shipping out."

Hugh's face fell.

Now it was the sailor's turn to swallow from his drink. Noticing his new friend's disappointment, he gave Hugh's request a bit more thought. "Tell you what," he finally said. "We'll do it when I return, as soon as I get back."

Hugh, though some twenty-five years older than the sailor, was as excited as a child. "Can I try it now?" he asked. "Can I just see what it's like?"

"Sure, buddy. Sure."

Hugh threaded his arms through the accordion's straps. He was ready to start. Given the choice and the ability, Hugh would have played all afternoon and into the night. I'm sure of it.

My father stared at his reclusive uncle with disbelief. He leaned toward the sailor. "I've never seen him so happy," he said, straining above the noise of the crowd. Then he stood up straight, clapped the gunner's mate on the shoulder, and announced in a still louder voice, "You're in the family now!" and everyone within earshot guffawed and took another drink of Tom Collins.

I ran to tell Sheila.

This was it.

I jumped and jabbed punches at the air.

The party on the porch was exactly the kind of thing I'd been hoping to see. No car fire, no hit-and-run death, no bottle throwing. No old man waiting mysteriously. Just an amiable slice and a happy insight into my family. Wonderful stuff.

I'd learned how our family and Mr. Peacock met.

I'd solved the mystery of the accordion, from party to ocean floor to Hugh's disappointment.

Now for the baseball. Another step or two back in time—I was certain that was all it would take—and another family tale would be complete, wrapped up, ready for me to tuck away into my vault, that brain where I stored whatever it was for whatever reason I stored it.

Of course, in my excitement I was conveniently forgetting my brother's death and whether there were any precursors in this happy story to that sad one. But I'd worry about that some other time.

At this point I simply ran, bursting. I wanted Sheila in my world. I wanted her to know. She deserved to know.

Besides. Jab! I just couldn't keep this damn secret to myself. Not any longer.

Now to pause for a moment, I've got to say: I couldn't help noticing just a few minutes ago here what Sheila was saying about yin and yang. She'd always been the listener; I'd always been the observer. Different, but a pair. Funny she should say that, because I'd had much the same thought. A good scout (okay, a semi-good scout), telling all he knows (okay, mostly), and a mystery lady, sometimes with secrets. Yin and yang, ebony and ivory, potato-potahto, tomato-tomahto. We were a matched set all right. But I don't know how she kept up her end.

Whenever I tried to keep a secret, I was constantly and painfully aware that sooner or later I'd tell. Sheila always knew when I was lying. I did it so seldom and so poorly that after a very short while, there was no longer any point. The question was always the same: not whether to reveal my hand, but when was the best time to do it?

Certain events I did hold close. The burning car, my brother's death, my great uncle's funeral. These mysterious, hurtful, and sad events from my own life I could hold longer than others.

Mr. Peacock's welcome-home party—that one could have been okay to reveal. Except for Walter Lee's "follow me" gesture. That one confused me. Maybe I should stay quiet.

But the right time for the right secret had bit. It appeared out of nowhere, took a big chomp, and I knew. An accordion played, Tom Collins swirled on chipped ice, and my father clapped his new sailor friend on the shoulder. "You're in the family now!"

It was time for jumping and jabbing and running home. It was time for Sheila to join me for the party.

s e v e n t e e n

SHEILA

The trouble with Eddy: give him a little encouragement and he won't leave you alone. And I do mean a little. All I had to do was listen to his story about the porch party. It didn't seem to matter what I had to say in return; he just kept talking. And here I'd been, worried about what he knew, wondering how long it would be before he'd finally open up to me. Be careful what you wish for.

To one extent or the other, I suppose we all do what Eddy was doing. We become so absorbed by the sheer wonderfulness of something or what we think is the wonderfulness of something that we can't see that precious few others—maybe not even one other person—feel the same way. Love is the classic example. "Love is blind," it turns out, has many meanings, including blindness to whether your friends and family give a flip.

So I wasn't surprised, I wasn't surprised at all, when a week or so after he told me about the porch party Eddy dropped a second piece, a new and different piece, of what he'd been experiencing in my lap. Except that this time, it was more than just Eddy telling a story.

This time, I saw it happen.

It could have been the rosemary that set him off. In those days, we kept a big patch in the garden, and whichever of us the mood struck would bring an armload into the kitchen. I loved its aroma. We'd put sprigs in a vase and whenever I passed, I'd rub the leaves between my thumb and index finger, then press my fingers to my nose. I once read that rosemary was therapeutic. It was supposed to enhance perception. That night, at least, it lived up to its reputation.

That night Eddy clamped a big bunch he'd just cut under his chin as he fumbled with a vase and his briefcase. Then he stopped. I thought at first he was just overcome by trying to do too much. He'd already given up on closing the pocketknife he'd used to harvest the herb. He'd set it down, open, on the kitchen island. Now he set the vase, rosemary, and briefcase beside it.

"Baseball?" he asked. "On the radio?" And I knew he was off. Eddy stared blankly for a moment, then walked out of the kitchen and into the parlor. A sleepwalker with his eyes wide open.

He returned a few seconds later, as if he'd walked into the other room and immediately turned around. That's all he'd had time to do. Any more time and he'd have had to be in two places at once. Maybe he was. At any rate, when I saw him next, he was shaking with excitement.

I'd say he should have been shaking with fear, but what did I know? Probably more than Eddy. He was thinking about the wonderful family day he'd just seen and the joys he might see next time. I should have given him a good slap. I should have scared him straight. I should have reminded him how he felt after seeing his brother die. But I couldn't. At that point, Eddy still hadn't told me about Stan's death, his most personal part of the family story. I wished he had. I could have used the ammunition.

Here's what Eddy did tell.

The scene he described took place in this house, in the old Victorian, with its period piece of a parlor (Eddy seemed really taken with its overstuffed furniture and antimacassars), its looping porch, and its maze of upstairs bedrooms. And it had a familiar cast. There was Eddy's great grandfather, the Confederate veteran Old Jacob. There were the sisters, Eleanor and Lillian, schoolteachers living at home. There was the family's baby, Hugh, a young adult by now. I'd heard a lot about Hugh, but I didn't know him. No one did.

So let's begin.

"It's Ruth to the plate," a voice said as Eddy stepped into history again. "The Babe hasn't done much all day," the voice continued, and Eddy entered the parlor.

The room was dark. The wooden slats of the Venetian blinds were closed against the afternoon sun. The light in the room came instead from the glow of a big tabletop radio. With its black metal case, its collection of toggle switches and fat dials, and its insides filled with glass tubes, the radio looked like some sort of shortwave rig. In the era suggested by the room's décor—Eddy told me he guessed late 1920s or early 1930s—big was necessary for even the simplest transmissions.

"The count is two and one. Now the Babe takes a swing at a low outside pitch . . . he drives it hard toward first . . . the baseman Leary takes a step . . . ."

An old man who had been bent over with an ear turned toward the radio sat up, removed his pipe from his mouth, and waited, military straight. The cat on his lap dropped to the floor. The dog at his feet picked up his head and stared at the man, anticipating whatever dogs anticipate.

". . . and the ball hits the bag! It caroms off first base out of reach into the stands! Ruth pounds around the base, but the second base umpire is holding up his hands. It's a ground rule double!"

The dog set his head down, as if he'd heard enough of what he was waiting to hear. The man sank back into his big upholstered chair, disappointed. The cat disappeared upstairs.

"Well, the local boys battled hard all afternoon," the radio voice said. "They held the barnstorming celebrities scoreless for most of this exhibition game, on this beautiful springtime afternoon. Now they're down four to two in the top of the ninth."

Babe Ruth was still on second as two Yankee batters grounded out, and the side was retired. The old man nodded in approval to the radio, and when the local boys came to bat, their fortunes were looking up. "It's a scorching ball down the third-base line!" The runner was safe on first. But hope was brief. The visiting New Yorkers put the next three locals out with a series of pop flies and simple grounders, and the game was over.

"A shame, a crying shame," Eddy told me he heard the old man saying in the empty room. "You agree, Gene?" The dog pricked up his ears, head still on his paws, and the man switched off the radio. The pair sat in the silent dark.

Time passed, Eddy couldn't tell me how much, but as the room grew still darker in the gathering evening, the old man made no effort to turn on the lights. He reached across the table beside his chair and felt with the flat palm of his hand, fingers splayed. He picked up a pouch of tobacco, refilled his pipe, and struck a kitchen match on the bottom of his shoe. In the flare, Eddy could see the man's face, his neatly cropped beard, and his stare into the darkness. This man was blind.

"Father!" A woman of about forty rushed into the living room and threw her arms around the man's shoulders. "Did you hear it? Did you hear it?"

Eddy could hear the clang and rattle of the departing streetcar down the hill.

Another woman a year or two her junior and a man younger still, perhaps ten years younger, stepped through the Victorian's front door. The young man methodically set about switching on the floor and table lamps. "They picked Lou Gehrig off first," the young man said and without a word more, he followed the cat's retreat upstairs.

"Did you hear the end of the game?" The woman was excited. Eddy recognized her as Eleanor. "Did you hear Babe Ruth's last hit?"

"Yes, dear," Old Jacob spoke softly, but Eddy told me he had no trouble hearing.

"Did the radio say what happened?"

"Yes, dear."

"Oh, Hugh was wonderful," exclaimed Eleanor. "The ball went straight to first, and then it bounced toward us."

"Hugh was a hero," gushed Lillian. "He jumped so high. I've never seen him do anything like that. Twenty men must have had their hands in the air, but Hugh got there first."

"And the ball?" asked Old Jacob.

"The ball is here," beamed Eleanor. She opened her purse and carefully lifted out the stitched cowhide. Eddy took a step forward to see as his great aunt placed the ball in her blind father's hands, which were cupped as if to receive something precious, something transitory, a liquid perhaps that he didn't want to slip away. Slowly, Old Jacob closed his fingers around the ball. He rolled and kneaded it as a pitcher might.

"It's real," said the old man.

"It's signed," exclaimed Lillian. "After the game, we went to the Yankees' dugout. Mr. Ruth was so gracious. I didn't think someone so famous would be so kind."

"I hear he likes the ladies," said Eleanor.

"Sister!"

"Well, it's true. But he signed the ball, right between the stitches." Their blind father ran his thumbs along the seams that framed the famous name. "Then we went over to see our boys, and we had the young pitcher who threw the ball sign it, too."

"It's right there on the other side," said Lillian, "opposite Babe Ruth, like players from two teams should be. Albert Cara. He pitched the entire game. Our boys almost won. It was just an exhibition, but it was a grand game."

It was a grand little vignette. Grand in its simplicity, in its ability to recount something memorable in everyday life and to reveal personalities so long gone and so easily forgotten. As Eddy told me the story, we were seated in the parlor, the same room where Old Jacob had listened to his game. It would be a stretch to say I could almost hear the radio. That kind of thing was Eddy's domain. But as he spoke, I mentally walked the room, looking for connections, maybe for personalities.

There was a picture on the wall. In it, family members were seated on the front steps of our house, cat on Old Jacob's lap and dog to one side, Eleanor, Lillian, Hugh, and their other brother, Eddy's grandfather, who had moved across town, gathered around. Roses climbed a trellis behind them. The people looked rather dour. I suppose the photographer told them not to move, but I almost had to laugh at their expressions. Because now I knew about Hugh leaping to catch Babe Ruth's hard-hit ball. I knew about the blind Confederate calmly smoking his pipe and accepting the evening darkness he did not know was falling. I knew about the sisters giggling at a mild innuendo.

Don't people disappear fast? And when those who knew them are gone as well, what remains? I have to be honest, I'd never cared much for that photograph. It gave the McBrides such a cold face. The camera trapped the family in a single pose, locked them into a single image, even though that image was not who they really were. That day I saw, through Eddy's eyes, that they were more.

But mostly what I saw that day was Eddy himself. Eddy showing me a little of what it's like to be him, a little of what he was seeing in the world, and a little of his enthusiasm for what he was experiencing. I was beginning to think that once Eddy got beyond his brother's death, maybe he wasn't on such a bad track, that what he was seeing was what had always struck me as the important part of life. When he told me about the porch party, he'd been revealing the fabric of living, events that were memorable but weren't life-altering, small events that make life what it is just as much as, or maybe more than, the big events. If I were going to see the past, that's what I'd want. The worm's-eye view, from the ground up. What was the danger in that?

Heh. For a few minutes there, Eddy had me going.

The more he talked, the more he made it look like the McBrides wouldn't be bad companions for the trip Eddy was taking. Hugh was odd, but the others seemed okay. Life was good, whether they were happily home from a ballgame or cheering up a lonely sailor on his way to war.

I almost bought into his vision. Until I looked around the room. And I couldn't find the baseball. Eddy was talking, filling in more details about the story I suddenly knew enough about, and I was staring at the mantel.

Where was the baseball? It usually sat just to the right of center, turned at an angle to minimize the view of the bullet hole Eddy's father had put into it, but proudly displayed nonetheless. It had been there so long that I usually didn't see it. But this time I really wasn't seeing it.

By now I wasn't hearing a word Eddy was saying. He'd just finished telling me how his uncle Hugh had caught the ball; I remembered that. It was an amusing little family story. But the ball's disappearance was telling me something different. It was telling me that there were a lot of stories and a lot of meanings I still didn't know about the McBride family. And it told me that I'd better keep my guard up.

eighteen

EDDY

How many times have any of us left out details when we were telling a story? Dozens? More than that. Hundreds of times? Yeah, the big number. Maybe we did it because details were too confusing, didn't make sense. If the story was a dream, maybe we just couldn't explain some weird thing we'd seen. Maybe we were afraid we'd upset someone. Or embarrass ourselves.

Well, I hate to admit it, but I was beginning to leave out details. As soon as I became overjoyed with what I'd been seeing, I began to have doubts about being so open. I experienced the past, the past became real, and reality became truth. But the past could be upsetting to all concerned. Besides, leaving out details wasn't untruth. At least that's what I told myself.

My stories were little dramas, little theater, and I could make all the sweet scenes I wanted. What happened up on my stage was framed by the proscenium arch I'd carefully built around it. It was a perfect approach for the benign domestic drama I'd just pictured. But even in this, I had to be careful about what I showed. It was looking like Sheila already suspected unpleasant twists to my story. She wouldn't have liked what was about to happen next and what was going on in the wings, the parts I'd cropped out.

So let's continue. Curtain up. Scene Two.

"I'll fix us some supper," said Lillian.

"Oh, not for me," giggled Eleanor. "I ate too much Cracker Jack at the ballpark." She gently put her hand on Old Jacob's shoulder. "But Father must be hungry, and Hugh will want his tray up in his room."

I turned toward the stairs. The family cat had reappeared, sitting on the bottom step as if on guard. But when Lillian left for the kitchen, the animal followed and I seized the open opportunity. I took the steps two at a time with a long, loping stride.

"They picked Lou Gehrig off first," Hugh was saying. My mysterious great uncle was in his room staring out the window. "They picked Lou Gehrig off first, and they hit a home run."

I stood in the doorway. I'd been doing a lot of this recently, stopping just short of entering peoples' lives, observing from a distance. Sure, there'd been the burn on my arm at the car fire, but in other instances, I'd moved through events pretty lightly. I'd stood in the nighttime dark at Mr. Peacock's welcome-home party and I'd floated through the crowd at the porch party before he went off to war. Maybe I needed a one-on-one. Now here I was with Hugh, alone with that opportunity.

When I was a child, my great uncle had been a complete unknown. I've said that. But the more I saw of him now, the more I felt an affinity. We both tended to stand to one side, observing. In doing that, we both gathered—or at least I assumed he was also gathering—insights into the family that we weren't saying out loud. Difference was, I had no one to tell my insights to. My parents and my brother were gone. Sheila didn't want to hear any more of my ponderings and musings. Hugh, on the other hand, still had his sisters and his father. And Eleanor and Lillian put their brother, childlike as he was, on a pedestal. I wished I had that.

"Hugh," I ventured from the doorway.

Nothing.

"Hugh." I stepped forward. I stood behind his shoulder and slowly raised my hand. Dare I touch? "H . . . ."

But I stopped short. Through the window, I could see another figure, another man of about the same age as my uncle.

This man had not enjoyed a ballgame. He had worked until dark, and in his dirty, sweaty overalls, he was packing up his tools by the light of the curbside streetlamp. He hung his hoe on a peg inside the carriage-house door. He rolled up the garden hose and draped it over the spigot below the Victorian's long porch.

"Walter Lee," I whispered.

"They picked Lou Gehrig off first," Hugh said.

Hell, these men were both mysteries. Maybe that's why I left this part out of the story I told Sheila that day. But it's important to the complete story we're putting together now.

The blind old man and the maiden aunts and the baseball made sense. These two didn't, though Walter Lee the stranger at my door had turned into a person well known to the family, and he was beginning to make sense as the one constant, the one red thread I'd been looking for that was woven throughout the story.

Walter Lee would mourn at Hugh's funeral and he'd play the saxophone. He'd salute a sailor's welcome home and he'd motion me to follow. Hugh may have been mysterious, almost vacant, but Walter Lee seemed to know things. And he seemed to have some destination in mind. A destination for the both of us.

Forget Hugh. It was a one-on-one with Walter Lee that I needed.

I lowered my hand behind my uncle's shoulder as I saw the hired man begin to climb the stairs to the carriage-house apartment.

I whispered louder. "Where are we going?" That's what I needed from Walter Lee.

I ran down the stairs, thundering across the treads as quickly as my feet would carry me. Across the living room, through the front door, onto the porch.

It was quiet outside. All I could hear was my own breathing. Now that the noise of my running footsteps had subsided, it was quiet inside the house, too. Where was everyone? I walked back through the parlor. What had happened to the overstuffed furniture and the antimacassars? I entered the kitchen. A ceiling fan was slowly and silently turning. The moving air felt cool, though the oven was hot. The air conditioning was on and it was Sheila, not Lillian, who was cooking dinner.

Sheila held out her hand, absently waiting for a sprig of rosemary. Getting no response, she looked up, saw me, and dropped a hot pan of spaghetti sauce on the floor. "You've done it."

I wasn't sure whether we were thinking about the same "it" or not. I didn't know how she might know. But I couldn't keep a secret; I had to confess. I assured her everything was okay and asked her to come into the parlor and hear me out. To at least hear the part I wanted to tell.

***

That night, I took to meditating. After I finished telling Sheila what I'd seen, the two parties, my safe, edited version of the old ballgame but not the disturbing, more recent events from my own lifetime, I began walking our long, dark porch, placing one foot in front of the other, moving very deliberately, very slowly. Only one problem: I hadn't emptied my mind the way a meditator should. I never could do that.

What was this? I stooped to retrieve a ball of cat fluff lodged in the gap between the porch railing and the floor. It could have been the same fluff that rolled off Ike the day I'd petted him and stepped into the porch party. "Hello, friend!" I raised the little ball and puffed gently, like a child blowing on a dandelion, and it sailed into the yard. Where to now? Some random destination. Or maybe not. Maybe fluff knew exactly where it was going. Unlike me.

I'd had some success in observing present-day details. I'd watched them closely enough to bring the past into view. But I hadn't had much success determining which view I'd see. Days and events popped up as inexplicably as the reclusive Hugh or the ghostly Walter Lee. The good news was, since I'd moved to the years before my brother's death, my visions were as light as a fluff of cat hair. They were nothing to worry about. Not really.

Then why was I worried? Why had I kept this most recent bit of family fluff hidden from Sheila, these inconsequential glimpses of my reclusive uncle withdrawing into himself and the cryptic hired man toiling behind the scenes? Now I was worrying about worrying. I was worrying because as I pondered the behind-the-scenes action of my family's little play, I knew there had to be more coming.

I climbed into the hammock on the porch and there, lying on my back, I looked at the ceiling. I knew it was painted blue and it was made of grooved, beaded board, but in the dark it was featureless. I peered around the eaves at the sky, which I knew was filled with stars. On this evening, clouds completely obscured their lights. But I knew these things were there, just like I'd learned that the past is still there.

So I meditated on the ceiling and the sky. I meditated on what I already knew about them and what I could see now and what facts remained to be learned.

I meditated on keeping facts to myself and on how I was indulging in a luxury, this meditating and pondering, and on how luxuries were personal and how a personal anything had meanings that I could not pass on to others no matter how much I wanted to. I meditated on how I wanted to see, how I didn't want to see, and how all and any of this affected my vision of the truth, whatever the hell that was becoming these days.

And I meditated on how telling Sheila what I'd been doing may have been the biggest mistake I could have made.

nineteen

SHEILA

That night, I fell asleep on the couch. Pregnancy was beginning to get the better of me, and I was tired early. But couches are a poor substitute for beds and an hour later I was awake. I lay on my side, one arm curled under my head, staring across the room at a gray something on the wall. The symmetrical Rorschach shape was about the size of an old half-dollar. I watched for movement, but there was none.

I sat up and examined the window behind me. It stood wide open in honor of what we used to call Indian Summer, those delightfully warm and beautiful autumn days and those cool, approaching-cold autumn nights that demanded we pay attention before winter shut us down. Eddy and I had dutifully obeyed. All the windows of the Victorian stood wide open.

There was a small hole in the screen. I reached across the cat, who was lying quietly on the windowsill, happily watching bugs, and I plugged the hole with a bit of paper. I turned back to the room. "Now you're trapped," I told the shape.

"Who's trapped?" called Eddy. I hadn't realized he was right outside, in the hammock.

"A night visitor. A moth."

"Get a rag," he said. "And don't make a splot."

I'd never do that. I'd never kill a creature we had seduced with a hole in the screen and lights in the room. Coming inside hadn't been his fault. So I swooped down on the moth, lightly wrapped it in a dishrag, and gently held the bundle in both hands. I pushed open the screen door with my toe, walked to the porch railing, and let the creature go over the shrubbery.

The moth fell, wobbling uncertainly as if it, too, had been asleep. Then its wings caught and it angled across the coil of our garden hose, down into the damp air rising from the bedding mulch, and away into the shadows.

Responsibility discharged, I gave the rag a quick couple of shakes, then remained at the railing, slowly folding the rag in the cooling Indian Summer air. I was thinking that I should have given the moth a name. I should have called him Eddy.

Eddy, seduced by hidden times and places. Eddy, freed back to his own life. Eddy, not doing such a good job of hiding himself on a white wall but, aside from what he'd willingly revealed, pretty successful at hiding the details of his adventures.

I couldn't say with any certainty what Eddy the moth may have been trying to accomplish in his visit to our house. But I gave a little prayer that Eddy my husband hadn't accomplished anything on his own travels.

As I approached the hammock, I could tell that while I'd been capturing and releasing the moth, Eddy had fallen asleep. It was getting late. Across the yard, the lights of our neighbor's house flicked off. Street and animal sounds had almost entirely stopped. I watched Eddy. I didn't want to disturb him. If it didn't get too cold, he'd stay the night here. He'd done it before when he was upset or when he was feeling nostalgic for his boyhood.

I pushed down gently on the side of the hammock and climbed in. Eddy rolled onto his side, and I balanced carefully. Lying against his back, I put my arm around his chest, pressed my hips against his, and settled my knees behind his. Spoons in a drawer. My belly was getting a little poochy, but the baby wasn't so big yet that it came between us. I could feel Eddy's heart and my heart and I could hear our breathing.

It was my heart as much as my body that was in a family way. Eddy was in his hometown, though he'd been emotionally adrift for years. I was far from any place I'd ever called my own. But the two of us had been building a life. We'd clung together tightly, carving out our own stories. Here's one: We were children ourselves, the lonely boy and lonely girl dropped off at some foster home or orphanage. Like you see in old movies. Well, that was a start. But there was some truth in it. Eddy and I did cling together—when we weren't pushing apart. We were so close to each other that we felt every rough edge, and every rough edge hurt like crazy. I leaned on Eddy a lot. He did have a strength and a certainty about him. But Eddy could still be lonely. He didn't always touch the rest of the world, not the way it touched him. I just wanted him to pay better attention to the present.

And now I needed him to pay attention to the future. My mind was swirling with baby's first steps and first words, with an endless round of homework and violin lessons (or would it be piano?), summer camp (mountains or coast?), driver's ed (that's scary), high-school graduation, and then off to college (where?). But Eddy was still in the past.

Eddy had told me a sweet story about a long-ago ballgame, and as far as it went, it was okay. In the dark, I dropped one leg over the hammock's side to the floor and gave a little shove with my foot, like rocking our baby. But the present and the future are what's really sweet, and that's what I wanted him to know. "This is enough," I whispered. "You and me and baby make three."

I'm not sure whether my words got through. Eddy lay still, sleeping soundly while I was still squirming to get comfortable. There was a lump of something in the hammock. Something hard had shifted out from under or beside Eddy and now I was right on top of it. I unwound my arm from Eddy's chest and shifted just enough to reach. And as soon as my fingers touched it, I knew what the lump was. It was our baseball. So this was where it had gone.

Oh, what's Eddy up to now? Cradling the missing baseball. Was he like a child with his teddy bear, seeking comfort in a familiar icon, pining for the good times? Or was he mourning the bad?

In the darkness, I found myself nervously running my thumb along the ball's seams just as Eddy had described his blind great grandfather doing. I, too, kneaded the ball. And between the seams, right where I knew Babe Ruth's autograph was, I felt a tear in the surface, a spot that, when I rubbed it a little more, was quite obviously a little round hole.

Eddy, damn it. Was he missing his dead brother or understanding his runaway father? Was he wishing for the simple way things used to be or finally seeing the tangle of details that led to family tragedy? Damn it, he could have shared. But this hiding the ball, this keeping the things that touched him most closely all to himself was hurting me, too.

Eddy had no right to do this to me. He had no right to do it to himself either. Eddy was indeed acting like a child. For my benefit, at least, he was acting like everything he'd been seeing was some jolly game of hide and seek. But I knew better. I knew it was a dangerous game and he was seeing it all wrong.

What frightened me was that sooner or later he might see it right. And then it wouldn't be just a family at a baseball game. It would be a family that was still affecting our lives. But he'd go mucking about anyway.

Now mucking about and changing the past didn't worry me. That was the stuff of science fiction, not real life. What worried me was his coming back and mucking about and changing the present. And that change would be just as hurtful as if he'd inserted himself into history and altered the outcome of some event. In fact, it would be more hurtful. Because he, I, our friends, our families—our child, for crying out loud—would have to live with the consequences. Maybe live with them for years. And he thought he could just hide what he'd seen, whatever that was.

I climbed out of the hammock and stood again beside Eddy. I wasn't so generous this time and I wasn't so affectionate. A quick step down on the hammock's edge would dump him out onto the floor. Maybe that would make him sorry. But then he'd be awake and he'd follow me into the house and he'd want to talk and talk and explain and explain. No, thank you.

So I just gave him a kick. Right on the bottom side of the hammock where he hung the lowest, right on his backside. He rolled over but didn't wake up. Fine. I returned to the house and slammed the door. Eddy could spend the night outside. For all I cared, he could freeze his ass off in his goddamn hammock, dreaming of his goddamn family.

I wouldn't have been sorry about that at all.

twenty

SHEILA

Am I a bitch or what? Not for what I'd done. Up to this point, even that night when I kicked Eddy in his low-hanging hammock, I'd mostly just been dropping heavy hints about my displeasure. But for what I was about to do.

This time, I was about to be mean.

First to Ike. It was late afternoon the next day, and he was lying on the bed, getting cat hairs all over the sweater I was planning to wear. His head was down like he was trying to hide, but his eyes were turned up. Cats know when something's afoot. He wanted to keep things the way they were. I wanted everything to change. But passive aggressive wouldn't work for the cat. I lifted Ike by the middle and dropped him on the floor. It wouldn't work for me either. Not any longer.

More important, I was about to be mean to my friend. I was planning to trap an innocent bystander and there wasn't much I could do to avoid it. I couldn't confront Eddy. I couldn't scream the hurtful things some couples find so easy to say. "I don't want to be married to you anymore!" But that wasn't me, and that wasn't how Eddy and I operated. Eddy could be infuriating, but I'd always managed to pull my punches and pull myself back from the edge.

No, what I needed was help. I needed someone to do the dirty work for me. I needed whatever it would take to set Eddy and me free from the rapidly approaching disasters I knew were in the past and that I knew could destroy the future. Even if it meant expanding this messy web to someone who had been—and by all rights deserved to remain—only marginally involved in our story.

"Any brand," I told the clerk at the corner store. I hadn't bought cigarettes in years, not since I'd started running, but that day I was a mean bitch. I needed to be responsible, responsible for saving our lives and our marriage, but I didn't want to act responsibly. Before I returned to the car, I'd lit my first, and as I inhaled, as the car's side mirror reflected my growing midsection, I hesitated. Then I finished my smoke.

In the parking lot behind the office, I lit I don't know how many more, but responsibility had staged a comeback. I'd take a puff, stop myself from inhaling, and stub it out in my never-used, virgin ashtray. I'd light, puff once, and stub. Light, puff, and stub. Before long the ashtray was overflowing. The foil package lay empty and crumpled on the floor. Evening arrived. And I waited.

Soon, only one light in the building remained on. Then the light clicked off.

"Tim!" I called when our partner emerged from the building.

"Sheila." Tim paused in the midst of buttoning his suit jacket against the chill. He changed direction and walked toward me.

I leaned across the passenger seat and shoved open the door. I could barely reach, but it opened far enough for Tim to know what I wanted. He climbed in. The spider and the fly. But he didn't know that part yet.

"I haven't seen you at work," he said.

I shrugged and drove, fishing a nearly whole cigarette from the ashtray, lighting up, and smoking the whole thing. Tim rolled down his window.

He said nothing about the smoke. I said nothing about the cold air.

And when we finally cleared the rush-hour traffic, I drove quickly. We crested a familiar hill. We came around a familiar bend. We saw a familiar sign. Villa Capri. My next destination was a motel, but my intent was innocent. Sort of.

The room we checked into may or may not have been the same room, but Tim and Eddy and I had spent quite a bit of time at the Capri in our student days. We and our friends all lived in old apartments without any amenities, and this was our getaway. It was an inexpensive place that we pretended was a resort. Here, any number of people could escape for a day or two on the cheap.

We'd swim. We'd drink beer and red jug wine. When the stars came out, so did the reefer. Then we'd swim some more. We never seemed to sleep. Those were our "*Rashomon* weekends." That's what Tim always called them, everybody in the same place at the same time, but nobody remembering events the same way. Like that Japanese film.

Most of those old friends were professionals and business people now, with families and mortgages and an eye on the future. To them, the Capri was far in the rearview mirror, a wide place in the road on the way to real life. But I'd known for years that those long-ago weekends were as alive to Tim as being in this room on this night. For better or worse. That's why I'd brought him here.

What a bitch.

I stood staring through the sliding glass door at the kidney-shaped pool and its surrounding round tables. The tables had been stripped of their umbrellas, and the pool had been drained and covered for the coming winter. Rainwater on the tarp was dirty with fallen leaves. The management had turned floodlights on the scene anyway.

I knew exactly what Tim would do. He'd make a quick dash to the liquor store next door for bourbon and ice, and he'd return with a sack clutched tightly to his chest. His baby. He'd slip paper wrappers from short, stubby motel glasses and pour two drinks. He'd hand me one and I'd continue staring.

"We've been here before," I finally said, swirling the ice in my drink with one finger.

"In another life," Tim answered. He stripped off his suit jacket, tossing it onto the bed with one hand as he loosened his tie with the other. Tim took a sip from his drink and watched me. He was wondering, I'm sure, what was up.

Not much was up with the room. The carpet was new, but that was about the only thing. The forty-year-old attempt that the furniture made at being modern—Danish Modern, were they kidding?—made the place seem ancient.

"Tim." I looked him in the eye. "It was in this life. It's just that life is very damn long." I sat beside him on the bed. Tim finished his drink and poured himself another. I set mine down untouched on the bedside table. Preggers, girl. Remember that. I thought about Tim going the other direction, toward drinking as much as he could.

I guess he noticed me looking. "You know why I like to drink?" Tim asked. "I like to drink because even if life is long, the past is never so far away. And I don't want to notice it anymore. I like it when the edges get soft. I don't like it when everything is in focus. Or when I think it's in focus."

"Your pictures are in focus," I said.

"My pictures . . ." said Tim. He took another swallow from his drink, punctuating his idea as if he were giving a lecture or an interview. "My pictures show the world the way I want it to be, the way I want to see it. Pictures stop the world, and what's in the photo is my world. That and nothing else."

Tim contemplated the disappearing bourbon in his glass, but now he set it down without another taste.

"Sometimes I see too much of the world. I see it too clearly . . . ."

"I know too well." I reached for my drink and finished half all at once. Time to join Tim's game. "I've been blocking it out with willpower," I said. "That doesn't work any better."

By now the room, and not just Tim's comments, had a tangible chill. Outside, the temperature was falling fast, and I realized we were sitting in near darkness.

I flicked on a lamp on one of the bedside tables. Tim turned up the thermostat on the through-the-wall heater below the window.

Tim topped off both our drinks and we returned to sitting side by side on the bed.

"When you saw the past . . ." I began, directing Tim toward the place I needed him to go.

". . . it was chemically induced, " he interrupted. "But it was very real. It was very wonderful, and it was very frightening."

I'd known for years that Tim had seen the past, that his experiences had begun and ended here at the Capri and that he'd been very careful ever since not to discuss what had happened with anyone. Not with anyone, that is, besides me. At first he'd thought it was the drugs. That was the point, wasn't it? To heighten perceptions. To go somewhere else, see something else, at least in the mind. Tim had wanted it to happen, hadn't he? Maybe he still did, but secretly. I was betting on that. And maybe I was right. Without any more prodding, Tim eased into his tale.

From bits and pieces he'd let drop over the years, I'd put the whole thing together long ago. But the tale wasn't for me, was it? It was for Tim. I needed Tim to relive what had happened. And for that to happen, I knew he had to be here. At the Capri.

"The first time was good," he told me. The sounds of boys and girls at the pool shouting "Marco" and "Polo" had showed him a day when the motel was new, when a woman in an aqua, one-piece bathing suit lay on a reclining, beach-type chair and stared at him over her sunglasses. Long-legged. Thirty-ish. At her feet on the deck, a bathing cap adorned with floppy rubber flowers. The woman sipped a drink with an umbrella in it. Tim ran his fingers nervously through his long hair, which he grasped with his fist to make a ponytail, then let fall loose, framing his face. The woman seemed puzzled by his hair, but she smiled. And when modern shouts of "Marco" and "Polo" pulled him back to our *Rashomon* weekend, Tim had in his hand a matchbook inscribed with her room number. "I still have the matchbook," he told me.

The next time, he said, was less good. A puff of wind bearing the smell of freshly turned earth landed Tim in the middle of a construction site. The unfinished motel stood alone beside the highway. The city's growth had not yet caught up, and with no competition from speeding diesel out front or frying hamburgers next door, the earth smelled warm, wet, and sweet. Three men were digging the swimming pool. Now Tim could hear the grunting of the workers, the swoosh of thrown dirt as it slid from the shovels into a growing pile. Now he could hear the hammering of the roofing crew. Tim shaded his eyes and looked up just in time to see a hammer fly. It bounced on the dirt pile and struck one of the digging men in the thigh. "Faster, boy. Work faster," roared a roofer, and the other men on top of the new motel cheered and jeered.

But then Tim learned he would never be safe at the Capri. It was a dark, new-moon evening, as he described it, and he saw only a faint glow of the city over the hill. The music coming from the old roadhouse bar drew him inside. There was no motel yet, but there was hospitality. There was a country fiddler and a guitar picker and bottles of beer and a game at the pool table. Tim stood against the wall and watched. He drank a beer made by a brewery that by our day had long since gone out of business. He drank another. This was amusing. Until the lights went out, the shouting and shoving started, and Tim finally pushed his way outside.

He was bleeding.

He never went back.

I put down my drink. I gently took his glass and set it with mine on the bedside table. I held both his hands flat between my palms as if praying. Then I unbuttoned his shirt cuff and shoved the sleeve up as far as it would go. At the elbow, the fabric bunched, but I'd gone far enough. On the inside of Tim's forearm was a long scar.

"It's fading," I said. I hoped the pain of his memory was fading, too.

Tim looked down. "Maybe." He gently removed my hands and rolled his sleeve back to the wrist. "But I notice it every day. Every day I feel like I'm back in that crowd. There's stale beer on the floor, and there's crappy country music over in the corner, and there are all these assholes who just want to fight, who think fighting is just the most damn fun in the world, and who think a knife is nothing more serious than a fist. They don't care if a guy is just standing there watching. Everybody's got to join in. And somebody's got to get hurt."

Then I knew. I knew that for Tim the past had not faded at all. It had a stronger hold on him than I'd ever imagined. Even if he'd been there only three times. I knew what he'd seen—no, it's not that simple; make that what had happened to him—was why he still sought distraction, in photography when inspiration struck, toy cars in his office, or liquor constantly. Maybe even in his crush on Libby. I knew Tim needed help. I knew he was hurt. I knew he needed to get out of that old roadhouse and stay out.

I knew my plan wouldn't work, but I still wasn't ready to let it go. It was all I had.

I crossed the room and pulled the draperies shut. The floodlit ghost of the pool disappeared. I handed Tim his drink, which he contemplated and again set back on the table.

"Are you okay?" I asked. I really was a rotten bitch, feigning concern, digging one more time when my friend had just been through so much.

"Maybe we should stop keeping secrets," he answered.

Instantly, I knew what he meant. I knew Tim was challenging me the same way I'd challenged him. And I knew I had to hit back hard before Tim landed another hit on me. "I'm not ready for that," I replied through pursed lips.

"Don't you think that's part of your problem with Eddy? You've got this . . . ."

"I don't want to talk about it."

"No, you never do. But I know what you've seen. What you saw years ago."

I stared hard at the closed draperies. It was as if I were trying to see through them.

And when Tim took a breath, when he acted as if he were going to continue, I put my index finger to his lips. Silence, please.

More silence.

"You and I," I finally said. "We know what could happen. We know what horrible things Eddy could do, even if he doesn't mean to. We know how bad things could be."

"Sheila," Tim said sternly. He waited to make sure I was paying attention. "I'm not going back."

Now he did reach for his drink. He reached deliberately, like he needed it and like he wanted me to know I'd pushed him toward it.

I tried gentle. I tried hopeful. "We can stop everything."

"No, we can't. We wouldn't have a clue where to look. The past is big and Eddy really hasn't told you much about what he's seen. What am I supposed to do, just go and hang out and wait for Eddy to come strolling by?"

"He's looking at the wrong thing. He always thinks he's finding the truth, but all too often, he misses the truth that matters."

"So you're saying I should try."

I perked up, nodding my head hopefully. I noticed only at the last moment how tightly Tim was gripping his glass.

"The answer," he said, "is still no."

"But Tim . . . ."

"Sheila!" Now Tim was angry. "If you feel so strongly about going back and stopping Eddy or changing things, why don't you do it yourself?"

I stiffened. "I told you," I said. Now I was the one who was angry. "I told you. I don't want to talk about that."

"But you can do it."

I held my hands over my ears. La-la-la-la-la. This was not how I'd imagined our conversation going. I'd been sure I could convince Tim to do what I needed, but he'd cut me off before I could even make my case.

"You can do it just as well as I can," Tim said. He rose and pulled open the draperies. The floodlights around the swimming pool were so bright that we barely needed the light we had on in the room. Tim plopped back onto the bed, massaging his old wound. "Better, actually. You can see things no one else sees."

"I don't want to hear it."

"Eddy's seeing one past. But you can see the present and the past together. Maybe even the future and the present and the past. Eddy's only partway there. But you've seen how bad things back there can be."

"Go to hell." Tim had called my bluff. I rose and stomped out the door.

"No," said Tim. I was still close enough to hear. "Don't go anywhere."

The parking lot was cold, but I just stood by the car, keys in one hand, the other leaning on the roof. I was ready to go and wanting to stay. "Tim," I pleaded under my breath. I knew he couldn't hear me. I'm not sure I wanted him to. I still needed his help, but I knew I should stop asking. I knew these things because I knew Tim was right. Stay out of the freaking past. Tim had been right about that for years.

twenty-one

SHEILA

How did that go? Not so well, I'm afraid. Not for me. Not for Tim either.

Among friends and family, there's always so much that's understood, so much that doesn't need to be said. That makes it difficult to clean up our messes. How do you get rid of the dust bunnies you know are under the couch if you never see them?

Holding back, of course, makes cleaning up a mess more than difficult; it makes it impossible. Tim was talking about things I'd seen and things I'd known years ago. Those, I'd never discussed. There was the burden of backstory, which I not only carried as well as I could but held as close as I could. But I was beginning to see that backstory's time had come. What did Eddy call me? A mystery lady with secrets? I'm not offended. A mystery lady was who I wanted to be for quite a long time. But it was time for that lady to quit, time for the mystery to end.

So listen carefully.

Just in case there's too much that's understood but never spoken or too many secrets going on around here, I'm going to explain this. And I'm going to explain it only once.

I'd seen for myself what Eddy had been seeing. I'd seen it many times.

Damn it, the past sucks, especially when I see more than Eddy. Back on that day when Eddy opened all the windows in our house, the curtains fluttered and that was all he seemed to notice. Eddy was an observer. But Eddy should have felt the chill that came in on the breeze, the chill that went straight to the bone. I did.

At the time, I hadn't been able to do anything about it. I couldn't become absorbed in events that had already happened. Someone had to take care of our life. Take care of the present and plan for what might happen next. For the baby, if nothing else. Maybe the past would just go away.

No such luck.

I may not have been able to do anything about it now either, but I was still worried. Truthful Eddy was keeping secrets, and that was not a good sign.

I'd been hoping Tim could give me some help in stopping Eddy's crap before it was too late. All I'd wanted was to stop my husband before he went too far. Because I could see what Eddy apparently could not. He'd grieved for his brother, learned about his relatives, had some fun. But my own experience showed that Eddy's explorations really would reveal nothing good.

Eddy was so annoying. He called me a clean slate. "You never think about the past," he'd say. "Were you really there?" One problem, Eddy thought, was that I wasn't anywhere near my family. He thought I simply preferred the anonymity of the present, the lack of a defining backstory. And of course, Eddy being Eddy, he had it backward. It's not the present that's anonymous. The present is where we engage other people and where that engagement defines who we are.

No, the problem was not that I wasn't anywhere near my family. The problem was that my family had been everywhere and nowhere all at once. Dad had been a wandering academic. We'd moved every time a university didn't grant him tenure, or we'd preemptively moved whenever he thought he could find a place where tenure would come more easily. Life was all impermanence. We'd moved so often, we left few traces. We built few relationships. How do you build a family story on that?

There were, of course, individual stories that grew into memories. I remember old nursery rhymes with odd meanings: "Ring around the rosie / a pocket full of posies / ashes, ashes / we all fall down!" (At which point, all the kids would jump into a swimming pool, let out all their air, sink quickly to the bottom, and see who could stay down the longest.) I remember watching with amazement as adults yukked it up like children, passing Life Savers candies on toothpicks they held in their teeth at a Labor Day picnic. (I think, in retrospect, that they were probably all drunk at the time.) I remember sitting in a power-out, candle-lit house as a hurricane passed overhead, my father out of town at some conference or looking for some job and my mother reading out loud from a book of folk tales to calm me down. (My favorite was the one where the farmer and his wife traded jobs, and he put the cow on the roof with a rope down the chimney to his ankle, and the cow fell off and the farmer was dragged up the chimney. It still makes me laugh.)

So my family life was all very normal. If I had the ability now to revisit those days, I don't believe I'd see anything out of the ordinary. Meat-and-potatoes stuff, hold the gourmet ingredients (or the arsenic). My memories were my preferred worm's-eye view of life, ordinary events from the ground up. What you see is what you get. Nothing complicated, nothing far-reaching, nothing that changed the course of the world. There didn't seem to be any need to spend time pondering.

Then I saw the broken tree.

On the day of my high-school graduation, I woke up early, and there, a dozen yards outside my window, shining clear as the rising sunlight, a big oak's bright yellow insides were showing themselves. There'd been no storm. The tree didn't look like it was sick. But a big limb had snapped off and now lay on the ground. I believed it had just grown too big to support its own weight. That happens. And now it was as if the tree's viscera were exposed, exposed and vulnerable like a human tragedy.

Even at my tender high-school-graduating age, I knew time and the elements would seal the wound and that the tree would live long with a tough scar, but the loss nonetheless appeared very painful. The oak was an ancient thing. The limb had been decades older than anyone I knew alive. History had been diminished.

Or had it? I went outside and lay my hand on the nub that remained and I realized that the oak's exposed guts told their own story. I realized that a person who knew how to see, really see the ripped and wrenched splinters, could know the damaging event all over again. To the person who knew how to see, there was little difference between an event from just a few days previous, an event from deeper in the current lifetime, and an event from another generation. History is never diminished. It's still here.

Then I went away to college. I never knew the stories that old tree promised. My parents lived in that particular house and that particular town for only a few more months, and then we all were gone. My family never seemed to have the time or the context to built its own story, so we were left with a lot of episodes. Disjointed chapters. No continuous story that I ever saw.

But Eddy's family, now there was a story. And there was continuity. When I arrived at college and the two of us wound up in academic programs that were different in their expression but still complementary in their essence, much like our romantic selves, we imagined, I stepped deeply into history that a family had made. Or was that a family that history had made? It works both ways, doesn't it?

Like Tim, the first time I saw the past was at the Capri. Sitting by the pool, I had my nose in a book, a classic Sheila pose everyone still says, but I was spending as much time peering over the top, focusing on my boyfriend, Eddy, as I was with the text. I lowered my eyes. Raised them. Took a sip of wine (I was on about my third glass by then; this was, after all, a *Rashomon* weekend). Stared. Stubbed out a cigarette on the pool deck. Lowered my eyes. And then, refocusing on where he should be, where he'd just been, I didn't see Eddy at all. His chaise was folded and placed to the side, leaning against the wall. The air had a chill. And I could hear a football game coming from the television in a nearby room.

It was a familiar sound, that cadence of the announcer's voice. Familiar game, too. I knew the final score. Knew the score? I put down my wine. But before I could ponder that one, Eddy leaned over from behind me, over the back of my chair, and kissed my forehead. He was there and the air was warm. It was June; I'd watched that game the previous October. I'd had only a quick glimpse, a flash of another day that went by so fast I might not have noticed it or I might not have remembered it.

I might have thought it was the wine or I might have taken it for a memory. These were both entirely plausible, if it weren't for the lingering chill I felt on that early summer day. It was the same chill I'd feel years later when Eddy opened all our house's windows.

The first time I saw the past unassisted and unmuddled by wine—and the first time I did more than observe, the first time I physically moved, as Eddy would describe later, through two places at once the way a person's mind can move through simultaneous thoughts and observations—was in Eddy's old neighborhood.

He'd yammered on when we were dating about the Victorian house and about daily life there, but it took some serious badgering to get him to show me where he'd grown up. Eddy didn't want to be there at all. He'd told me only the bare bones story of his brother. But I'd insisted. I wanted to know all about my boyfriend. And finally he'd driven us down from school for the weekend. He almost dumped me out of the car, and he remained sullen, sitting behind the wheel, as I walked down the street.

I was paying very close attention, just as Eddy later would say he'd done, when an earlier day appeared. I'd been catching the aroma of a barbecue in someone's backyard, brushing my hair back out of my eyes in the breeze, listening to the shouting and laughing of moms and kids as they unloaded cars returning home from errands. And then there was another car. And then there was its horn: shave-and-a-haircut-two-bits. And then all around me, people were running, hurrying to see what the automotive fuss was all about.

"Well?" asked the driver as admirers crowded around. "Well? Here she is. Just in from Detroit. Just today."

"Is that real leather?" someone asked. "What else?" the driver grinned. He pushed open the passenger door and straightaway he was giving rides around the block. Kids first. A boy and a girl. Another boy watching and waiting. Stage whisper from me: "Eddy?" I knew nothing yet about Stan or Libby.

Now if this was a day Eddy had told me about, reminiscing and carrying on as he tended to do, I might have passed it off as a visualization of his story. But he hadn't said a word about the new car at that point. And it certainly wasn't a reminiscence of my own. I hadn't been there, of course. Not until now. I looked back toward where Eddy had parked. He and his car had disappeared, just as he'd been gone from his chaise at the Capri.

Back on the street, the man in the new car was giving another ride. A dog trotted alongside, barking happily before returning to the crowd, where he nuzzled the neighborhood children, one after the other.

And then came the day when I realized I was seeing the past in my own unique way. I was stepping out for lunch from a downtown design firm where I was a student intern. I recall being in a rush for a quick takeout sandwich so I could get back to my drafting station and impress the boss with my diligence. But haste doesn't always work. Circumstances change. And as soon as I stepped onto the sidewalk, a cold, piercing wind and a blast of horizontal rain slapped me hard.

Then it stopped.

Across the street, a woman walked with her umbrella furled. No rush. A car passed with its windshield wipers on slow, intermittent mode. A puddle on the sidewalk was shallow and small. A few tentative raindrops fell, but before they could touch the surface the wind blew them away.

Then the wind and rain slapped me harder and took me someplace else.

Beside me was a man. I couldn't see his face. He was cupping his hands around his eyes, peering through a barbershop window at hulking chairs of chrome and leather, at razor strops, white porcelain sinks, and oak-framed mirrors, at shaving mugs lined up neatly on shelves and deer antlers hanging on the walls. He acted like he'd never seen such a place before. He was probably right, because when he turned and started walking down the sidewalk, out into the blowing wind, stepping around puddles that were suddenly much bigger and dodging the on-again-off-again rain, I recognized him.

"Eddy!" I called. "Eddy!" But the man kept on walking.

Walking through a city I knew but didn't know, its streets lined with two- and three-story buildings, shops below, arched windows above, a low, horizontal masonry city, a city as it once had been, full and complete.

A few doors down, walking Eddy passed a grocery where sidewalk stands held pyramids of apples. The proprietor stood in the doorway, arms crossed over his long, white apron, guarding against greedy thieves and hungry boys.

Lightning flashed. The light was barely noticeable at midday, but the boom of thunder that followed made me jump and made the grocer look up.

A moment later, I saw walking Eddy stuffing an apple into his jacket pocket. What was that? Stealing was so out of character.

But then he was gone.

A streetcar was disgorging passengers into the street.

A woman stepped into an ankle-deep puddle.

And in the shelter of the doorway, I jumped again.

Okay. I was new at this business, but I could have sworn that this woman in the rain was the little girl I'd seen riding in that new car. It was the oddest feeling. I had no idea where it came from. But after listening to Eddy tell us what happened at his uncle Hugh's funeral, how the aunts recognized him even though he was a man, I'm thinking now that I was seeing the same way. I'm thinking maybe I was seeing some kind of essence that was the same for this girl and this woman no matter how old they were.

Anyway, one thing I did know: Judging from the car and the clothes, that other time was the 1950s. And this was not that time at all.

At the corner, a very wet horse stood patiently tethered to its buggy.

This was a long time earlier.

I was growing worried. Now I was not only seeing this long-ago place with its own people, but I was seeing it with people from the present. It was all very strange, confusing, and a little bit sinister.

Out on the avenue, the streetcar was stalled in a rising flood. Water above its wheels, climbing the steps, rolling across the floor inside.

From a hotel's front porch, a wicker chair had blown into the street. If the water rose much higher, that chair would float, sliding away in the stream.

And down the way was a commotion, a crowd standing where the avenue dipped and where two converging side streets dumped their own rushing contributions into the principal flood.

"A tiny woman like that?" I could hear a man saying. "What in the world possessed her?"

It was a story I'd heard before, a family story Eddy loved to tell. The crowd parted and an elderly man in a white suit emerged from the flood on horseback, an exhausted woman lying in front of him.

It was a grand rescue. Grand heroics. So why didn't I feel good about seeing it?

Maybe this was my visualization of Eddy's family story. Except that it was off-kilter. Eddy had been there. So had that woman from the streetcar, that girl from the neighborhood. I could still see her, but she'd walked a block in the other direction, unaware of the drama on the avenue. She was screaming at someone's house. Something about what people were doing and what she was doing. Something I couldn't quite hear. At the time, I still had no idea who she was either. But what I did know was that she was very angry and she was very, very upset.

The evening traffic had thinned, but driving back from the Capri with Tim took longer than the trip out. I wasn't in any hurry. I hadn't accomplished what I'd wanted. All I'd done was open old wounds and get Tim pissed off. Then there was the weather. A thick fog was rolling in.

In empty downtown, we passed office windows that glowed in a hazy blur and stoplights that oozed red and green. Stopped at a mess of red, I could make out the edges of a small park, the one by the county courthouse. It had a bandstand in the middle, shaded by a canopy of oaks. This I knew. I'd been here many times. But I couldn't see that structure. The fog was too thick.

Then near or far—I couldn't tell in the fog—I heard voices. I rolled down my window. I heard hammering. I heard sawing. And in one corner of the open space, in the dark under the trees, between the slow beats and the smear of the windshield wipers, I could just make out a pile of lumber. But I couldn't make out what the men were building. It was too deep in the gloom.

"Why are we stopped?" asked Tim, who'd been riding with his head tilted back against the headrest. He neither opened his eyes nor moved his head. He seemed to think the answer would be either no surprise or of no consequence.

"You don't hear?"

"I don't hear." His eyes were still closed.

"Then it's nothing."

"I can see the color of the stoplight. Through my eyelids. It's green again."

I pulled ahead gently. Rain had begun to fall, and I rolled up my window. Tim was in his own moment. The edges of his world were still fuzzy, the way he liked them, I supposed. And I supposed he'd forgiven me. The next time I looked his way, he gave me a wan smile. The time after that, he was staring at the car ceiling. He did seem worried. And Tim did seem knowing. About my encounters with the past I'd had on my own, about the noises I suspected he'd heard with me in the park, about what was about to happen to all of us next.

It was nothing, I'd reassured him, but I couldn't reassure myself. Whatever was out there in the park, it wasn't going anywhere. One of us would come around and discover it soon enough. Tomorrow, most likely.

twenty-two

EDDY

I loved cool autumn mornings. My favorite thing on those days, when the air was thin and crisp, when the few yellowing leaves that still clung to the trees provided a reminder that life was about to take a break and sleep for a little while, thank you, my favorite thing was to take my newspaper and coffee to the porch. I'd settle into one of the rocking chairs and become one with the atmosphere.

And if I was lucky, when the wind blew from the west, I could hear drums. I'd scrape my old wooden chair around to the angle that best caught the beat. Ike would remain in his spot, perched on the railing behind me in the sunlight, eyes closed, ears up. *Boom, boom, ba-BOOM.* The marching band from the high school would be going through its early drill. How odd, I'd often think, that the heaviest music would float farthest on the air, across the city and through the trees, that the drums would come a mile or more to my house while I never heard any other instruments. There were no clarinets in the air, not even a trumpet, but what I did hear was enough. It was all I needed in order to know the syncopation and punctuation of the entire drum line, the bleat of the trombone section, the tittering of flutes, the stomping and shuffling of feet. Drums were enough to bring the band to life.

I'm sure Sheila was tired of hearing me recreate that scene. It struck me so powerfully each time I experienced it that I'm afraid I described it over and over. But on this morning, when she made her bleary-eyed, fluffy-slipper-and-terry-robe way out from the kitchen, fully expecting to be lulled by my familiar ramble while she sipped her herbal tea, I had a different tale to tell. I don't believe she liked it. I know I didn't. But it was a tale of such magnitude, a tale that may well have set the direction for a hundred years of my family history. I'd known as soon as I encountered it that this was a tale that had to be told. And that my flirtation with the pleasant side of my family, with parties and ballgames, was over.

Earlier that morning, I told her—while Sheila absently, a little bored, stared into her cup, reflecting, I suspect, on the proper amount of honey

149

or whether or not to remove the tea bag—I'd been sitting, reflecting on the band when other sounds had followed it. It wasn't just the usual songs of birds and the usual traffic on the street. Over those sounds, I'd heard voices. But it wasn't the singular voice of a neighbor calling her dog. And it wasn't a collection of laughing individuals, each crying to be heard amid a pack of teenagers. What I heard sounded like a crowd, and it was a crowd with a purpose. A crowd that was anxious and excited. A crowd that was moving, though I couldn't tell its destination. The sound faded in and out, like waves. It was a moving force. A flood.

The crowd had been somewhere just outside the neighborhood, but I hadn't been able to fill in the gaps the way I could when I heard a drumbeat. Hundreds of people, all men it seemed, were in the streets, but exactly who, where, and why, who knew? For five minutes, maybe more, I turned toward the voices, straining during the lulls, amazed when I heard them again that the voices sounded so close.

So I put down my newspaper and my coffee. I gave Ike a quick scratch behind the ears. He stayed put on the sunny railing. Ike seemed to know that home was the better place to be, but I couldn't help but follow the sound.

"Don't do it," Sheila said, suddenly ignoring her tea and fully engaged.

"Too late," I replied. "It's done. And I've returned."

Sheila shook her head as if to say that I had it wrong. The return didn't make up for the going. But like I said, it was too late to stop what I'd seen.

So I told her how I'd descended to the sidewalk, how a green streetcar had approached on the cross street, how it had rumbled from the right and exited left without stopping.

How surprised and delighted I'd been and how I'd immediately begun walking faster.

Sheila tried to hide now behind sips of tea, but I could tell she was distressed.

I was sorry to have to hurt her again, but I had to tell what I saw. This was something important. Here it is.

At the corner, I saw the streetcar, stopped but already full. Men pressed together on the rear platform and clung to poles on the steps. The long queue at the passenger stop pushed forward anyway. A few more squeezed on board, the conductor rang his bell, and the streetcar glided ahead.

The men who were left behind, men in stiff collars, bowler hats or straw boaters, dark suit coats or waistcoats, began following on foot. I was dressed more simply in plain, modern shirtsleeves and gray wool trousers, but no one seemed to notice. I danced a little jig to avoid a steaming pile of horse dung in the middle of the street, then fell in behind the crowd. The men were talking excitedly. I was happy. I'd found my voices.

The procession moved quickly, and I thought of marching bands and football games. This was that kind of day when crowds convened to share their passion for a single event. Outside the crowd and the event, the world went on as if nothing special were happening. People shopped at the market, mowed lawns, read books, took naps. People cooked, ate dinner, argued, made love. All in a normal day. But inside the circle of the event, the rest of the world ceased to exist. All attention and energy had one focus. Only the event mattered. It was all-consuming. I was approaching that maelstrom.

The city, while in an era different from the one I inhabited, looked familiar. Two- and three-story buildings, none taller, lined the streets and avenues. A disorganized spaghetti of electric wires crisscrossed overhead. Horse-drawn delivery wagons lined the curb downtown. The year? I had no way of knowing what year it was, but some major event, maybe a historical event, seemed to be occurring. And the crowd was growing.

Then, seven or eight blocks along, everyone came to a halt. I was confused. I should have recognized this place. Across the street stood the courthouse, unchanged, the same one I'd visited many times. I should have been at the little city park, the one with the bandstand. Except that a massive, dark-stone building stood here. A sign over the entrance said county jail.

Hundreds of men were milling around on the street, their voices growing louder. They seemed to want something, seemed to be debating their options, competing for something. I worked my way forward.

"Hey, mister, give me a hand with this." I was standing at a side door to the jail. I looked around. "You, mister." A man was gesturing toward me. "Give me a hand with this and you can come in. You won't need a ticket." The man and two others were bending over, working their hands under a long, plain box. It had no handles and they needed a fourth to lift it. The box was a coffin.

I followed instructions. On our shoulders, the coffin was light. It was empty. And when we four pallbearers stepped through the door, I found myself in the jail's exercise yard. It was smaller than I had expected from the mass and height of the walls, and it was nearly filled by a crowd of two hundred, maybe two hundred and fifty men. In the middle stood something I had not expected. In the middle of the yard stood a gallows.

"You're in, mister." The man with the coffin clapped me on the back, and I thought of my father, welcoming Gunner's Mate Alvin Peacock to the family. "Those poor buggers outside might hear the trapdoor drop—if they shut up long enough to listen—but you're here now. You'll see that bastard get what he deserves. You'll see him swing."

The scene was terrifying and fascinating. I shook the man's hand. I tried to say "Thanks," but my throat closed up tight.

Sheila interrupted to say she should hope so. At least I was properly appalled. But I let her remark go. She could have her modern reaction. I was just trying to follow the past.

So I told her how men all around were jockeying for position. How some crowded to the front, where deputies pushed them back from the scaffold. How others perched on top of tool sheds and a row of single-story cells ringing the yard. And how I wanted to disappear into the back wall.

But I also wanted to know about the case, so I stayed with the crowd. I tried to eavesdrop on conversations. Most of what I heard were references to the condemned as a "bastard" or a "sonofabitch" or a "goddamned fiend." The men smoked cigars and laughed and cursed some more. "Goddamn good night's sleep." "Chicken and goddamn dewberry pie . . . ." The speaker spat out "goddamn" as two harsh and distinct words: ". . . God damn last meal." The group lit more cigars.

I learned little of the condemned man's story until a man nearby pulled a rolled-up newspaper from his hip pocket, asked his companions if they wanted to read any more, and tossed it aside when they shook their heads. I pounced on the news.

"The gallows was tested yesterday," the story began, "and Sheriff Henry Montegut's man will pull the lever this morning, sending the condemned murderer to the fate he sealed for himself when he added so horribly to the tragedy of last month's flood."

I learned that the condemned was a farm laborer who had been found guilty of pushing a woman from the branches of a tree where a dozen or so people had sought safety from floodwaters. The victim had disappeared into the torrent. Her body was recovered only after the flood receded five days later. The year was 1906.

"I am not guilty of murder," the man had told the reporter who wrote the story. "I am only guilty of trying to escape that flood."

I learned that the governor had dismissed an appeal for executive clemency with a simple declaration: "Let the law take its course." I also learned some names. The victim was one Caroline Simms. The condemned man was one Alexander Lee.

My God. I'd heard that one.

"If you want to know about Hugh, you've got to understand about Alexander Lee," Great Aunt Eleanor had told me at her brother's funeral.

I sat in the dirt as if to hide, certainly to ponder, thankful for the forest of legs that obscured the gallows. A few men glanced my way, wondering, I'm sure, why I was sitting, but their attention was short-lived. The hour of execution had arrived and the men around me grew loud. "There he is." "Sonofabitch." "Woman killer."

I stood.

In the present, Sheila set down her empty cup and placed her hand on mine. I let it remain. I did need support.

Two deputies, one on each side, were leading the condemned from his cell. The man's hands were cuffed in front of him, but he was dressed in a new, tailored black suit, white shirt and collar, and black tie. Someone near me said that it was tradition for a condemned man to be neatly and closely shaven. When he reached the foot of the gallows, two preachers stepped forward from the crowd. Alexander Lee shook their hands, stepped out of the prison slippers he was wearing, and slowly mounted the scaffold in his stocking feet.

Atop the platform, the sheriff, more deputies, and the executioner waited. Again, deputies flanked the condemned. They were ready for him to collapse. The crowd hooted. Alexander Lee showed no sign of weakness or fear. He promptly, calmly took his place on the center of the trapdoor, which one of the carpenters had marked in chalk with a large X. No one wanted the man to fall crookedly. A straight fall and a clean snap of the neck were always better.

A deputy unlocked the handcuffs. Without waiting for instructions, Alexander Lee folded his hands behind his back.

Sheriff Montegut leaned close but spoke loudly so the assembled specta-
tors could hear. "Do you have anything to say, Alexander?"

The condemned raised his head and fixed his eyes on the crowd.

"Only a short speech, Sheriff. Only a short speech."

"But it's got to last for eternity," someone shouted. "Get on with it,"
another called. I was shocked. A man was about to die and they were acting
like this was entertainment. How would they feel later? Would they regret
their behavior? What would they tell their sweethearts, their wives, their
children? Would they brag about what they had done?

"Go ahead, Alexander," the sheriff urged in a gentle, even voice. "Have
your say."

The crowd, which had been steadily shuffling closer, stopped moving.

"We are all dead men," the condemned man began. "Enough time passes,
we're all dead."

The crowd grew silent.

"Enough time passes . . . ." Alexander Lee's voice trailed off.

"But," he abruptly started again. "Some are hastened along their way.
Some have the help of a state that rushes a trial. Some have the help of juries
with made-up minds. And some have the help of men who bear false witness.
The man who convicted me to drop here," he said, pointing to the trapdoor
below his feet, "was a false witness. The state didn't do right. The jury didn't
do right. But it was a false witness that convicted me to drop here."

Alexander Lee stood quietly, eyes burning into the crowd. Men began
shuffling their feet again, looked around, stuffing their hands into their
pockets, pulling them out again.

"Are you ready, Alexander?" the sheriff finally asked.

The condemned man nodded.

As deputies bound his wrists and ankles and wrapped a long length of rope
about his legs, the two preachers offered prayers. Their voices were low, meant
only for Alexander Lee and his God. Until the clergymen began a hymn:
"Yes, we'll gather at the river, / The beautiful, the beautiful river."

Alexander Lee's lips moved with the music, but if he actually sang, his
voice was very faint. I could not hear him.

Neither could I hear what transpired next, as the condemned turned his
head and spoke to the sheriff. The men's eyes met, the two nodded at each

other, and I thought I saw the gleam of a tear on Alexander Lee's cheek. A moment later the sheriff stepped back and the executioner took his place.

He slid a black hood over Alexander Lee's head and shoulders.

From under the hood came a single word. "Goodbye."

The executioner dropped the noose over the hood, over Alexander Lee's head, and around his neck. He adjusted the knot behind the left ear. Maybe I'd read it in a book or seen it in a movie, but I recalled somehow from somewhere that this left ear position was the way to break the man's neck quickly when he fell, to kill him instantly and without any suffering. I didn't know what to believe. I didn't know much about hangings. But if this had to happen, I certainly hoped the knot would work that way.

A small group of men in a corner of the yard gave a small cheer, but their voices faded quickly. The crowd stood in awe of the condemned man's behavior. Of his incredible politeness.

"Goodbye," he said one more time.

The executioner pulled the lever.

Alexander Lee shot through the trapdoor, fell eight feet, jerked sharply upward with an audible snap, and began to sway, like a pendulum making circles.

I braced myself with a stiff arm and one hand against the exercise yard's stone wall, leaned far over, and closed my eyes. The bile rose quickly in the back of my throat and I threw up.

twenty-three

EDDY

I thought Sheila was going to throw up, too. Her skin was waxy and white, and her lips were quivering. It was not such a good state for a pregnant lady. She stared at me for the longest time, her eyes unblinking. Then she began to cry.

Crying was good. Certainly it was better than throwing up. And it was confirmation that I'd done the right thing. Once again, I had not told Sheila the whole story. I'd given her only the basics of Alexander Lee's execution, the public story you read or hear, not the hidden, personal story you see. For Sheila's sake, I was glad I'd held back—even if it meant being less truthful than I've always wanted to be.

I didn't know how she'd take the truth. And I didn't know how I could have told it. I could taste the bile again, so I shut up. What I know now is that I can't hold this secret any longer.

I'd told the beginning of my hanging story pretty much as it happened, though I'd left out the part about the golden retriever. As I left the Victorian, our neighbor's dog, Alice, ran with me for a block or so, trotting alongside like my best friend, intrigued perhaps by the cat smell of Ike, then peeling off and returning home like a jet fighter leaving formation. Alice wasn't important to the story. I just remember those things.

What was important, but which I'd also left out, was the lantana. As I passed a little bungalow a few houses down, I noticed the purple blooms of the spreading, trailing plant cascading over a retaining wall in front. The fragrance was strong and unmistakable, a smelly, oily kind of sweet that seemed like it would follow me if I touched the plant. Maybe it was that peculiar smell that heightened my senses that day. Maybe it added smell to my hearing; maybe lantana joined those voices to put me into the past with an intensity I'd never felt before.

Anyway, it was right after I smelled the lantana that I also smelled the ozone sparking from the streetcar wires. I know Sheila wouldn't have been interested in that. It was a small detail. But the ozone definitely was with me, and by then I was definitely somewhere else.

Problem is, every time I smell lantana now, every time I see a wire spark or men in waistcoats, every time I hear the sound of a crowd in the distance or a gospel hymn nearby, I still think of what I saw that day. Snap! And the inert body of a man, alive only a few seconds before, swings like a pendulum once again. It's more than a memory. It never fades. But there's one thing about it. I can make this story change, depending on which version I recall. The one I told Sheila. Or the one I kept to myself. This one:

In the exercise yard of the county jail, the man talking with his friends tossed his newspaper aside.

"I don't know," he said as he turned back to his friends. "I just don't trust that sonofabitch witness. He made the poor bastard sound like some kind of goddamn fiend."

"Alexander Lee is a good man," one of the others nodded.

"Then why the hell are you here?" asked a third.

"That's a good goddamn question." The second man struck a match and re-lit the stub of his cigar. "A good goddamn question."

The crowd's clamor outside the walls, the cursing, the smoking, the general bravado of those who'd gained admission, all were attempts, I was beginning to think, to hide an extraordinary sense of unease, an extraordinary nervousness. Who, I wondered, were the real condemned here? This hanging would have a lasting effect on everyone who saw it.

Nonetheless, even the men who suspected Alexander Lee might be innocent felt they were drawn to witness. As did I.

So when the hour of the execution came I stood from where I'd sat behind the forest of men's legs and stepped away from the center of the crowd. I skirted the periphery of the exercise yard, following the stone wall until I was at the front, as close to the gallows as I could be. Behind me, the crowd pressed forward. I inched ahead some more. I craned to the left, watching the cellblock door, waiting for Alexander Lee to appear.

A big man in shirtsleeves stood tall at the front of the crowd, crossing beefy arms over a barrel chest like he was proud of something. Or someone. Like Alice the dog, he may not have been important, but I had a suspicion about him.

"The boy's a man," Barrel Chest was saying to a fellow standing nearby. "I had an extra ticket to this here, and he'd been doing a good job sweeping up the store and he wanted to come. So I give it to him. It's something he needs to see. It's justice. Ain't nothing wrong with seeing justice."

I had my doubts about the wisdom of this, but I said nothing. Neither did anyone else. It turned out the man was a grocer, a mild profession for his muscular build and belligerent attitude, but his neighbors seemed cowed by his manner. They looked down and shuffled their feet, trying to pretend that either they or the big man weren't there.

"Ain't nothing wrong, don't you think?" The grocer stared straight at me, and I stood motionless, wordless. I was hoping I'd fade back into the crowd or back into the present time.

Until I remembered something from Uncle Hugh's funeral. "The grocer," Great Aunt Lillian had said. "I wish none of us had ever laid eyes on that one." I laid my eyes on the grocer hard, examining intently, but it seemed as if I was getting my wish. The grocer acted as if I weren't there after all. Or at least as if I didn't matter.

"Come here, boy," he said, turning back to the crowd, away from me.

Proudly, a ten- or eleven-year-old youth stepped forward. The man draped a big arm around his shoulders.

"You'll grow up today," said the man.

"Yessir," said the boy.

The man took off his bowler hat and put it on the boy's head. The boy grinned, but I sensed an uneasiness about him.

"Shut your yap," whispered a man standing to my right.

I looked his way.

"You don't know what you're doing," the man said under his breath, glaring at the grocer. Then he redirected his gaze downward like the others, away from me. He spoke to someone else in a still lower voice. The other was a preacher, one of the men who would counsel Alexander Lee before the hanging. Beside him stood another boy two or three years younger. This boy was not trying to act proud. He was holding back, trying to disappear. He was frightened.

And in an instant, I knew that this man and maybe the others and certainly the boys were not random details. They were not Alice the golden retriever.

Oh, God, I thought. This boy with the preacher was Walter Lee, who I'd been following. Then I had another flash. I turned back to the grocer and his protégé. That boy was listening intently to the others around him, following them closely with his eyes, trying hard to be a man. Acting big, I thought, but acting big nervously. "Shit," I said and this time I said it aloud. "Hugh."

The boy took a pull on a cigar and coughed. The grocer slapped him on the back. The boy tried again. Everyone laughed.

Everyone but me. I knew what was about to happen. "Hugh, Hugh," I whispered. I thought of the reclusive young man alone in his room the day Babe Ruth came to town. I remembered the shy, middle-aged man who brightened for a moment at the thought of playing the accordion, but who remained a cipher, the aged shell I'd known in my own youth. Oh, Hugh, I wondered, will you ever laugh again?

At the far end of the exercise yard, a door clanged open, and deputies ushered Alexander Lee to the base of the gallows. The preacher stepped forward and shook his hand. And something else I had not told Sheila: The boy Walter Lee ran forward and threw his arms around the condemned man's waist. The boy's face was wet, but he was quiet. Alexander Lee stared straight ahead, and I wondered where he fixed his eyes so intently. On the crowd waiting for him to die? On birds overhead flying free? On God, wherever God was?

Alexander Lee put the palm of his big hand on the boy's small head and tousled his hair, and I knew he was seeing the world and all its connections. The man's face betrayed no emotion, but I could sense the affection in the gesture. Walter Lee continued to hug his father. The relationship was not something I needed to ponder. Then the boy relaxed his hold.

Father and son knew the end had arrived. Two deputies gently but firmly took the condemned man by the arms. A third put his hand on the boy's shoulder and walked him toward the exit.

At the door, the boy looked back one more time. His father was standing at the base of the scaffold, stepping out of his jailhouse slippers.

I looked to my left, at Hugh. The boy's eyes were wide, fixed on Walter Lee.

"Do you have anything to say, Alexander?" the sheriff was asking.

Hugh seemed to be in shock. The reality, the eternal finality of the event suddenly had dawned on him.

"Enough time passes . . . ." Alexander Lee began.

"Listen to him squirm," the grocer told the boy.

But the condemned man kept his dignity. As a deputy bound him with ropes, and as the preachers prayed, Alexander Lee stood still. When the hymn began, he joined in singing. I was close enough to hear that Alexander Lee not only knew the words, he felt their meaning. He felt it with deep emotion. I was close enough, too, to hear what Alexander Lee said when he leaned back and spoke to the sheriff. "You're a good man," said the condemned. "You're a good man."

The sheriff nodded and wiped perspiration from his brow.

"Goodbye, Alexander," said a number of men near me.

"They got a good Manila hemp," the grocer was telling the boy. "It's all treated with oil so it's good and flexible, like a fine fishing line."

The boy was quiet.

The sheriff stepped back.

The executioner sprang the trapdoor.

Alexander Lee fell. His neck snapped. He began to swing. He kicked.

He was not dead.

And I tasted bile. I threw up. Had I arrived in hell? Every time I opened my eyes, I saw one thing more terrible than the other. For those in the back of the crowd, and in the version I had told Sheila, the scene appeared clean, antiseptic. It looked like justice. It looked like a history lesson. But from here, from where I really stood, everything was different. I heard the condemned man's whispered confidences. I saw his family's anguish. Now I was watching a slow death, as kicking turned to twitching, as Alexander Lee clenched a fist one time and let his hand go limp, as life ebbed.

At six minutes, three doctors employed by the jail felt for a pulse in the dying man's wrist. The heart was still beating, and they released the body to resume its slow arc in space. At eight minutes, they felt again. The pulse was slower, the doctors announced, but there were still signs of life. Finally, ten minutes after the trapdoor was sprung, the medical men pronounced Alexander Lee dead. As deputies cut away the ropes that bound arms and legs, a pair of undertakers moved a coffin under the gallows, and the body was lowered into the box.

I recognized the coffin, of course. It was the one I had helped carry, but I no longer sensed that I was in the event. Watching the coffin's lid close over Alexander Lee, I stood alone, as if the crowd around me did not exist. Or perhaps my presence was what did not exist. But invisibility was only what I wanted to believe. I learned the truth of my situation the hard, physical way as the crowd surged, shoving me so forcefully I nearly fell to the ground.

All hope that the crowd might have retained some sensibility, some tiny shred of decorum during this horrible event, instantly disappeared. Men reached out to grab pieces of rope. They wanted souvenirs, and someone up front was obliging them by cutting into short pieces the long length that had bound Alexander Lee's arms and legs.

Men fought over five- and six-inch pieces. They shoved and punched, they bullied and stole, and they had no shame. As they left the jail yard, many pinned the pieces to their lapels or stuffed them into their waistcoat pockets so that the ends dangled outside like watch chains. Those lucky enough to have longer pieces draped the rope around their shoulders, dangling in front like an untied necktie. Or a hangman's noose. As I said, who were the real condemned?

At the foot of the gallows steps, the big, burly grocer picked up Alexander Lee's discarded jailhouse slippers and stuffed them inside his coat. He calmly walked from the yard, lighting a cigar, joking with his friends.

And where was Hugh? "Oh, Hugh," I said in a sad whisper. "Hugh!" I called aloud, but I didn't see the boy anywhere. Though the crowd departed rapidly after the gates were opened, the exercise yard was still churning. Men from the crowd outside were flowing in to take their fellows' places. They were looking for leftovers, for some tangible evidence of the event they had missed. What they found was ordinary trash, ragged newspapers and stepped-upon cigars, wrapping papers from a few dozen lunches and one abandoned straw boater, its brim snapped by the crush of shoving men. But the crowd remained hopeful that it would still see death and it remained thick for so long that I gave up hope of finding the boy.

"Well," a man walking behind me was saying as I finally left the yard. "That's the end of a horrible story."

I was overcome with grief. I was torn every which way, feeling for the hanged Alexander Lee, for his son who would mysteriously stalk me as an old man, and for my great uncle who would hide from the world. For I knew this was not the end, not by any means. I knew, as the man behind me apparently did not, that events lived for years, and that they could resurface in the most unlikely places, with the most unforeseen results. Even then, I could feel the heat of Mr. Peacock's burning Cadillac. I could hear accordion music on the front porch. I could touch my brother's blood. There was a connection. I knew there was. I just wasn't sure I wanted to see it anymore.

And then I saw Hugh. The boy was wandering through the crowd of men, his face filled with panic and shock, far beyond emotion. His eyes were glazed, red from spent tears and now nearly catatonic. I watched the boy leave the jail and make his way out into the city streets. He did seem to have a direction. Physically, Hugh would arrive home safely. Emotionally, Hugh was not safe, not at all. Hugh would never really leave the hanging behind.

I knew exactly how the boy felt. From fascination with my family story and a feeling of safety in those years before I was born, I had made the short step toward despair myself.

twenty-four

TIM

"The time has come, the walrus said."

I've been sitting here listening to Eddy and Sheila deliver their takes on this story, on what happened all those years ago. So much of it is a McBride story that I've been quiet. Sitting here, I've been in and out, hanging around, waiting on the edges for I don't know what. Now I'm joining the dance.

Eddy said something not long ago that struck me. When he began his tale of Alexander Lee's hanging, he was in the crowd moving down the street. He was totally consumed by what he was seeing right around him, but he was talking about the world outside going on as if nothing special were happening. People were cooking and making love, he said. I appreciated that nod to the larger context, because, yeah, I was in that context. Making love is about as consuming as you can get.

And, you know, I think what I experienced could have been that same day. It was certainly some day about that same time, as best I remember.

Libby was lying on her back, in her bed, next to me. She was making her best guess at how to adjust my New Orleans Zephyrs baseball cap without a mirror. The results were crooked but cute. We were in a very good mood.

"I saw something," she said. She stared at the mirror over the dresser, but it was too high to reflect her image. She saw the corner of the ceiling instead.

"You snored," I said. I was thinking about cooking some eggs, but I was reluctant to leave the bed. I was feeling a part of this person, so much a part of her that I could be wholly open and honest.

And I was astounded at my luck. Here was this delightful woman, a client who was in and out of the office regularly, my partner's childhood friend, a person I had worked with side by side for months. It should have been business as usual, and it should have been business only, but our relationship had never been that way. Not even that first day at the pub.

There had been little signals, a touch here, a nod there. There had been a flirty little smile, Libby's sad kind of flirty smile, every time we saw each other. And when Libby had phoned the night before with a cheery but somehow lonely invitation for dinner at her carriage house apartment, I'd immediately understood how much she needed companionship, how much she really needed someone in this time as she returned to this place. After my visit to the Capri with Sheila, I was feeling pretty much the same. Lost.

Libby rolled over and pulled the blanket almost to her shoulders. She cocked an arm at a 90-degree angle, elbow on mattress, head on her palm. The posture knocked the cap askew. "I don't snore," she said, her eyes now fixed on me. "I wasn't even asleep."

I was the one on my back now. I hugged a pillow over my face, pretending to hide, like a child who thinks he can't be seen because he can't see anyone else. "Oh, yes," I said, raising the pillow an inch or two for air. "Fingernails on the chalkboard." I lowered the pillow.

"Not all night."

Pillow up. "Only the parts when I was awake."

"I don't snore," Libby repeated. Then she added: "I saw something."

I tossed the pillow to the foot of the bed. "Was it good?" I asked, wrapping an arm around her waist. She rolled in my direction, on top, and as she bent to kiss me, her long, silver-blonde hair cascaded across my face, containing me like a tent.

Later, as she was falling asleep, Libby whispered again. "I saw it."

I lay awake for a while, absently running my fingertips along the scar on my arm and thinking not so much about what each of us had said as about what we might say next. I was thinking that the conversations that follow sex can be as interesting as the sex itself. The electricity of sex changes a relationship. Conversations are its new revelations.

When I emerged from the shower, Libby was wearing a big, loose robe and watching an old movie on television. She pointed wordlessly at the kitchen, where I found an assembly of two plates, one upside down on top of the other, toast and fried eggs in between. I picked up the plates and held them carefully, like an athlete balancing a discus. I removed the top half. How had she known what I wanted?

"Remember the first time you saw this?" Libby asked. I looked up from the plate, where I'd been contemplating breaking yolks. She was excited, as if she wanted to share something she'd never shared before.

On the television, three young people reclined near an empty swimming pool. One was talking about eavesdropping on his parents fighting when he was a child.

No, I'd never seen that one. I sat on the bed beside her, fork poised.

Rebel Without a Cause," Libby said wistfully, not moving her attention from the screen. "Remember?" But she spoke more to herself than to me. The young man on the screen was now talking about how his dead father had been a hero in the Navy.

Oh.

This sailor father sounded just like Libby's, but I held my tongue. Libby was a fragile person, up and down with cheer (a cry of "Wonderful!") and sadness (despair at her father's mackerel sky). Her bravado was on the surface only, and she could be hurt easily. Eddy never understood that. He seemed to think she was still the tree-climbing tomboy he knew when they were little. Or the quick-witted society fixture she became when she moved away.

But the Libby who returned home was somewhat shattered. She was looking for something. And she needed help. I understood that pretty quickly, though beyond the loan of a ball cap and the giggling and the physical closeness, I'm not sure I was doing much to provide it. Or maybe I was. We seldom know about these things.

"They're all dead," Libby said without turning.

"They died in the movie?"

"In real life. Assaults. Accidents."

"Famous people," I said, trying to keep the conversation away from real people, especially away from her dad, "people in the movies, on TV, in politics. What's the difference? They get to the point where they're just faces and bodies. They're puppets. You wonder if there's anybody inside."

I think Libby knew exactly what I meant, but I don't believe she wanted it to be true. She sat so quietly, so absorbed in watching.

"What's the point," I asked, taking a different tack, "once you've seen the movie the first time?"

Libby's eyes never moved. Some people, she explained, watch a movie a second, a third, a fourth time because each time they see something new.

She'd tried that, but she was always disappointed that she'd caught details already. She was disappointed, too, when she tried to recapture the emotions she'd felt. An old movie never brought back the past.

But the present! That's why Libby watched old movies, and every time she came across one of her favorites, the experience was too comforting to resist. The questions that the characters raised had already been answered. The suspense had been smoothed out and resolved. She could laugh, she could cry, she could love, she could hate, and she could do it all so freely. Libby could simply settle into the life of the film. The familiarity became her new present.

It happened every time. Maybe I was right about actors as hollow puppets, but in Libby's movie-watching present, the characters—and it was always the characters who were important, not the actors—characters did have substance. They did have life.

The female character on the screen was asking her male friends what they thought a woman wanted.

What indeed? What does any one of us want? By the time I was dragged into this story of McBrides and Peacocks and now, though I didn't know it at the time, a hanged man named Alexander Lee, I'd been watching their drama unfold for months. Like its own movie. But not with the comfort and ease that Libby felt as she sat in front of a film.

First came Eddy. Maybe he felt obligated, but he also wanted to see and know and understand everything, regardless of where it would take him. Saw himself as so damn smart. Didn't know shit.

Then Sheila. She wanted to keep moving into the future. She'd seen some disturbing things in her earlier years, but she refused to admit they existed. No one could put the past behind her like Sheila.

Me, I'm in Sheila's camp. Not going back. Never again. But that doesn't mean I don't watch the train wrecks that the past makes of other peoples' lives. I can't help it. I suppose that's why I was rubbing the scar on my arm more than ever in those days. Those things that had happened, to me and to everyone else, just wouldn't go away. I eyed an empty bottle of wine from the previous night. If only some were left. I'd nip over and finish it right away.

And Libby? That one, I was still figuring out. There was something about her father and something about Eddy's brother and something about her return to town that tied it all together. Some kind of regret, a thing done or a thing not done, who knew? It's a terrible thing to be racked with regret, and almost as terrible to love someone caught in regret's trap.

Where was that wine?

I reached across Libby's line of vision and flicked the television off. She gave a peep of protest, but it was only a peep. The present of the film was gone. The actual present had returned. She gave me a kiss.

"Timmy, I think I'll call you Timmy," she exclaimed, jumping to her feet. "You're so serious. You need to be a little kid again."

Well, a bit of fun, a bit of playfulness as an antidote to regret and sadness, was just fine with me. You know how relationships are. Give whatever is needed. I gave her a kiss.

"What did you see?" I asked.

"Timmy, Timmy. I saw it. I dreamed it. Whatever happened, I can hardly tell the difference. The difference isn't important."

I grabbed the pillow, put it to my face, and collapsed again onto the bed. Of course the difference was important. It was damn important, but I couldn't tell that to Libby. She'd been raising the subject all morning, hinting that she wanted to talk. I'd finally responded just to be polite, just because I knew that's what she wanted. But I didn't really want to talk, not about her father, not about Eddy's brother Stan, not about what else she might have seen or dreamed or imagined.

So I lay in silence. At that point, dead air in the conversation seemed like a damn good idea.

Except that now from outdoors came a plaintive little voice. Libby crossed the room and opened the door. Ike sat staring.

Libby reached down and lifted the cat, her thumbs under his armpits. She always called a cat's front legs his arms. She was cute that way. But Ike wanted none of it. He wriggled free and ran down the carriage-house steps and into the yard. Libby shrugged and closed the door.

Easy come, easy go. We'd had our electricity and we'd had our revelations and I may have been her Timmy now, but our relationship hadn't changed the Libby I'd met. Sometimes she was detached, aloof like the cat. Sometimes she was in her own world. Or she was trying to get to some other world. That's what worried me, under my pillow. Other worlds could be a damn big deal.

twenty-five

TIM

Libby and I climbed into her Land Rover. "We're going over to the East side," I said. "Take the old iron bridge. I'll show you the way from there."

"I remember," she replied.

"Of course." And I slunk down in my seat. Pretty stupid giving directions to someone who'd grown up in this town.

"Timmy," she said and reached for my hand. "Timmy, Timmy."

As soon as I'd mentioned that I needed to photograph an old house at the river for one of our firm's projects, Libby had asked if she could come along. Maybe she wanted to make a small contribution to my art, but I flatter myself. More likely, she was searching for something of her own. Ever since Eddy had cornered her about her father's car fire, Libby had been looking differently at places she might have known.

Her new perspective hadn't been much of a leap, either. Somehow she'd found out what Eddy was up to with the past. It wasn't from me, I promise. It must have been Sheila, trying to enlist her to stop him. But Libby had immediately put the pieces together. Eddy had seen something. Eddy knew something. Now Libby wanted something, too. She wanted just what Sheila and I had been trying to avoid.

Eddy just didn't know when to stop. He had to pull in other people. And you know what? The last thing I wanted was to hear more about the damn McBrides.

But a trip to the river, like my Timmy name, well, that was something new and different. It was something away from Libby's old neighborhood and it was something away from the McBrides' Victorian home. I didn't believe Eddy had ever mentioned this place. A drive seemed harmless enough.

I knew only a little about the old house. It had been damaged in a flood a few months back. Voilà. Architect needed. But Libby knew more.

When she was a girl, Libby told me as she drove, this part of town was out in the country. Over the years, the city had swallowed it up, overlapping and merging the way cities do, and the area was now considered a historic neighborhood. Libby laughed. I could go on and on about board and batten siding, center hall vernacular architecture, and such. I could throw myself into documenting and then restoring the structure. Libby just called these houses plain and simple, as ordinary as they could be. But she wanted to see. When I'd described the location, she'd acted as if it sounded familiar and as if she needed to find out why.

We turned at the center of town and rode in silence, holding hands like teenagers. I stared out the window, scanning neighborhoods as we left the affluent areas and made our way along streets lined with big, off-brand discount stores and small, mom-and-pop restaurants and bars. These soon gave way to pawnshops, used car lots, and waste-paper recycling centers. This was where end-of-life goods went. Here, everything had a story, often a long and complex one, and over the past few months, as I'd begun photographing again, I'd searched with my camera several times for whatever I could find. Jumbled, tumbled environments were prime spots for seeing and documenting the city my way, with the messy vitality of people. But as we drove, even those disappeared.

We pulled up in front of the flood-damaged house and a flock of grackles rose from the yard. As the grackle flies, or as the river flows, we were only about a mile from downtown, but it had taken twenty minutes to drive here. We'd left the city far behind.

I walked to the rear of the Land Rover and began plucking equipment from the luggage compartment. Libby didn't budge from the driver's seat. She wore a puzzled look, as if this place was both very familiar and not familiar at all. Libby seemed sad. I guess her premonition had been wishful thinking. "This place . . ." she murmured, digging through her recollections. "This place . . . ."

Then I suppose she quit worrying. I was on the porch, sorting through a big ring of keys when Libby walked up and gave the door a hard, tomboy shove. It opened slowly. The floor was covered with an inch of silt deposited by the flood. The door left a mark like the wing of a snow angel.

I immediately held up my arm, horizontally, waist-high, in front of Libby. "Don't." I raised the camera that hung on my shoulder. Libby took a step backward. "No," I said. "Come up here, right up to the door. Do you see that? Out there in the middle?"

There were no curtains on the windows, and at this morning hour the low sun was coming straight into the room, making it almost as bright as the outdoors. The sun cast sharp shadows from two wooden, straight-backed chairs. It glanced across a wiggly, feathery line that cut the silt from one end of the room to the other. I leaned into the room, clicking my shutter. I stepped back, changed lenses, and began again. The heavily shadowed, overlaid patterns of glancing light and feathery tracks looked like the design of a lithograph. Libby crouched for a low angle on nature's art.

"Snake," she whispered.

I leaned farther into the room.

"You better not do that," Libby cautioned.

I have to admit I found the prospect of a snake exciting. I stepped completely into the room, making my own impressions in the silt. "Maybe he's still here," I suggested. "That would really be something." But I was a little worried, and I exaggerated my bravery when I looked behind the door. "Not here," I said waving an arm like a magician at the completion of a trick. I was relieved.

Libby pushed her way in, tromping straight through the house and out the back. "Not here," she called through the screen door. "Whatever it was, it's not here anymore." And without pausing, she set out across the open land behind the house.

Watching her go, I guessed she was still frustrated by not finding what she'd expected. Disappointed at finding snake tracks instead. But maybe what she needed was near. At the tree line by the river, she stopped, turned, and gave me a big arc of a wave. Libby was doing okay. I needed to get to work. I began setting up my tripod.

I was preparing to record the details of this single structure. Libby, though in the broader landscape, seemed to be focused even more. How different, yet how similar. A view of details. A discovery of truths. Differences, of course, can share the truth.

That's why I'd begun looking at life through a camera, to get different views and find a common thread. And it's why I found myself distracted from architecture that day and focused on this woman. After only a few minutes with the old house, I swung my camera in Libby's direction. I attached my longest lens.

I could see Libby sitting on a stump beside the running water. She told me later that she'd been remembering swimming in the river as a child, but she'd swum in so many places. She'd backstroked across the still pools of deep water and sat in shallow rapids while whitewater splashed across her legs. She'd burned her skin red in bright sunlight and shivered and raised goose bumps under dark cypress trees. She'd floated on inner tubes and air mattresses. She'd jumped off docks. She'd waded along sandy shoals. Which had this been?

Through my long lens, I could see Libby pick up a stick and start drawing and digging in the mud at her feet. She started with an "S," then quickly rubbed it out. I knew she'd gone years without thinking of Stan, that she was angry at Eddy for bringing the dead boy back into her life. She was frustrated that she could not let go again.

I could see Libby bouncing the stick on her knee. Then she used it to push aside a layer of blackened leaves that had caked during high water. She dug deeper. Her tool was ill-suited to scraping a wide hole, but it was ideal for probing. With leaves removed from the surface, the mud underneath would have been easy to penetrate.

The object that stopped her stick appeared to be three or four inches down. Later, she told me she thought at first that it was a small stone. She tried to slide her stick around it but kept hitting resistance. Finally, she pulled the stick from the earth and started digging with her hands.

Libby told me she'd been only marginally curious about what she might find. She was mostly killing time while I finished my pictures. If she'd known that I wasn't photographing the house, she probably would have given up right then. But she kept digging. Soon she pulled a glob of mud from the ground. She wiped away the muck, and it was not a stone at all.

It was a watch, a pendant-style watch, the kind that ladies a long time ago pinned to a blouse or a dress. Shirtwaist was the garment she told me came to mind. Just above the twelve on the watch was a metal pin in the shape of a ribbon.

Libby rose and walked to the river's edge. She washed away the remaining mud. She dried the artifact on her shirttail and held it up in the sunlight for a better look. Lost a long time ago, no doubt, but under what circumstances? When, how, by whom? she recalled wondering. All unknown, all perhaps unknowable. Libby appeared to be pondering the time. Then she put the watch into her pocket.

I was packing up my equipment when Libby returned to the house. I feigned ignorance. "So have you been here before?"

"No," she said. "I don't think I have." She opened the car door. "Though I do feel a connection. I just don't know what it is."

"Nothing at the river?" I could see the lump in Libby's pocket.

She shook her head. "No."

"It was worth a try."

I returned to the house for another load of equipment, but I paused inside. I stood half hidden by the door, and I raised my long lens again.

Libby had pulled the watch from her pocket. She was turning it over slowly and rubbing the crystal gently with her thumb, as if to gather some tactile knowledge that a visual inspection would not reveal. Maybe there was meaning in the hour. I could see now that the watch was stopped at 10:36. Was that morning or night? Now I was curious. What year? It was a puzzle for sure.

I saw Libby slide into the driver's seat and reach across to the car's glove box. She extracted her burned baby doll. I let out my breath, almost in a whistle, then caught it, afraid Libby might hear.

I hadn't seen the doll in months, not since Libby had discovered it that day we began work on the florist shop. She must have been carrying it around all this time.

Libby lay the scarred figure on her lap. For a moment, she looked like a child playing at diapering a baby. Then I saw that she was simply freeing her hands for the detail work of opening the watch's ribbon-shaped pin. Pin open, she held the watch in one hand. She raised her doll with the other. She jabbed the open pin into the naked chest of her doll, who now looked like a dead soldier wearing a medal.

Even to me, a relative newcomer to Libby's story, this seemed like the right thing to do. I don't believe Libby knew all the details of the car fire and the day her doll had died. She certainly knew nothing of the watch. But she was acting as if the watch and the doll were valuable reminders, leftovers from devastating tragedies. Libby returned the doll to its resting place and closed the glove box. If she was right, mysteries and tragedies were now conjoined.

twenty-six

EDDY

"The past just sort of sneaks up behind you," Libby was saying. We were at the florist shop and she was standing behind me, floating her idea. She put a hand on each of my shoulders. "It comes from back here, where you can't see it at all." She began tiptoeing around toward the front, slowly circling me. "It sneaks around the side, where you begin to see it, out of the corner of your eye . . . ." Then she jumped. Right out in front of me. ". . . and suddenly, Bam! It's out here, staring you in the face."

We stood face-to-face.

"Is that the way it works?" Libby wanted to know.

I was flabbergasted. I'd avoided Libby for weeks until I was confident that I'd fully tested the waters of what I'd been seeing with Sheila. I hadn't wanted this to happen yet, maybe not ever, especially after Alexander Lee's hanging. But as soon as I began telling Sheila about what I'd seen, as soon as I let out the secrets I could keep no longer, as soon as I'd told the truth or my version of it, I should have known the result. Libby would hear, Libby would call, and innocent Eddy would have no choice but to do as she asked.

Libby'd told me she wanted to discuss the sofa in the dumpster. The damn thing was still there, and I really did think at first that that was what she had in mind. When I arrived, I saw she'd dragged out the same dirty cushion that I'd crammed through that little green door. She'd dropped it onto the ground and there she sat, waiting.

"I don't know how you work in such a dysfunctional industry," Libby announced as I came up the front walk.

"You get used to it," I replied, reaching out to help her to her feet, hoping the renovation was all she wanted to discuss, but letting my mind go to another place anyway. I was distractedly staring down the street and listening for something I hoped wasn't there. I was listening deep in the cosmos, searching for the low clang of the rattling dumpster door that the sofa cushion made the day I saw my brother die.

Of course I wasn't the only one looking elsewhere, and of course renovation wasn't on Libby's mind at all. It was just her bait. And now Libby had snuck around behind. Now she'd floated her own theory of how all this business worked.

And I hate to say it, but the only thing that surprised me was the timing of her jump.

Letting adventure pass was entirely out of character for the girl I'd known in childhood. Libby had always been the pushy, outspoken type, the leader of the neighborhood kids who grew up to grab for the high life in the big city, who lost her grip, who was searching again for the edge where she needed to live.

She may not have had her own life back together, not yet, but she'd nailed my life. She'd nailed what I'd been seeing.

Right at the time when I didn't want to see any more.

The work at the shop had progressed to a point that clients and architect alike always found exciting. Studs and insulation and wiring and plumbing all were now covered by drywall, and it was possible to feel the spaces that all this work had created. Libby and I walked through the old showroom and the office, now transformed into dining area and kitchen, and we stepped into the living-room greenhouse. Dramatic as hell. I'd said it before: This was my ticket.

But one thing I noticed right away: the shop was quiet. Mysteriously quiet, Sunday quiet. Except this was the middle of the week and the middle of the day. In the quiet, empty space, Libby explained, "I sent the workmen home. I didn't want any interruptions while we talked."

I was only lightly listening as I scanned the greenhouse and considered its relationship to the rest of the spaces. Some of the rooms felt larger than I'd expected and some felt smaller, but it was all good. We'd done well. Meanwhile, I hadn't noticed Libby growing reflective. But when I did notice, it became very obvious: She wanted to discuss something different.

"I have to do it," she whispered. "I have to do it, too."

Hell, here it was. I couldn't ignore her now. But I didn't want to hear what I knew she was going to say. I really didn't.

"Libby." I turned her way and forced a smile. I was trying to make light of her circling around me and her tiptoeing and her Bam! now history's in my face. "No wonder we followed you around when we were little." I gently socked her arm.

The gesture didn't work. It's pretty impossible to build camaraderie by yourself.

"You want to know what really happened the day our car burned?" Libby asked. "I haven't told the whole story, but you need to know. You need to know so you'll understand how much I was hurt back then and how much I need to do what I need to do now."

And all I could think was: No, I don't want to know any more, and no, don't put this on me. I've seen a man hang. I've seen my brother run down. None of this was my fault and none of this was my responsibility.

On the other hand, somehow it was. At least the part that lingered in the present, the part that still caused hurt for Libby, for me, and for everyone else.

I took a deep breath. "It was something about your running away, wasn't it?"

"You do remember," Libby said.

"I remember hearing people talk."

"Yes, they did." And after a beat she continued. "I fell apart that day. I looked through the screen door at the car in flames, and I looked back at my father, and he was crying. He was really crying. It wasn't just little wet spots in the corners of his eyes. He had his handkerchief out and when he saw me looking at him, he blew his nose. I guess he was trying to hide how he was feeling, but it didn't work. It just upset me more. I started to run toward him, and he probably thought I was going to stop, maybe give him a hug, but I couldn't do it. I kept going, out the back door. I was so upset and I was so confused I just wanted to disappear. And for a while I did."

"And no one could find you. People were looking all up and down the street."

"No, they couldn't," she agreed. "They couldn't find me because I wasn't on the street. I was in the cemetery."

I tried not to show my surprise, but I could feel the flushing, the heat of blood and the prickling of nerves rising to my face, old emotions returning.

"Stan's grave," Libby said, paying no attention to me. "It seems damn theatrical now. The flight of a preteen who was growing up fast. You know. Ophelia drowning herself. Morbid stuff. But that's where I was. I sat on the ground for hours, until it got dark, until a couple of hours after dark, actually. I wanted to be with Stan. The grave was still fresh; it had been only a couple of days since the funeral, and I wanted to talk to him. But I never said a word. I just sat and waited and nothing happened. Then I went home."

"No one ever knew."

"And now you do. You're the only one. Maybe that's good. Maybe it's good that I've finally told someone, but I wish to hell you hadn't made me remember. It's your fault, you know. But what did I think was going to happen? Everything I've experienced has been just another in a long line of failed expectations." Libby ticked off the list, touching each finger of one hand with the thumb of the other. Money, society, divorce, death, both Stan's and her father's.

"All the time," she mused, "all this time we think we're building a future, but what we're really doing is creating the past."

I cocked my head. I'd never seen this side of Libby before. Libby had always been the upbeat, indomitable one. Everyone assumed events never bothered her. Now something had changed her. Maybe I'd changed her. She'd just said what she was feeling was my fault, and that hurt me.

"We live on hopes and dreams. We live in the future," she continued. "Then suddenly—whoosh! When we get close, whatever we were trying to make happen pauses for just a tiny moment in the present, a ridiculously tiny moment, and zooms off, and then it's back somewhere behind us. Whatever we experience as it goes by, it's never what we thought it would be, and then it's gone forever."

Libby was staring me in the eye. All her playfulness—Bam! the past is right out here—was gone and she was dead serious.

"Except for you," she said. I was afraid she actually was going to point a finger at me. That accusation would have hurt all the more. "For you, it's not all gone." She gripped my arm just above the elbow, then tightened her hold. "I have to apologize. I have to say I'm sorry to Stan."

I protested. The accident had not been her fault.

"Yes, it was." In a heartbeat, Libby had moved beyond wistfulness to remorse. Anger couldn't be far behind.

I repeated my protest, but she wouldn't let me finish.

"You have to help me."

But that was something I couldn't do. It was something I wouldn't do. I wanted so much to disavow my own experiences. There was no way I wanted to encourage someone else's.

"There's no future for me unless I apologize," Libby replied. She crossed the greenhouse and pulled a hammer from a tool belt that was lying in a corner next to someone's empty lunchbox and a well-worn set of plans.

"Do you understand?" she asked.

No, I didn't.

Libby began walking the length of the new living room, gently tapping the walls, walking, pacing. A couple of taps in the center of each wall, one at each corner. The sound was rhythmic. And at a hollow, dull thump, she stopped. Libby tapped again as if she were sounding out the wall for a stud, looking for a solid place to hang a picture, but the sound she wanted seemed to be the opposite, an empty pocket of air. When she found it, she shifted to a two-handed grip on the hammer, raised the tool high above her head, and brought it down with all her strength.

The hammer sank up to its shaft in the smooth, gray surface. She yanked at the handle. The head was stuck. She yanked again and again, and when it came free, the hammer brought a foot-wide chunk of drywall with it. Libby gazed at the ragged piece that had landed at her feet, and she seemed pleased. She repositioned her grip, raised the hammer and buried it once again in the wall. Then she walked away. The worn wooden handle—some carpenter must have owned the thing for years—protruded like a small sculpture. Dadaist, the artist and architect in me would say. The absurd. Or maybe it was nihilist. Dead and gone and hopeless.

"Do you understand?" she asked. "I have to find out if there's any meaning in what happened. Otherwise, there's no future. There's no point in doing any of this work."

I crossed the greenhouse and put my arm around her shoulder, but the gesture didn't last. Now things were flipped around. Libby was the one with the power. I felt like a hostage. I was the one who should need consoling. Her demand was pretty straightforward: Show her how to go back to the time my brother died and we could move ahead with this work. If not, we stop right here.

But there was no way I could do what she wanted. No way in hell. I gave her a hug; then I gave her another. It was all I could offer.

But I don't think paying better attention to Libby would have prepared me for what was about to happen. Libby the friend was nothing but surprises about our past, and Libby the client was nothing but surprises about the future. And none of her surprises were good. I understood that she missed my brother. I understood that she'd figured out that events were still swirling out there, somewhere in the cosmos. I understood that I may have given her the idea back on the apartment steps that I could do something about those events.

But hell. There was too much for me to handle. A bird was suddenly chirping whatever she was chirping near the top of the greenhouse, and now I was worrying about a hole in the glass. I was worrying about Libby's state of mind and the state of my drywall and whose hammer that was anyway and whether a neighbor dog might get in at night and eat whatever food was left in that lunchbox over in the corner.

I couldn't take much more. I was beginning to feel like hiding in the damn cemetery myself. Hiding from the past and whatever truth it might have brought. Hiding from the prospect of Libby pulling the plug on my work. Maybe hiding for a long, long time.

twenty-seven

EDDY

"I have a plan," I told Sheila. I balanced on one foot, then the other, as I pulled off my shoes.

She flossed her teeth and spat into the sink. "It won't work."

"I've figured out how I can control what's going on."

"It won't work," she repeated as she crossed from bathroom to bed and settled under the blankets. "Just a couple of days ago . . ." she lay back and closed her eyes, ". . . you watched a man die, and now it's too late. It doesn't matter what your plan is. There's nothing you can do to avoid the fall-out from something like that."

She was right, of course. Sheila was right about the fall-out and she was right in her suppressed irritation. I just hoped she wasn't right about the futility of my plan.

"And while you're at it . . ." she added, eyes still closed. Sheila wanted to make her point, and she wanted her word to be last. This was her cue for me to shut up—not being good liars, we had to be good actors; we had to know our roles—and this was her cue for me to avoid confrontation regardless of what she had to say. "There's a baby, you know. But don't let that get in your way."

Sheila turned off the light and rolled so her back was toward me. "I miss you, Eddy," she murmured, but I chose not to respond. How could I? This time, I was struggling with more than an old married couple's argument. I honestly didn't know where to direct my attention.

"I need some help here," I mumbled, but reaching out didn't work so well in the dark.

Finally: "C'mon," I whispered to Ike. I grabbed the cat from the foot of the bed. He dangled loosely in my hands as I descended through the darkened house.

Like my blind great grandfather, I knew where the furniture stood, how many steps there were between the parlor sofa and the coffee table and between the coffee table and the armchairs. I sat by the window in one of those chairs and squinted at the silhouette of the porch. I left the lamps unlit.

I hadn't had the chance to tell Sheila the details, but yes, my plan was this: to remain in the dark.

The idea had come to me the night after Libby had bashed her fresh, new walls. I'd been worried about the shop and worried about what she'd said, and I'd lain in bed wide-awake, listening to the silence. Finally, I'd given up on sleep and walked downstairs to read. Four hours later I'd climbed back into bed. The sun was coming up. And I'd noticed something.

Awake in the dark and sleeping house, I'd noticed that life was suspended, that the world stood almost still. The motionless air had no force. It carried no scents and, aside from the sometimes woof of a distant dog or the throaty muffler of a solitary passing car, it carried few sounds. I noticed that in the night, my senses slept.

All I had to do to keep from entering the past was be less observant. All I had to do was stay up at night. In the dark, I would see, hear, and smell less. And when daytime returned with its sensory stimulations, I would sleep. I would sleep all day, unaware of events and people I had come to know all too well.

Maybe now I could control my pondering mind. Maybe I could balance the swinging, jumping, yammering, jabbering monkey in my head that sampled a thought quickly, then leapt wildly and promiscuously to the next. My monkey mind didn't care for balance. It was distracting and annoying, though generally benign. But the places my mind had swung to recently, now those were an entirely different matter. I really needed to do whatever was necessary to avoid seeing those places again.

The hanging had been devastating enough, not only the innate violence of the event but the portrait of catatonic Hugh and my introduction to the orphaned Walter Lee. My brother's hit and run, his blood puddling in the street, seeing that tore me apart. Put those together with my present-day run-ins with Sheila and Libby and it was all rapidly becoming more than a person could bear.

Sheila was constantly stressed. And Libby, she seemed to think she could do some good by visiting the past. I couldn't imagine what that might be, but maybe if I put a halt to my own experiences, maybe that would stop Libby, too. Assuming it wasn't already too late. Who knew what else was lurking among the McBrides?

Ike jumped onto the sofa. So now my life would be nocturnal, like a cat's. The cat and I stared through the window, across the porch, and into the night sky, which was filled with a raft of puffy clouds, white with the reflection of city lights, uniform in size, regularly spaced, marching from the south with almost military precision.

Darkness, of course, was not devoid of events; it just lacked the kind of events that had connections. The clouds advanced quickly as if on a mission, and I found myself tracking them across the sky. A cloud appeared in the distance, moved overhead, and was gone. Distant, overhead, gone. Too small for rain, carrying nothing, though in their gaps they did show stars.

As the clouds passed, the stars were covered, visible, covered again. I changed my focus from foreground to background to foreground. I felt pulled upward by the three-dimensional sky.

I stared into the room. This was what I needed, a darkness more intense than outside, a one-dimensional blackness I could wrap around myself, a cloak I hoped would keep out other sensations. In the dark, I finally would be alone.

But the world always intruded. It began with rolled newspapers flopping onto the ends of driveways. They sounded like thrown fish. And just before morning light came the garbage.

I could hear the trucks in the distance, the stop and start as they went from house to house, the rattle and clang of upended refuse bins, the smoothly oiled crushing and squashing from the pneumatic arms and heavy gates. The trucks circled the block. They came closer. I imagined predators.

By the time a truck reached the Victorian, daylight had broken and I could clearly see the driver. The man pushed a button and a mechanical arm reached out, snatched the bin we'd put at the curb, upended it over the truck's open back, and gently returned bin to earth. The truck moved on. Alone, one man was able to collect the city's remnants.

From upstairs I heard Sheila's alarm clock. Her feet hit the bedroom floor. Her footsteps made their way to the bathroom. Water ran in the sink. Clothes hangers jangled in the closet. And Sheila descended to the kitchen.

The teakettle sang, eggshells cracked, the toaster popped.

I began angling toward the stairs and my day of sleep, but Sheila was waiting. She intercepted me at the kitchen door, holding out a plate of toast. "Breakfast?" Her peace offering.

"Dinner." I took a slice. "Whatever." I managed a tired smile. "Thank you."

Sheila stood on her tiptoes and quickly gave me a kiss. I gently brushed her growing belly with mine, but I left the future unspoken between us.

"Goodnight," she whispered. Then she laid a hand on my arm. "You know, you're a good egg."

"Good scout."

"That, too." Sheila smiled as she kissed me again.

SHEILA

I missed Eddy. I really did. And if this were an old movie, I'd add a line like: "The big lug." I'd say he really was well intentioned, but where do good intentions get you? Nowhere, in my book. Not if good intentions turn out to have unhappy results. I missed having him involved in whatever way a father could be involved with our growing baby. I missed the simplicity of dealing with the present and the directness of aiming toward the future. I missed how we used to be. I hadn't thrown a pillow at him in months. His recent obsessions had worn me down just too much.

Oh.

Now I, too, was worrying about the past. Eddy was drawing me into his world. He was drawing all of us into his world. It began in earnest that morning.

Eddy had disappeared up the stairs and I was about to leave for work when the first attempts at a knock came at the front door. It was a faint little tapping, actually. Then Libby gingerly poked her head into the foyer.

She stepped inside and closed the door against the morning chill. "You're up," she said. "I didn't know whether I'd wake you or Eddy or both of you."

I gave her a quick explanation. Eddy had been up. Now he was down. I didn't want to confuse Libby with details, and she seemed okay with that much.

"I guess I didn't need to worry," she said.

I gave her a smile and pointed her toward my pot of tea. She shook her head. Toast? Eddy hadn't eaten it all. Marmalade? We had a new jar of home-made. She shook her head again.

"Or maybe I do need to worry," she said. "Because I've seen something."

I put a cup of strong tea into her hands, whether she wanted it or not. I aimed her toward the big Morris chair in Eddy's office. "What? Where?"

"All over."

"In the apartment?" I thought about Eddy's sketchbooks in the closet and how for me, their discovery had been a prelude I wished I'd missed.

"No. The apartment's just empty, and it feels like it's always been empty."

"At the shop?" All of us at the office were hoping that work on her fancy renovation would start up again. Maybe Libby had been giving it some thought, too.

"I go over there a little." Libby slid forward to the edge of the chair and cast her eyes nervously around the room. She stared at the lamp on the table beside me. Or maybe it was the books on the shelves behind me. I could tell she didn't want to talk about the shop, but something was up. She was acting as itchy as Eddy when he was observing his surroundings. She was casting her eyes around in the same way he described a while ago when he talked about his behavior at the shrink's.

Libby and I had been in this confidence-sharing mode before, back on that day she ran and hid and I found her in the greenhouse. So I kept quiet. Libby would talk when she was ready. And if she'd talk to anyone, I knew she'd talk to me.

"I tried to talk to Tim," she said. "A few mornings ago."

Okay, so I wasn't the only one. But her attempt with Tim did make sense. Given what she told me next, it also made sense that Tim had not listened. I hoped she hadn't taken his deaf ear personally. Tim was very good at blocking conversations that appeared to be driving where he didn't want to go. He was almost as good at avoiding the past as Eddy was at rushing toward it. The two men shared one trait, however. Now that Eddy had seen the hanging, now that he'd been injured emotionally on one of his visits the way Tim had been injured physically, neither wanted to help anyone else go there.

Libby seemed to know that, but she wasn't letting it bother her. Not now, at least. Because now she thought she'd been able to make a visit all on her own. And this is what she told me she'd experienced:

"Will you meet me after school?" a voice asked.

Libby blinked. She was inside a school bus, its arching, yellow, tin-can ceiling as plain and featureless as ever, its young cargo cranking up the decibel level so loud she almost missed the question. But she did hear it, and she saw the boy. It was Stan, sitting on the other side of the aisle. Or was he? Libby was on the bus, and she was off the bus. She was in the scene, and she was watching it from outside. She tried to speak, but she knew the din would drown her out.

As Libby slid across her seat and stood to cross the aisle, the driver turned hard to round a corner. Libby lurched, swayed, and landed with an undignified plop beside Stan. Embarrassed at her clumsiness, she hung her head, searching for something to say, waiting for Stan's response, but he said nothing. When she got up enough nerve to look his way, Stan was gone.

Libby was in her neighborhood. It was a beautiful springtime day. Tulips were blooming on each side of her home's front walk, trees were fully leafed out, and boys were playing baseball in a front yard down the way. Libby's father had stretched the garden hose to the curb and was washing his new Cadillac. He smoked his cigarette to a nub and tossed it into the puddle in the gutter. The butt washed along the side of the street, bumping its way around a soggy clot of leaves and bouncing over an uneven joint in the pavement. Libby thought it looked like a boat riding a rapid. Was it a boat? Did she see it sprouting a mast and a sail? Or was it a car, floating in a flood? Libby looked up, alarmed. Across the street, she saw Eddy's father, hands jammed deeply into his pockets, arms pulled tightly against his sides. Were his arms disappearing? A rolling baseball caromed off Libby's foot and disappeared under the Cadillac. One of the boys ran from the game and slithered after it. "Stan?" she called. "Stan? Stan?" Libby could see only his sneakers, and when she reached down and grabbed one, it came away in her hand. There was no boy at all.

Libby was at the courthouse. There were no leaves on the trees, the air was chilled, and she was circling the building, again and again and again, reading inscriptions on tall monuments. At her eye level were the boots of a granite firefighter. He was holding a child in his arms. Was Libby sinking? The ground felt very soft. Was she falling? She had no footing at all. Two men, one in a straw boater, the other in a bowler hat, emerged from the building. "The jury is never right," said one. "I have a shovel," said the other. He handed the tool to Libby and she began digging. "We might look for the remains of my son," said Bowler Hat. "We might touch the blood," said Straw Hat. "We might touch the ground. It will be sacred." Libby dug deeper. She was down in the hole and couldn't see out. When the handle of the shovel snapped, the sound was as loud as a large beam breaking or a heavy wooden trapdoor falling. She threw her arms over head to protect herself.

Her story finished, Libby wriggled in the Morris chair and rubbed her hands over her face. She stared at Ike, who was sitting on Eddy's desk. Ike stared back. "I've done it," Libby whispered. I sat quietly.

Ike jumped to the floor and ambled into the hall, where he stopped. Libby saw only his tail around the doorjamb. "No, I haven't," she admitted.

"No, you haven't," I agreed.

Libby wanted so deeply to experience the past. She needed so much to do something about Stan, but this had not been it. She had been asleep. She had been dreaming. Now she was crying. Libby pulled her feet up onto the chair, put her head between her knees, and hugged her balled-up self tightly.

Outside, the sun had risen to treetop level. I crossed the room and gave her a hug. "I'm sorry," I said, and she turned her face up. She looked very alone and very vulnerable.

Long ago, as a child, Libby had loved Stan. Until she was twenty, she'd had the constant of a father. In her adulthood, she'd taken a husband. That cheating bastard. Then she'd come home to rebuild her disappointment of a life in her father's empty florist shop, but now the shop seemed dead, too. Maybe Tim could fill the void. Eddy and I could help a little, but only a little.

"Thank you for listening," she said, rising from the chair. Libby turned off the light in the study and went to the kitchen, where she distracted herself with puttering about, pouring a fresh bowl of water for Ike and moving the teakettle from burner to sink and back again. She wiped away the tears remaining on her cheeks. She seemed not to notice that I was still there.

Which may have been just as well. I was embarrassed. Of course I was sorry about what Libby had seen—or not seen—but I was also trying to make apologies for an exit. I had a meeting. Clients in the office. Modern life. In the present. It may not have been what I needed to do to help our friend, but it was what I needed to do to keep going in the right direction. I was the practical and efficient one. No one else seemed to want the role.

I gathered my briefcase and left. I let Libby and her failed vision stay where they were.

twenty-eight

EDDY

I was happy to report that for the next several weeks, time passed exactly as I'd hoped. I rose late each afternoon, made a pot of coffee, and ate a bowl of cereal. It was surprising how easy it was to meet the day, or the evening. Certainly the absence of fear, the lack of worry that any unwanted events would intrude, didn't hurt.

Happily traveling against the rush-hour traffic, I'd drive my truck to the office and meet with my staff. They'd soon depart in the other direction, toward their homes, and I'd get down to business. Some evenings, I'd work into the wee hours, sometimes I'd stay all night, but my usual plan was to gather up my work and take it back to the Victorian. I didn't want to become a complete recluse, but it was rapidly becoming clear—not only to me but to Sheila and Tim as well—that my being at least a partial recluse was a good thing for all of us.

Tim could go home on time for a change, because I was finally pulling my weight. And I'd be home for a late dinner. "Fashionably late," I liked to call it. "Frantically late" was Sheila's term since I was always wide-awake and full of energy. For us, 7 P.M. was the new 7 A.M. But it was good. I had the feeling that I'd finally kicked a bad habit.

And when Sheila went to bed, all my daytime entanglements simply dropped away. In the night, my study seemed to be the only place on Earth. It was as if the room was not surrounded by a larger house and the house was not surrounded by a larger world. Unable to see or hear the city around me, I felt I was floating utterly, delightfully free. My plan had done more than put me in a single room in the dark. It had put me squarely in the present.

Head down over a sketchbook, squinting into the computer screen, or empty-headed daydreaming through a night-black window, it didn't matter what I was doing. I knew the past was still there. I could access it if I wished. All I had to do was return to the daytime. But I didn't wish. Most important, it wouldn't come unbidden after me.

To mark the change, I'd play this little game. The clocks would pass midnight, then one o'clock, and I'd approach the sharpest of dividing lines, the one that used to occur every night at about this time.

I'd hold out one hand, palm up. This was day. I'd hold out the other, also palm up. This was night. Bam! Bam! Bam! I'd clap three times, remembering one particular night back in college when the day went completely black. It was the night I saw three television stations leave the air, one, two, three, as I spun the dial. Television sign-offs used to be a big-ass deal. No more, but years ago the Air Force would be flying fighter jets on one channel and the Navy would be plowing the ocean on another. Army marching bands would be blasting out the national anthem and there'd be flags everywhere.

And then even the invisible television signals would be gone. And night would settle in.

The world was not at all like it is today, with its constant barrage of visible and invisible stimulation. There used to be a difference in where we put our attention. Wakefulness in the day and evening. Final surrender in full darkness. Never the twain shall meet.

On that long-ago night, the night I watched three sign-offs, I sat totally alone and I surrendered. I couldn't move. I fell deep into the night, as if into some kind of abyss, down to its very bottom for maybe an hour, maybe two, maybe four. The night was empty. It was wonderful.

Alone in my study, remembering, I sat again at the bottom of each night's abyss. "Wonderful," I'd repeat to the empty room as I worked. There was a near insanity about sitting alone in the night, an insanity that was strangely appealing. "Wonderful," I would say, "incredibly, wonderfully wonderful." Okay, I'd seen the past. So what was I supposed to do with that information? Satisfy some curiosity? From what I could tell, it would be hard to use what I'd learned for anything good. The drop of a trapdoor. The snap of a neck. Never again. So I'd punted. Straight into the abyss.

There was, of course, that nagging parallel between these nights of mine and the entire life of Great Uncle Hugh. At times, I thought Hugh had hit on something good with his hiding out, living as alone as he could with his family. But Hugh was much sadder than I ever wanted to be. He spent as much time as he could living in his single room, sometimes staring out his bedroom window, watching Walter Lee at work. Walter Lee, with whom he had shared the formative event of his life.

No, I didn't want to be Hugh, but I understood what he felt. The hanging had changed everything for him and it had changed everything for me. Sometimes I looked up from my work wistfully. For a brief time, sandwiched between the tragedies of my youth and the tragedies of my family, the days when ballgames were the center of the universe and young men came safely home from war had been wonderful. No more. The good past had disappeared as certainly as the television sign-off that divided day from night.

So I kept where I'd been and what I'd seen at bay. And when I had to direct my attention anywhere, I directed it toward the future. Sometimes I had to force myself. The past pulled hard. But I kept telling myself the future was what my work was about—somebody's dreams for a school or a business or an office or a house that would be better than today's. I told myself that's where I should be.

I made one sketch and balled up my paper. I made another and put it aside as a possible solution. I reached for my calculator to figure the slope of a house's driveway, a house on a steep and unusually shaped lot. What if the cars came in from the right? What if they came in from the left? What if I turned the house at an angle to the street? Hell, obsessing on the "what ifs" of the future was a pain in the ass. Maybe that's why the past could be so appealing. It was established. It was real. The future, no one knew.

But that's also the future's appeal, isn't it? Tonight, the house I was designing was not yet a house. It was flat, a two-dimensional shape on a piece of paper. It was potential. This was certain to be a good house. I was a good designer, and Tim was a good businessman, and Sheila could turn a chewed-up construction site into a landscape that looked like only God could have made it. For the few weeks those nights alone lasted, I felt certain I'd stepped beyond the past. I felt I was finally back in my groove. With my wife and my friends and my business, just as Sheila had pleaded. I felt like I'd hit bottom with my damn family history and bounced back to normalcy. Now if only I could figure out where to put the damn house on the damn lot.

———◆———

SHEILA

I was pretty well frazzled after a day of meetings, but when I returned home, I couldn't rest. Libby was waiting for me on the porch the way an anxious pet might wait, bouncing with excitement. In the short time it took me to pull into the driveway, she must have sat in one of our rocking chairs then bounced to her feet four or five times. She was nervously fingering something pinned to her shirt. And as I approached I saw it was a pendant watch.

"That's beautiful." I managed a slight smile as I trudged up the porch steps. "Nice antique."

Libby fingered the timepiece even more excitedly. "You'll never believe this," she said. "I found it out by the river. It was buried in the mud."

"You went to the river? Today?"

"Time is stopped. 10:36," Libby said. "No, I found it a while ago, when I was out with Tim."

It was then that I noticed her blue jeans were soaked to the knees. "But you went back today."

"This watch belonged," Libby whispered as if she and I—and also Ike, who sat on the porch railing with his eyes closed but his ears pricked up— were in cahoots. Conspirators. "It belonged to a woman who drowned."

"And you know this how?"

"I know this because I saw her."

Libby just couldn't leave well enough alone, could she? The other day, she'd thought her dreams were real. Now it was something about this watch. I felt the burden of unwanted information rolling down from my husband to our friend and landing squarely on top of me.

I sighed. Why hadn't Libby been able to tell Tim? Isn't sharing what relationships are for? Then I remembered the distances that lived in my own relationship and I kept my mouth shut. I parked my briefcase on one of the chairs, leaned against the porch railing, lightly rested my fingers atop the cat's skull, tickling him nervously just the tiniest bit, and listened.

It had been windy earlier in the afternoon, out at the river, she said. Gusts were whipping up waves in the water and Libby made a point of being glad— she remembered this so distinctly—that she hadn't worn a hat. It would have sailed downstream. Such a trivial thing. So small. But the lack of a hat wasn't all that took her attention. Libby told me she was noticing other things in ways she hadn't noticed them before. There was something unusual, she felt, about the wind and the air at the river. There was that smell.

Despite the wind, the air was musty and dank, like it wasn't moving at all. If she hadn't been standing in the bright sunlight, Libby would have thought she was in a dense swamp. Mosquitoes and alligators and Spanish moss. Libby approached the trees that lined the river. Big, sturdy cypresses but without the moss. And the smell became stronger. It was the smell of rot and decay. It was the smell of death.

Listening to Libby, I squirmed where I stood, gazing at my briefcase, which was now out of reach. I should have stayed at work.

Then in the distance, through the wind whipping the water and rustling the trees, Libby had heard voices. Three or four men. They seemed to be calling to someone.

As she talked, Libby nervously sat and stood a couple of more times, one hand always on the pendant watch. I was wary, but she was increasingly excited as she told me how she stepped into the water and walked slowly and carefully along the shoreline, following the shouts.

"Carrie!"

"Caroline!"

"Caroliiiiiiiine!"

Her first thought, Libby recalled, was to join the search. Libby cut across a small spit of land, passed through a patch of trees, and emerged at a little cove created by a bend in the river. There, exposed to the broad unbroken stretch of water, she almost fell. The wind was blowing that hard. She regained her footing and stopped splashing. She could hear the voices again. There seemed to be a boat out toward the middle of the river.

"'We waited too long,' I heard her say. Those were her last words."

"Lord, Lord."

"Do you see something?"

"Caroliiiiiiiine!"

Then softer: "Oh, Lord, Carrie. Where are you?"

The water was higher than usual and there was a lot of junk floating by. Sticks. Branches. A broken section of fence. A cane-bottom chair with hardly a scratch. A dead rabbit. It was as if Libby were seeing the end stages of a flood. The rabbit caught in a small whirlpool, made three full rotations, and continued its way downstream. Libby knew that dead animals would not be unusual in a flood. But through the muck, she could see that the rabbit was white. It had been someone's pet.

Then, off to the left, so far to the side that she almost missed her, Libby saw the woman.

"Hey!" she shouted. The call was instinctive. Libby turned uphill toward the house, half expecting to see Tim at work with his photography, but that had been weeks before. Maybe the men in the boat would hear. Libby turned back in that direction. They were close now. "Hey! Over here!"

Libby took a few very long, very quick strides toward the floating figure before abruptly stopping. She could get no closer than twenty feet. A deep, swift current stood in the way, but she could see clearly that the woman was dead. She floated face up, her long hair tangled in brush just below the water's surface, her feet pointed downstream. Anchored this way, the body swayed slowly from side to side, like a dancer.

"Caroliiiiiiiine!"

Libby turned toward the voices, saw the approaching rowboat, and noted that she had been right. There were indeed four men. The two not rowing scanned the river, front and back. The one in the front held an old-fashioned megaphone. "Caroliiiiiiiine!" The voice was much louder now. The man in the back called less clearly: "Carrie!"

"Caroliiiiiiiine!"

"Over here!" Libby cried. "Over here!" No one in the boat heard.

The megaphone was an odd thing. It certainly worked, but in this day and age, who besides cheerleaders used a megaphone? Odder still was the men's clothing. The man with the megaphone wore a soft cap, the kind taxi drivers wear. One of the rowers was in his shirtsleeves and an unbuttoned waistcoat. The others wore suits. They all wore shirts with what appeared to be celluloid collars.

Libby turned back to the body. The woman's dress was familiar, with its lacy bodice and high neck. Gibson Girl. A photo of Eddy's grandmother wearing the same style hung at the Victorian house. Libby had seen it many times. The photo had been taken in 1906.

The men's voices came across the water sharply and clearly.

"We could see her and the others up there, up in that tree. It was dark as the devil. Dark as God. Damned. Hell."

"We could see them in the headlamps," one of the men said. "I had my automobile pointed right at them."

The man with the megaphone stood and channeled his plea directly at Libby. "Caroliiiiiiiiine!"

And that was when the fishermen arrived. Their modern-day powerboat roared down the river toward Libby, churning its own waves. *Rrrrrrrrrrrrrrrrrrrrrrrrr.*

"Then she was gone," said a voice faintly from the old rowboat, which had returned to mid-river. "Some of them were still up in the tree. Carrie was gone."

RRRRRRRRRRRRRRRRRRRRRRRRRRRR and the powerboat passed, completely obscuring the voices.

Libby turned toward the body. It was gone. Back toward the searchers. They had vanished.

Rrrrrrrrrrrrrrrrrrrrrrrrrrrr the powerboat headed downstream.

Libby told me she stood there for a minute, maybe more, confused and lost and still. The musty smell in the air and the rustling sound in the trees were the only reminders of what she had seen.

That and the watch. Still knee-deep in the river, Libby dug the watch out of her jeans pocket and pinned it to her shirt. The men's voices were still ringing in her ears. She could still feel the vibrations. "Caroliiiiiiiiine!"

As Libby finished her story, I could feel the vibrations, too, and they were not good. I finally reached my briefcase and extracted a pack of cigarettes. I lit one, but baby told me to stub it out and I did.

Libby made a feeble gesture toward the smokes, but I'd already sent the pack sailing over the railing, across the bushes, and bouncing on the lawn toward the garden. If Ike had been out there, he would have been startled; he would have jumped and run at my toss, but the cat had left just after Libby began her tale. I believe he knew better than either of us humans to keep his distance from what Libby's had seen.

twenty-nine

EDDY

Sometimes my afternoon coffee turned out horrible, but I drank it anyway. Sometimes it hit me; hell, sometimes it attacked me. It was not just bitter; it was hard. It was nasty. But I was never surprised; I was never upset. I'd become pretty successful at turning my feeble breakfast into an important part of my night-is-day ritual and turning my attention to something else. That afternoon, I turned to the kitchen window, the trees outside, and the wind. Wind had blown in surprisingly strong while I'd been asleep. And it had the strangest smell.

I sipped and stared at the piece of landscape that the window framed. Funny how a piece of a view can be more artistic, more striking, even more real than the entire thing. A piece never tells an entire story, but it certainly can tell a hell of a truth.

In my framed little drama, the wind tossed the lid off a neighbor's garbage can and scattered fast-food wrappers into our yard. I didn't care. I was watching the tree limbs, which had begun to sway in every direction. It was a frenzied, random pattern, and from inside the house, the trees appeared to have free will. If I'd known nothing about wind, if I'd gained my entire knowledge of trees through the window, I might have thought they were moving on their own, in any way they wanted. Perhaps they were dancing to some rhythm they alone heard.

I rubbed my eyes and thought about the events I'd seen in the past. I wondered whether I'd seen the world as it really was or whether I'd simply seen it through my personal window. I'd been there, I knew that, but aside from the car fire that had singed my arm, mostly I'd been a detached observer or only a very slight participant.

I stretched and twisted my back. Sleeping during the day never completely relieved my weariness. At first I'd enjoyed my all-night isolation, but now I was wondering if I could keep it up. The night was a young person's time, enjoying it was a young person's game, and I was rapidly leaving youth behind.

Ike appeared at the porch door. I opened it just enough to let him in, and the cat bounded to his bowl, took a sniff, and walked away. He scraped his sides against my trousers, rubbing off onto me some bit of the world he'd been visiting.

"Seen enough?" I asked.

"Are you talking to me?" Sheila called from the parlor. I choked on that horrible coffee. Ike continued to circle my legs. I almost tripped over him as I went to see what was up with my wife.

In the dimming early-winter light of the late afternoon, Sheila was stoking a fire in the fireplace. Libby sat in one of our armchairs, feet propped up on an ottoman, aimed at the warmth. She'd left her wet shoes just inside the front door and removed her socks, but her jeans still clung to her legs and her feet were still wrinkly and wet. Sheila put down the poker and retrieved a bottle of red wine from the sideboard.

Something was up, and I suspected I really didn't want to find out what it was. The time was near for me to leave for the office, but I was Eddy, semi-good scout Eddy, almost truthful Eddy. I couldn't stop myself from wanting to know.

"Finally awake?" Sheila brushed me with a kiss as she passed wine to Libby who had been nervously fingering a watch pinned to her shirt. 10:36, it said.

"That's a good goddamn question," I said. The phrase was my secret. Ever since I'd heard it at the hanging, I'd been running it through my mind. Especially when I knew the answer was going to be no damn good.

Sheila poured another glass and handed it to me. Wine for breakfast. I was guessing I'd need it.

"Libby," said Sheila, "tell Eddy your story."

I took a place on the sofa and listened, and when Libby reached the conclusion, I asked, "Could it be your imagination, or another dream?"

"Don't be patronizing," said Sheila.

"What is imagination anyway?" reflected Libby.

The two were talking on top of each other. Then silence.

Libby leaned and massaged her feet. "And what is seeing? Or dreaming?" she asked, alone with her ideas. "None of us can perform a lobotomy on ourselves. We can't cut out what we're thinking."

"Some people can," I said, thinking about Sheila's refusal to live anywhere but the present. I turned her way: "And I'm not patronizing. I'm being logical." Logically, I was also glad I was sitting at the far side of the room. At the dining table, whenever I talked about subjects Sheila preferred to ignore, I felt her opinion on my shins.

"You know," I said, turning toward Libby as if we were childhood buddies again, "what we think about the past is very different from what it really is."

Sheila was rolling her eyes and mouthing the word "patronizing," but I ignored her.

"I never say after I've seen it: 'Everything was exactly the way I remember.' There's a better chance that I'll say: 'I never knew this shit before.'"

"But," Libby said, "*I* want to see." She almost shouted the word "I."

"Libby." I tried to be gentle. "You don't."

"Yes I do. And you know why? Because now I can. I've never been able to look back at things that happened and deal with what comes next. I've never been able to face the continuum. Big word, huh?" She laughed, then cut the humor short with a drink from her wine glass. "But that's part of my style, isn't it? Make a joke. Cover up the real feelings. Then run away."

Anyone who knew Libby knew this, but I was surprised to hear her admit it.

"I ran away from my failed marriage. I ran away from your questions about our Cadillac car."

Libby was hitting close to home and I was getting nervous. I put one hand into my trouser pocket. Office keys, loose change, notes to myself on scraps of folded paper. Oh, yes. Buy cat food.

"You've always seen things others don't see," Libby was saying.

"No, I haven't."

"Yes, you have, goddamn it. And you're stingy about sharing what you see."

I looked toward Sheila. She was the one Libby had confessed to. She was an inside player. Could she intervene, maybe? But Sheila gave her head one slow, sad turn side to side. No, she was afraid not.

Nonetheless, I did have one glimmer, and I brightened for a moment. Since Libby had finally seen the past and Libby had now told her story, could I wash my hands of her wishes? Was my role finished? But glimmers, by definition, disappear and this one went fast. What I hadn't counted on was Libby landing in the wrong place, Libby missing the time and place she wanted, Libby continuing to seek my assistance. What I'd misunderstood was that even while my nocturnal lifestyle had prevented me from seeing the past, it had had no effect on others. Libby had gone right ahead without me.

"Remember when we climbed the church steeple?" Libby asked. I was worried again, just as I'd been at the shop, that she was going to wag an accusing finger. At least there were no hammers lying about for her to bash into the wall.

"That's not . . ." I began.

"Let me tell this story, will you? Just for once. Just one goddamn time."

I held up my hands in surrender.

Libby took another sip of wine and settled down. "I was about seventeen and you were thirteen or fourteen," she said. "You'd figured out how to get into the steeple and we climbed all the way up to where the bells were. All the way up to where we could see for miles, out beyond the edge of town. There were rolling hills and they were very green, extra super green, and there were farms. But what I remember was the way you looked at it. I saw green and a few dots of houses. You acted like you saw a different world."

I waited for her to continue. Waited a bit longer. "That's it?" I finally asked.

"What do you mean? That's my story. I've told it a thousand times. Now you tell yours."

"You're partly right," I conceded.

Libby nodded.

"I did stare off into space when we got to the top," I said, "but I wasn't really looking at anything. I wasn't seeing anything."

"Bull," Libby enunciated, "shit."

"Look, Libby . . . ." I was feeling my way slowly, unsure whether I, too, could be angry and defensive, or whether I should be conciliatory. Libby already thought I was holding out on her. She knew I didn't want her to experience the past, and maybe I was as self-centered as she thought. A patronizing boor. Either that or I wanted to protect her.

"This is the truth." Libby was adamant. "You saw something and you kept it to yourself. For no . . . damn . . . good . . . reason."

"If you were to go back and see the past again," I ventured, "well, that's the problem with this crap. You might see your story. You might see somebody else's."

"So if my story is about being up in the top of the steeple, up by the bells, looking at a bunch of the stupid little farms, what's your story?"

"It's different."

"And how do I get there?" Libby demanded.

Without a word, I crossed to the window. Until recently, until I'd started seeing disturbing things in the past, I'd tried hard not to keep secrets. Not good scout Eddy. But for this one I'd long ago made an exception. I'd held this one inside for years, and I still felt a need to keep it mine. Mine alone. Libby would never understand. But Sheila apparently did. In her reflection in the window glass, I could see Sheila draw her fingers across her lips as if she were closing a zipper.

"We crawled through the attic," Libby said, prompting.

"And we climbed the ladder inside the steeple," I replied.

Sheila clapped her whole palm over her mouth. Speak no evil.

"And that's all?"

"That's all."

"Fuck you."

Okay, I'd take that. Libby's curse was less painful than my memory of the dark and narrow walkway, just two shaky boards laid across joists in the church attic. Her curse was less painful than balancing, trying desperately to stay on those boards, fearful that I might step off onto the fragile top side of the ceiling. And it was a hell of a lot less painful than what I saw when I stopped halfway across. Walking in front, Libby had continued. She was intent on the distant doorway that led to the steeple. She was unaware that she'd left me behind.

I'd stopped cold. I'd been unable to move.

Looking through a big air vent into the sanctuary below, with hot air rising from the apex of the ceiling and streaming around my face, I was terrified and mesmerized. Because what I saw was Stan, my brother who'd been dead for six years. It wasn't like he was doing anything special. He wasn't stealing money from the poor box or drinking the communion wine, and he wasn't floating around like an angel, behaving like a dead person should maybe behave. He was just walking around looking at the stained glass and thumbing through the hymnals, like he was waiting for someone. And he looked young. He looked like Stan at the time that he died. He was younger than I was.

A door opened and Stan turned. "Libby?" he said. But it was Walter Lee. I guess the yard man also did odd jobs for the church. Maybe chasing boys out of the sanctuary was one of his duties. Especially boys using the church as a rendezvous point with girls. Walter Lee was waving his arms, Stan was running, and I had this huge urge to step into the vent or onto the ceiling, break through, and fall.

I'd break through a high two stories above the sanctuary floor and fall past the balcony and over the pews. I'd come to my brother's rescue. Or I'd kill myself. I wouldn't hit the altar. That would be too neat, too conveniently symbolic. I was no martyr. Instead, I'd land in the aisle, maybe hit my head on the corner of a pew somewhere near the back, somewhere unremarkable. The forgotten younger brother, returning to do good.

I'd fall back into the empty sanctuary, into a place I'd been many times, into days when my brother still lived. Or whatever was going on. Damn. The force pulling me down that day was stronger than any I'd ever felt, and the prospect of falling scared me like nothing else.

I jerked my head. I stared wild-eyed into the parlor.

"Are you all right?" I heard Libby asking. "Say something."

Sheila rushed across the room and shook me. "You didn't . . . ?"

"No, no. It was a memory. Just a memory."

"Thank God." Sheila hugged me tightly as if to hold the past in, to keep it from taking me to some dangerous place. But I'd already been there, years ago. It may have been a memory on that day with Sheila and Libby, but it was a memory of the first day I'd seen across the years. It was a memory, if you want to be scientific about it, of that business my shrink would tell me about, the one where I noticed too much. It was also a memory, if you want to be spiritual and emotional about it, of wanting to be with my brother again so deeply that I'd almost been willing to die.

I hugged Sheila, mother carrying our child, even more tightly. What happened that day at the church would stay where it belonged.

And over my family's shoulder, I saw Libby stand. I saw her roll down the legs of her jeans, pick up her socks, and walk to the front door. Then she was gone. Gone alone.

I was sorry to have disappointed Libby, but you've got to remember: Stan didn't come to me as a dead boy's ghost or something. That's what you'd think would happen. Instead, I went to my brother's place and my brother's time. And the memory of that visit was just too frightening for me to tell. Even good scout Eddy couldn't handle it. Because it could happen again. And even as a boy, I'd felt deep down that it would.

So that was the day the good scout learned the hard way that he really did need secrets.

Now it was Libby's turn to discover how to handle whatever demons were frightening her.

TIM

I felt like a cuckold. Romantically involved, intimately entwined, and last to know. But that's what we cuckolds do, isn't it? We ignore and hurt our lovers until they look elsewhere for comfort. Then they turn around and hurt us. Surprise! It's our own damn fault.

I'd refused to listen to Libby in the early stages of her visions, when she was mooning over an old movie and dreaming of men in bowler hats and a boy who disappeared under her father's car. I didn't want to be hurt by what she'd seen. So when she stopped dreaming and found the real deal, she told her tale elsewhere. And I was hurt all the more.

"I needed someone to listen, so I went to Sheila," Libby explained that evening when she finally told me about the dead woman. "God knows Eddy doesn't listen." I hadn't even shut the door yet when she started in, criticizing her old friend.

"He's so damn wrapped up in his own experiences, he's not thinking about anyone else's. I just want to make up for the day his brother died. Can't he let me do that? Can't he help me? Of course I want to do it for myself, but I want to do it for Stan, he was a true friend, and I want to do it for Eddy, to put Stan's death behind us. Eddy's such an asshole."

She'd spoken without stopping. I took a big breath for both of us.

"Did you hear me?" Libby turned my way. "Or are you not listening either?"

Ah, it's the cuckold's fault. My fault that she'd stepped into the past, come back excited and happy, found a sympathetic ear in Sheila rather than me. My fault that Eddy had treated her in his all-knowing Eddy way. My fault that she now felt like crap.

But it was her fault that she didn't quite understand what this vision-of-the-past thing was all about. She was overlooking the tight links between past and present.

"So tell me," I said. "What's really bothering you?"

Libby shut down. I wasn't surprised. Ever since she'd learned what Eddy had been doing, she'd wanted to do it, too, and now that the past was happening for her, she was upset that she hadn't seen what she wanted.

I crossed to the kitchen and pulled a bottle of beer from the refrigerator. I was about to break my own rule about not dealing with the past. I'd break it for Libby.

I told her that seeing was never an accident. That specific times and places she could visit may have been unpredictable, that what she could see may have been uncontrollable, but that they were never unexplainable. Think about it, I said. She'd found the pendant watch. She'd been wondering, maybe even caring, about its owner. It was the dead woman she'd never met, not the dead boy she wanted to see again, that was there for her now.

"You can't always get what you want," I said. I waited for her thanks.

"Go to hell," she snapped. "Quoting the Rolling Stones is a little shallow, don't you think? And don't lecture me either. You're as bad as Eddy."

Gee, I thought a little rock 'n' roll would cheer her up. She used to be so playful. But maybe I really was Eddy. Maybe I was tactless. So I let it rest. "You take your time," I said. "All this may lead where you want to go, to some other place out there in some other year, though God knows I wouldn't want to go there."

Libby gave me the finger.

And that hurt. Libby may have been able to focus on what she wanted, able to focus on Stan, but when it came to my own regrets and memories and understanding of the past, for better or worse, I'd never forced the issue. In Libby's case focusing and forcing did appear to be for the worse.

"Caroliiiiiiiine!" I did have to admit, that cry from the rowboat had gotten under my skin the way few things did. It irritated and chafed, and I wanted to scratch, but I didn't know exactly where. I didn't know its entire history, only that Libby had said one of the men in the boat had talked about seeing the drowned woman clinging to a tree.

Now I was worrying as much as Eddy might worry. I was thinking about how afraid this Caroline must have been. Hell, I was afraid when I thought about the scene. It was pretty obvious she'd fallen. What I didn't know was what type of fear she'd experienced in her final moments. Up in some tree, climbing above the floodwaters, she may have been afraid because she didn't know what was going to happen. Or she may have been afraid because she did know. Had she looked down into the flood and seen her fate? I wondered whether she had surrendered to the future or whether she had fought, whether she had sunk quickly into the waters or whether she had risen to the surface only to be carried deeper.

Hell, this hurt. Fear was exactly why I avoided the past.

I pulled another beer from the fridge and worried that all of us, like poor, dead Caroline, might have been on our way to sinking so deep we'd never rise again. But I knew only about myself. I tipped the bottle up and drank half the beer. A little drink should help me rise. I drank the rest. And when I turned back to the living room, Libby was gone.

thirty

EDDY

We all replay stories in our minds, especially when we've made a mistake. And I was the king of replay. King Eddy. That's me.

"Do you understand?" Libby had asked that day we met at the florist shop, and I'd stood there like a lump, not understanding at all. "I have to find out if there's any meaning in what happened." And she'd smashed away at the wall.

Now I was back at the shop—back in the daytime, as I'd known I'd eventually have to be—thinking guilt and embarrassment and apologies and reparations. I was trying to make up before too much time elapsed.

The hammer hole was patched and sanded. I found a painter's drop cloth and flung it open, like a man spreading a blanket for a picnic. I waited patiently while the cloth settled, the air bubble underneath gradually escaping.

Painting would be my friend. It should please Libby. More immediately, I was hoping it would give me both the uninterrupted time and the uninterrupted mind I needed to think about repairing my world, healing my relationship with my childhood pal, falling a little more in love with my wife, getting this project back on track for my business partner. And soothing my soul.

I found the painting crew's old, paint-splattered radio. I carried it to the center of the room, its long cord stretching from the wall socket like a leash. I clicked it on. A country singer sang, and as sunlight warmed the greenhouse on that calm, quiet, early-winter day, I stood tall on the ladder and worked.

For about half a song.

When the singer stopped in mid-chorus, I twisted to look. Standing behind me, below me, radio in his hands, was Tim.

"Very nice radio," he said. "It suits you."

"Grab a roller."

Tim raised his eyebrows in an "Are you crazy?" attitude. He wore a camel-hair overcoat and business suit. Not dressed for a jobsite, I'd say, though Tim seldom was. Sure, in our college days, he'd worn a long Army greatcoat, thick as a horse blanket. He'd also carried the makings of a Manhattan cocktail, the rye and the vermouth and the maraschino cherries, in the coat's pockets. Now

Tim was spiffier by the day. He'd taken to wearing his hair long and flowing, something like the architect Frank Lloyd Wright, who favored long hair and a cape. Tim had become more self-assured as an architect and more secure as a person. Love of a woman will do that. Even when you have differences.

"Come on down," Tim said. "Libby needs us more than this place does."

"Good? Bad?" I asked, disengaging the roller tray from the ladder and pouring paint back into the can. So much for apologies; so much for reparations. I'd taken only one swipe at the wall, which now looked more forlorn than ever.

"Or indifferent," said Tim hopefully. "That's what we have to find out."

TIM

Eddy knew right where to go, which surprised me. For a guy who usually seemed to be paying attention to everything but people, he sometimes understood people cold. Or at least he understood their patterns of behavior.

"Libby runs," Eddy explained as we drove across town in his truck. "She's run here before, but it was a long time ago. I thought she'd be over that by now."

"I don't think Libby gets over things," I replied. "Mostly she just covers them up."

Eddy raised his eyebrows a couple of quick times in a Groucho Marx "You should know" attitude, and we let that line of discussion go. We drove in silence and after a dozen blocks we pulled up at the gates of City Cemetery. There was no need to raise my eyebrows in return. This was Eddy's town and Eddy's history.

City Cemetery was a beautiful place, conveniently located if unimaginatively named by early citizens who set aside what was then a plain, weedy patch for burying their dead. Over the years, trees had grown tall and broad, and mourning families had filled the landscape in with roses, azaleas, camellias, hydrangeas, oleander, all kinds of favorite flowering plants. It seemed like there were always people in there pruning, watering, and spraying, caring for the departed past, the painful present, and memories they hoped would last into the future.

Of course, there were counterforces, too. There were lichens on the tombstones, rust on crooked spigots, and holes in brick walkways. The world was relentlessly wearing itself down. An endless cycle of the quick and the dead passed through these gates. Eddy and I complied, carrying our respective worries into the cemetery, I my concerns about Libby's state of mind and Eddy his obsessions with what he could know and what he should and shouldn't tell.

It took us only about ten minutes of searching, and when we found Libby, she was simply wandering, pausing at the occasional tombstone, curiously studying lives and visiting those whose lives were receding into little more than a carved name and a couple of dates. She seemed calm, lazy, aimless, but Eddy and I would have to wait to see if we were right about that. We didn't want to interrupt if we didn't have to. We kept our distance.

I felt like I was back at the river watching Libby through the camera. Or back in the apartment, watching her watch television. But even from a distance, I could tell there was something very intense, much more intense, going on. Libby was a person who came and went. Into the city, out of the city. At the shop, now in the cemetery. It felt like she was always yearning, always wanting to be someplace where she wasn't. Libby was my playful lover in our bed, but she was also the contemplative woman digging for whatever she might find in the river's mud. Now she was the runaway reading tombstones of people she didn't know.

Ambling, Libby turned a corner in the paved walk and continued between rows of small, neat, identical stones. Soldiers' graves, decorated with tiny flags slowly waving, all faded, many tattered.

In the next sector, she paused to right a broken urn. She bent over, lifted, froze, and with a low thud dropped the urn back to earth.

Caroline Pfeiffer Simms, 1871–1906

Libby's hand went to her breast, to the pendant watch she was not wearing. Then it went to her pocket. Libby withdrew the watch and, backing away slowly, sat on the wrought-iron bench at an adjacent grave. She could have been simply moving carefully, but I don't think she knew what she was doing at all. Libby was acting as if her mind were somewhere other than in her body.

The sun slowly dipped lower, first obscured by a cloud, then glaring into her eyes, but Libby never stopped staring at the monument. From where I stood at a short distance, her hands were obscured, held between her knees, but I knew what she was doing. Libby was hypnotically running her thumb in a circle around the pendant watch's face. On a day in 1906, the time was forever 10:36.

A small bird, a wren, I believe, landed on Caroline Simms' memorial. It hopped nervously, its torso a tight, still ball but its head twitching nonstop, looking, watching, searching. But stone holds nothing a little bird needs, no bugs, no seeds, no whatever this particular species prefers, and she flew. It was probably a coincidence, but Libby stood at the same time. Or it wasn't a coincidence at all. I thought I heard her say, "This is not what I want." She resumed her walk.

Without a word passing between us, Eddy and I agreed that the time to intervene had come. Our strides were long and determined. Libby was the ambler, not us. We soon caught up and slowed to her pace.

The three of us continued around another corner, when Libby suddenly knelt and put her hand on a small, carved lamb. "Our dearest angel. April 1911." A lamb was the symbol of a dead child. Libby spoke without looking up. "I see you've been there."

"We walked around," I said, keeping my hands behind my back.

"Timmy, Timmy," she said. "But I think I'll have to call you Timothy now. Timothy when I'm disappointed and sad." When Libby looked up, she eyeballed me as if I were some kind of traitor.

"You don't have to hide it," she continued. "I'm the one who left it there."

I held the scorched baby doll in front of me, my hands tight around its ankles. I bobbed the doll up and down nervously.

"Don't do that," she snapped.

I held the doll still, but stillness made me uncomfortable. I wanted to run, but I knew I couldn't do that. We'd come here to help Libby.

I handed the doll to Eddy. Libby may have been my lover, but what we were experiencing, these stories of automotive arson, a drowned woman, and a dead brother were his history. If anyone was going to untangle this mess, it would have to be someone who'd lived it. Or whose family had created it.

EDDY

Ahead to one side, hanging heavily over the walkway, stood an ancient and massive live oak tree. "I think this is as far as I want to go today," Libby announced as we approached, and she dropped onto another bench. "You can put the doll back on Stan's grave when you leave. Burned Up Baby is taking my place."

"You come how often?" I asked. I gazed at the trees that divided the cemetery as if I could see through them. I wanted sincerely to be on the other side, over where Stan was buried, over where I could find so many people I knew: my childhood music teacher, the man who'd been the police chief, the owner of the store where I used to buy shoes, a big-band crooner. My parents had owned all the crooner's records. I wanted to be where both life and death were more familiar. Mostly, I wanted to be away from the things Libby seemed intent on discovering.

I shifted the dead doll from one hand to another. And me, about to be a father. Burned Up Baby, or whatever Libby was calling it now, was the last thing I wanted. But there was a reason why I had to take the doll, and there was a reason why Tim had recruited me to help him, and there was a reason why I had to see this mess through. Tim was right. This was my history.

"You know . . ." Libby interrupted my thoughts, taking the doll from my hand. She stroked Baby's burned stubble as she talked. "Something must have been wrong with the car that day. It was very hot. I think it was spontaneous combustion."

"Probably so," I lied. The appearance of the doll had suddenly pushed the drowned woman deep in time. Or had it? The dead, I guess, are all just the dead, all in it together.

"Daddy used to love cars so much and we had so much fun. Do you remember riding around with the top down? We'd just ride and ride. Especially on Sundays. We'd go out into the country and we'd cruise up and down the hills, around the bends. We'd ride out to new subdivisions and look at the houses. People don't do that anymore, do they?"

"That ended a long time ago."

"Yes." Libby stared down at the doll. "It ended." She was bobbing her burned Baby up and down between her knees just as Tim had done earlier. He and I were watching, and Libby noticed. She set the doll on the bench.

"Daddy was so sad after his beautiful new car caught on fire. He was sad all the time, and he made me sad."

"It was not his fault," I said.

Libby exploded. "Yes, it was, goddamn it!"

Tim and I jumped.

"Yes, it was!" she cried, "He was always at work. He never came home. He burned up my Baby in his goddamn car, and then he had to go and kill himself."

I expected at first to see tears, but then it was obvious that Libby had been through this before and had wrung out all the sadness. Only the anger remained.

"Goddamn it," she cried again, leaping up from the bench. Libby grabbed her doll and held it close, as if she were holding a real baby, only she held it tighter, much tighter. She paced in front of the bench, only a few feet from Tim and me, but she was speaking to herself. "Everyone goes away," she said. "They build me up, they get me started feeling good, and then they leave. They just fucking leave."

Tim reached for her hand, but Libby pulled back, continuing to fume. Tim looked at me helplessly, searching for some way to calm Libby down, but I had nothing to offer. It was then that she kicked the bench.

"Fuck you, Stan." She kicked again. "Fuck you. Fuck you." She kicked a half-dozen more times, directing some, I'm sure, at her cheating husband, some at her former city and society's slight friends. Then she stopped speaking. Fuck you, Daddy was beyond her ability to say, but it was what she was feeling; I knew that. She took one more kick and finally let Tim take her hand. He began leading her back toward the seat.

"Burned Up Baby is right at home here," Libby suddenly cried, pulling away again. She held her doll at arm's length, facing away, across the cemetery. "She can be best friends with the drowned lady. She can be best friends with the hit-and-run boy and the hanged man." Libby paused and turned, locking her eyes on mine. "Tell your secrets to one person, and they don't stay so secret, you know." Libby let the silence hang and centered her gaze accusingly before breaking away and resuming her rant. "Burned Up Baby can be friends with my goddamn father who killed himself."

And suddenly, I saw it, too. Libby had made a connection between all these tragedies, the ones in my history, the ones in hers, and the ones we shared. She may have seen only a tiny slice of history itself. She may not have known the details. But she instinctively felt, in her heart, in her gut, certainly not only in her head, the emotions and the soul that tied life and its events together.

Libby waggled the doll side to side like it was dancing. She sang: "The worms crawl in, the worms crawl out, the worms play pinochle on your snout." Then she held Baby high: "Look at her. Queen of the Dead. Burned Up Baby surveys her empire."

She landed on the bench, exhausted.

Tim and I sat on either side, each with an arm around Libby's shoulders, but neither of us knowing what to say. The three of us remained silent for ten, twenty minutes as the sunlight slipped away.

The best thing to do would be to demonstrate, despite what other people in her life had done, that Tim and I were here to stay. Especially Tim. But that was hard to do. Tim told me later that he'd tried transcendentally or telepathically or simply with his eyes and his heart to send her some love and some help. Words didn't seem the right thing just then. As for me, I was mostly just trying to avoid another of Libby's outbursts. I'd been the one to begin this obsession with the past, so maybe removing myself would help the most.

I watched the cemetery squirrels come and go, digging and scratching. In the distance, an old man in overalls was tending a grave, plucking away autumn's dead leaves and fallen branches. Walter Lee? I shouldn't even think that, but it did seem in character, this old man and his work, removing the dead from atop the dead as he pointed the way toward earlier times and other lives.

I tried to hide my feelings with play. I reached for Burned Up Baby and gave her a waggle.

"Don't."

"Sorry."

Dusk was upon us, and around the borders of the cemetery, streetlights were flickering on. Cars turning at the corner stop sign cast their headlights across the tombstones and through the trees, reaching almost to our bench before they swung away. But not quite; not that far. The three of us sat in the growing dark. Had we not been friends for so long or known each other so well, we might have had difficulty recognizing each other's faces.

thirty-one

TIM

At the cemetery gates, children were playing. They were shouting and laughing and chasing each other around under the streetlamps. From someone's driveway, there was the rhythmic, hollow thump of a dribbled ball, and the clang and bong of an off-target shot at the basket. From the street, there was the grinding whir of a skateboard. It began down the block, passed before us with a jump—I could hear ball bearings spinning in its airborne wheels—landed with an uneven, uncertain, asymmetrical crash-clank, and receded into the night.

"The future dead," said Libby tipping her head toward the children as we emerged from the cemetery. And then, as we turned down the sidewalk and headed for Eddy's truck, she put her hand in the crook of my arm. "Let's go home," she said. "Timmy." I kissed her on the temple, happy my tenure as Timothy was over. Libby gave me a smile. She was sweeter now. Maybe it was exhaustion. Maybe it was her on-again-off-again nature. Or maybe it was something as simple as the weather. A light, drizzly rain had begun to fall. Maybe she wanted shelter of all sorts, physical as well as emotional.

It wasn't long, though, before drizzle turned to drops, big drops, audible drops. Each struck with a distinct splash. All around us, shoes slapped pavement. Running feet were loud, and in the wet they grew louder.

"Boys!" a woman's voice called from one of the houses. "You come in out of the rain. Right now, you hear?"

In the dark came a slightly deeper male voice, taking charge like an older brother: "Come on, fellas. You heard your mother."

Libby poked Eddy with her elbow: "We were never that obedient."

I draped my overcoat across Libby's shoulders: "It's starting to come down pretty hard."

EDDY

Our boy Timmy was in love. Lucky guy. Lucky for a while, at least.

He gave Libby another kiss, and she smiled. She stopped in front of a small cottage, paused briefly to stare at its front porch, turned her face up into the rainy sky.

And then she ran.

Libby shucked Tim's camel-hair coat, dropping it onto the sidewalk without a thought, and disappeared into the darkness.

When Tim and I caught up three blocks later, Libby was drenched. Her hair hung limp and droplets of water clung to her forehead, cheeks, and lips. With one hand, Libby pushed her wet hair back from her face, flattening it against her scalp. She wrung out a fistful of water. With the other hand, Libby reached to steady herself on Tim's arm.

I knew immediately that in the few moments she'd been separated from us, she'd gone to an earlier time and returned. It was the same as my experience that day I'd seen Old Jacob listening to the radio. I'd left Sheila for the briefest instant, but I'd seen a complete slice of history. Only Libby wasn't nearly so pleased with her adventure. She had the look of a woman who had suddenly awakened, a woman pulling out of a vivid and bad dream to sit bolt upright in bed.

"It's not where I wanted to go," was all Libby would say. "It's not."

"I know," I replied.

In Libby's eyes, I saw all kinds of hurt. There was the confused hurt of the boys Hugh and Walter Lee at the hanging, the weary hurt of my great aunts at their reclusive brother's funeral, the desperate and helpless hurt I'd felt myself as I knelt over Stan and his puddle of blood.

"I don't understand," Libby said, "why I saw Caroline." The particulars of what she'd seen were missing, but I knew they weren't as important as the context. They weren't as important as the consequences either. Because when I looked at Libby, I found myself looking into a mirror. I was seeing from the outside, seeing for the first time, what effect all these visits back in time were having on our little group. I knew the frustration of trying to protect a person who wouldn't be protected. And I felt the unavoidable rumble of whatever was coming next.

None of it was pleasant.

SHEILA

I discovered the three of them sitting on the porch steps when I stepped out to retrieve the morning paper. "You were quiet," I said, nodding toward the coffee pot that sat between them on the floor.

"Mice," said Tim. Eddy shrugged. Libby rose slowly and thanked Eddy for the ride home. She gave Tim a little peck of a kiss and handed back his overcoat.

It turned out that they'd ridden around in Eddy's truck most of the night, warming Libby with the heater on high. Libby hadn't said much. Mostly she'd just sat, slumped in her seat, feet on the dashboard. Eddy, accustomed to staying up all night himself, told me he hadn't pressed for her story, that he thought she could use the overnight hours just as he did, to decompress, to settle down, to put some distance between herself and whatever sounds or smells or feelings had taken her to the past.

At a coffee shop before dawn, Eddy told me, they'd stood like disappointed children, peering through locked glass doors at chairs upturned on tables, ceiling fans spinning, every light glaring. Libby had ventured some ideas about the last man at that shop, the one who wanted everything bright, who wanted to see what he needed to see as he mopped up. Perhaps, she'd said, this was someone more alone in what he was doing and in the life he was chasing than she was. Eddy and Tim told me later that they'd taken that idea in, pondered it a bit, but said nothing. It was looking to them like Libby was the lonely one.

We stood on the porch, and Libby pointed Eddy toward the door, into the house.

She sent Tim back to his place, not hers.

She turned to me. Here, with me, here on the porch, she'd stay.

"Good sprout," I gently joked as Eddy left. I had a brief laugh at my scout husband's expense, but Libby was more serious. Eddy and Tim meant well, she said she understood that, but Eddy turned everything around to be about himself and Tim recently had taken to lecturing. I was the only one who listened.

How I wished she'd dismissed me, too. But this scenario was feeling familiar, this patiently and attentively listening to Libby's tales and revelations. Libby was a mess, and I'm not talking about what the previous night's rain had done to her hair. I simply couldn't *not* listen. I couldn't blow her off. Somehow I knew this would be her most serious revelation yet.

It had begun, Libby recalled, with the sounds of children playing and a mother calling her boys. Just the way Eddy and Tim and I all had entered the past when we zeroed in on smells and sounds and the brush of a breeze, Libby saw three brothers bounding up steps and flinging open the front door when she listened to the voices.

"The rain has stopped. Honestly, it has," Libby heard one of them say. A woman emerged from the house, stood on the top step, and looked at the sky. Big clouds were moving quickly. Receding lightning flashed with a slow glow on the horizon. The moon was a blur, but it was out.

Libby saw the woman put her finger to her lips. "Don't disturb the neighbors," she said, and the boys ran off, feet slapping the wet sidewalks. The woman raised one hand to her blouse and, under the electric light, checked the time on a pendant watch.

My God, Libby told me she'd thought. Caroline Pfeiffer Simms, 1871–1906. Libby looked at the darkening sky. What year was it?

"Caroline!" Libby called. The woman was doomed; she needed warning (oh, God, she needed warning!), but she could no more hear Libby than the men in the boats had heard her that day at the river. The screen door slammed. Clouds thickened. The moon disappeared. And Libby smelled the rain before she felt it. This time, the rain came hard.

As Libby stood at the curb, watching the house, she was barely aware of the wet, and she was completely unaware of the passing time. When daylight returned, Caroline reappeared on the porch. She looked again at her watch. She seemed hurried, worried, as she raised her umbrella. She stepped into the storm, and Libby followed.

The streets were almost deserted, Libby noted, as Caroline made her way to the streetcar. In the two-block distance, they met only one horse-drawn carriage and a half-dozen pedestrians. The men and women they passed walked with their heads down under hats or umbrellas. No one seemed to notice this person in blue jeans and a sweater.

But when Caroline climbed aboard the streetcar, Libby hesitated, afraid that in this close space she would not be so anonymous. Caroline handed a coin to the conductor and received a ticket. Libby hung back, one foot on the top step, fumbling in her pocket for money while knowing, she told me, that any modern coin she had to offer would be different than Caroline's, that it would be recognized, questioned, and rejected, as would she. Libby dug deep before she realized she had no coins at all. She wiggled her fingers. And she realized something else also was missing. Here in the past, the pendant watch, which she'd removed from Burned Up Baby and taken to carrying with her instead, was back with Caroline where it belonged. All very interesting, she thought.

Then Libby gathered her courage, stepped quickly into the streetcar, and moved toward the rear.

The conductor paid no attention. "He didn't see me," Libby whispered to other passengers who didn't see her either.

The streetcar made its way to town, swaying gently, stopping regularly to take on wet passengers and send semi-dry ones splashing into the flooded street. When Caroline's turn came, she alighted into a puddle and in her haste forgot her umbrella. Libby thought to remind her, but remembered: Caroline could not see or hear her. Libby could not affect events. She could only follow.

The houses on this street were much like Caroline's. Small, single-story Victorian cottages stood close together. Porches crossed the front and sometimes ran down one side, decorated with fancy railings and jig-sawed cutouts.

But if Libby had her bearings right, these houses and yards had long since disappeared. She watched as Caroline knocked on the door of a large home at the corner. This house, in Libby's and our present day, had been replaced by a vacuum cleaner repair shop with a blue roof. Its neat flowerbeds had disappeared under paved, front-yard parking.

All very interesting, Libby thought as she sought brief shelter under a sapling. She knew this tree, too. It would grow tall and lush. Then, when it blocked the repair shop's sign, it would be unceremoniously cut down.

All very interesting back here in time. But what was the point? "I really don't care," she said aloud. Libby gave the sapling an angry shake, and its leaves let loose a spray of water. In the storm, Libby barely noticed. "I don't care about this woman." Libby started toward the streetcar again. A passing bicycle cut through a deep puddle, leaving a skinny wake and little waves that lapped against the curb.

"Visiting her sister, cheating on her husband." Libby's conjectures were like curses. "I don't want to know." If she were to see the past, Libby told me, she wanted only one event. But that event was a half-century away. More than a generation of people would be born, live, and die before the day she needed would arrive.

And there was no hope of getting there from where she stood. The streetcar might take her downtown, and it might take her back to Caroline's house near the cemetery, but the neighborhood where the florist shop stood, where the hit-and-run accident had occurred, was still a farmer's field. It was not yet the place where Stan had died. It was not yet the place that had shaped her life.

In the rain, Libby glanced back at the house on the corner. "What are you doing in there?" she shouted. "What am I doing here?" she asked softly.

Libby raised both arms toward the sky as if to grab the rain or reach for the clouds, stood silently a moment and let them fall with a heavy, dead weight. She turned and began walking back the way she'd come.

And as she walked, Libby noticed a lump in her pocket. It seemed an elusive thing. It was there. And then it was gone. But as she grew closer to where she'd begun, as she neared her own place and time, the lump stayed. It was round and hard and flat against her thigh. And with each step Libby took, the pin on the pendant watch gave her skin a little prick.

I sat quietly as Libby concluded her tale and I held my silence as she stepped to the porch railing, poured her cold coffee into the shrubbery, and returned to sit beside me on the steps. From the far end of the porch, Ike joined us. He rolled over to expose his belly. Libby gave the cat a scratch. Ike playfully nipped at Libby's hand.

"He'll bite you," I warned. I was thinking as much about myself as I was about Ike and Libby. There was no way I was going to tell her, but years ago I'd visited this same date in history. It was that time I talked about not long ago, that time I discovered Eddy peering into the barbershop and Libby hollering into the rain.

But that had been long before Eddy entangled us with Libby, I hadn't felt good about what I'd seen then. I didn't feel good about it now, and I certainly didn't feel good about what might come from it.

"It's okay," Libby said. She scratched Ike's stomach and the cat purred. Then, true to my prediction, purr turned to hiss, a deep hiss from somewhere behind Ike's back teeth, and the cat lunged, catching the outside of her hand at the base of the pinkie. Libby gave Ike a shove. "Don't hiss and bite at me." Ike skittered down the steps, feet sometimes touching wood, sometimes pedaling air, and he ran across the lawn toward the trees.

"That wasn't very nice," I said.

Libby examined her pinkie and pressed it into the hem of her jeans, blotting the drop of blood that Ike had raised.

"You know," she began, "Eddy talks about the past like it's a movie that's constantly showing at some theater. Sometimes there's an audience, sometimes there's not, but it's always there when you want to go in and see it."

She wiggled her nipped finger at a still distant Ike.

"He's not coming back anytime soon," I said.

"But . . . ." Libby ignored me. "I wonder if it isn't more like a play. If it's a play, we can jump out of the audience and join in. We can add our own lines, we can punch the actors in the face, we can . . . ."

"We can set the theater on fire," I interrupted again. "But setting a fire or even shouting 'Fire!' in a theater is never a good idea. All hell breaks loose."

"All hell deserves to break loose. It's the only way anything will change." Libby stared at her finger close up, then blotted again. "Each time I've seen this woman, the one who drowned, I've been at the movies. Next time, I jump onto the stage. I join the play. I've got to move the story ahead."

What Libby was saying was the worst I could imagine, and I'm afraid I probably sat there frozen, glazed on the outside with a paralyzed look but churning on the inside with panic. She was headed, I was sure, for something unspeakably horrible.

Meanwhile, Libby was rambling on. "You know, Tim was right. We see what we know and what we care about. And Eddy's right. We go to the same physical place where we begin. I saw that woman because I began at her house, there across from the cemetery. But maybe Tim's and Eddy's expectations are too low. I'd take it a step further. I'd say that once we get to the past, we do have a choice."

Libby was back to watching Ike and Ike to watching her. Her stare was idle, but his, well, Ike was staring as if he were listening, intent as she worked out her ideas. "So what do you think? Maybe they'll see me next time. That's what happened to Eddy." Now Libby turned and spoke directly at me. Her face was inches from mine. "What do you think about doing more than observing? What do you think about making some changes?"

As I said, it was the worst I could imagine.

I took a long time to answer.

A long time.

"Libby," I finally replied, "What you've been doing and what Eddy has been doing is dangerous enough. It's frightening enough."

"Or maybe . . . ."

I could tell Libby wasn't listening.

"Maybe something good can come out of this. What I've seen so far isn't what I wanted, but maybe it's good. Maybe it's teaching me how to see."

Libby was running fast in the direction she'd already decided to go.

"Libby." I had to try again. "Stop it."

"I want to see Stan."

"The past is . . . the world is a lot bigger than Eddy's brother," I countered. "Trust me. There are so many things going on, so many events that are all interconnected. We can't see it all. But we can't look at just one part, either."

"Don't you lecture me."

"You carry Caroline's watch. Who knows what that's all about, but you're obviously concerned about her, too."

"I don't think so," Libby snapped. "I don't care about her at all." She stood, jammed her hand into her pocket, and pulled out the watch, balled up in her fist. She held her arm straight out, fingers facing downward.

"Take it," she said.

I hesitated. The watch must have had some meaning, even if it was only a reminder that the past existed. She had nothing of Stan save memory, but for earlier years and another time, she did have this watch.

"Take it."

I reluctantly held out my hand. Libby dropped the watch into my open palm.

"I don't give a shit about that dead woman," Libby announced. "She's your worry now."

PART III

Then came the fire

That burned the stick

That beat the dog

That bit the cat

That ate the kid

My father bought for two zuzim

CHAD GADYA, TRADITIONAL PASSOVER FOLK SONG

thirty-two

TIM

"Timmy," she said. Libby was in my office guest chair, leaning with one elbow on my small conference table and playing with one of my toy cars. Something had happened since that evening at the cemetery, something with Sheila. But I wasn't entirely surprised. Sheila had always been Wendy the mom to lost boys Eddy and me, helping us figure out life. Why not Libby, too?

Whatever it was, some face-to-face or heart-to-heart, I didn't know at the time, it seemed to have removed some old burden or pointed Libby in some new direction. On this day, Libby and I had been in my office for an hour or more, and we were just enjoying sitting, a contented old couple. You heard me. Contented. More upbeat than she'd been in weeks. Libby sat back in the chair and tossed the car from one hand to the other. She was a child playing stunt driver, until she dropped it on the floor.

"Timmy," she said, bending to retrieve the car and sitting up again. I was behind the desk, quietly snipping open invoices. Blueprint company, copy-machine rental, software licenses, all those. It was my businessman ritual. I'd tap the return-address end on the desk, hold the envelope up to the bright light of the window, and when I was assured the papers inside had safely settled, I'd raise a pair of long shears and with one stroke I'd snip just outside the stamp. I'd remove the contents and brush the snipped end into a pile of other snipped ends. Then I'd take up the next.

"Timmy," she said, reaching for my pile of snipped ends and arranging them into a neat bundle in her hand, like straws with their ends all lined up and even. "You know what we ought to do?"

I slid open my deep desk drawer and extracted a pint of bourbon and two paper cups. I poured a couple of ounces for myself. I left the bottle uncapped in front of me and ceremoniously dropped the other cup upside down on its neck. Libby stared at the bottle's brown glass.

"Not that," she said, standing and crossing the room. She kissed me on the top of my head. "Silly."

On the windowsill lay a piece of granite that some sales rep had given me, and there Libby began carefully stacking snipped envelope ends in log-cabin style. Adding the last end, she stood back and examined her work. My first thought was that she'd made a little architectural trophy, a little building displayed on fancy stone, some little pat on the back for me. She picked up one of my cameras and held it out in my direction.

I leaned close and took a couple of shots. At first, the city outside was more in focus than the snippings cabin. Now the cabin was in focus and the city was the blur. Shifting depth of field. I'd figure the final selection later. Now Libby's hand was in the frame, bearing a lighted match. I looked up, almost puzzled. But not quite. I saw exactly the image she wanted.

The little blaze caught slowly. I clicked the shutter. The snippings flared briefly. I clicked again, and I didn't stop even as the fire died. Smoke continued to rise and obscure, then not obscure, the city behind.

When I finished, Libby did reach for a drink and the pair of us stood there sipping, watching the disappearing smoke and the fragile pile of ash, and thinking about the usual things, I'm afraid. Our lives before we met, our current relationship, our ongoing worries, our respective obsessions, how little one person could ever know about the histories of others, and what in the world might be coming next. Also why the fire alarm hadn't come on. I looked up at the sleeping smoke detector and shrugged.

I gave her a kiss.

"What was that all about?" I asked. I took another sip of bourbon, feeling almost post-coital in my reverie.

"We ought," she said, decisive, like she'd been planning this for a while, "to have an exhibition of your work. Start with this little fire. It's a fresh start."

I couldn't say no. I just looked at her in amazement.

"You've seen lots of things. You've heard things, too. Or so people say."

"I'm a normal guy," I protested.

"Timmy. You're not so normal. Not the last time I saw you behind the camera, making pictures no one else sees. And you know exactly what I mean."

Guilty as charged. I was discreetly running my thumb along the scar on my arm. I did know what she meant, especially the allusion to why maybe I had drinks and why maybe I saw and heard things differently, even though I'd tried for years to push those things behind me.

"You're a guy who sees differently and feels differently," Libby continued. "You disguise yourself as a businessman, but you're not a normal guy. That's what I love about you. Now, we do something about it."

"An exhibit," I repeated.

"Look," she was saying, holding up her hands like a magician proving no trickery. "There's no past here. I promise not to do that. Only the future."

Libby must have been paying attention to how I did business, because she'd developed the most impressive way of making her point while making me feel good about it. She went on and on about how she wanted to see the world of my photographic vision and see it all together, how she wanted to share me with everyone we knew and for that matter with everyone we didn't know, and how we could do it right here at the office. We'd clear out the reception area, hang my photos, and we'd have a big old opening.

I guess I was still kind of blankly staring.

"Say 'Thank you, Libby.'"

"Thank you, Libby."

She gave me a deep, formal, comic curtsey, and when she rose, she threw her arms around my neck. Libby was in grand spirits.

I, on the other hand, couldn't keep from wondering what was behind it all. Okay, there was nothing up her sleeve. Or was there? Because I kept noticing one thing. As soon as the smoke cleared, as soon as the dramatic little event Libby had created and I'd recorded was over, as soon as the purging of the past that the burning of the snippings cabin was supposed to have symbolized was complete, the city behind had come in clearer than ever before. Nothing out there had been purged at all.

Libby spun me around a couple of times, still the comic, still with her arms around my neck, and she ended with her back to the windows. So I don't believe she saw. But just outside, right there behind her, was the low, flooding place in the avenue where Eddy's great grandfather, Old Jacob, had made his famous horseback rescue. A couple of blocks in one direction stood the park, now with bandstand, where Eddy had told us he'd seen Alexander Lee hanged. About a mile in the other direction was the neighborhood where Eddy had seen Mr. Peacock light his own purging fire under his new Cadillac car. Where Eddy's brother had died.

"It'll be great," said Libby, and she planted a big kiss. "You'll be a star."

I thanked her again. Yes, I said, the show was a great idea, it would give us a new focus, and it would be a lot of just plain fun. Yes, I thought, it would be a great distraction from any unfinished business. It would, I sincerely hoped, purge what needed purging, make it disappear like a puff of smoke. If it didn't, I feared, the past might end up more real than ever, just the way the city had emerged with new clarity outside my office window.

Now, that's a photographer for you. Seeing all the angles.

And I chose . . . well, fun was easy and distraction was necessary and both were what everyone needed. Especially Libby. She needed me to put faith in what she was doing. So I did. I gave her another kiss and told her to start planning.

EDDY

As soon as Tim's work went up on the wall, everyone agreed how good it was and everyone wondered why we'd waited so long to put it on display. "I know you're usually the art guy," Tim had said to me after Libby had hatched her plan. He'd apologized for being the business guy. I'd told him to screw the apology. This was about art. Also about friends. And I was happy to put my drawings into storage to further the cause. To prove the point, I took them down from the wall myself.

We sent out a hundred or so invitations, pushed around the reception area's antique furniture, and hung the photos. Tim and Libby seemed to have a plan for what went where, and they swore it would become self-evident once all was in place. I was sure it would. But hammering nails and leveling frames hadn't given me time to discover it yet.

"Where's Libby?" I asked Tim a few minutes before start time.

Tim shrugged, then pointed me toward a photo he'd given a place of honor by the entry. "What do you think?" Waiting for my reply, he plunged his hand into a tub of ice and came up with two bottles of beer. He opened both, took a swallow from one, and stood watching, hanging onto the other almost as a prize or bait for me, pending my answer.

I stared at a dark, black-and-white photo of what appeared to be a house of cards on fire, out of focus in the foreground but with the city skyline sharply focused behind. I didn't move my head. I tried not to blink my eyes. But I did hold out my hand, palm up, like a waiter expecting to balance a tray. Tim stood the bottle where I wanted, and I closed my fingers around the cold.

"Someone bought it," I said, indicating a red dot on the wall.

"Libby," said Tim. He'd moved farther down the wall to straighten another photo.

"And she's where, again?"

"Right there." By now, Tim was a couple of more photos down the line, but he pointed back my way. "Her spirit, at least. That photo was her idea, her doing, actually." He turned the corner into the conference room. "But you can buy it, too," I heard him holler. "I'll print as many as there are dots." Then Tim popped out again, hanging onto the jamb of the conference room doorway. "And she'll be here," he said. Tim tossed his empty bottle underhand into the trash bin beside the bar, and I winced at the image of Libby's dad with his overhand throw at the welcome-home party, of the beer bottle flying toward my head. "This," said Tim, "is her baby."

Guests arrived, and each of us fell into familiar roles. Sheila the marketer would work the room for business. She'd steer people to Tim if they wanted to talk about photography, to me if they wanted to talk about architecture, and to our receptionist, whose desk had been turned into a bar, if they wanted a drink.

A lot of people wanted drinks. A lot of people wanted to meet the photographer. The success of the evening was assured.

For Sheila, the mission wasn't so easily accomplished. Her pregnancy had progressed to the point where she was having trouble maneuvering through tight spots in the crowd. From time to time, she had to sit and rest. Sheila wasn't working prospects very hard, but that was fine. This was Tim's night.

As for me, a few of our existing clients cornered me to talk architecture, searching in a non-subtle way for some non-billable advice. I had fun kicking around theoretical musings, historical precedents, and artistic flights of fancy as I avoided commitments that would mean altering any of our designs. But mostly I was free to roam.

"That's the place, isn't it?" Sheila appeared behind my shoulder and pointed at the photo before us. "That's the restaurant," she repeated, "the one where the three of you tried to buy coffee."

"It is," I said. The chairs were upside down on tables like when we were there. The lights were on. The ceiling fans were spinning.

"But look there," said Sheila, handing me the ginger ale she'd been drinking and leaning toward the photo. "In the back." Sheila was waving her hands lightly over the framed photo like a medium summoning images from a crystal ball. "There's a guy."

She was right. Far in the background, visible between the upended legs of chairs as if he were behind bars in prison, stood a lone man with a bucket and a mop. He'd inserted the mop head into the pressing mechanism fastened to his bucket and he was pulling hard at the lever, squeezing out the water he didn't need.

Of course. In the world according to Tim, architectural spaces were always occupied, even when no one but the photographer seemed to notice. The life they included may have been small. It was never insignificant. The man with the mop could easily have been overlooked, but once Sheila and I had spotted him, he became central to the picture's story. These were Tim's photographic truths and I loved them, truth maven that I am.

The little cat Ike was a soft corner where railing met column on our porch.

The man who collected fees at the city dump was barely visible through the door of his guard shed, but he was king of the bulldozed moonscape behind him.

The nude figure lay in bed. Flower-papered walls, a curtained window, a white expanse of cracked plaster ceiling all loomed around her.

I looked closely. It was Libby.

"Where *is* Libby?" Sheila asked, retrieving her ginger ale and turning back toward the crowd to search.

And as I scanned the room with her, I had the oddest sense of recognition. Directly across from me stood a paunchy, middle-aged man in a janitor's blue cotton shirt. I knew that man. I also knew the man who had dressed up his jeans and black T-shirt with a herringbone sport jacket. I knew the tall blonde that one of our draftsmen was chatting up near the front door. I knew the college student leaning on the bar and helping himself to another beer. But I had never seen any of them before this night.

"Come here," I overheard Tim saying through the crowd. Tim put one hand on the janitor's shoulder. "I want you to meet someone." He inserted Blue Cotton Shirt into the conversation between Draftsman and Blonde.

And with that motion, I saw the truth of the images Tim had recorded and the event Libby had staged.

The Blue Cotton Shirt was the man with the mop, and Draftsman's blonde friend was the loan officer from Tim's photo of a bank.

In a photo of a new library lay the college student, asleep on a couch, book open across his belly. At a store in the mall stood the man in the black T-shirt. He was buying the very sport jacket he wore tonight.

I returned to the front of the room and began looking at the photos again. Tim's photos captured people in moments, froze those moments, stretched them across time, and deposited them in this very evening.

Across the room, I saw that Sheila had wandered into a group of real-estate developers by the restaurant photo, where she again juggled her ginger ale as she shook hands. I was glad she was occupied. Now I could focus on my hunt for images of people I'd overlooked earlier. I returned to the walls, my back to the crowd.

The people in Tim's photos changed almost as often as the buildings, but it didn't take long to spot the pattern.

I was examining a man crossing the street in front of a pawnshop. Wait! Was that Walter Lee? Was he one of Tim's subjects? I stepped quickly to the next photo.

It was a pattern that seemed devised just for me.

Walter Lee was patting a dog tethered to a tree outside a supermarket, he was eating a sandwich on a stone wall that bordered a downtown plaza, he was crossing a footbridge over the water-lily pond in a Japanese garden. He was reading a newspaper as he stood on the sidewalk in front of McBride, LeFevre & McBride.

I felt I was being followed.

Tim sidled up beside me.

"This old man . . ." I began.

My partner the photographer tipped his beer and took a long drink. "You noticed."

"Why is he always there?"

Tim shrugged. "Libby's idea. She was as surprised as you the first time she saw these, but she said she remembered him from when she was little. Said something about the only living link."

"That son of a bitch," I said. "Whenever you see him, you're about to see something bad."

Tim closed one eye, squinting his question.

"Something from long ago," I explained. I leaned closer to the photo of Walter Lee in front of our office. "When did you first see him?"

Tim shrugged. "He came and went. I was looking around for people I could catch off-guard in my pictures, and for a while it seemed like I ran into him every day. Then he was gone. But he was a great subject. He had this strange appeal. And I found myself actually looking for him. Until I realized that the hunted was really the hunter. I think he was looking for me."

You're not the only one, I thought.

I hadn't seen Walter Lee in weeks, but it was looking now like he'd been there all along. I wasn't surprised to know that the dark figure who'd stood behind me outside Seaman Alvin Peacock's welcome-home party, the hired man I'd seen from Great Uncle Hugh's bedroom window, and the newly orphaned boy at Alexander Lee's hanging—my red-thread person, Libby's living link who'd seen everything I'd seen, and probably much more—was always around.

Tim had finished his explanation and begun to angle toward the bar, but I'd lost eye contact with him anyway. I was gazing more or less absently across my partner's shoulder, still pondering the odds that Tim had recorded the same old man I'd been seeing. It was then that I made a more important connection.

Of the subjects in Tim's photos, Walter Lee was conspicuous in his absence from the evening's festivities. The same was true for Libby.

I set down my drink and began pushing through the crowd. I should run to the elevator. I should shout out the window. I should throw open the fire door and dash down the stairwell. Walter Lee was a manipulative son of a bitch and he was dangerous. I had to find him.

I reached the elevator lobby, which seemed eerily empty and quiet after the din of our guests at the exhibit. Through the windows, I could see the sun was setting and the streetlights were coming on. I thought of the night Tim and I chased Libby and Burned Up Baby to the cemetery. What if she'd run again? But where this time? I was spinning, turning as if trying to see through the walls and across distance, hoping desperately to locate her. But my questions were moot.

Because that's when Tim burst out of the office. His face was ashen. Behind him, I could see Sheila at the reception desk, telephone to one ear, listening without saying a word, hand pressed against the other ear, blocking out crowd noise.

"It's Libby," Tim said. "The hospital is on the phone. There's been an accident."

thirty-three

SHEILA

In the hospital waiting room, Tim was standing at the television. "You don't want to watch this," he said as Eddy and I entered. We sank into a couch and watched.

At first the picture was a close-up of a young woman reporter, wireless microphone clipped to her lapel. But as the camera pulled back, it revealed her location. The story was coming from the florist shop, from the street where, as the reporter put it, "A local woman named Mary Elizabeth Peacock was found lying by the side of the road, the apparent victim of a hit-and-run driver."

The reporter took a dramatic pause, and the three of us responded with hopes that the story would end right there.

I held my breath.

"No," whispered Eddy.

"Stop," commanded Tim.

The story continued. "Police have no leads in the case . . . ."

Relieved, we relaxed.

". . . and if the bizarre story the woman told the paramedics is correct, they probably never will."

We tensed again.

The reporter walked to the curb and looked down with an expression that worked hard to mix serious contemplation and are-you-kidding-me disbelief. She scuffed the sole of her shoe against the pavement. High drama. She returned to face the camera. "As you can see," she said, "there is no glass from broken headlights. There are no skid marks. That's because the car that hit Mary Elizabeth Peacock has been in the junkyard for forty years. And the driver? Well, if this accident took place in some other dimension, he's probably in the graveyard, too." Another pause. "Or so the woman claims."

We all were speechless. Tim and Eddy were rock-still. I rose, crossed the room to an outside window, and leaned one hand on the sill, stiff and straight and angry, the other hand protectively cradling the baby in my belly. Wearily, with my back to everything I wanted to put behind me, to my companions, the newscast, and this damn business about seeing the past, I studied the comings and goings in the parking lot.

"Turn it off," I finally said, forehead dejectedly on the glass. When the reporter continued, I spun and raised my voice. "Turn it off! Turn that damn thing off!"

When I wasn't looking, Tim also had stood and now was in a low conversation with a nurse. He excused himself, stepped to the television, and hit the power button hard. He turned to Eddy and me.

"Libby can have visitors now," he said. "We should be upstairs."

EDDY

Libby was more alive than we expected. I thought she'd be knocked out by painkillers if not by her injuries. Her face was bruised and she had a couple of blooming shiners that were destined to be beauts. Her scalp was wrapped at the hairline with a bandage that looked like a white gauze bandana. It made her look like she'd been working in the garden. But her collarbone was splinted, her arm was in a sling, and I could only guess at the damage under her gown. Nonetheless, Libby was sitting up. She was stabbing the air in front of the television with the remote, changing channels as fast as she could.

Apparently Libby had seen the same news broadcast we'd caught downstairs. She was muttering about know-nothing paramedics, reporters chasing sensationalism, and how she knew damn well how to keep a damn family secret. Then when she saw us she changed. "Hey," she called. "How was the party? How was the show?"

Tim gently took the remote, kissed her on the forehead, assured her that both party and show had been hugely successful, and eased her back down onto the bed. If not seriously injured, Libby for sure was seriously distraught and seriously exhausted. She closed her eyes. "Thank you, Timmy." She kissed the air in his direction. Then she sat bolt upright. "But I almost did it. I almost saved him."

Now I'm sure that despite what Libby may have said at the scene and the bizarre activity (wink-wink) the reporter had described, the police and the doctors had their theories. No broken glass? Probably she didn't hit the headlight. No skid marks? Probably the driver never touched the brakes. A car from long ago? Certainly this woman was in shock.

Tim and Sheila and I, of course, we all knew exactly what Libby meant. She was surprisingly forthcoming, given that events hadn't turned out in her favor. And so each in our own way, we all listened to her tale—I probing for ever-more detail, Tim quietly holding Libby's hand in comfort, Sheila staring out the window wishing, I'm sure, that the present would stay the present and the past would stay where it damn well belonged.

The day's events, Libby told us, had begun simply enough. She'd gone to the florist shop, where the unfinished renovation still gave off the chalky smell of taped and floated drywall. Everything was new. Leaving, she pulled the door closed, but she didn't bother to lock up. She couldn't see anything worth taking from the renovation. No history there.

Libby walked down the shaded sidewalk toward her childhood home. Each house along the way had a history. Each had its own family, its own view from the porch. But Libby told us she was looking for one view.

Libby picked up an empty, green soft-drink bottle lying beside the curb. Who would leave this here? She shook the bottle and held it upside down. The last drops of cola drained onto the ground, followed by the soggy end of a cigarette.

That was when the old man had appeared. The yard man, trimming shrubbery next door, put down his clippers and walked over to where she stood. He took the bottle from her hand. That was in character. Yard man keeping things neat. But then a car door slammed, and the man nodded in its direction, indicating that Libby should turn and look.

Libby didn't know what to think. She held her breath, turned, and there, directly on the other side of a big tree, directly in front of her family house stood a parked car, a blue Cadillac convertible with the top up. Libby just watched, awestruck and dumbstruck, as a man in the street wearing pleated khaki pants and a dress shirt, sleeves rolled up above his elbows, leaned through the driver's window and spoke with someone behind the wheel. The man stood and lit a cigarette. The man was her father.

Mr. Peacock pushed down the button to lock the driver's door and circled behind the car. He climbed into the front passenger's seat. The engine screeched as the driver turned the key, trying to start the motor that was already running, but finally, the car eased away from the curb more or less properly. The Cadillac gained speed, and at the corner stop sign, the driver tapped the brakes lightly, Libby told us she saw the rear lights flash, but the car barely paused. The Cadillac disappeared around the block.

The street was quiet as Libby took in the scene. She'd wanted the neighborhood of her youth. Now she had it.

A hopscotch game lay drawn in chalk on the sidewalk. Libby walked over and tossed a pebble onto the grid. The stone bounced and came to rest at the far end, but Libby stood where she was. During the few short months when her family had owned the car, she'd been twelve years old, and twelve was too old for hopscotch. Twelve, she thought, remembering her growing attraction to boys at that age, twelve was almost grown up.

Boys and whispered secrets, crowded and raucous school buses, empty and quiet streets. The street where Stan had died. Oh, God, she thought. This couldn't be the day of his death, could it? That wasn't the day she wanted. If Libby were to make up to Stan, she needed some day earlier.

Libby scanned the distance for any sign of a school bus. No need to panic. This might not be the day. This might not be the hour. Or it might. She wanted to run to the corner where the Cadillac had disappeared, but Libby was frozen. There was a car moving through the neighborhood streets. A big, fast, poorly driven car.

Libby told us she searched her memory hard for some account I might have brought back from seeing this day. But she couldn't recall, and that was entirely correct. I'd told stories of my trips to the hanging, the big Victorian house with baseball on the radio, and parties on the porch. But I'd never spoken of visiting my own life. Libby found this inconceivable. How could I have missed a day so important? If I'd been there, how could I have kept it to myself? She was angry. She also was hurt. And as she recalled events she'd just experienced, I saw a tear forming in the corner of her eye.

Then she recovered. She didn't even wipe the tear away. She continued her story.

There in our old neighborhood, Libby stood worrying. She stood with her eyes closed. She stood as if she were praying, mind blank and open to her senses, the cosmos, the sounds and smells and energies around her.

Then from across the street, came a tinny grind, a clank, and a squeak. Old brakes rubbed metal against metal. Hinges that needed oiling creaked as doors swung open. And Libby knew. Damn it. She knew what she did not want to know. The loud throb of a big motor filled the background.

The chaos of children's voices raced toward her. A school bus had arrived at its stop.

"Sit down!" she heard the driver shout. Libby didn't have to open her eyes to see what was happening inside the bus, the football throwing or the arm punching or the book stealing. But Libby did have to open her eyes to find out if this was the day of the accident. She squeezed them tighter. But she couldn't wait forever. She needed to know. And she cautiously opened her eyes and looked about, at old trees arching over the street and new trees young families had planted, at crepe myrtles budding in yards and green lawns cropped with the greatest of care, at the picture-book serenity of suburbia.

At the yellow bus sputtering at the curb.

At the Cadillac car approaching from the far end of the block.

At the boy leaving the bus and heading for the street.

Libby took a step toward Stan and paused, surprised by her own calm. The boy was just now in front of the bus, not yet in danger. The car was still a half-block away, toy-size in the distance. But the boy was beginning to run and the car was beginning to accelerate and Libby stepped off the curb. She took another, faster step toward the middle of the pavement.

In the perfect plan of her mind's eye, Libby told us, she saw herself crossing in front of the car with plenty of time to spare, forcefully but lovingly grabbing Stan by the shoulders, and guiding him to safety. The car would slide by. It would dangerously ignore the signs on the bus commanding "Stop," but in the end all would be well. There would be no accident.

Libby fixed her eyes on Stan and walked ahead faster, almost at a run now. The boy was not looking her way. She had no idea where his thoughts were, but now he, too, started to run. Stan will be thankful, she thought. This will make up for the emotions and intimacy never shared, the goodbye never said.

Libby never knew where Stan went next, whether he veered left or right, slowed down or speeded up, how he moved from her line of sight to the front of the car. How exactly he died.

What she knew was her own wrenching pain. Eyes on Stan and not the road, intent on heroic rescue, Libby had run nearly full tilt into the side of the speeding Cadillac, bounced off the driver's door, and hit the pavement in agony.

From the middle of the street, Libby slowly picked herself up and inched toward the curb. Behind her, there was no Cadillac; there was no school bus. Around her, all the trees were taller, the houses were shabbier, and she knew she had returned to the present. "Stan!" she cried. Libby sat up carefully. Something in her shoulder felt as if it had snapped, and her arm hung limply. Behind what were certainly a number of broken ribs, her lungs felt as if they would burst. Her stomach cramped. Her head spun.

Libby laid herself down carefully and watched the grass from insect level. She was only vaguely aware of the world beyond, but she was intensely aware of what she'd seen in the car.

Libby had recognized the Cadillac's driver, frozen with fear, unable to turn the wheel to change the car's trajectory or move his foot from accelerator to brake. And she had stared into the eyes of her father, not the driver after all but a passenger too far away for her to reach. A man whose guilt and fears she now understood but who she could help no more than she'd been able to help Stan.

TIM

Jesus, I should have known she was up to something. On the day when she proposed the exhibit, as the smoke curled up from our little fire and then cleared to show the city in a way I'd never quite seen it before, I should have taken the hint. Libby was claiming that she was no longer interested in the past, that she was aiming toward the future, when in fact she was still looking backward and she was still searching for Stan.

I laid Libby's hand on the bed and gave it a squeeze. Sure, there was affection in the gesture, but I was harboring a lot of anger, too. I was wondering whether Libby had set me up, whether she'd set us all up, whether she'd arranged my photo exhibit as a distraction so she could go off and do what she wanted. Because that's exactly what she'd done. She'd gone off on her own, she'd hurt herself when things went wrong, and she'd hurt us all. So as she talked, I stepped back. I stroked her hand a couple of times, gave one more squeeze, and joined Sheila in staring out the window.

How ironic. Sheila (her confidant) and I (her lover) were the ones who detached the most from Libby's hospital-bed tale. Eddy had played the we-were-kids-together-so-I-know-best card, not in so many words but suggesting it damn hard, and now he'd wrangled himself into the center of events. Eddy jumped in as if he were that news reporter, thinking, as he always did, that he was the one best suited to finding the truth, putting together its complete details, and telling it right.

"You finally found Stan," I heard him telling Libby.

Well, yeah. But he and Libby could have that.

Sheila laid her fingertips on the Venetian blinds, about eye level. She pulled down gently on one of the blades until the metal snapped into a creased V, opening a wider view of the street.

Across the way, an old man sat on a bus-stop bench. He was bundled in a woolen coat, overalls, and heavy, muddy boots, but he held his hat neatly on his lap. In the winter sun, he turned his wrinkled face up to take advantage of the warmth.

The man turned to look into the distance, down the street where the city bus had not yet come. He seemed to sigh. He stood to begin what Sheila and I instinctively knew would be a long walk, a trek to what was sure to be an empty, solitary home, wherever that was.

I knew this old man. He was the dog-patting, sandwich-eating, street-crossing figure I'd photographed so many times, but this time he was the observer watching us. Because before departing, he turned our way, staring directly at the window where Sheila and I were standing. He held his gaze for a long time. It was as if he had a stake in the outcome up here in Libby's room.

"Walter Lee?" whispered Sheila. She pulled the blade lower until it dragged others down with it. Probably none of them would snap back straight. What did that matter? "Walter Lee." A person or an event would come along, small or large, and the world would not snap back either.

Sheila kept staring out the window. This seemed to be the first time she'd seen the old man, but it was clear that Eddy had talked and talked about him the way Eddy tended to do. It was clear that she understood: The old man's appearance meant the past was near. "Walter Lee," she whispered, and it was as if he heard her. Walter Lee was still staring at our window. He gave a salute. Then he walked to the corner and disappeared from view.

Sheila let go of the blinds, and I saw that I'd been right. They didn't snap back into shape the way they should.

thirty-four

EDDY

During the night, Libby took a turn for the worse. No one called me, I had no sense of midnight foreboding, and as much as I wished I could have done something about it, I just didn't know until I arrived the next morning. Then I was stranded.

I was waiting in the hall among the folded wheelchairs and shrink-wrapped trays of emergency equipment. Facing a world of morphine drips and heart failures, ruptured organs and broken bones. Fearing the hemorrhaging specter of bad news, often very bad news, from impassive physician specialists.

Through the open door, I could see a nurse lower the bed's side rail, pull the sheet up to Libby's waist, and clank the rail back into place. She turned and thanked me for waiting.

As I entered the room, I felt as alone as Libby.

Beside the bed, monitors beeped and blinked a ragged line that rose and fell with each beat of Libby's heart. The lights were low, but I could see Libby clearly. She did not look good. Her eyes had turned much blacker in the overnight hours. And she looked old. She was only four years older than I was, but she looked like she'd been around a lot longer. Been around longer and seen a lot more.

"Daddy?" she asked. Libby stirred under the sheet, then kicked it away. "Daddy, let's don't do this."

The sheet landed in a lump around her ankles. I gingerly pulled it back into place and tucked it in at the top, where I was standing. Yesterday, the doctor had called Libby's injuries "blunt-force trauma." I'd found a distressing lack of caring in that stock phrase, but I couldn't come up with a better way to describe what had happened. Or to describe how she looked. I'd been there once, seen that already with my brother. God help me, and God help Libby.

"Daddy!" Libby was twisting from side to side and shaking her head as if telling someone, No!

In the office across the hall, the nurse looked up from her paperwork. She seemed to be considering returning, maybe bringing medication, something for pain or perhaps a sedative, but Libby fell quiet. The nurse smiled a sympathetic smile, snapped shut the chart she'd been working on, and looked at the clock.

In Libby's room, the monitors softly beeped. Machines and people all were waiting, simply waiting with a deadly, dreadful anticipation for improvement or not, whichever was to come.

"Stinks, doesn't it?"

The voice behind me was Sheila's. She'd come into the room quietly. "Stinks what she did to herself," Sheila repeated. "Trying to follow your example."

There at Libby's side, I felt I should do something for my friend, but the only one I could help was myself. "Oh, no," I protested. "You can't lay this on me."

"You take this," Sheila put the pendant watch into my hand, "and you think about that."

"Everything," I said, lowering my voice but speaking very directly and very distinctly and I'm sure very defensively to Sheila, "is not somebody's fault."

"A neighbor found her lying on the ground," Sheila said. "Your friend almost died. That's not something that happens all by itself."

From the bed came a single word, weakly. "Daddy."

Sheila turned toward Libby. "Is she back there again?"

Dream, hallucination, actual seeing back into time, Libby could have been experiencing anything, but I was beginning to have my suspicions. I'd seen so much in so many past and present times that I couldn't help but think about the nature of the connections, links, bridges, whatever it is that ties our universe together and makes this seeing possible. I'd not only seen but I'd also stepped back and forth so often, as simply as if time were one continuous place, one house full of rooms, that I'd naturally wondered about the physical nature of what I'd been doing.

Until now, there hadn't been much evidence to support any kind of theory. I'd been alone each time I'd gone back. There was no one with me on the street when I saw my brother killed. No one with me on the porch when I descended and followed the streetcar to Alexander Lee's hanging.

The night I saw Old Jacob at his radio, I stepped into the parlor briefly, alone, and then returned to Sheila in the kitchen. That time Libby followed Caroline Simms, she ran ahead down the rainy street. By the time Tim and I caught up, she'd already been there and back.

But here in the hospital, past and present were occurring simultaneously, and we were watching Libby come and go. It was as if one aspect of Libby, or

Libby's consciousness or Libby's essence or Libby's soul or whatever you call it, stepped back in time, while her physical aspect remained in the present.

All it required was some kind of gateway, some scent or sound or movement of air she could ride. Something anyone could notice. Was it that ever-present, distinctively antiseptic hospital smell? Remove the bed and the monitoring equipment and Libby's room would be wrenchingly empty, a room that gave nothing to the senses. But it did have history. People died here, had miraculous recoveries here. They screamed in pain or slipped into the pre-eternal silence of a coma here. Whatever gateway she'd found, Libby had stepped through to her own troubled past.

Still she remained, occupying two times and two places at once.

And suddenly she was sitting up, eyes wide open. Just as she'd done the last time she was awake. The effect was startling, a sudden resurrection of the dead more than a curing of the sick.

Sheila, resting in a visitor's chair, rose and started toward the nurses' station, but I laid a hand on her arm. Already, Libby had sunk back to her pillows.

"That's just like you, Daddy. It's a very nice thing to do." The tone of Libby's voice was calm, one side of a perfectly civil conversation, but it worried me. At her bedside, the monitors continued their rhythmic beeping and their steady graphing. They had, in fact, never changed their pace. Despite Libby's sudden burst when she sat up, the monitors had shown neither spike nor dip beyond normal. It was as if she'd always been still. From the monitors' point of view, Libby's sudden jump could have been made by another person.

"That's very nice of you," she said, "offering to teach Hugh to drive. But something terrible is going to happen."

Sheila dropped back into the guest chair carefully and asymmetrically, supporting herself on one chair arm at a time in the way heavily pregnant women do. (Eight months down, only weeks to go.) But she was barely aware of her actions. Focused so completely on what she was hearing, Sheila seemed as disembodied as Libby.

"Oh, Uncle Hugh," Libby laughed, coyly, girlishly tittering. "Uncle Hugh, you don't need to drive. You get around fine already."

The monitors beeped.

Sheila sat still. I remained quietly standing.

And Tim arrived.

I saw him in the hall, carrying a bunch of flowers, giving a cheery little wave to the nurse, blissfully ignorant of what was transpiring in Libby's room.

But as soon as he entered, Tim knew Libby had gone to a different place. It was obvious to any of us who had been there ourselves. He quietly closed the door. This was no time for the nurse to intrude.

From the bed: "No, learning the accordion was different. Nobody gets hurt when you play the accordion."

I turned to Sheila and Tim. "If she really is there," I said, "it's just before my brother's accident. But who knows. I can't tell if what she's seeing really happened."

"You don't know?" Tim asked. He laid his bouquet on Libby's bedside table, but he was facing me. "You don't know, Mr. Expert-in-the-Past?"

"I don't . . . ."

Sheila bristled. "I know you've seen the accident." She was guessing, but of course it was a very safe guess. "This is what's important, so this is where you've been."

"Not this part."

"What do you mean, 'Not this part'?" Tim was trying hard to keep his voice down. "It's one accident. It happened one time. You were there."

Actually, I wasn't so sure it had happened only one time. And I was increasingly unsure that the past was one continuous thing. There's no reason why it wasn't exactly as jumbled, just as much of a complex, confusing, many-angled, every-man-for-himself, entirely screwed up *Rashomon* experience as the present.

"Eddy," Sheila said with some force. "There's no point in your keeping secrets. Not anymore."

"Don't tell me I could have prevented this. You don't know."

"No, I don't. And guess why. You tell me everything you see when you go back to a party or a ballgame or a hanging, when you go back where there are people we don't know. But you haven't told me shit about what's closest. You haven't told me about your brother's accident. So you're right. I don't know about that."

I remained silent. The time and place of my brother's death were important to a lot of people. To me. To Libby. Mr. Peacock. My long-gone parents. That much was true. But there was no reason why I should feel responsible for either my or Libby's actions. That's what I tried, and tried hard, to tell myself. Libby never could come face-to-face with her problems, and that's a fact. Her style had always been to run away. Running this time had nearly killed her.

And the monitors beeped.

And Libby moved onto a different time.

It sounded like she'd landed months after the accident.

"I know, I know," Libby was saying. She seemed exasperated. "You destroyed your car. What else could you do, kill Hugh?"

"No! No! I'm not suggesting . . . Shit, Daddy, Hugh was nuts. Maybe he wanted to get sick. Maybe he let himself die . . . .

"No, Daddy, it's not your fault. It's not your fault about Stan, and it's not your fault about Hugh. Just believe me, will you? It's not."

Tim leaned against the door. He was blocking it shut with all his weight, but he seemed oddly relaxed and relieved.

We all did. There was a kind of buzz that jumped between us, a long-time-coming relief in knowing what had happened. Libby had talked in circles. We'd heard only one side of the story. But Sheila and Tim and I knew with the kind of knowing that comes from the heart, from deep in the soul, from intangible universal truths, we knew my great uncle was the one who'd killed my brother.

Mystery number one, solved.

Then Libby spoke again, and it seemed to be years later.

"Look, Daddy, you can't go . . . .

"I know it's raining. It's raining like shit, and that's why you should stay home . . . .

"Just believe me: It's not your fault and I'm not going to tell you again . . . .

"No, Daddy, you stay home . . . ."

Libby leaned back over the top edge of the pillow, facing the wall upside down at the head of the bed. Her chin was pointing toward the ceiling. Tears were streaming from the corners of her eyes and across her temples.

Mystery number two, solved as well.

Now Libby was sleeping. I was imagining my dream, and again we all knew—all of us including Tim and especially Sheila, who'd lived with my dream almost as intimately as I had. Flood gauge, creek bank, rising water, low-hanging branches, a big arc of a waving arm.

And in the end, a salute.

"It was suicide," whispered Sheila.

I put my arm around her. "It'll be fine."

"No, it won't," said Sheila, wriggling free.

I could see my image of Mr. Peacock's car upside down, awash in muddy water. In my pocket, I closed my fingers around the pendant watch. I knew Sheila was right and that Tim agreed. Two mysteries, two deaths, now were solved. But at what cost? Certainly, we'd not learned those facts in any way we'd want to repeat.

We'd learned those facts because Libby had tried to change them. Libby had tried to save Stan. She'd put herself in danger in the middle of the street. When that failed, she'd tried to prevent her father from teaching Hugh to drive. Then she'd tried to talk her father out of the remorse that had driven him to his own death.

I could only think about how many more facts and truths, events and people, were out there. Because I had to agree with Sheila's pessimism. I'd felt the depth and the pull, I'd felt them at the hanging, and I knew the past could swallow a person whole. Libby needed to return to our time, and she needed to do it soon.

thirty-five

TIM

"Walk with me," Sheila said, and I held open the door.

"Bring me a coffee?" Eddy asked. "Cream and . . . ."

On its pneumatic closer, the door swung shut, silently closing him off.

So we left Eddy where he needed to stay, watching over Libby and pondering the fruits of his actions. At least we assumed he'd ponder. He'd damn well better ponder. If there'd ever been a time for Eddy to think something through, to seriously wrestle with an outcome and take responsibility, this was it. But we'd see.

We headed for the elevator. "You and I, we had the past under control," I said.

"Did we?" Sheila asked. "Did we, really?"

"Well, yeah. Some of our methods may have been suspect."

Sheila gave me a sideways look to let me know that alcohol wasn't any kind of proper method.

"Well," I answered, "your being a total control freak wasn't so pleasant either."

Sheila pressed hard on the elevator call button.

"But until Eddy went back to those parties . . . ."

"You mean," Sheila corrected, "until Eddy went to his brother's accident. Or wherever he went before he started talking about those parties."

"Until then," I agreed, "we had it under control."

We stepped into the elevator without another word.

In the hospital cafeteria, Sheila and I took a table without taking any food. She directed me to a spot way in the back, as far from other patrons as we could get, stuck in a windowless corner, down there in the hospital basement, a place without character or history. That's what we wanted.

"No Danish modern here," I said.

Sheila drew a blank.

"No frozen swimming pool," I ventured. "No floodlights shining in the window."

It looked like I needed to spell out what I intended.

"The last time you wanted to talk. At the Capri."

Sheila and I sat looking at people eating at tables around us. I'm sure we both wondered—I know I did—what kind of horrible story each was carrying. Hospitals are like that. Stories everywhere. Everyone hiding them in the public areas because they have to spill their innermost souls, or witness their loved ones spilling their souls, in private. We were the exception. We spilled our souls everywhere.

"The problem with Eddy," Sheila began slowly, "is that he thinks he's dealing only with the past."

"The problem with Eddy," I fleshed out her thought, "is that he could have killed Libby."

We looked around a bit more until I could hold it no longer. "Clueless bastard." I was so glad to be out of Libby's room. I might have punched Eddy if I'd stayed longer. And not just a playful bop on the arm.

"How are you feeling?" I changed the subject, but I smiled to let Sheila know the next step was hers. She told me she was fine, that the baby was healthy, that she actually would have been able to sleep if it weren't for the other traumas in her life, but our discussion of the present ended there. As we'd made clear at the Capri, Sheila and I shared worries about the past, and I knew where she'd take this. Sheila leaned as close to the table as her belly would allow, as if she were about to share a confidence with me, as if she were about to say something she didn't want even the baby to hear.

"He was there, you know. And so was she. I saw them both. Eddy and Libby were there."

"A boy and a girl," I replied. "A new car. A ride around the block."

"No. Well, yes, I saw them then. But this was much deeper, much longer ago."

Turns out, she hadn't been worrying only about Eddy stepping back to his childhood.

Sheila told her tale of the man at the barbershop window, the walk down the windy sidewalk, and the woman stepping off the streetcar into the rain. Of the day Eddy saw his grandfather rescue Caroline Simms from the flood, the day Sheila watched Libby angry in the storm. But I'd known all that for years.

In earlier times, I'd freely shared my experiences. Sheila had shared, too, especially the times when she'd recognized Eddy. They were dating by then, so recognizing him was easy. She'd had no clue who Libby was. Just another person out of time. Me, she never saw. I'd never gone to the dates she visited, and I believe that made me someone safe to talk with. Sheila told me she was afraid to approach Eddy after she returned to the present. What she'd seen of him was pretty benign, this walking around in the storm business, but she worried that Eddy would feel invaded or betrayed or spied upon.

Of course, later she changed her mind. She must have been stewing for years over things she'd seen—and recently over things Eddy had seen—but something had also frightened her. That night at the Capri, when I not only refused to help her change the past but dared her to try for herself, Sheila was visibly shaken. Now she seemed to wish she'd tried.

"'We waited too long,'" Sheila said, staring again across the cafeteria. The cashier was staring back like she was trying to will us to order some food or get the hell out, but neither of us was focusing on her. "Libby said those were the last words of the woman she found in the river. Now I've waited too long, too. I've known for years, damn it. I've known for years that something bad was coming and that I should have tried to stop it."

"You didn't know what Eddy was going to do," I said. "Did you?"

Sheila then continued with another explanation. I must have been really showing my frustration with Eddy and my disapproval of this entire chain of events, because an extended monologue was so unlike her.

"Years ago," Sheila began, "I saw Eddy at a time and place that wasn't so benign. I saw a man helping to carry a coffin, a man who was dressed a little oddly for the time, who seemed nervous and out of place. But he mostly had his back turned to me and I lost him in the crowd. It wasn't until a couple of months ago when Eddy told me he'd just been there that I knew what that day meant and that he was the man."

"And Libby?"

"You know, I hid that I didn't like her and that I didn't trust her when she first arrived. I even lied about it," she admitted. "And I'm sorry, I really am, because you do like her."

I have no idea what kind of emotion I was showing at that. I may have nodded.

"But no, I didn't. I didn't want Eddy to take the florist shop job. I didn't want him to get involved with Libby. Because as soon as I saw her at the pub I realized I'd seen her before. I'd seen her in this part of the past as well, and I knew . . . ."

I waited.

Nothing.

I was growing impatient.

"That's all," Sheila said, slumping back into her chair. "You know the rest."

But what did I know? And how could I have known it? I leaned my head back, massaging my neck as I wondered. Until the last few months, we hadn't talked about the past in years. Not since that time in our student days when Sheila had become hysterical over something she'd seen. She was eyes-wide-open frightened in a way that made everyone around us think she'd had her own bad experience with drugs. Something extra in the smoke, maybe. Sheila and I decided a little misunderstanding among our friends wasn't so bad. It was good cover. But I was the one who knew drugs, and I was the one who was reluctantly coming to know the past myself. I understood that what she'd seen had been no hallucination.

And now I understood. "Ohhhh," I whispered, exhaling long and opening my eyes. "Libby was that woman." I twisted in my chair toward the door, as if I could see all the way back to Libby's room. "That one you saw."

"That woman," Sheila repeated, finally admitting. "The one who tried to kill Uncle Hugh."

SHEILA

It was indeed that time I'd become so frightened in college—and I remember it now like it was yesterday.

"Libby tried," I explained to Tim in the cafeteria, "but she couldn't bring herself to kill a child. Not even a child she knew would grow up to hurt someone she loved."

My vision had started simply enough. We'd just returned from a weekend at the Capri, and a bunch of people had decided to continue the party at my apartment downtown. They were upstairs drinking wine. I went outside to lock up my car. And there was this crowd. Just like Eddy would describe his own crowd, the one he followed when he stepped down from our porch years later, I saw men in the street, I followed them, and I came to a stop outside some kind of courtyard surrounded by tall, stone walls.

That was when I saw Eddy helping carry the empty coffin, and when I lost him in the crowd. The thick pair of wooden doors in the stone wall closed and I guessed he was on the other side. The men left outside where I was were milling about; they seemed anxious to get going on something, to be doing or seeing something, but there was order. They all faced the same direction. They kept staring at the blank walls and the wooden doors. On the other side, voices spoke louder. Then silence. Then the thumping of heavy timbers. Then more silence, inside the walls and out, almost a religious, respectful silence.

Afterward, the crowd wandered the streets, now aimless where they once had a common agenda, now full of bragging and obviously forced bravado. I knew there'd been a hanging behind those walls; I'd heard that in their conversations, and a lot of the men were carrying bits of rope that had bound the condemned man. They should have been satisfied, but still they were restless, looking for something to fill an unspeakable need.

I felt invisible as I wandered among these men.

Until, at a corner, I encountered another woman.

Men walked by unnoticing. This woman also seemed invisible to them, and she seemed to carry a sense that she also was out of her time. The woman carried an aggressiveness and a determination. She carried something modern, a big piece of the future's complexity, its accumulated layers of years, into what should have been a simpler time.

Then amid the formless, wandering crowd, the woman suddenly took off as if she'd spotted something, as if she were in pursuit. I followed, keeping two or three men between us so I wouldn't be noticed. The woman's gait was fast. We passed loiterers and braggarts on the sidewalk. And when a gap in the crowd opened, I spied her goal. A half-block away, I saw a boy alone.

The boy was more than lost. He stood as if he belonged no place in the world. His face was streaked with the tracks of tears. Dust kicked up by passing horses and a very few but very obvious early automobiles had left a gruesome film over the marks of his crying. This was a boy whose eyes had no soul left, who had no desire to see the world.

"But you told me this years ago," said Tim. "What's different now?"

"Well . . ." I said, trying to get comfortable with a story I'd always found uncomfortable. I was also trying to explain how I'd finally put people and events together without sounding like I was bragging. Because my story was very sad. It wasn't something to brag about.

"Well, what's different," I said, "is that Libby has come home. She's here, back in this city. I didn't know her then, and I'd only recently met Eddy. I had only a rough idea of who the members of his family were and who his friends were, and I knew nothing about the McBride family story. Nothing about poor, damaged Uncle Hugh. And only a little about what happened to Eddy's brother."

In my version, my vision into the aftermath of the hanging, Libby was walking faster toward Hugh. He was off the curb, a few feet into the street, his back to the people on the sidewalk.

"What I was seeing," I continued, trying in the same way Eddy would try to focus on the logic and the details of events rather than their emotion. "What I was seeing in a bizarrely circular kind of way was that the same thing that happened to Stan fifty years later could have happened to Hugh. All Libby had to do to rescue Stan was push Hugh into the street. One boy into harm's way would move the other out. A neat little logical action. Except none of it worked."

"She could have changed history," said Tim.

"I think that's what she was hoping. She'd failed to save Stan back in the neighborhood. Now she was trying again, and she must have been coming from her bed upstairs, after she talked with her father, after she saw Hugh driving. It could have happened five minutes ago. We don't know because we didn't hear it. There wasn't any conversation, no talking. But she must have one simple idea: no Hugh, no driving lesson, no accident. Stan would be alive."

"But she didn't," Tim said. "So don't be mad at Libby. Be mad at Eddy. She wouldn't even have known going back in time was possible if he hadn't done it. Libby didn't do anything wrong."

"Tim," I said, resting a hand on his. "I know you don't want to hear this." I lowered my voice. "But she meant to. Libby really did mean to kill Hugh."

From where I'd stood in the past time, I'd seen Libby approach the boy and I'd seen her raise one hand to shoulder height, elbow bent, palm facing out, ready to shove. Hugh stepped off the curb, catatonic after the hanging, heedless of the people and the traffic around him. Horses. Wagons. Early automobiles. The street was filled. Even without Libby's interference, he seemed doomed.

And then everything stopped.

"Hey!" A high-pitched, pre-adolescent voice cut through the noise in the street. "Hey, boy! Hey, you! Watch out!"

Hugh looked as if he were emerging from a dream. He backpedaled slowly, retreating from the crowded street, and his heels hit the curb. He stumbled, and he sat down hard on the sidewalk.

Now Libby could do nothing. She could not shove the sitting boy. She, too, took a step backward. She paused. Then Libby turned and ran into the crowd.

Across the street there was a delivery wagon. It seemed ordinary enough. Its wooden sides were weathered. Any paint had long since disappeared. The graying horse that pulled it stood quietly, eyes closed.

In the back, in the wagon's bed, lay a long narrow box. It was six feet long, maybe more. It was not decorated with flowers, not draped in the final solemnity of black. The deceased was ready for perfunctory delivery, a quick burial, dust to dust.

A boy in the wagon's seat, next to the driver, was staring at Hugh.

Hugh, seemingly unaware of his clumsy fall or any pain in his landing, stared back at the boy, hypnotized.

The wagon's driver flicked the reins and the horse took a step forward. The boy in the wagon, the new orphan, gave a little wave. Then, without waiting to see if Hugh responded, the boy faced straight ahead, stoically. Walter Lee—because that's who the boy was—sat watching as the buildings, the people, the entire city slipped from foreground to background.

The nursing shift must have changed while Tim and I were in the cafeteria, because as we approached Libby's room, I saw a new young woman, a frazzled and frantic-looking one, emerge. She rushed to the nurses' station and began urgently dialing the phone. Libby's door stood slightly ajar.

Then the smell struck. It was some kind of poultice or inhaler, some pungent rub of camphor and menthol, or perhaps an antiseptic. It was something that touched and treated the body in an older, organic way.

"Holy Mary," I said, as I pushed the door open wide. Tim slunk back into the hall, escaping, backpedaling just as the boy Hugh had done in the street but backpedaling more quickly and more effectively, virtually clawing his way, holding onto the present with his fingertips. Just in time, too. As for me, I'd already slipped into an older time.

Now, when I'd opened the door, I still didn't understand what had happened. I'd thought Eddy would be there, sitting to one side, in one of the room's guest chairs, right where Tim and I had left him. But after Tim's panic, when I turned back to the room, there was no Eddy. And the room itself, well, when I entered I saw that other things also were missing.

There was no rhythmic beeping of monitors. The principal sound now came from a window fan whirring the stuffy sick-room air. A lighter sound came from the half-open Venetian blinds, which clinked occasionally in the feeble breeze. To one side stood an over-the-bed table, a tray of hospital food growing cold under a squat, stainless-steel dome. I waited for my eyes to adjust to the dim light.

A green curtain hung by tiny chains from a track in the ceiling. A stainless-steel pole, the kind used for hanging bags of intravenous fluids, waited in the corner. And against the side wall, motionless and perfectly quiet, stood Libby. She was clutching a pillow to her chest.

My eyes went to the patient. Uncle Hugh lay motionless. The bed was cranked up to a gentle angle, but he was flat on the mattress. No pillow. I turned to Libby. Back to Hugh. Was he breathing?

Libby was shaking with emotion, a violent shake of the type that could be relieved only by a complete surrender to tears. Or rage. She hugged her pillow tighter but she was focusing on Hugh. She seemed to be both willing and fearing some result.

The door swung open and a doctor entered, brusquely. The frazzled nurse followed.

Automatically, Libby and I stepped behind the curtain. Libby didn't say a word, but when she turned my way, she presented the saddest face I'd ever seen. She acknowledged my presence, it seemed, with a tear that slid from the corner of one eye and ran down her cheek. And in that tear, I saw Libby's lonely world.

I saw the way she'd thrown herself into the lives of others. And for all the self-assuredness she wore on the surface, I saw the way Libby had taken so much of her identity from those people. From artsy Eddy, from her cheating husband, from her self-destructive father. It happened whenever she was crazy about a man. Most recently, there'd been Tim, good and kind Tim who was trying hard but with limited success to make Libby happy, to make her independent, and to help her stand on her own. And for long, lingering years, there'd been the memory of Eddy's brother Stan, now returned to the center of her life.

I saw in her pitiful and plaintive face the kind of desperately needy look I'd seen in our little cat Ike whenever he'd been sick, the kind of helpless look you'd see in any creature who wasn't communicating verbally but who was asking for forgiveness and love and grace and assistance all at once.

Libby had thrown herself into all her men's worlds—quite literally thrown herself into that last day of Stan's life—but she hadn't been able to help anyone. Her obsession with changing events had left her alone with the status quo. All she could do was take one final shot at doing away with Hugh. It was a meaningless gesture, as Hugh lay dying of pneumonia, but desperation and frustration and anger and the need for revenge each had a hold, and she couldn't help but do what emotions commanded. She had to try again. Even if, from where she stood in the sequence of things, Stan was already gone. Even if Hugh's death would come too late to make a difference in the chain of events.

And now she was left without even that.

"This man has been dead for an hour," the doctor announced after a cursory examination. He jerked the sheet to cover Hugh's face, but he pulled so hard the bottom came free and settled around the dead man's knees. The doctor berated the nurse for not calling earlier, slapped the chart into her hands, and stalked from the room. The door stood open. The nurse cast a resentful glance at the covered body, then followed.

Immediately, something flew and tangled in the curtain. The chains emitted a jangling skree, the curtain slid to the end of its track, and a pillow dropped from its folds.

"Goddamn it," cried Libby. "Goddamn. Goddamn."

I expected the nurse to come running, but there was no response. The fan whirred and the breeze continued to gently shake the blinds. I crossed to the window and clicked off the motor.

The room was silent for a moment, until the beep-beeping of Libby's monitors started up again.

thirty-six

EDDY

"I don't know," said Sheila, dropping onto the parlor sofa in a pregnant heap. I'd gone straight to the kitchen and was emerging with a cup of herbal tea. Sheila politely accepted my offering, took a tiny sip, wrinkled her nose, and placed the cup and its saucer on the end table. She explained what she'd seen at the hospital. "I don't know whether Libby was just standing there trying to get up the nerve to do it, or whether she'd already put the pillow over his face."

I'll grant Sheila this: She was damn good at keeping secrets. All those years of her seeing the past, and me left in the dark. Libby tried to kill Hugh when he was a boy? As her nerves calmed down and she told me the secret she and Tim had shared, I thought she had to be kidding. But she wasn't. She wasn't kidding either about Libby's latest attempt at revenge, the clutched and thrown pillow. More horrible stuff, but with a difference. Because this second time, there was no mystery to it. Tim standing in the hall and I sitting by the bed, we'd both known immediately that Sheila was in the past.

As Sheila explained, she had no sooner entered the hospital room than she backed up a step and let out a gasp.

What Tim and I saw with Sheila was just like watching Libby in her bed, a person in two places at one time.

Sheila pressed herself against the wall, as if she wanted to escape through it. She narrowed her eyes to a deliberate focus and twisted her head from side to side. She paused briefly at the end of each arc as if she were waiting for something to happen or someone to speak. Tennis match. Then she took long steps, quickly and deliberately, to the back side of the room. She snapped her head to face the window, eyes wide open, waved a hand in front of her, and reached through the Venetian blinds as if grabbing for something.

Then Sheila was blinking, rubbing her eyes, running her fingers through her hair, once again in the present.

I'd immediately hustled her into the hall. I needed to get her away from what she'd seen, help her escape before she saw more. But I was too late. The past had come to Sheila all in one piece, and it had come fast. The entire experience had taken ten, maybe fifteen seconds.

At home now, I began massaging Sheila's neck and shoulders, trying to calm and comfort her, kneading three, four, five deep times. She pushed my hands away.

"'Goddamn,'" Sheila whispered after a long silence. Tim sat at a respectful distance at the far end of the sofa. I'd moved across to an armchair. We pricked up our ears.

"Libby said, 'Goddamn.' She was just as late getting there as I was."

Sheila paused, nervously raised her tea as if she were looking for something to do, but she set the cup back into its saucer without even putting it to her lips.

"Neither of us could do anything," Sheila was saying. "Libby couldn't kill him, and I couldn't prevent whatever she wanted to do. I saw the intent. I saw how desperate she was to make things different. Who knows? Maybe next time, maybe somebody, maybe one of us, will be able to do something."

Sheila grabbed one of the sofa pillows and hugged it in a conscious or unconscious imitation of Libby. "Good damn luck to them."

SHEILA

The three of us sat in silence as long as we could bear it, avoiding eye contact. At least I guess that's what Tim and Eddy were doing. I had my eyes closed, still seeing Libby standing over Uncle Hugh with that pillow. It didn't really matter, did it, whether Libby wanted to be in the past or not? It didn't matter whether she was on some mission to save Stan or on a vendetta against the driver who'd killed him. We couldn't leave her wandering around who knows when while her body lay disconnected in the hospital.

Eddy did break the silence once to ask if I wanted more tea. But I'm sure he was just trying to change what we were all thinking. When I didn't reply, he walked to the kitchen and turned off the light. Not that it was a significant gesture, but anything to change the topic.

Tim had a better strategy. Just at the point when it seemed like the tension might snap with some cosmic, wrenching force, maybe even with an audible sound, he stepped into the dining room and retrieved a bottle of bourbon from the sideboard. He poured two fingers straight up into a wine glass— Why not? It's what was handy—and swallowed with one gulp. He poured another and carried his drink and the bottle into the parlor, where he added a splash to my room-temperature tea.

I couldn't help but follow Eddy's eyes as he looked from the teacup to my pregnant belly, up to my eyes, over to Tim. My stare warned Eddy not to say a word. I needed help to be in a place where there was no past or no need for the past, and that's what I was going to get. At that moment, unchecked stress was a greater threat to my health and well being than a bit of booze. No doubt about it.

I swirled the drink in my cup and took a sip. This was better. I finished the spiked tea and held out my cup for a refill, but Tim had already set the bottle on the floor, out of reach at his end of the sofa. Oh, Timmy. You take such good care of others, but you still have problems of your own.

Meanwhile, at the open window behind me, Ike had jumped to the outside sill. His tail was in the air like an antenna. I scratched at the screen, and Ike pressed his cheek against the scratching place.

Eddy smiled. Ike was making me feel better, and my husband should have, too, but I knew what he was thinking and that made me worry. He'd told me about the night he watched Libby's father, sailor home from the war, throw that beer bottle. He'd told me about the divide a screen makes between inside and outside and the divide he'd breached between present and past. For Eddy, everything was so symbolic and connected, so much cause and effect. Too much. And now I was beginning to think like him.

Hey, Ike, I thought. Can I be like you? A gentle rub on the cheek. A bit of purring. Life would be so much simpler. But a contented purr never lasts, and it wasn't long before Ike jumped back to the porch floor and settled by the railing, watching birds peck at our feeder.

"It's a complicated business," I said, staring at the cat, whose simple life calmed me down, but addressing Eddy, whose help I needed more. "For years, I've seen people from the present in the past, but now it's getting worse. Libby may be lying in the hospital here, but she's trying to commit murder back there. And she's doing it right now."

"No . . ." began Tim. He wanted to defend Libby, he seriously did, but we were all coming to know what was what.

"Hugh was a dying old man," Eddy said, inserting the one defense he knew. "He wasn't leaving the hospital alive no matter what." Eddy then began a detailed explanation of how his reclusive uncle was dying of empathy and guilt, how nursing Eddy in his measles and coming down with pneumonia had been more than a kind gesture; it had been Hugh's suicide. Or his execution. Eddy explained how Hugh didn't have it in him to run the way Eddy's father had, how he'd already descended into unhappiness, into a touch of madness really, with the execution of another man, how he wanted to atone with self-execution for killing Stan and how events didn't really have any choice but to play out as they did.

At which point, I wriggled my pregnant self to standing and headed for the bourbon. "We get it, Eddy. You've pondered and figured it all out. Hugh was a dead man. But we still don't know . . . ."

"We don't know what?" Tim was eager, hoping for a crumb that would absolve Libby.

"We don't know," I said, picking up the bottle and pouring a large share into my empty teacup, "whether or not a person from the present can affect the past." I held the drink up to Eddy in a little toast, a dare really, hoping my message would hit between the eyes, but it lost some of its impact, I'm afraid, when I sloshed bourbon into the cuff of his trousers.

Eddy dabbed at the spill, then stood and gently and politely took the cup from me. We sat. Eddy nipped at the liquor, but Tim seemed to sink his entire face into his. He'd been there before, with the dare I'd given him that night at the Capri.

Okay, boys, follow me, I thought. I'll lead this dance.

I turned to Eddy. "You want to know why I haven't told you about what I've seen? It's very simple. The past and the present and the future are all mixed up together. And that scares me. It scares the hell out of me."

It looked like Tim had had enough of fear, too—he'd said as much not long before—because now he went looking for the cat. Tim walked to the front door and kept going onto the porch. It looked like we all wanted some simplicity; we all wanted to stay in the present. But humans don't necessarily have the choice.

"Of course," I turned to Eddy, "it wasn't all bad. One time I was waiting for a bus at a shopping center and I saw a man getting out of a Cadillac convertible. Two boys in Cub Scout uniforms and a girl in a sundress were in the back seat, and I remember what the man said to them. He said, 'You mind Silver, cowboy.' He must have known what would happen, because as soon as he was safely inside the shop, the boys climbed onto the backs of the front seats and straddled them like horses. 'Hi-Yo, Silver!'"

"I don't remember," Eddy said.

"It was a little thing," I answered. "We forget. Let's try another."

I told Eddy about the time I'd seen him in the long-ago storm. He'd been on one block, and Libby'd been around the corner. Just recently, Libby had confirmed that she'd been there. She remembered too well.

"I don't remember," Eddy repeated.

"I never told you," I said. "It was a long time ago, the year I was a student intern. But more importantly, I couldn't tell you, could I? I couldn't tell you when you were in your twenties what you'd be doing when you were in your forties."

"No, you couldn't."

"What if I'd seen you as an old man? Would that have been good? To reveal you lived a long time? What if I'd stopped seeing you? Would that mean you were dead? Or just disinterested?"

Eddy shrugged.

"So I waited. And now I know. You don't remember being in that storm because you were coming from a time that hasn't happened yet. You and Libby weren't together. She'd come into the past from last summer. You came from when? It could be later today. Or tomorrow. Or sometime soon. It better be soon, for Libby's sake."

"I don't have much choice . . ." Eddy began, and I could tell he was off to pondering. But after a minute, he said he saw two choices. He could go wherever Libby was and bring her back. Or he could go somewhere earlier and change events so none of this would happen in the first place. "Two shitty choices," he said, "for our good friend."

"You do what you think is best," I said. "You still have that watch?"

Eddy removed the pendant watch from his pocket and held it on his flat palm for me to see. I looked for a nod, any sign of agreement, as Eddy closed his fingers around the watch, but he was showing nothing. Maybe later.

"I can tell you one thing," I said. "We've all been almost there. It's just that none of us has gone far enough or stayed long enough."

I rose, took the teacup, and swallowed the last drop of bourbon. "And I'll tell you another. I believe that years ago, I got closer than anyone else. I can't go there now because of the baby. But I just might be able to show you where you need to go."

I leaned toward Eddy, balancing the empty teacup with one hand on the little shelf that was the top of my belly. The baby kicked and the cup bounced. Some other time we would have had a laugh at that, but I'm not sure Eddy even noticed. I put my other hand on his. I gave Eddy a kiss.

And with that, I went up to bed.

Pausing at the window on the stairwell landing, I saw Tim slowly making his way across the lawn to Libby's apartment, where he'd pass a lonely and no doubt tearful night.

Turning back toward the parlor, I still had a glimpse of Eddy. He was gathering up the afghan we kept draped over the back of the sofa and wrapping himself against the winter chill.

Eddy would pass his own fitful night in the porch hammock accompanied by a starry sky, the intersection of events, and a head full of ponderings—hundreds, thousands of options and plans and worries, if I knew Eddy—about a future and a past that both seemed so inevitable.

thirty-seven

SHEILA

Up early and off to work first, that was usually my style. But when I stepped onto the porch the next morning bearing a cup of coffee for Eddy, he was gone. It didn't take much to see I'd been right about the nighttime pondering. When I pulled away the afghan he'd left in a clump on the hammock, the Babe Ruth baseball bounced to the floor.

Now Eddy could have brought out the ball again as a reminder of an easier and simpler time. Eleanor and Lillian and Hugh at the game. Comfort food, or its equivalent in story. He could have been pondering a dark day. His father shoots and the ball is scarred forever. But what I was hoping was that he was using the ball as some sort of talisman, a tool, a gateway, a link to the connections he knew he had to make. Rubbing his thumb round and round the bullet hole. Eddy doesn't have any choice but to help his old friend. Open sesame, and he's on his way.

I followed the ball's path over to the top of the steps, where I picked it up. I was pleased. Eddy still had a fascination with the past. He wasn't Tim, fighting against it. I gave the ball a little toss. This time, if I'd found Eddy asleep, I wouldn't have kicked him. I'd have kissed him. Eddy was thinking the way I wanted him to think. He wasn't using the night as an escape anymore. He was figuring out where he should go and what he should do next.

EDDY

You know what I was really thinking that night in the hammock? Well, it wasn't what Sheila imagined. Somehow she'd got the idea that I'd bought into her plan. Somehow she thought I was happily planning, toying with a head full of options, creating a foolproof scenario for how I'd bring Libby back. Not so fast. Sheila's charge to me wasn't something I could ignore. But first I had to spend some time at another place, with another time.

What I was really thinking about was an entirely different day when I'd been standing quietly in the Victorian house's parlor, watching my family. The date, I guess it was sometime after Old Jacob went blind. The 1920s sometime. The event, that was nothing important. I was just there, and they were just there. My great grandfather tapped his pipe on his ashtray and spilled out the last of the burning tobacco.

Then he turned my way. "I want to walk," he said, reaching for my arm. I was too shocked to deny my presence, and I was quite uncertain how I should behave. I simply went along.

As we crossed the yard, the pair of us bundled in coats and rolled up in scarves against approaching weather, I wasn't sure he knew who I was. He could have thought I was Hugh. He held my elbow the way he held Hugh's. He shuffled along beside me the same way, too. He didn't seem to need to speak.

Old Jacob and I made slow but steady progress as far as the carriage house, where he stopped and turned toward the apartment window. I followed his cue. It was as if the old man wanted me to see something, as if he were guiding my seeing eyes with his blind ones. And I suppose he was, because just then a curtain rustled and Walter Lee appeared, holding the drapery to one side.

Walter Lee could have been doing something simple, checking the weather maybe, but he wasn't. He was staring straight at me. I wish I could say he simply nodded. For anyone else, that would have been the most natural. But I'm afraid his gesture was uncomfortably more. Walter Lee gave me a salute. Then he let the drapery fall.

Old Jacob was pulling at my arm. "Come on boy," he was saying. "Weather is coming, and I want to walk." And so we did.

I rolled the memory of our walk around in my mind that night in the hammock, how commanding the house's hilltop site was back then, how the trees were so much smaller than they are now. From where I lay on the porch, staring across the garden and at their dark silhouettes, the trees now blocked out a good portion of the world. But in that earlier time, I could easily see the surrounding land. It was completely bare, cleared of the fall harvest and waiting for spring planting. The city hadn't grown out to this hilltop yet. And I could see fog in the river bottom. You know how fog settles on a river in the morning? There wasn't a dam and a lake like there is now. The river was just a gentle little stream. But the fog was thick that day, and it defined the river pretty well.

"It's not much bigger than the creek where the fighting was," Old Jacob said that day. I was certain he could not see the river, but he was staring right at it.

It was then that ice began to fall. One final gesture of winter as the season turned to spring. It was making a hissing sound, and Old Jacob began jerking and ducking his head. Ice fell, *sssssssssss*, and Old Jacob ducked again. "It sounds," he whispered, "like The Cornfield."

Of course, I knew the old man wasn't talking about wind rustling in the family garden or the hired man plowing under the dry, dead stalks of winter. Old Jacob was a survivor of The Cornfield, the Civil War massacre at Antietam.

The ice kept coming, and Old Jacob stood straight, as if he were at attention, and I imagined he was seeing that other morning. It was 1862 and he was twenty-one years old. "The corn was taller than we were," he started to say, "and we stood in formation. The enemy was only a hundred paces away, but could not see us. We fixed our bayonets. We waited."

Sssssssssss. "Two armies stood almost face-to-face. 'I believe my cousin may be on that side,' whispered the boy standing next to me, and the boy began to shake."

Sssssssssss. "When the shooting began," my great grandfather said, and he turned to me, "the bullets sounded like hail coming through the corn."

I lay shivering in the hammock, remembering Old Jacob's story. "The man in front of me," he'd said, "the man in front of me went down, and I knew I was a dead man."

Damned if I could have survived. I felt the cold and terror wrapping me up more completely than my afghan. I'd have been a dead man, too.

On the hilltop that day, Old Jacob took my elbow again and pushed me straight ahead, angling toward the river. "The Cornfield was filled with smoke," he told me, "but I could see the enemy clearly. We yelled like hell and we ran at him. And then I couldn't see anything. I was lying in the plowed field and my face was bleeding and my eyes were blinded. All I could do was lie there and wait."

I curled up in the hammock as I remembered that talk, shivering like crazy with my own fear.

On our hilltop, my great grandfather had turned his face to the sky. "The fighting," he said, and I thought in the freezing rain that I saw tears in the old man's eyes, "the fighting went back and forth, killing men in one direction, then the other. I don't know what happened to that boy. Two armies stepped on me and stumbled and tripped over me. They lay in the dirt and died beside me, I knew that much."

What a horrible damn thing for me to be thinking during a long, lonely night.

"By the time the fighting was over," I recalled Old Jacob saying, and I recalled that he, too, was shaking, "my sight had come back some. But I wished it hadn't. Not a single stalk of corn stood. The field was planted with dead men."

Around us, the freezing rain was harder now, and the sky was rumbling in the distance. Early-spring thunder. Or ancient artillery. And then thunder crashed so loud I thought I was one of the dead. I squeezed my eyes shut, and I felt as blind as Old Jacob. I was scared. I was really damn, pants-pissing, knee-crawling, mother-pleading, helpless scared.

I really did think I was going to war. Or that the damn war was coming to me. That it was going to swallow me up and I'd disappear like that young soldier at The Cornfield. Walking there on the hilltop, I felt so exposed. I felt that any event had the power to just reach out, grab me, and kill me dead.

And this was what I pondered in the hammock, this one terrifying thought, not the thousands of happy options that Sheila imagined. Shit. Where would events land me? Shit. Could I avoid it? Should I avoid it? Did I have any choice?

I could think only one thing: Don't make me do this!

Rising from the hammock and walking out to the garden, I closed my fingers around the pendant watch in my pocket. I wound up to throw—more like an outfielder aiming a long ball home than a pitcher in his precision windup—but when I came around I kept my fingers closed. No. History deserved better than this. The watch shouldn't come to a meaningless rest in someone's backyard.

Libby deserved better, too. As much as I wanted to stop, as much as I needed to stop, I couldn't do it now. I had to keep on doing what I'd been doing, even if events completely swallowed me up. I couldn't run. I couldn't disappear and avoid responsibilities the way my father did.

There'd been a time when the past seemed so simple. One version of the hanging, the one I'd told Sheila, was clean and antiseptic. In that case, simple justice. Isn't that the way the books tell it? Wars back then didn't hurt, not like wars do today. Bull. Shit. Just ask Old Jacob. Hell, just ask Mr. Peacock. A young sailor bobbing in the ocean is not so unlike a young soldier lying in a field. Now it was my turn.

It had become painfully clear, as I lay in the hammock that night, that I was on a fast track to seeing the complete story, the final links in the chain of events that made my family and friends what they were: Caroline Simms's drowning leads to Alexander Lee's hanging, which leads to Great Uncle Hugh's depression, which leads to a childlike obsession with the accordion and former Seaman Alvin Peacock's offer of driving lessons, all of which lead to my brother Stan's . . . .

I just lay there in the dark and remembered and worried. How far would I have to go? Two, three, four decades? A hundred years? To my own Antietam?

In the morning, a light came on in the carriage-house apartment, and someone dragged the curtain aside, checking as Walter Lee had done to make sure the world was still there. The curtain fell. The light went out. The door slammed. Tim descended the stairs and began walking toward town, aiming to absorb himself in work. Everyone does it, I thought. Everyone copes the way they have to.

Truth. I thought. The word lay in front of me like a lump I wanted to kick. And the more I thought, the more certain I was of where I was going next time. I was going into a time and place where events were true and already determined. But the truth of what I was about to do there wasn't certain at all.

thirty-eight

SHEILA

I caught up with Eddy at the florist shop. His presence in Libby's space looked promising to me, but I wanted to make sure. "This is not a Ouija board," was the first thing I said when I arrived. Eddy nodded. "We're not asking the advice of ghosts." He nodded again. "You're going, right?" He said he was. But first, he needed to attend to the kitchen cabinets. I sighed.

Eddy told me that working at the shop helped him think about Libby. He said he hoped that finishing the job was a step that would take life back to the way it was when work was going well. So he stopped around regularly, looking forward to milestones like the installation of kitchen cabinets. Here at the shop, he could focus simply on getting the work done. Maybe even on moving into the future.

I, of course, reminded him that the cabinetmakers and carpenters were still a good half-hour away, which left plenty of time for me to lay out the work I needed from him first. I sat him down under Mr. Peacock's front-yard tree, where early spring's budding leaves were just beginning to show themselves. I put a cup of coffee into his hand, and I told him to shut up and listen.

I told Eddy I was going to explain what I'd hinted at earlier, about my seeing him come into the past from a time that had not yet occurred. I told him I was going to fill him in on the historical events I'd witnessed. But really, what I wanted to do was point Eddy in the direction he needed to go. Libby was out of commission. Walter Lee was who knew where. It was up to me to give Eddy the shove.

It had been a foggy day, I told Eddy, when I'd gone out from my internship job for a sandwich and had come back soaking wet. It was a day we hadn't talked about in years, but it was a day Eddy should remember.

"How'd you get so wet?" everyone at the office wanted to know when I returned. Some turned toward the window, which was lightly streaked from mist. "It's just fog out there."

"It's coming down harder than it looks," I whispered. My throat was scratchy from the rain, and I began to sit my soggy and exhausted self into the boss's chair. A gasp of "Don't!" went up from the interns gathered around, and Eddy saved me from embarrassment with the toss of a towel. I draped it over my head like a prizefighter between rounds and remained standing.

Yes, Eddy said after I told that part. He did remember that. It was an amusing little story.

What he didn't remember, of course, and what wasn't so amusing was what happened back where I'd been. Because for him, it hadn't happened yet. And because for all concerned, it was something deadly serious.

What I'd found so startling about that long-ago day, I explained to Eddy as we sat under the tree, was the first-hand realization that the past was more than a movie of days gone by. I'd seen that movie already, or scenes from it, on earlier visits. Now I saw the past as a story about present and future, just as the present and the future are stories about the past. Seeing the full story, I told him, was about learning what other people saw. It was about knowing forces that unspooled endlessly, forces that never went away.

I guess I probably looked pretty nervous as I then put the big question to him. "You're going, right?" I was worried I may have said something that would change his mind. But Eddy nodded. Yes, he'd still go, he said. So I began unrolling my story map that would take him there.

At first, I told him, I'd been alone. In the rain. Following Eddy. This part I'd told him before. "Eddy!" I'd called as he stood at the barbershop window, but he walked away and kept going.

As I followed, we passed a grocer standing in the doorway of his shop.

We passed a streetcar disgorging passengers into the flooded street.

We came to a crowd, and that's where I lost Eddy. But it was a familiar scene, an elderly man on horseback emerging from the flood with a nearly drowned woman, a police officer wrapping the woman in a blanket. The elderly man told the officer to take the woman safely home. He did, and I followed.

With no umbrella and no hat, I was soaked and I was cold, but at least I was unencumbered. There was no need to dash into dry doorways, no need to keep to a path that ran under trees, no need to avoid puddles. I could freely follow the horse-drawn carriage that bore the officer and the woman on its slow, directed walk away from the center of town.

As the carriage and its passengers progressed, with me the lone trailing pedestrian, Main Street gave way to neighborhoods, businesses gave way to houses, and with the exception of an occasional stable or corner store, the city became residential for blocks and blocks. All gone, of course, all invisible to us today.

The procession crossed a bridge over a swollen creek, then turned a corner. One block and it eased to a stop in front of a small Victorian cottage, its yard lightly but completely submerged in an inch of water.

An automobile ran up the street, its tires cutting a pair of wakes in the steadily rising flood.

"You know," I paused in the story and told Eddy, "I think it was the car. It looked a lot like a buggy and kind of like a bug, some spindly, gangly insect. The car and the horse and the old buildings and the clothes these people were wearing—what year was it?"

He told me it sounded like 1906, the year we'd heard so much about. Enough people had cars, he recalled reading, that the city already had paved a couple of dozen streets with brick.

"Good to know," I murmured, only lightly interested in Eddy's collection of facts.

I continued with my story. "It was getting dark by then, and another car went by, but it was barely moving. The rain wasn't coming down so hard anymore, but the water was rising, and I was thinking about what must have been happening upstream, about all the rain that had fallen miles away and that was just now reaching us in the flood, when the woman I'd been following . . . ."

"Caroline," Eddy interrupted.

"Caroline," I repeated, and started again. It was then that I saw Caroline open the front door and come out of the house. She walked straight up to me and spoke. "Have you seen him?" She grabbed me by the arm. Her eyes were frantic. "Have you seen him? He's late." She said it again. "Have you seen him?" Then she turned and walked away, as fast as she could go, down the middle of the street. The water was up to her ankles.

In the growing darkness and the deepening flood, I followed, sloshing after Caroline and asking who the woman was looking for. Caroline just kept walking.

Down the neighborhood street, back toward the bridge that spanned the creek, I stayed as close as I could, followed Caroline with my questions but I got nothing in return. I wondered whether Caroline and the man had quarreled. Whether Caroline would be able to find him. Whether she'd be able to stay with him.

I had the distinct feeling, the unhappy knowledge, that this man was not Caroline's husband.

And all the while, the water continued to rise, bouncing off a high bluff on the creek's far side and flowing through a low spot in the near bank and into the neighborhood.

The water had risen almost to knee-deep when Caroline and I at once saw the man coming and Caroline churned forward. She made a wake just as the automobile had done. She stumbled and almost fell, but she kept going. Caroline left me far behind as she went for her lover's arms. He was not a tall man, but he appeared to be a powerful man, with a barrel chest and thick arms that engulfed the woman.

The lovers came together just as the flash flood arrived, a rolling, boiling wall of muddy brown.

And I forgot Caroline and ran. I ran as hard as I could without regard for hazards that might lie submerged and hidden. Barely ahead of the water's leading edge, I struggled in the deep water to the closest house and climbed the porch, a short flight of steps to a dry floor and a sheltering roof where I could stand above death.

Leaning on the railing, my heart thumping, my breath wheezing, I scanned the floodwaters. I ran the length of the house. I could see the entire property, but I saw nothing of Caroline and nothing of the man with the barrel chest. Tossed in the waves, a dog swept by, struggling to save itself. A wooden wheelbarrow crashed against the porch foundation, hung for a moment as if resting, then bounced and was carried away.

Rain fell with a new ferocity. Lightning flashed, and in the brief moments of illumination, I did gain some hope. At the point where a neighbor's yard met the swollen creek stood a massive live oak tree, its ancient and twisted branches hanging low, bowing to within easy reach from the ground. In the tree were a number of people. As the waters rose, they climbed higher.

It was at about that time that a pair of automobile lights came to life across the creek and shined on the tree. I hadn't been aware that there was anyone watching. The automobile's driver emerged, waving his arms and shouting. In the storm, I couldn't hear words, but in the beam of his headlamps, I could see the tree better. The barrel-chested man had climbed onto a stout branch. Caroline was clinging to a smaller branch. The man leaned, grabbed her around the waist, and pulled her to just below his perch, above the flood.

Across the creek, a young boy emerged from the crowd and ran to the edge of the embankment. The boy cupped his hands around his mouth as if calling to someone in the tree. The boy waited, but no answer came.

I felt powerless. All I could do was cry out, too. Then cry louder. I put both hands on the porch railing, leaned into the storm, and added my voice to the shouts from across the water and the cries from the big oak tree.

"And the next time lightning flashed," I told Eddy, "I was standing on the deck at that café, the one down by the creek."

"The one that sometimes still floods," he prompted.

"But not in the present time that day. I just stood for the longest time, staring out into the day's fog that had replaced the past's rain and trying to pull myself together. Then I walked back to the office. It was all I could think of to do."

"But you never saw Caroline fall."

"No." I whispered. "I didn't. And I should have."

"You didn't have to."

"Yes, I did." I raised my voice, then dropped it again to a whisper. "I knew she needed help, but I couldn't do a damn thing about it, standing there on the porch of that house. The water was too deep. The flood was too strong. I couldn't help her because I was just visiting—visiting the freaking past, damn it—from my freaking present. But at least I could have been a witness."

Eddy closed his eyes. After a few moments, he conceded. "Maybe so." But he kept his eyes shut.

I was worrying about what he was thinking. Was he having second thoughts about Caroline's death, wondering whether he really could follow the doomed woman, whether he could save her life, whether he could change this entire chain of events? I sure as hell hoped not. Even if he had doubts, I knew exactly where he needed to go and exactly what he needed to do.

"I just wonder." Eddy paused.

"What?"

"I wonder what happened up there. I wonder if that witness at the trial was lying when he said Alexander Lee shoved Caroline to make room for himself, to save his own life. I wonder if the county executed the right man. I wonder how everything back in 1906 affected all the years that followed and how it still affects us today."

"You know the answer to that," I replied. "It's the root of it all. So when are you going?"

thirty-nine

EDDY

Here's something I haven't told. (Bad scout.) Quite often, very often, in fact, I saw past and present together. It wasn't what Sheila saw, her visions of people from different times. It was more like what Libby experienced from her bed at the hospital, two places at once, only more benign. If I parked my truck just so in our driveway, for example, avoiding the open area directly in front of the carriage-house door, I could leave room for the McBrides' touring car to appear. The one the family had owned in the teens and early 1920s. The deep royal-blue car with wooden spoke wheels. The one the family had bought when Old Jacob's sight was still good enough for him to drive, that Hugh had never driven—in fact was afraid to drive—and that Eleanor and Lillian occasionally sneaked out for a spin, though they were forbidden to do so. Objects don't just sit there, you see. Like the old car, they do contain stories.

And so it was a few days later, when I arrived home. Tired at the end of the day, I remained in the cab of my truck, motor switched off but still making gentle pings and hisses as it cooled. I leaned forward, folded my arms across the top of the steering wheel, and rested my cheek on my wrist. Facing left, I saw the world ninety degrees from normal, and as the touring car appeared, I wondered about a world that was not so refined, one that was firmly part of the imperfect past. The vehicle's canvas roof still looked like the top of a carriage. How wet the driver and passengers must have gotten as they struggled to raise it in an unexpected rainstorm. And yet for its day, this was current. This was new. And this was good.

I turned and faced right. A missing panel revealed the inner workings of the truck's passenger door. Here was the latch that turned the lock and handle; there were the crank and gears that raised and lowered the window. On the floor lay a pair of needle-nose pliers, a vise grip, and a screwdriver, each representing a failed attempt to grab or twist or force a piece of machinery to work.

So there I was, pondering the wisdom of forcing events or letting them come naturally. The present was ragged and battered, but with a patina. The new and somewhat ideal past showed the very best it had to offer. The two eras fit. Except the past didn't have a clue how change would work. Not a damn clue what was coming.

I sighed and sat up straight, grabbed my briefcase, and pushed open the truck door. The touring car was still there. This was strange. Usually, these visions of side-by-side objects or events were fleeting, little more than moments of déjà vu. This time, when I turned around, it was my truck that was gone.

I looked into the sky, hoping for something modern, a jet contrail perhaps. I listened for the neighbor's television, usually too loud beside his open window. I sniffed for the fried scent of the donut shop that had recently opened on the next block. But there was nothing to pull me back to the present. Well, that's what you get when you make promises. A scout is obedient. My job was to watch, to follow, and when the moment was right, to seize the opportunity. Then run like hell back where I belonged, back to the present.

That was when Old Jacob and Hugh came up the front walk. The Confederate veteran held the crook of his son's elbow, just the way he'd held mine in the ice storm. He hesitated as he walked, but I don't believe he was fully blind yet. I was trying to calculate dates—early 1920s, I guessed—when I heard the clanging bell of the streetcar down at the curb and gave that my attention. Not the most gentle form of transit for an old man, with its bumping and swaying and jostling, I thought, but I was getting to know Old Jacob now, and I was certain he'd have wanted to handle whatever came his way. I was right. Once clear of the front steps, Old Jacob shook off his son's guidance and took himself to a rocking chair down at the far end of the porch.

Hugh stood by slightly bewildered, as if hoping for a "thank you" but knowing from experience, I suspected, that the old man needed his independence and that waiting for him to acknowledge help would be a long wait indeed. Hugh turned toward the door, pulling off his jacket in the process. Underneath, he wore a white uniform.

"How was the doctor?" asked Lillian, wiping her hands on her apron as she came from the kitchen.

Hugh shrugged.

Lillian turned to her father. "How was the doctor?"

"I'm still going blind," the old man replied. He reached into his pocket for his pipe.

"And the boys at the hospital?" asked Eleanor, putting an arm around Hugh's shoulders. "How are the boys today?"

Hugh shrugged and wriggled free.

His sister pinched his cheek. "I hope you talk to them more than you talk to us."

"I do."

"I hope so."

Eleanor and Lillian followed Hugh into the house, but I didn't need to hear more. I'd seen the McBrides enough to know, as family members always know, the shorthand and brief mentions that carried stories on their backs.

Even though I'd just arrived, I knew that "the boys at the hospital" were soldiers returned from the Great War, amputees with their wounds visible, and shell-shocked soldiers with their wounds deep inside. From bits and pieces of overheard conversations, I knew that Hugh helped men from their beds to wicker wheelchairs and gave them a place in the sun on the hospital's broad second-story verandah between its fat, white columns. I knew that Hugh carried their bedpans when that was necessary, read letters from home when the men were lonely, and cried with them when they were afraid of dying.

Their stories were tragically sad. A whistle blows. Soldiers rise from their trenches, "over the top" it was called, advancing toward enemy guns. Of course there was a pattern here. Earlier, soldiers stared at death in a farmer's field. Sailors floated alone, helplessly riding the ocean's swells. A very definite pattern. A man nurses a boy with measles. The boy heals and the man succumbs. It's about duty and loyalty and honor and following what has to be done.

"Brother," I overheard Lillian in the kitchen.

"Yes?" replied Hugh. Peering through the window, I saw him standing by as Eleanor stoked the fire in the wood stove and Lillian vigorously pumped water until it poured from the well spout in the sink. Hugh handed Lillian a cake of soap and stepped aside.

"Have you seen the new nurse?" asked Lillian, scrubbing under the cold water.

"I hear she is peculiar," said Eleanor, standing by with a hand towel, waiting her turn to clean up.

I stepped closer to the window to hear better. "Who's there?" called Old Jacob, turning toward my footsteps.

As quietly as I could, I lowered myself to sit on the porch floor, hidden as well as I could manage behind the row of chairs. Old Jacob stared toward me, furrowing his brow and drawing down his eyebrows, but eventually relaxing. He returned to his pipe and his rocking. He faced the sun.

"Where is she from?" Lillian was asking. "Have you heard anything?"

"She says she's not from here," replied Hugh. He paused for the longest time. From the floor below the window, I couldn't see him, but knowing Hugh as I did by then, I imagined him doing something routinely obsessive, like drying the cake of soap. "But," he finally said, "I have the strangest idea that she is. She is from here."

The sisters found this hard to believe. The woman, they said they'd been told, wore her hair in a length unlike any other woman her age. It was not uncut, but it was not "bobbed" short either. She arrived at work in trousers. She spoke to men on their own terms and carried herself with a certain insolence. But mostly, she seemed out of place because she seemed physically lost. The story was that she did not know how to crank the telephone. She did not know where to find the farmers' market. When she rounded a corner downtown, more often than not she'd stop in her tracks, staring at a building that had stood fifty years as if she'd never seen it before.

"I've seen her," said Hugh. "I think she has something to prove, and to do it I think she has to be from here."

Damn right. Libby was from here and so was I. This news was manna from heaven. This gave me the chance to complete my own mission. I was thinking I'd landed here because this was a time and a place that was important to me. That's how seeing the past worked. I didn't need to know what year Libby was in. Sheila'd been wrong about that. Not 1906. Fifteen years later was the ticket. All I'd needed was to let the past take me.

I slid toward the porch steps and commenced walking. Smoothly. Briskly. Apparently not so quietly. Old Jacob sat up straight, old-soldier straight, pipe in hand, pointing with the stem in my direction. "Who's there?" he called as if he were a Confederate again, standing picket and challenging an enemy in the dark. I did not slow my pace.

Across the street from the hospital, under an ancient oak, I took up my own sentry station. Another bit of the past gone, I thought, as I slowly circled the trunk, trailing fingertips around its bumpy circumference. It wasn't so long ago that I'd replaced this tree myself with a professional building for some bunch of doctors. I hadn't really wanted that to happen. It was just the way of the world.

But sometimes the intersection of past and present brought exactly what I wanted. Now it was Libby, alighting from a streetcar a half-block away and walking in my direction. I took a step forward and stopped. This was how Sheila had always seen the past, dotted with people from the present. I'd been fully in the past by myself, and I'd had those fleeting, parallel glimpses of two times at once, but this total immersion in the same time and place as others was new to me. Even as Libby drew near, I couldn't tell whether she was aware of me or not. She seemed focused elsewhere. Then when her eyes finally caught mine, an astonished look came over her face. Libby clasped one hand on the wide-brimmed hat she was wearing and ran the remaining way. As she threw her arms around my neck, the hat danced into the street. There was a chill breeze blowing. A chilly look of disapproval, too, from people walking nearby.

I didn't know how to take Libby's greeting. Was she simply amazed at finding me at this time and place? Or was she clinging to a friend from the long lost future? Was she afraid to let go, afraid that if she didn't hold on to my present time that she'd slide permanently into the abyss?

I reached behind my neck and gently untwined her arms. "How long have you been here?"

"Days, maybe weeks," she said.

"And?" I asked over my shoulder as I stepped quickly to retrieve her hat from the street.

"I have a room in a boarding house. I come to the hospital. I go back to the room. Life is very simple."

But life was not simple. It never was.

At first she'd been frightened, she told me, by her separation from the familiar. She'd feared she might never see her own time again. But as the days passed, her fear went away. So I'd been wrong about her clinging. Libby may have been embracing me as an almost-lost friend, but she'd also embraced her new time and her new people. Libby told me she knew them more intimately than she'd known anything or anyone before.

Libby said she knew the patients in the hospital, the boys home from the war but not at all where they'd been a short year or two earlier. She knew Uncle Hugh, working as an orderly beside her but frozen into a childlike state. The other nurses had been quick to tell her about the trauma he'd suffered nearly fifteen years earlier from seeing a man hanged. She knew the outpatient Old Jacob, physically almost blind to the present, but holding on to the sights he'd known from the previous century, and in his own way keenly aware of the world.

"What do you do?" I asked.

"Nursing. Cleaning," Libby said. "Anything that helps." Whatever she did could have greater meaning, she told me she'd discovered, if her actions were small. Sometimes living and working here seemed her punishment for trying to kill Hugh. Sometimes it seemed her reward for not succeeding.

"Is it enough?"

"I've learned how to cope with disappointment," Libby said. "The boys in the hospital, Hugh, Old Jacob. Life is not what they thought it would be, if they'd ever thought it would be anything. Hugh was so young at the hanging. He didn't have a chance to make any plans. Then he had to live with what he saw. And in the end, he lived with it for a very, very long time. He had more impact on the future than anyone else in your family."

I looked up at the columns that lined the front of Libby's and Hugh's place of employment. I squinted into the brightness and thought how Hugh had killed my brother Stan, and then I relaxed as a bank of clouds moved across the sun. From the horizon, darker clouds were moving our way.

"Libby," I began. I turned back toward my friend. No, her hair was indeed not bobbed, but she did have a look about her of a simpler time, a look of peace that I'd never seen on her face before. Hell, it was a look I'd never seen on anyone's face. Should I stay out of this? Is this the way the world wants to be? I thought of the other Libby, lying in her hospital bed. "It's time to go home," I said.

"I am home," Libby replied.

Now that did seem true. But I knew from Libby's previous behavior, from her short-lived attention to the florist shop, from her tendency to run—run back home from a failed marriage or to the cemetery clutching Burned Up Baby—that events seldom turned out as she thought they would. Save Libby from herself? You bet. This life she'd found, nursing or atoning or whatever it was, looked suspiciously like running again. So saving Libby was exactly what I had to do. Bring Libby back from the past or change the past. It was a choice, but only a slight one. I had to do something. Otherwise, she'd never wake up in the hospital.

How to save her was another matter. Keep her close, for sure. Make certain she noticed what I noticed. If I looked, I could find something in the air that would break into our awareness of the past, something that would take us to the present with its own power. We'd be safe. But I said it before: Life was never simple.

"I can't do that," Libby said, as if reading my mind.

"What do you mean?"

"I can't leave what I've started. I can't go back to my old ways."

They're not such bad ways, I thought. Well, maybe they were, but they were the ways we'd all evolved to and they were the ways she needed to follow.

"Eddy, Eddy," she gently scolded in an old-fashioned kind of way. "You're always so transparent. You're the one who always told the truth, who believed everyone else was telling it, too."

And why not, pray tell? Libby was acting so straightforward, but she was living someone else's life. I wanted to grab her by the shoulders and shake some sense into her.

A block away the courthouse clock began to chime. "Look," said Libby. "I've got to go."

I thought of throwing a burlap sack over her head, slinging her over my shoulder, and heading for . . . where? Instead I asked, "Are you okay with this?"

She nodded.

"Really okay?" I asked again.

"My shift's beginning right now. What are you going to do?"

I shrugged.

"No, of course not," she said. "You've been to this time and this place, but you don't really know them." She put the palm of her hand against my cheek in a gesture that could have meant either affection or discipline. She could have been the adult now and I could still have been the boy she'd known long ago, the boy whose faithfulness and support she needed.

"Don't worry about me. I'll be fine," she said. "You just go. But be careful. You be careful." Libby turned, gave a quick, second-nature glance at a car approaching from a block away, and sprinted across the street, her hand again holding her hat in place. At the hospital's entrance, she paused and waved. I sensed a hint of melancholy, a hint of bittersweet in the gesture, but before I could be sure, Libby disappeared through the hospital doors.

In the distance was the throaty bass of rolling thunder. No more puffy clouds. Blackness was stretching across the sky, horizon to horizon. I could smell the rain.

Up on the hospital verandah, between the columns, a nurse appeared. Libby? But the figure never showed her face. She quickly leaned over to unlock the brakes on a patient's wheelchair, and when she stood again, she was already spinning the chair around in retreat.

I felt the temperature falling with the weather. The wind sent loose papers skipping down the sidewalk and leaves spinning upside down in the trees, showing their bellies.

So Sheila had been right after all.

I'd really hoped I could bring Libby back, change just this one person's actions, and avoid disrupting the full history. But Libby's work in the 1920s was not the time. Sheila hadn't shown me the flood and told me what she knew of Caroline's death because she thought it made an interesting story. She'd pointed me to 1906 because she knew that's where I needed to go. And because changing all of history was what I needed to do.

forty

Ahead of the rain came the dog and the cat. The pursuer was a dirty, brown cur of a thing. That's about all I noticed. The animal meant little to me; it registered no familiarities; it made no connection to anything in my life. The pursued was another matter.

The cat flashed by faster than the dog, but I saw it all, this subtly tiger-striped creature, gentle little yellow tabby, Ike's near-twin, running for its life. Or Ike himself. Ike! I took a step, two steps, as if to rescue it, then stopped short. Where was I? Yes, the hospital sidewalk. But what time? I was lost, as disoriented as if I'd dreamed without realizing I'd fallen asleep. Had I bounced again to the present? Was this Ike at all?

From down the block came a yowling scream. I stiffened. I saw the brown dog backing away from the foundation plantings at the side of a house, whipping its head hard, snapping a neck, killing something small. The rain began to fall and the dog continued to shake the lifeless body. The rain fell harder as I approached. The dog ran. On a windowsill above sat the yellow tabby, sheltered from the weather, face never betraying emotion, looking impassive in the cat way, not telling what it knew about the killing and the victim, though surely it knew something. Maybe it knew a lot. But the dog was gone and the cat was mute and I was again without any clues as to my time and place.

I couldn't help but think of what Tim had said that day he'd stalked and photographed Ike. A cat makes a good subject because it can be your cat or your grandfather's cat. A person dates a scene. A person tells you exactly where and when you are. Something like that.

No, it was exactly like that. And as soon as the people appeared, I knew where and when I was. I also knew what I had to do.

At a shop downtown, it was just as Sheila had told me it would be. The barrel-chested grocer was guarding his wares. "Good afternoon," I said, trying to be civil, but civility was hard. I recognized the man instantly as the cigar-smoking son of a bitch who'd taken Hugh to the hanging. Lightning flashed and the grocer looked skyward. Screw civility. I palmed one of his apples, stuffed it into my pocket, and headed down the street.

I'd arrived just in time. Only a moment later the grocer threw a tarp over his sidewalk apples and shoved his display against the building. Closing early, it appeared. The grocer hoisted his apron over his head with one hand while lifting his suit jacket from a peg by the door with the other.

I paused and in the reflection of another store's window pretended to be buttoning my shirt and adjusting my coat collar against the rain. Behind me, I could see the man reflected clearly.

Now he was walking in my direction, only a block away. He seemed in a hurry, still wrestling into his suit jacket. Preoccupied with some destination and dodging streams of rainwater that ran from shop awnings and splashed onto the sidewalk, he'd been successful at getting only one arm into a sleeve. He stopped as I had, sheltered by an awning, water streaming behind him, staring at his window image. He finished with his jacket. Then he was straightening his lapels, smoothing his hair, adjusting his derby hat. Handsome, barrel-chested devil. Vanity takes precedence even over haste, I suppose. And when he was satisfied, this man's man, ladies' man, fighter, lover, or whatever he imagined himself to be turned and stepped with distinct purpose into the full force of the storm.

Watching the grocer's routine closely, I absently and somewhat automatically took a bite of my illicit apple. It was mealy.

I shouldn't have been surprised that this man would sell fruit beyond its prime, and when I spit out my bite onto the sidewalk, I was sorry he wasn't close enough that I could get it on his shoes. Well, stealing an apple had been worth the try. It had been a puny effort, but I just couldn't leave the shop without doing something to avenge Hugh.

I'd done what I could for Hugh the boy with this boyish gesture, this prankish theft that seemed suited to this simpler time and place. Except simple was about to move toward the future, and simple was about to grow complicated. After the hanging, Hugh would never be the same. Our family history and my friend Libby's fate would be set in motion. Unless, of course, I could put a stop to events.

I turned and stepped into the rain and the darkening night. Now I was stepping with a purpose. And now I was stepping lively. I needed to move fast to keep up with the prideful grocer. He had a couple of blocks' lead. We both faced wind and rain. I kept my head down.

Time is a river, right? Maiden aunts in the parlor, baseball on the radio, a sailor going away and returning from the war, these were the events of midstream. They moved smoothly and steadily. Then they were gone.

A brother dies, and the river takes a sharp turn.

But time isn't just the shining surface ribbon where we float, maybe smoothly and safely, maybe fighting the current. I think that if time is a river it is something that travelers are submerged in, and I think that time hides whatever travels with it. There's silt and there are fish and there is lots and lots of trash. Then along comes a person who can see underwater, like a swimmer in a clear stream. Maybe it's me. That person can see, maybe even reach out and touch, all the events that make a life. He can see the currents of life swirl over holes on the river bottom, around the pylons that support bridges, across the tree stumps and tumbled stones of submerged garden walls if the river has grown beyond its original banks or been dammed into a lake. He can see the sunken beer cans, the underwater automobiles, all the lost and rusty memories and ruins that most people hope never to see again.

But that's what floats through the present. To really see the past, the swimmer has to go upstream. Up to the headwater.

Sheila had said to go deeper, and I had. For the first time, I'd jumped straight from one past event to another, like hopping logs floating in that river without first returning to shore. One moment, I'd seen Libby outside the hospital; the next, I was chasing the source of our family tragedy. Above, thunder became the cannons of Old Jacob's Antietam, but I was no longer worried about being dragged deeper than I wanted to go. This was the deep time and the deep place I needed. Hell, it was the time and place Libby needed and Stan needed and most of the people in our family needed. This was as far as I needed to go. I was sure of it.

Thinking and walking, I really didn't need to look up. Sheila had pointed me in the direction I should go, aiming me toward the big tree at the flooding creek. But keeping my head down ended up being a mistake. Because the next time I did look up, the grocer was gone. And I could walk no farther.

I was standing at the top of a bluff, the high, six- or eight-foot creek bank overlooking swollen and rushing waters. The flood was moving swiftly at the base of this cliff and its channel was deep. Across the way and twenty yards or so downstream, the flood was streaming over a lower embankment, sneaking out to slowly drown yards and gardens and city streets.

There was a bridge, but if the grocer had crossed, he must have been one of the last. By the time I arrived, the bridge itself was still clear, but water had flooded the neighborhood on the opposite side so completely that police had blocked passage. Even pedestrians were forbidden from crossing. Atop the bluff, a small crowd was beginning to gather.

"We won't be getting across here," a man said. He was climbing down from an automobile that had pulled to a stop in the middle of the street. It was just as Sheila had described it. Cars did look like spindly, gangly bugs, with their awkward black bodies and wide eyes for headlamps.

"How long does this usually last?" I was growing anxious. Among the people gathered at the creek, I alone knew what was about to happen, and my self-assurance was disappearing fast.

"Hour. Maybe less." Now the man was climbing back into his vehicle, under the shelter of its canvas top. In the dry car, he rolled and lit a cigarette. "It's best if we wait."

"You live over there?" I asked, gesturing at the other side of the water.

"I do. Me and the wife and our three boys. They should be at home now."

"Is your house . . . ."

"It's a block from the creek. Everyone should be safe."

Standing here in the dim glow of fading daylight, here at the top of the bluff, I could do nothing more than watch the floodwaters rise. Tragedy would fall with the night. I would see Caroline Simms die. I knew it would happen. I stood with a blank mind, staring into the rain, which had let up enough for me to stand out in the open, not thinking this time, just feeling. And waiting.

"Robert Simms," said the man in the automobile. He put his cigarette in the corner of his mouth and held out his hand. "Men's haberdashery. Accessories mostly. Collars, cuffs, ties. What's your business?"

I shook the offered hand limply. "Architecture."

"Anything I'd know?"

But I did not let go of his grip. "No," I offered softly. "It's all somewhere else." No, this man would not know my work, but I knew this man. At least I recognized the name. This was Caroline's husband. Poor, doomed Caroline. Poor, unknowing husband. My grip grew tighter and I held Robert Simms's hand longer than I really should, until Simms pulled back and I quickly let go.

The salesman removed the cigarette. "You all right?" he asked.

"Oh," I answered. "Sure. I was just thinking about something else." I nodded toward a pair of black-leather cases in the automobile's back seat. "Your samples?"

Simms was a talker. He told me about his line of haberdashery and his territory and how he'd bought his automobile as much to impress his customers as to get around. There were a growing number of automobiles in the city, but his arrival still drew a crowd, always sparked conversation, always gave the impression that this was a man who knew what he was talking about. If he was up-to-date when it came to automobiles, wouldn't he be up-to-date when it came to haberdashery?

Or up-to-date with greenhouse horticulture and teasing jokes and white, convertible car tops, I thought. It's all too familiar and not what it's cracked up to be, isn't it, this hard-won cheer before a change-everything loss?

"My wife's not too happy about all this," Simms admitted, immediately proving me right. But he was matter-of-fact about it. He spoke as if he had confided this personal detail so often that it was no longer personal, as if he had learned to live so well with a difficult arrangement that it was no longer difficult. "I'm away too much, she says."

I nodded. Over Simms's shoulder, I was watching the rising flood. And I was still looking for the grocer.

On the city streets beyond, an automobile and a number of horse-drawn buggies had passed earlier, but the streets were quiet now, just water. Hard rain was starting up again. And the flood continued to rise.

"Caroline?" Suddenly it was Simms staring, like me, across the water. He appeared stunned, as if someone had slapped him. He stepped slowly, almost robotically from his automobile, tossing his cigarette into a puddle as if ending one occupation to make way for another. His eyes were riveted across the river.

There, a woman was wading through deep and rushing water, and when lightning flashed, her identity was clear. Caroline Simms had left the safety of her house and was pushing her way toward death.

"Where?" her husband whispered. "Where is she . . . ?" The woman stumbled in the water, as if she had stepped in a hole or bumped the curb. Simms gasped. Then his wife was walking faster, almost running. A man was helping her, a man with a big chest and dapper clothes and an assured manner and the strength to climb into a big tree and pull her up after him.

"Caroliiiiiiine!" Simms called and the crowd turned his way. Simms was shouting and waving his arms. "Caroliiiiiiiine!" Above the roaring waters, no one on the other side could hear.

Now Simms was cranking the engine of his automobile, and when the motor caught, he was running to take the wheel. He was backing the vehicle and training his headlamps on the tree. The evening was growing dark now, but if we couldn't hear, at least there was a way we still could see.

The salesman was an optimist. He reached out and clapped his hand on my shoulder. "She's safe," he exhaled heavily. Simms was breathing hard from his fear and from the exertion of cranking the engine. "And that man saved her. Thank God for that man."

Not really. I knew Caroline was going to die. I remembered that son of a bitch grocer hadn't been so damn noble at the hanging. I couldn't imagine him a hero now. I wished I had another way to get at him, something more than stealing a mealy apple, but I kept quiet.

"Caroliiiiiiine!" Simms continued calling as if his voice could somehow ride the beams of his headlamps to the tree. Maybe it could. Sound definitely could ride the wind, and snippets of voices occasionally drifted over from the tree to the bluff.

"We waited too long," one of the voices said.

"That's Carrie! That's my wife!" cried Simms. "Wherever she was going . . . ." He spoke as if his wife were headed on a simple errand, as if he forgave her for an ordinary mistake in timing.

I suspected differently. Perhaps Caroline was wishing she'd run an errand earlier in the day, though I knew, as her husband didn't, that whatever she was trying to do earlier had also trapped her in a flood. Or perhaps Caroline had wished to run away. Perhaps she'd long sought to escape a lonely marriage to a mild and courteous salesman and run to the strength of another man, a rougher man. In those circumstances, how long was too long to wait? A week, a year? Any wait was too long now. In a storm, too long could be a matter of seconds.

10:36. That's what the pendant watch said, and that, it was obvious now, was the hour of the tragedy. I raised my wrist to look at my own watch, but quickly folded my arms, wrist in armpit, everything modern out of sight. The time was near; that's all I needed to know. There was nothing I could do.

And the waters kept rising.

A dog struggled and a wheelbarrow floated in the waves. The same that Sheila had seen. I stepped to the edge of the bluff, the better to scan the houses across the water. Rain was falling hard, but there in the distance, on the porch of a cottage, I could make out a figure. There was a young woman, a twenty-something woman, calling and crying. The keening sound of her frantic and mourning voice was broken and interrupted in the storm, but enough made it across the waters for me to know Sheila.

She was seeing the tragedy from one side of the flood and from her youth. I was seeing it from the other side and my present day. Sheila was shredding her throat out of fear and frustration. I was continuing to quietly watch and listen.

In the fading light, a mattress, buoyant but ungainly in the water, wallowed in the waves, and I wanted to ask who'd slept there. Whoever they were, they were gone now. I recalled accounts I'd read in the newspaper I'd picked up at the hanging. How had the writer put it? "The bodies of strong men, delicate women, and innocent children."

I forced myself to see whatever I could see.

forty-one

Now a small boy, maybe seven or eight years old, ran to the edge of the bluff and joined the wailing chorus. He was one of many who knew souls in the tree, one of many as frightened and anxious as Robert Simms. They all wanted to help, but like the boy, they all were helpless. They could only cry and watch.

That, I also could do. And I could learn. The past is a big and complicated story. As is the present. As is the future.

The day I'd seen my brother snapped and dragged by the Cadillac, I'd witnessed the unity of the world around me, the flamingo-decorated screen doors, the playing cards in bicycle spokes, and the concrete ducks waddling across a lawn. I'd seen the details that make a time a time and a place a place.

But it had taken Libby to see the entire event and solve the mystery of my brother's death. I was glad she'd done it. I just wished the price hadn't been so high. Especially since I could tell we weren't finished paying.

Now there was a hand on my shoulder. And I did not need to turn to know who it was.

This was not Robert Simms, not a character who would appear briefly and walk away. This was the one person who tied all these years together, and I was not surprised to meet him here.

"You have to do it, you know," Walter Lee said.

I still did not turn.

"You have to save my father."

The boy at the edge of the bluff continued to shout into the night, and I knew that these two, the man and the boy, were the same. The innocent boy Walter Lee, about to be orphaned by events that were out of his control. The intruding adult Walter Lee, who hoped against hope that his fate, for years sealed, could now be reopened and reversed. Like me, he had journeyed to the headwaters.

Walter Lee gestured for me to come closer. I recognized the "follow me" wave from our other vigil in the darkness, that night we'd stood outside Mr. Peacock's homecoming party, and it startled me. "You help my family," the old man said, "and you'll help your family."

I was incredulous. "You're bargaining with me?" I shouted into the wind. "Right here, right now, when people are in danger of dying, you're bargaining?"

"Where did you think all this was leading?" Walter Lee replied. "Some interesting tidbit about your family? A little something to satisfy your curiosity?" Walter Lee leaned close. "This is not about you. It never was."

"Papa! Papa!" called the boy at the edge of the bluff. He cupped his hands around his mouth, but no one across the waters could hear. And no one on the bluff other than the adult Walter Lee and myself seemed to care. Each person had his own worries.

"If you want to save your friend," Walter Lee said, "you have to do it."

Do what? Sure, a condemned man deserved as much compassion as an innocent one. I knew that. Walter Lee's father was as much a tragic figure as Caroline Simms. But do what? Alexander Lee wasn't about to drown. It was Caroline who needed saving.

"Caroliiiiiiiine!" Simms was calling.

Walter Lee put his hand again on my shoulder. "I can't swim," he whispered.

This was no deal he was offering. The old man had boxed me into a corner, and he'd boxed me in damn tight. Walter Lee had a plan, he'd had it all along, and I was his means to that end. He had a mission, and it would, damn it, it would be followed.

It was then that the automobile's headlamps began to flicker. Simms slapped one of them with his open palm and the beam shot up into the dark, rainy sky.

"Put it back!" Walter Lee cried, immediately tearing away from me and raising one hand as if he were about the pummel the salesman. He was pointing frantically at the tree with the other. "Put it back now!"

Simms made another attempt at an adjustment, forcing the headlamp into more or less the right position, then climbed behind the wheel, maneuvered the car slightly, and the scene we'd been watching went totally black. Had it not been for the wails and cries for help coming faintly across the waters, the tree could have disappeared from the earth. Simms pulled his automobile ahead, closer to the edge of the bluff, stopping beside the boy above the flood.

The refocused headlamps shone brighter on the tree and we all breathed a sigh of relief.

"Edward McBride," commanded Walter Lee returning to my side. "You have to do it. These events and this place have been waiting. If you want to help your family and your friend, the time has come."

What had that old bastard done? Was Libby some kind of hostage to events? Was she some kind of bait for me? It sure looked that way. I needed to know, I needed to consider what he'd done, I needed to ponder my options, but hell, there was no time for any of that, no time for me to be Eddy. Because when I turned toward Walter Lee again he was gone. Only this time and this place remained. Those and an expectation. More than ever before, when it came to Libby and history, I had no choice.

In the lights that shone on the tree, I could clearly see Caroline Simms clinging to safety. I could see others as well. Above Caroline, on a larger, sturdier limb clung the dapper, barrel-chested grocer, grabbing mightily for his own life. Below Caroline, holding the trunk and standing precariously on the nub of a broken limb, was a painfully familiar man in a farmer's working clothes. Maybe a half-dozen others were scattered across the tree's remaining limbs.

And the tree began to move.

Slightly at first, listing toward the water.

People screamed and three or four scrambled to branches that were high or away from the rushing water.

And the tree stood still.

And rain fell harder.

"Caroliiiiiiiiine!" cried Simms.

The boy on the bluff cupped his hands once again and shouted whatever he was shouting into the night, into the fury that swallowed all but its own sounds.

My God, I thought, how frightened the people in the tree must be. I looked down into the waters at the base of the bluff and heard what they heard and saw what they saw. The dark only thinly masked roaring and swirling and certain death.

Robert Simms's headlamps flashed across the waves revealing whitecaps and whirlpools and the debris of life. A chair, a broken fence. Hell, the gable end and a large section of a roof arrived like a raft, crashed against one of the supporting columns of the bridge, and disappeared under the waves.

Simms was shaking with fear. "Oh, the baby, the baby."

And at once I knew, just as I'd known my shared family histories and the stories of shell-shocked boys. I knew that this tragedy also had its secret. Libby had sensed it that night in the cemetery. There should have been a little stone lamb at Caroline Simms's grave, a lamb for the baby that was never born. A lamb for the baby that was the child of . . . was it Robert Simms? Or the grocer?

"Oh, the baby," Simms whimpered, and I knew that the baby was the grocer's, that Simms did not know this, but that the kind and gentle salesman would forgive his wife anything. Whether she would forgive herself, and how the grocer would fit into the puzzle, the answers to these were about to go to the bottom of the flood with Caroline.

And they would go now, right now, as the tree shifted again and the refugees in its branches screamed and Caroline lost her grip and began to fall. And I once again saw events all together, beginning with a glimpse of another man's watch. He pulled it from his pocket just then and flipped it open. The time was 10:36.

I saw Caroline slip slowly, almost tentatively, from her place on the tree, and I could see a look of surprise more than fear on her face. She could have been tumbling toward a dunking in a favorite swimming hole on a hot summer's day.

I saw the grocer tighten his grip on the limb above. He made no move to reach out, no move to save his lover. Son of a bitch. He's big and he's strong and he's a coward. But more than that. Because the next thing I saw was a thin flash of a smile, maybe a smile of relief, and I realized that the grocer was willing to let Caroline go. And with her, the problem of his child. "Ain't nothing wrong with seeing justice," the grocer had said to his friends at the hanging. The words had rattled around in my head for months. Now I understood their cruelty. There was no justice here.

I saw the farmer below, the man who seemed familiar, reach out with one hand from his own precarious perch and grab Caroline's wrist as she fell. She dangled a moment and grasped with her other hand at the man's strong arm. But one arm was all he had to spare, and Caroline was writhing and jerking with too much force. She knew her fate now, and she wanted none of it, neither its certainty nor its finality. She writhed too hard and jerked too many times and the farmer could hold her no longer. Caroline Simms dropped into the muddy, brown flood and disappeared beneath its waves.

Exhausted, the farmer pulled himself onto the branch that Caroline had occupied. "I am not guilty of murder," Alexander Lee would say before he was hanged. "I am only guilty of trying to escape that flood." But in the eyes of the law, he was indeed guilty. Doomed to drop through the gallows' trapdoor in a matter of weeks, he may as well have dropped into the flood with Caroline that night.

The barrel-chested grocer, the false witness, would see to that.

Now I knew what had to happen.

"You have to do it," Walter Lee had told me. "You have to save my father."

And the old man was right. Walter Lee, the red thread that ran through ninety years of our shared story, had seen it all. It was indeed his father who mattered.

The key to stopping the serial tragedies of my family and friends was not simply in saving Caroline Simms and her unborn child. It was that saving Caroline would spare Walter Lee's father a death sentence. And if Alexander Lee were spared hanging, well, there'd be no need to worry about Uncle Hugh and my brother, Stan, and Mr. Peacock and Libby. Especially Libby. She'd return to the present. There'd be no need for her penance in the past. I could stop the entire chain of trauma and depression and hit-and-run and suicide.

Oh, to hell with events as I'd known them. Over the top!

Any hesitation and I, too, would have waited too long.

So I advanced to the edge of the bluff, glanced almost casually at the flood below, and stepped into the air. A scout is brave, I thought as I fell. But that was to encourage myself. In reality, a scout just does what he has to do.

I landed the way a lifeguard lands, feet first, legs scissored front to back and brought quickly together as I hit the water, arms spread like wings at the shoulder so that on impact my head would not go under. It worked. From water level, I looked up at the tree and the bluff looming tall. It was a perspective that made me feel small and lost. Freaking Alvin Peacock, a sailor waiting to be picked up and floated home. I held that thought a moment before a wave roared by and I went under.

I wondered whether Caroline had submerged quickly. I wondered whether she had tried to swim.

I bobbed to the surface and twisted in every direction, trying to spot her above the water.

Another wave, and I sank again. I wondered if Caroline had been carried too deep to find the surface.

Now, it's quite obvious that swimming in water is different than walking through air. It's not our normal process. But people do it all the time. Was Caroline listening? Water's just thicker. Caroline, where were you? And so it is with the past, I thought as I sank deeper, and so it is with the present. We can move from one . . . .

I remember interrupting myself. Pay attention! I was under water, the night was dark, the suspended mud was almost solidly opaque, and I was completely disoriented. I had to quit thinking and act. Otherwise, I'd drown with her.

I blew air from my nose, opened my eyes, and watched the bubbles rise. I knew the direction to swim. I broke the surface and gasped.

Three submersions and you're out, that's the popular wisdom. I'd had my two. But what does an old saying know? I sank and surfaced many more times. Each time I lusted, desperately lusted for breath, and each time I knew—I did not have to think; I instantly knew—how the past and the present, the people in each of those times, my own visions and efforts, how all of them fit. It was more than my life. It was the entirety of time, as it were, passing before my eyes.

I knew a duty to the people whose lives I could save. It was the duty a person undertakes when stepping into danger is the only option. It was a knowledge that danger happens every day, that it happens emotionally and that it happens spiritually even if it is not so dramatic as a war or a storm.

I surfaced, breathed, and was pulled under again.

I knew the futility of blame. The tree had shifted and Caroline had fallen. Alexander Lee, who did not know her, had innocently tried to save her. Her lover, who'd fathered her unborn child, had selfishly sat and watched. But she was already gone. Sometimes even the most horrid events were just events and sometimes there was no human cause.

I surfaced and sank.

I knew it wasn't any one thing that had killed Caroline. Underwater, I heard each raindrop plonk on the surface. The sound was like crinkling cellophane. On the surface, raindrops stung, as if they were ice pellets. Plonks and pellets. Sure, raindrops made the flood. But it was their collective force that did the damage.

I thrashed. If only I could save Caroline. That would be duty fulfilled, justice achieved, worldly forces overcome. But it also would be just another event. Just an event that had happened.

One time I brushed against something soft, a flowing and diaphanous thing, a dress or a net or maybe only the water. I grabbed at the muddy wave where I'd felt it, but nothing was there. Whatever it was—or maybe it had been nothing at all, another movement, another worldly force—it was gone forever.

I never did see the drowning woman.

What I did see, or what I dreamed, was a car floating in the flood only a few yards from where I was swimming.

The driver sat in the window, terrified, and when the car began to roll, I dived deep to avoid being trapped under the vehicle's mass. I dived deeper than I'd ever dived before.

I'd never seen this part of my dream, this long-ago reality of Mr. Peacock's drowning, this hallucinated version. I thought I should stay underwater, hug the bottom, and remain in the past for a good damn long time. Maybe I should drown after all.

But I couldn't do that. I couldn't give in to a dream, a hallucination or the past, I couldn't give in to any of them, and finally, on surfacing one more time, I willed myself toward a scrubby bush at the edge of the water. I grabbed hold and made it my anchor. Caroline was gone; I knew that. She'd stayed deep in the flood, deep in her own time. And there was nothing more I could do. Nothing but save myself.

I crawled as far as I could onto a sandy little beach, a calm and sheltered spot at a bend in the creek, but when I collapsed my legs still lay in the water, the waves of the flood washing over them. I rolled onto my back and let the rain fall in my face. The simplicity and immediacy of a gentle rain. After the flood's dunking and dragging and pummeling, it brought me back to the present. It was very nice, very gentle, very comforting. And it pissed me off immensely.

forty-two

Someone was scooping through the sand and grabbing at my armpits, reaching up from under my shoulders, dragging me out of the water, and lowering me to the beach. The person leaned over. Seeing if I was all right, I supposed. I blinked twice and jerked my head to the side. I felt terribly agitated. It could have been the water on my face. I just needed to shake it off. More likely, it was the fact that I recognized this person, this supposed Good Samaritan.

"Go away," I moaned. "Just go away." I rolled onto my stomach and pushed up to my knees. Walter Lee peeled off his heavy coat and draped it across my shoulders against the early-morning, wet-clothes cold. He tucked his hands behind the bib of his overalls and waited.

I gazed mournfully at the creek. I could just barely make it out in the cloud-covered, starless pre-dawn, but I could see that it wasn't rushing like it had been during the flood, like ninety years ago (hell, like about two minutes ago), when Caroline Simms had died. The water was flowing steadily, filling the channel from side to side, but it was staying within its banks. Very well mannered, that water. I stood and the coat fell to the ground.

I stepped into the water, ankle-deep, knee-deep, thigh-deep. Around me the surface was flat. There was only the slightest ripple against my legs, but I did make an impression. The water flowed around me, came back together, and stretched the long tail of a wake downstream.

All I'd wanted was to know the past. Then I could have had my way with it. If I'd understood it, I could have managed it, right? If I'd known the facts, I could have changed the ones that needed changing. I could have saved the people who needed saving.

Never happened. Because in reality, nothing had been in my control. The past had kept its secrets and it had spat me out. Like I said: I was pissed.

Returning to shore, I stopped shy of the little beach, still about ankle-deep. I gave the water a place-kicker, soccer-player, surface-skimming kick. Son of a bitch past. And my shoe, made slick and loose by being wet, went flying. It landed right side up in midstream, a little boat. Then it sank. It went down with the old tires and burger wrappers and whatever other kinds of crap were under there.

"Walter Lee," I said as I continued to shore, one shoe on, one shoe off and limping. I paused and wiggled my heavier foot until the other shoe plopped onto the sand. I threw it after its mate.

"Walter Lee, do you know what I hate? I hate it when some positive-thinking, do-gooder, Pollyanna busybody says that everything happens for a reason."

In the nighttime dark, my Samaritan stepped forward and draped the coat on me again. "Thank you," he said.

"You tell me. Why did I just lose my shoe? And then throw the other one after it? Why did Caroline Simms die? And my brother? Was there a plan?"

"Thank you," the old man repeated. "Thank you for trying to save my father. Thank you for trying to right a wrong."

"The world's about backstory." I was deep into my own thoughts and shivering now with both cold and anger. I pulled the coat tighter. "Backstory is sitting right there, holding us down, and pinning us in place, keeping us under its thumb with its unchangeable and immutable, its historical, already-locked-into-place self. There's no way events are looking ahead. If anything, they're looking backward. But we don't pay enough attention. We just take off blind and we go."

I pulled up my socks, buttoned the coat, and began walking toward town. "And then we crash," I muttered as I passed Walter Lee.

He handed me a handkerchief and I took a couple of swipes at the creek water (or had it been replaced by raindrops?) that clung to my eyebrows. I appreciated the loan, but enough was enough. "It's time for you to go away," I said. The hired man fell in walking behind me, and I stopped. We weren't even off the beach. "You nearly killed me."

I dragged the handkerchief across my face once again, wadded it up, and threw it at him. Weighted with water, the white square stayed a round ball and landed at Walter Lee's feet. He retrieved it from the mud and began methodically folding.

"Well, shit," I burst, "if you're not going to leave, at least say something."

The rain had stopped and the stars, what few I could see above the city's ground lights, were slowly making their appearance. Walter Lee looked up, away from me, just as the moon emerged from behind a cloud. The pale lunar light made him appear almost transparent. It made him appear as far away and ephemeral as the people and events I'd seen in the past. The way he'd appeared that first day at my front door. "It was your turn," he said now. "And you tried."

I shrugged. "It doesn't matter." I moved out ahead and tried to ignore him.

In a few minutes, we'd reached a sidewalk. I stopped again to pull up my socks. We were making slow progress.

"It does matter," the old man said.

I kept going.

"Everything we do matters," he added.

We passed through the former ballpark, still rutted and still populated with tall and spiky weeds. The chainlink fence was still broken open in some places and still bent toward the ground in others. I paused about where second base would have been and half-heartedly chucked a rock toward home plate. Toward the place where the theater Tim and I had designed was to go. One day, it'd happen, but who knew when? Appropriately, the rock fell short. I was losing control of the present and the future, too.

"So it was my turn," I mused, retreating to what had already happened. "I'd grown up to be the guy who noticed things." I paused to take another yank at my socks. One already had a hole at the heel. The other wasn't looking good. "Except you were the one who knew Libby was coming to town. You were the one who knew she'd put me into the right frame of mind. You were the one who knew I'd follow her and eventually go back to where you wanted me to go."

I walked ahead, crossing freely against red lights.

"Back to where you needed me to go," I corrected.

The city was asleep and there was no need to wait for traffic that wasn't there.

"I was the last of the McBrides," I said into the dark. "I was your last hope."

Walter Lee still wasn't saying anything. I turned, and like the traffic, just like before on the stormy bluff back in time, he wasn't there.

I sighed. Yeah, probably so. Any or all of those reasons.

Walter Lee and I had been on a mission, apparently together. Over the past seven or eight months, we'd done an awful lot of crossing paths and watching events and, on his side, saluting and suggesting and urging and guiding. We'd tried, but we'd failed to change events. He was outside history, looking in just as I was. But he was in history, too. Deeply in. My red thread. And as history always does, he'd return. I had no doubt about that.

By the time I arrived at the Victorian, the sun was up and I was pretty much dry. I was wearing the old man's coat loosely around my shoulders now, and as

I climbed the porch steps I slung it over one of our rocking chairs. Two chairs away, Ike sat in the strangest, calmest manner. He usually would have jumped and run from the coat, but he stayed put, wearing the same poker face I'd seen on Walter Lee. Ike appeared to be waiting patiently for whatever I was going to do next, waiting without any preference or judgment about the outcome. He curled his little kitty wrists, keeping his paws tucked underneath and out of sight just the way Walter Lee had held his hands in his overalls.

I was probably looking too hard for signs of the hired man, wondering about that next appearance, but it was as if Ike now was the one who knew something and Ike now was the one waiting to see how long it would take me to find it out.

What Ike knew was that Sheila was gone.

Finding out didn't take me a minute.

And in a flash, I was back out the door, a new pair of shoes in hand, screen door slamming, Ike springing for the bushes. He had no secret to keep.

I slid behind the wheel of my truck and read Sheila's note again.

Water broken. Labor begun. She'd called Tim. They were at the hospital.

I read it once more. Like a young man with his first love letter.

Yes, yes. Wonderful, wonderful.

Sheila was having contractions, and the note seemed to pause for each one while she regrouped and resumed writing. She was phoning Tim. Pause. She was grabbing the overnight bag we'd packed weeks earlier. Pause. I imagined Sheila looking at the clock and timing contractions. Pause.

It was then that I noticed the time on Sheila's note. "Not quite 11 P.M.," it said. And I realized the hour of her labor coincided almost exactly with my plunge into the flood.

It was as if she'd known where I'd gone, that this was where she wanted me to be, rescuing Libby, and that she'd believed, after the events of the night, that I'd be done with the past. It was as if she'd planned a welcome home that would take me directly into the future. She'd go to the hospital. Our child would be born. And we'd be on our way.

Or would we?

True, Sheila never again mentioned the mission she'd sent me on, not until we all sat here together right now, here on the porch. She never mentioned my missing the hour our new future began. Sheila being Sheila, I suppose she really did put all of that behind her.

Me, I did worry. I hated being set up. Manipulated. Walter Lee had done enough of that. What I needed was a way to put these whys and wherefores behind me. Or if not behind me, then at least out of sight. If there was anything I'd learned throughout this business of seeing and visiting other times, it was the necessity of keeping quiet and keeping secrets. Good scout Eddy, seeker of truth Eddy, had become just like everyone else in that regard.

So I stepped on the accelerator hard. The truck fishtailed on the dirt driveway and raised a rooster tail of dust almost as high as the old pecan tree.

There's a time for walking and pondering and looking at the starry night. There's a time for reflecting and observing. Figuring the angles. But this wasn't it. Now there was really only one angle that mattered. Emerging from the driveway like a bat out of some deep, dark, angry, and misunderstood place, emerging out of the past, I drove without stopping the entire way to the hospital. I drove like I was still the only one on the street. Racing. Entirely in the present.

―――――――――◆―――――――――

Mother and baby were, as the saying goes, doing fine, and when I arrived the two were fast asleep. "Baby Girl McBride" read the tag on the clear-plastic bassinet beside Sheila's bed. I gave my wife a gentle kiss on the lips and my daughter a kiss on the top of her stocking-capped head.

I was exhausted. The struggle in the river and the walk home and the adrenaline-fueled drive to the hospital had wrung me out. I'd had enough desperation and despair, counterbalanced with enough (for the time being, I presumed) unabashed joy. No more ups and downs, thank you. I needed to rest. So I let my little family sleep and walked back toward my truck. It hadn't been a long visit. Neither knew I'd been there. But for me, it had been just enough. My grounding.

It didn't occur to me to look in on Libby. That's what a baby will do to you. This little person has no past. She's all about the future, so the future is where you focus. I was only lightly concentrating on what I was doing, smiling as I emerged from the hospital into the parking lot, carrying images of my two lovely girls. No Walter Lee. No Caroline. No Stan.

Just me, my woolgathering, and what in a moment would be my broken nose.

Tim's fist came out of the early-morning light and landed squarely and hard, right on center. One punch, but it did the job. Blood splattered up and down the front of his camel-hair overcoat, and he didn't care.

"It was you," Tim whispered, grabbing my collar and pulling me close with one hand. His other was still clenched in a fist. "She was following you." Then he let go. He gave me a light shove in the middle of the chest and I began swaying in slow, little circles like a punching bag, one of those stupid inflatable toys weighted with sand in the bottom that always comes back, ready to take another lick.

"I went home," I mumbled, trying to right myself. I did have the sense to keep quiet about exactly what or where home was, the actual house, my wife and child in the hospital, or, God forbid, my long-ago family history. I couldn't admit that during the previous night I'd tried to change that history.

"Libby's gone deeper," Tim said. "Now the doctor wants to put her on a ventilator."

I closed my eyes. I thought I was going to throw up, maybe black out myself.

"One minute she was there, and then she wasn't. She didn't cry out; she didn't gasp or whimper or shudder or shake. She didn't say she was cold or do any of those things. She just sank down. It was like she'd never really been here, like she'd never come back to town, never spent time with us at all."

"Or like she'd come and then she was desperate to be gone," I said, imagining a prisoner escaping from jail, hanging from a window on a knotted bed sheet, dangling for a moment, getting up the nerve to let go, and finally dropping to the ground. Running like hell.

I opened my eyes to see Tim retreating as well. He shuffled his feet and accidentally stepped into the beam of light that controlled the emergency-room doors. They slid silently open, suggesting he enter, but what was there for him to do?

This was so like Libby, this going to another place and living another life. Running to mournfully drink coffee in her father's empty shop or cry with Burned Up Baby at my brother's grave. Libby had always been in the past, and she'd always been dragging me along with her. I could still see her back there, working in the hospital, doing her penance for attempting to commit murder and change history.

The chain of events and my failure to break it had turned into a slaughter of the innocents, but I wasn't as sure as Tim that Libby was one of them. He was one. My brother and Mr. Peacock, they were, too. I was even beginning to wonder about myself. I certainly felt slaughtered.

We stood there for the longest time, neither of us moving or speaking. Tim opened his mouth once, but it was as if someone had put a finger to his lips, to quiet his worry, to tamp down his anger. He stayed quiet for a while longer. And when he tried again, what he came out with wasn't the accusation I'd expected. His quiet time must have mellowed him, made him reconsider. "It's true," he said. "You weren't here. But even for those of us who were, we all waited too long."

I wished I could comfort my friend Tim. I wished I could stay with my family. But again, once again, damn it, I knew what I had to do.

No fear of Antietam this time, no trying to wriggle out of this. I had an obligation, and I knew it couldn't wait. I'd been back in the present only a few hours, but time had grown very, very short. Pissed me off. I had to return to the past. I started toward my truck. I had to return right now.

"Hey," called Tim.

I stopped short and exhaled deeply. Not a sigh, really. More a gesture of resignation and exhaustion. "What is it?" I asked without turning.

"You understand what will happen if she goes on that machine. She'll never get better. And we'll have to make a decision."

My nose was throbbing and my head was hanging down. I really didn't need to be thinking about pulling the plug on Libby. I seriously needed to be moving in the other direction. I needed to concentrate on life. On succeeding this time. Tim didn't need to stick in a knife and twist.

Or maybe he was just being as truthful and as transparent as I'd always thought I could be. There was a hint of regret, maybe some contrition and empathy in Tim's voice. I thought I heard concern for where I'd been, what I seen, where I was going, and what might happen.

"You be careful," he said. "You be more careful than Libby was or I was, more careful than any of us were."

forty-three

Months earlier, I'd begun a process for inviting the past into my house. I'd never really followed through back then, but now it was time to keep that date. I'd be the host and the Victorian would be the venue. I'd open windows and I'd open myself. I'd try again. And this time, I'd rescue Libby.

Walter Lee may have been right. "You have to save my father," he'd said. That would have changed everything and that, now, would still save Libby. My plunge into the flood hadn't worked, but I supposed I could return and testify at Alexander Lee's trial. On the other hand, why would I want to entrust Alexander Lee's fate to the system that had put him to death the first time around? That kind of intervention was a long shot at best, ineffective and sure to fail at worst. But I'd find something.

So there I was, flinging open windows and propping open doors as fast as I could. Home was the one place I could control the vapors around me. I was confident I could catch a breeze, ride a sound, or follow a smell that would take me where I needed to go. Something that would show me who and when and where I needed to see. If I couldn't do it at home, I couldn't do it anywhere.

Walter Lee, my frequent and longtime visitor, I just hoped he wasn't too far. Because while I'd been working on windows and doors, he'd become my plan. Follow Walter Lee. I was ready. I was waiting. It was time to go.

I sat on the sofa with elbow on knee, chin on palm, watching, examining, and quietly demanding that the house or something in the house come back to its previous life. The baseball stood in its honored place on the mantle, and I stared and waited and watched some more. If I'd had a Tom Collins, I'd have raised a toast.

To the 1920s. The best of our family times.

To Libby. Coming to get you, kiddo.

I stood, walked to the kitchen, and turned around. I moved slowly, purposefully, and meditatively, crossing the foyer and re-entering the parlor. This was the path I'd taken the night Old Jacob had listened to the radio. Maybe this would work.

But there was no ballgame, and there was no blind, old man. There was only Ike, and when I entered the room, he jumped with an ungraceful, uncatlike thump from the sofa, walked as slowly and intently as I'd been doing across the floor, and climbed the stairs. Ike's path and my previous experiences were the only clues I had, so I followed.

I found the cat waiting outside the bedroom where I'd once followed Hugh. "They picked Lou Gehrig off first, and they hit a home run." That day seemed like yesterday, but at the same time, it also seemed like years ago.

And when I opened the door, I did see the past.

Goddamn past.

Because what I saw was myself, the boy Eddy, sitting on the bed. Pitiful, young Eddy. I remembered this day, too.

"Hey, Stan!"

"Whatcha got?"

"Stay out of the garden!" the adults sitting and talking on the porch had called.

"Baseball!" I'd cried.

"You'll get a whipping!" The adults were on their feet.

But the ball had already left my hand and it was already flying over Stan's head. The family icon bounced on the grass and rolled as fast as if I'd been bowling to outwit a batsman in a game of cricket instead of tossing to someone I expected to catch the damn thing. It came to rest just inches from the freshly watered, muddy garden. Lucky, I suppose, though not lucky enough for me to avoid punishment.

In Hugh's bedroom, the boy Eddy was staring at a bedside clock, willing the hands to move. They did not. The boy fidgeted, bounced lightly on the bed a few times, and flopped on his back like a fish in the bottom of a boat. Then, like Hugh before him, Eddy the boy crossed the room and stood in a kind of vigil at the window.

I was right behind.

Goddamn past. My past. But this could work. I may have landed at a time later than I'd hoped, but I'd found Walter Lee outside this window once before.

The window stood open and the hot summer air was bouncing off the porch roof and rolling into the room. In the garden beyond, tomatoes were hanging heavy. A few rested on the ground. Tendrils of Bermuda grass had broken the boundary of the garden's edge and were creeping across the plowed earth. They wanted trimming.

And Stan was ignoring his chores. He was paying attention to Libby. In the shade of the pecan tree, she was whispering into his ear.

The pair had a gleam in their eyes. They were only twelve, but it was the same flirty gleam I'd seen in adult Tim when he'd first met Libby at the pub and the same gleam, I sincerely hoped, that I still showed for Sheila.

Of course, an awkward, youthful gesture could derail it all. It was only a matter of time before these two would go off into an uncontrollable frenzy of excitement or embarrassment or frustration. Some little gesture, a kiss or a roaming hand or a promise of either, could have been exactly what had sent my brother running from the school bus and into the path of a speeding car. Frightened. Excited. Mortified. Under the pecan tree, on the bus, anywhere or anytime. It always happened at that age, didn't it?

No wonder Libby felt guilty.

I raked my fingers through my hair. Adult Libby lay in the hospital, dead to the present and who knew where back in time. But she was also very alive here in her youth. Meanwhile, my nose hurt like hell. Could I change what came next? I had to.

I reached through the open window, unhooked the screen, and stepped onto the porch roof. I walked to the edge, where I stood, a gargoyle staring. Stan and Libby stood below, still whispering.

And where the hell was Walter Lee?

I went for a quick porch-roof walkabout. Around the corner, over to the front of the house, circling back to where I'd started. No Walter Lee. I nervously sat down to wait, heels in the gutter, where I'd have the best view. A man expectant.

On the roof beside me lay a stick about three feet long, and I fumbled to pick it up. I waggled it up and down the way I'd waggled Burned Up Baby at the cemetery.

I'd tried for so long not to make anything happen. For months, most of what I'd done was look and listen. I spoke, but just occasionally. I took a drink at the porch party. I did help carry that coffin. But Alexander Lee was always going to die whether I carried the coffin or not. And when I finally did try to make something happen, I failed. Or I succeeded at doing nothing, at having no effect. Life and time and the world, they all just kept moving along, moving very well without me.

I pointed the stick straight ahead, an old-fashioned schoolmaster with his ruler or a drill sergeant with his riding crop. Not this time, Mr. History. You either, Mr. Hugh, Mr. Stan, Miss Libby. You won't get away this time. I hauled back and slammed the stick hard into the gutter. The blow put a V-shaped dent into the metal's outer edge. It was something puny and inconsequential, this dent. A perfect symbol of the impact I'd been having.

Stealing an apple hadn't been much of a punishment for the grocer. And in the flood, I never even got close to Caroline. This dent in the gutter had had such a small impact that I could remove it, and that's exactly what Mr. Peacock and I eventually would do. I'd stand on a ladder right here, right under where I sat waving that stick, and undo my worthless impact.

Shit, the only time I'd done something big was when I'd put dents into my present-day relationships. My nose really did hurt.

I swung again and with another clang I made a second dent. This time I broke the stick and one half fell into the shrubbery below. I tossed the other half after it.

Stan and Libby looked up, but under the pecan tree, falling sticks were nothing unusual. The pair returned to their whispering.

Over my shoulder, the boy Eddy was still looking out the window. I thought of how none of them knew what was about to happen, how Stan would die in only a few days, how messing around with the ball was the last fun I'd have for a long time, how time was short.

How I urgently needed Walter Lee.

I was beginning to think I should go ahead without him. Climb down from the roof, dash over to the florist shop, and slash the Cadillac's tires. Steal the distributor cap. Anything to stop Hugh's driving lesson. If I couldn't save Libby, at least I could save Stan. I could do that.

But then it wasn't necessary.

Because just then, Walter Lee emerged from the dark of the distant trees. He took a few steps onto the lawn and raised his face toward my spot on the porch. I'd clanged the gutter with a stick, rubbed my magic lantern, as it were, and the genie had finally appeared. But there was no salute this time.

There must have been a breeze blowing my way. I heard Walter Lee as clearly as if he'd been on the roof with me. "I'll be watching," he said, "but it's not going to work. My family is dead. Now it's time for yours."

Back at the creek, I shouldn't have told Walter Lee to go away. Not so forcefully, at least. Now I was on my own.

Moving fast.

Down the stairs.

Into the parlor.

Where I came to a halt.

The parlor windows stood open, curtains were fluttering, and from nearly every tabletop the stink of stubbed-out cigarettes rose from overflowing ash-trays. Dozens of empty beer bottles lay about the room. I stepped on a broken phonograph record and picked up a fragment. It was that big-band crooner, the one my parents had liked, the one in the cemetery. A 78 rpm, an easily broken thing. There was no need to treat it carefully now, but I set it gently on one of the tables anyway. A little respect.

On the porch, a stack of American flags, carefully folded in their proper, tri-cornered way, sat on one of the rocking chairs, but a big banner, one made from a painted bed sheet, still hung from the eaves. I could read right through it, backward. "Welcome Home." The sheet flapped and slapped in the breeze, and a man was struggling to tug it down. It was Uncle Hugh. "Accordion lessons," he repeated as he grabbed at the corners. "He promised he'd teach me to play."

This was more like it. I'd moved another decade. I was on the right track.

In the yard, Walter Lee picked up a lone beer bottle and carried it to the porch, where he set it carefully on the railing. Shaking his head all the time. I could tell he didn't agree with my direction, not one bit.

forty-four

By the time I made it outside, Walter Lee was nowhere to be found. I'd seen him pick up the bottle, and then I'd seen him up on the porch. He'd been raising into place the window screen that Mr. Peacock had knocked out when he threw that bottle. But that job was finished. The flapping sign was also gone.

And where the hell was Walter Lee? I hoped I'd just stepped briefly ahead of him and landed in a slightly different time. I really hoped I hadn't been abandoned. I needed my guide. I wasn't nearly finished.

Up the stairs, two at a time, to the carriage-house apartment. Walter Lee had been in the window that day Old Jacob and I walked in the ice storm. But the rooms were empty.

Down to the garage on the ground floor. This was where Walter Lee kept his tools. But instead of the hired man, I stood face-to-face with the spectacle-eyed headlamps of the McBride family touring car.

A-ha. So I knew the time I was in and the direction I was going. That much was right. Thank God.

Emerging from the carriage house, and closing and bolting its heavy doors behind me, I walked slowly and consciously, as if I were tracing a labyrinth, only in as straight and quick a line as I could manage. Aiming now for the garden, I moved in much the same way I'd traced my path inside the house. I'd found my way then.

Now reaching the garden, I stepped immediately to its center. I stopped and waited where the head-high corn on one side met the waist-high tomatoes on the other.

The corn was thick, and a breeze rustled the stalks. I was beginning to know this scene, and I was half-expecting to see Old Jacob in his gray uniform. He'd have outgrown his tunic and it would hang unbuttoned. Or I'd see a younger version, Private Jacob McBride with his rifle on his shoulder and his bayonet glistening in the morning sun, aiming skyward at corntop level.

Except here in the garden was another young man. He was about the same age as the soldier would have been, twenty perhaps. It was Walter Lee. Carrying a hoe.

The young hired man approached through the corn, stopping occasionally to lift the tool from his shoulder and come down with a high swinging chop at an offending weed. I stood pondering his technique, wondering at the youthfully unskilled and inaccurate movements, lost as I habitually was in my ponderings, when before I knew it, Walter Lee stood directly before me. He stared, inches from my face, then turned and resumed work. Walter Lee took smaller chops at a weed under a tomato plant, but he still didn't seem to be paying very close attention. On one of his upswings, he knocked a tomato from a vine and it fell to the earth.

Slowly laying his hoe in the dirt between plants, Walter Lee lifted the fruit with both hands, as if caring for an injured thing. He turned and without a word handed it to me. I closed my fingers. I examined it well. The tomato was evenly weighted and symmetrical, exactly ripe, deeply red without a hint of green. But while I was examining, Walter Lee was practical. He took out a pocketknife and opened it. Then he reached and gestured for me to return the fruit. It was looking like he hadn't intended for me to commune with the tomato after all. Walter Lee had just needed to free his hands. He cut a wedge and passed it, balanced on the knife blade, to me.

I hesitated, recalling the last time I'd sampled ill-gotten fruit, that mealy apple I'd taken from the grocer's stack. The apple's taste had been as much a punishment for me as it had been an insight into that vain and cruel man.

Walter Lee, though young, looked at me with world-weary eyes. He looked down at the tomato wedge. Was there a reason not to take it?

But I couldn't take my eyes off the young man. What I saw was the orphan still mourning his father.

Unhappy with his lot, living the life he had to live, doing a job necessary to survive.

Never far from the events that had set his tragedy in motion.

I could've kicked myself for having so little trust. Walter Lee was the one I'd been seeking, even if it had been his older version. The wedge lay there, balancing on the knife blade, and I stood there pondering and worrying, contemplating the motivations and the meanings behind actions, taking nothing at the simple face value that it probably deserved, until . . . until, well, hell. Until I reached out, plucked up his offering with thumb and fore-finger, and popped it into my mouth.

And it was delicious.

Face value. For a change. For a damn change.

It was delicious in that fresh-fruit way, with the essence of a universal something that was still living, an unchanging something that my great grandfather and the aunts and Great Uncle Hugh had also cultivated and known in this very same garden spot, that I'd discovered in my childhood when I'd sneaked a taste between my meditative clod kicking and plant sketching, that Sheila and I had loved together on summer evenings eating dinner on the Victorian's side porch. It was that universal, unchanging taste that was exactly the opposite of those specific and unique sensations that conjured the past. It could have been any unchanging taste, maybe a classic or favorite cookie. This was no transient sound or smell or puff of wind. This was . . . .

Oh, what had I done?

I'd bit into a sensation that had brought me back to the present.

I didn't want to see the time I was now seeing. I needed to stop and think. Though it may have been too late.

Walter Lee had dropped the hint. He'd given me something that was the way it always was, not some point in time that was the way it used to be. It was not what I wanted. But I'd taken the bait.

Now the young man was gone. I warily slipped my gaze sideways from where he'd stood. It was just the way I'd stared past old Walter Lee that first day at the porch and just the way I'd stared across that psychologist's shoulder when I was a boy. It was the way I'd always observed what was around me, going beyond the object of everyone else's attention.

So I turned and took a broader view. From the place where the young man had stood, beyond the house, around toward the dry creek, and into the woods beyond.

My family or Libby or Walter Lee had called, and I'd fallen in line. Then they'd all gone away. I was left to myself. And I was beginning to worry that I'd end up—or maybe I'd already arrived—in the same position as Walter Lee. Seems he'd really had only one shot at changing events. I suppose that's why he'd recruited me, to make sure he had the best shot possible, though even together, we'd failed. But Libby was still out there. I had to go back. I had to change whatever I could. The question was: How many shots at change remained for me?

Even with my worries about time and the new urgency about Libby that I felt, my instinct was to sit in the dirt and wait. To ponder. Even with my broken nose, I wanted to take in what I could of the unmistakable smell of the manure that had fertilized the garden for years. I was waiting to hear the clomping of feet and feel the puff of wet breath from the mule I remembered, or the generations of mules that had been brought to plow before him. I was anxious to play dodge 'em as the mule flicked at flies with its tail, to be in that particular time and place and on that particular path to doing something about all that had happened.

I was ready to go as deep and as far as I needed to go.

So I sat, but when I did, I smelled and I heard and I felt nothing. Forget the deep past. I couldn't find the roll of thunder greeting a boy waving a gutter pipe at the top of a ladder. I couldn't find the cold wind pulling at my jacket outside a sailor's welcome-home party. I couldn't find the scent of streetcar ozone or lantana blossoms leading me to Alexander Lee's hanging.

The garden was quiet, deathly empty of all the senses as I waited. And then I jumped to my feet.

Because now, across the way, present-day, old Walter Lee was coming once again from the trees.

He walked with a casual gait, and when he encountered Ike crossing the lawn, he paused to pet the cat. Ike gave a hips-low, spine-long, now-I-feel-better-than-ever stretch and continued on his way without looking back.

And when Walter Lee reached the garden, he held out his hand. It was as if he wanted to greet me, too. Or give me some object. Or show me some unknown thing.

If it was a tomato, I didn't want it. Instead, I grabbed Walter Lee by the wrist, and I held on tight.

I couldn't tell what he was thinking, but it didn't matter.

I knew what I was thinking, and it wouldn't wait.

Walter Lee stood immobile. "The boy didn't know," he finally said. "The boy didn't do anything."

"The hell he didn't."

"He was right to send you back to the present," said Walter Lee. "But he had no idea who you were."

I shut up and thought. Maybe the old man was right. I was beginning to wonder who I was, too, whether a creature of the past or present or some indeterminate time. Of course, a return to the past would fix all of that, so I pressed my case. "You stopped everything," I said. "I was almost there. You owe me your help."

"I owe you nothing," replied Walter Lee. "It was an innocent gesture. The tomato was how you perceived it. There was nothing intended in the giving."

I jerked Walter Lee's arm. He resisted, and so I went straight to the heart of things. "You took Libby. That was something intended."

Walter Lee spoke as if each sentence explained it all, as if each word was some logical conclusion. "I needed to get your attention." He spoke as if he was not only responding to me but speaking some ultimate truth. "You just wanted to look, but that was not enough. I needed to save my father. Your friend was ready to follow."

"That was just cruel," I countered.

"Indeed." Walter Lee fixed his eyes on mine. "Now are you ready to know what I know? About how the world works? This is how it works. My father has his turn. I have my turn. You have your turn. The end."

Walter Lee pulled back. He wasn't struggling. He was simply moving away, as if he'd made another irrefutable point that should have ended our conversation.

"Take me where I can do something," I demanded. I was pulling again, trying to reel him in.

"It's over," Walter Lee said.

"You selfish bastard!"

"You had your chance." Walter Lee was calm. "And now the past is past. The dead are dead. My family. Yours. Everything is determined, and everything is the way it should be. Everything is now."

It was then that I looked down at my grip, and I realized I was holding the old man's arm exactly the way he'd held mine that first day at my front door. Maybe this was determined. Maybe not. But I did know that this was not what I wanted to do and it was not who I wanted to be. Manipulation was not my game. I quickly let go.

I must have surprised the old man, just as he'd surprised me that first day. He'd been continuing his steady pressure away from me, just as I had, and suddenly he stepped back, stumbling, a "now-look-what-you've-done" expression on his face. Add to that the "I've-failed-at-everything-I've-tried" thoughts I was having and it was clear what a bad place all this had gotten us into.

Pulling away, stepping back, Walter Lee came down with the side of his foot on the old porch steps I'd fashioned into my cucumber trellis nearly a year before, steps I'd fashioned so harmlessly, I'd thought. Shows what I knew back then. Now I saw options.

Walter Lee would fall, head to the corner of a step with a sharp crack of bone. I'd roll the body up in a blanket, sling the bundle into the back of my pickup, drive to the river, and drop him in the old, flooded house. He lived in that kind of place, I'd always imagined. So why not die there?

It would take time for anyone to discover him. Meanwhile, I'd visit. I'd lower myself to the silt-covered floor and sit beside dead Walter Lee undiscovered and drying up like a mummy. Or eaten by rats, a skeleton in his overalls. I'd apologize to him, a sad conversation between a dead body and the person who made him that way.

But it hadn't happened yet. It didn't have to happen at all.

I reached out and grabbed Walter Lee's wrist again. He steadied, took hold of my elbow with his free hand, and pulled himself to standing straight.

I couldn't let him fall the way he'd let me fall at my front door. Hell, I may not have been able to affect the long-ago back end of my family tragedy, but at least I could keep the present-day front end from totally unraveling. I'd be a good scout, and maybe the portal into the past that he'd offered me earlier would open again. My reward.

Wishful thinking, I'm afraid.

"Do not," Walter Lee said. "Do not think that I now owe you."

He let go of my elbow and took another step back, smoothing his hair and adjusting his collar as if he were concerned about the image he was presenting. As if he wanted a formal and final presence from which to announce a new direction.

"You are on your own," Walter Lee said. "All of you are. From here, your individual selves and your individual natures take over."

And with that, he turned and disappeared into the trees. Gone forever. Yard man and guide abandoning me for real this time with the same endgame dismissal that I'd been handed by my father. The same finality as my brother.

I'd reached the end of my one red thread.

Which prompted me to spend the night in the porch hammock once more, seeing myself in McBride history. I was the reclusive uncle damaged by what he'd seen. I was the misbehaving boy punished for what he'd done. I was my grown self trying desperately to sort out times and places.

The future was at hand. Twice I heard the baby cry. I saw the lights come on. I heard Sheila's footsteps cross the hall. I smiled in the dark as she sang a lullaby. I should have been there with her.

But the past held tight. Libby was still back in time, and I had that scout's obligation and that Eddy obsession with doing something about it. Even without Walter Lee. Even on my own.

Save Alexander Lee and de-traumatize Hugh. Two generations later, my brother lives. And Libby never goes near the past.

Yeah, yeah, I understood the theory. By this time, I knew my family story better than I'd ever expected, better than I'd ever intended. I knew the future I wanted to create just as intimately. Only I was beginning to have my doubts. The future would be clear. It would be bright. But it wouldn't be as real. For those of us left where we were, looking in from the outside, the timeline of history, the river of events, just stretches longer and more tangibly every day. We're here, at our own spot. Time after time, we're left on our own.

The day after I'd struggled with Walter Lee, I would once and for all lose my opportunity to help Libby escape the past. A doctor would come striding down the hospital corridor, his long, white lab coat swirling at his knees. Sheila, Tim, and I would be stranded in the waiting room, banished from any hope of helping in the present. And as we watched, we'd know with each step that the message could not be good. The doctor would hold the metal jacket of a hospital chart in one hand, and as he walked he would beat time against his thigh. Some formal ritual, I would suppose. Enforcing some regime. Anything to distract from an unhappy chore.

We'd be right. The doctor would begin by announcing that a ventilator would no longer be necessary. He'd say that he was sorry but the skill of the staff and wisdom of medical science had not been able to save our friend. Dispassionate bastard, ruled by facts. But of course, I'd recognize my truth-hunting self in his attitude. I used to be that way. All of us bastards, twined together by our inclination toward misguided understanding but ultimately not together at all. Each shrouded in an understanding that was ours alone.

forty-five

We buried Libby in a plot as close to Stan as we could arrange. I'm sure it wasn't as close as she would have liked, but we all agreed it was the right place. Libby now lies near the bench where she and Tim and I talked that night, where she and Burned Up Baby surveyed the dead and lamented the missing lambs, the night she took her first step into the past and her big step toward becoming a lamb herself.

If you look at it one way, she was a child deeply hurt by the people she loved. But if you look at it another way, well, she just seemed to be doing what she wanted and needed to do.

Or was that second option just what I told myself? Like the doctor with his time-beating, thigh-slapping chart, what I needed was something that could remove attention from the possibility that what had happened to Libby might have been my fault.

To one extent or another, Libby had always wanted the past. That's where she'd always been, and in my mind's eye, that's where I could still see her. I mourned my friend, I surely did, but I was feeling like I'd been prepping for this for a long time, like the outcome shouldn't have been a surprise.

I'd been following Libby as much as she'd been following me. Then in the end, she went off alone. Just listen to Walter Lee. It's our individual selves and our individual natures that determine events.

So we do what we can. One failed rescue, when I'd showed up in the 1920s and discovered that was the wrong time. A second failed rescue, when I'd plunged into the right year and into the flood but failed to accomplish what I needed to. And then I sat up front in a draped folding chair, right there on the artificial grass rolled out next to an open grave.

Libby had lived away from town for so many years that Sheila and Tim and I were the closest thing to a mourning family that she had. There were a couple of neighbors and a handful of people she'd met in the course of renovating the shop. I believe her banker was there. But I wished the funeral home hadn't sat us where they did. I would have preferred the back of the gathering.

Heaven help me. I'd started out trying to do everything so right, and now I hadn't done anything at all.

A tear rolled down my cheek and Sheila took my hand. "You okay?" she whispered.

I shook my head. My tear was not only for my lost friend Libby but for everyone in life I'd come to know and especially for those I'd hurt. For my broken brother, Stan. For drowned Caroline Simms, unjustly hanged Alexander Lee, blind Old Jacob, shocked and reclusive Uncle Hugh, guilt-ridden Mr. Peacock. Even for my great aunts, Eleanor and Lillian, seemingly happy as they puttered through each day, but passing on their own lives to take care of others.

For all those injured souls who had now receded far away.

Also for those in the present.

For Tim, sitting on the other side of Sheila with his eyes closed, head down, somewhere in his own world, a less painful world I hoped, the soft and fuzzy world of drink, I imagined. For that old bastard Walter Lee, following me, leading me around, and then leaving me with no answers at all. And because of Walter Lee, actually because of all of them, also for myself.

Sheila seemed to be the only one who'd escaped. And the baby, of course, new and innocent and unscarred, waiting at home this day with a sitter. Sheila gave me a loving glance, a look that said she understood how much I mourned my childhood friend. It only made me feel more distant. It made me think of the secrets I'd learned about others and the secret failures I'd gathered around myself.

And so I sat in my draped funeral chair, as stiff and immobile as a dead person myself, worrying and grieving on a sheet of plastic turf that only Burned Up Baby could have loved.

Now it seemed like we'd all traded, merged, and jumbled our places together. Musical chairs; duck, duck, goose; fruit basket turnover. I was Sheila moving toward the future. I was Tim blocking out pain. Unfortunately, I was also Libby, longing for something that could never be.

It was a day or two after the funeral that Tim, who'd always been so reserved about what he was feeling, started talking, and I, who'd always just vomited out whatever ran through my brain, fell quiet. That he became inexplicably calm, actually quite cheery, and I nervously clammed up.

I was adrift. I was an orphan, as I'd long felt orphaned. As my dead brother and disappearing father had left me a lonely child orphan. As my mother, who'd seen me to adulthood but moved from this sad town as soon after as she could, then passed away in her distant state, left me a grown orphan.

Even as Walter Lee, an orphan himself and the one constant in my story, now had also turned and gone. People I thought I knew well, Hugh and the aunts and Old Jacob, turned into people I knew only slightly. Then they turned into people who disappeared altogether.

Searching for context, I'm afraid I badgered Sheila mercilessly. On too many days, I followed her around home and office and interrupted like a needy puppy. I wanted to be happily in the present, but I was having a hard time knowing where to turn my attention. Ever since the past had slipped beyond my reach, I'd felt shell-shocked, like the boys from the Great War my Uncle Hugh had nursed. Guilty, like Mr. Peacock, for a boy's death he may or may not have caused. A victim of friendly fire—my own friendly fire—like Libby.

"You're a good man." Sheila looked up from her work at the drafting table as if she knew what I was thinking. But she could not have known what she was conjuring. You're a good man—that's what Alexander Lee had told the hangman. I hadn't been good at all and Libby's absence was proof.

Life did get better after Tim went out to the cemetery and placed a small statue of a recumbent lamb on Libby's grave. Libby's funeral, like my reluctant acceptance of my failure to save her, had not been a resolution. Her death had been so ambiguous. Libby was in the past and she was in the present; she was with us and then she was not. But the little stone animal, symbol of a child dead before her time, told anyone who cared that Libby's passing had been part of a larger and perhaps meaningful story. The tragedy of Libby was that the events of her childhood consumed her. But her childlike dedication to the boy she loved was something we all admired.

And to anyone looking in from the outside, the lamb did bring our world some peace. The symbol did the remembering. It took away any need the three of us had to talk about a death that never should have happened. None of us ever spoke of the circumstances of Libby's death again, and none of us ever mentioned any wish to go back to the way we were before all this crap about visiting the past had started. That was as it should be. We may have thought these things and wished these things, but stone was more tangible and more real. It was more permanent and decisive than any of our expressions.

As for me, I was also beginning to sense that I'd thought all the thoughts that were in me. I didn't want to get over Libby. I didn't want to let her go.

I certainly didn't want to forget. But that's exactly what was happening. Just the way it had with my brother Stan.

Then one day, newly wide-open and observant Tim planted new ideas and possibilities, some surprising facts that shook up all I'd learned about events. I don't think he was just trying to make me feel better, to break me out of my funk, though Tim certainly had found something that made himself feel better. What Tim had to say spun me completely around. It set me off in an entirely new direction.

I was standing in the doorway of Tim's office, holding the baby in her clunky, plastic seat. It was awkward and angular, like an oversize picnic basket, and I swung it as best I could, slowly, the way people do when they're trying to prevent a cry. Tim had about finished loading his books and toy cars into boxes. I lifted the child seat onto my partner's conference table, held a box shut while he taped the flaps, and set it aside on the guest chair.

I looked around for something else to do. Baby sleeping. Grown-up toys gone. I had to settle for nervous fidgeting. I shoved my hands into my pockets. I pulled them out. I crossed my arms.

"The theater's back on schedule," I said, finger now digging and scratching deep in my ear. "You know that, don't you?"

Formal, pinstriped Tim was looking like an old hippie in jeans, a black T-shirt, and the beginnings of a scraggly beard. He set down the tape dispenser and began gently running his fingertips through that beard, much the way he touched the scar on his arm, feeling his way as if he were reading Braille, as if he were breaking a line of code that carried some repressed message.

"All yours," he said, turning and gesturing at the window, the one with the city view, the view in his photo of the burning paper snippings cabin. "Tomorrow, I'll be somewhere else."

Tim, in fact, had been mentally gone for some time. Now, the time had come to add the physical. Shortly after the funeral, he'd informed Sheila and me that he wanted to take some time off. Bereavement leave, sick leave, vacation leave, sabbatical leave, or leave purely because he was one of the owners and he could take it. But he needed to go. Come back when the time is right.

Or never come back at all. Maybe take a permanent break from architecture. At that point, he didn't know, and Sheila and I didn't press the issue.

I couldn't help but think Tim was behaving like Libby, running from difficult circumstances. But maybe that was myself I was thinking about. Being in the present may have been the right thing, but the right thing wasn't necessarily what I wanted. The past was always present and I was always Eddy. I did tend to read too much into life, my own and others'. What Tim was doing was a lot simpler than the options my mind imagined.

Tim was going exploring, he was going photographing, he was doing exactly what he needed to do to change his perception of circumstances—exactly what he felt Libby would have wanted him to do.

And he was so damn peaceful, so matter-of-fact about it. Striking out in a new direction now seemed the most natural thing for him, though a year earlier I'd never have expected it from someone who'd guarded his life so carefully for so long.

It was at about that same time that Tim stopped drinking. Now I really didn't know what was going on.

Tim handed me another box to stack. "How are you feeling?" he asked. "How's the nose?"

"I'm okay," I said. The break had been set and healed; the bandages were off. "But I can't smell a damn thing."

"Just as well," Tim said.

"Pardon?"

"What did you learn back there, back in the past?" He handed me another box.

I shrugged. I'd learned too much, that's for sure. I'd learned too much and I'd done not enough and I didn't want to talk about it.

"You didn't really learn anything."

I shrugged again. Maybe that was true.

"You didn't really know those people." Tim put a hand over the scar on his forearm. "I never knew the guy who cut me," he said softly, eyes down. "It was dark and it was loud and I couldn't see a thing."

Life was so damn confusing. I should have learned more. "We don't know shit," I said. We control even less, I thought.

"Follow me," he said. "I have a present for you."

Tim squeezed by me in the doorway, giving my shoulder an encouraging and gentle pat on the way. I glanced at the baby in her seat. Still sleeping. So I followed Tim into the conference room. There sat more boxes, the photographs from Tim's exhibit along with others he'd collected over the years.

"Maybe a snapshot can show us something," he said, pawing through his framed photos. They were all standing up in their boxes, the way music stores used to stand vinyl records in bins. Tim put a finger on the top of each and flipped them forward one by one until he came up with the photo he wanted.

It was an old photo of Babe Ruth in a ballpark somewhere. There was a scoreboard in the background. The Yanks had won. And a half-dozen nurses in their white uniforms were lined up by the player's side. The two next to the great man each draped an arm around his neck.

"Look at the faces," said Tim.

I moved the photograph closer and squinted. I tilted it to one side to reduce the glare. I let go and it crashed to the floor. The glass shattered and the frame splintered. "It's Libby," I whispered.

"I bought this two years ago," said Tim.

"Before her father died. Before she returned to town." I was incredulous. "Before you even knew who she was."

"This was the life she began when she went back in time, back to work in the hospital."

"How long have you known?"

"Since a little after the funeral. One day I looked and there she was." Tim bent down to pick up the picture. He tilted the frame so the shards of glass slid to the floor.

In the photo, Libby looked disturbed and distracted, staring off into the distance as if she were focusing her thoughts on something other than this slight brush with fame. Focusing on her father, I guessed. And on my brother. Stan would have been a fan. On her sad life in the present. On her failed mission.

"You've been there." Tim was using the side of his shoe to sweep the broken glass against the baseboard, but his eyes never left Libby's picture. "You've seen Libby as a child at her father's shop, and you've seen her as an adult repenting her errors. Now you've seen her in her own time and place."

"And have you . . ." I began to ask.

Tim was already shaking his head. No, he hadn't seen her again, though he wished he had. She'd be an old woman by now. But that would be okay.

Tim had every right to be angry about what had happened and I told him so—as my hand went instinctively to my nose—but he said this photo had changed everything. Now he was comfortable with the passage of time, and now he could be calm about what had happened to Libby.

Well, partially calm. Tim had begun nervously fingering his beard again. "So whatever you were doing back there," he said after a long, contemplative pause, "if you were trying to save Libby, it looks like you didn't need to do it." Tim's fingers went higher, maybe hiding a tear, maybe wiping a tear away. "It looks like she was fine," he continued. "It looks like she just abandoned us and she just abandoned her body here in the present—like she didn't need any of that."

Tim handed the shattered photo back to me. "Keep it," he said. "I don't need a picture. But you remember Libby. You keep what happened to her here with you."

forty-six

When it came to picking a name for our baby, we didn't have any choice. Elizabeth. What else? Looking to the future, we thought it a wonderfully malleable name. Playful and childish Lizzie at first, maybe Eliza Beth later, then moving to a more complete, more formal, more serious and adult Elizabeth. Sheila and I could remember our friend. Our daughter could be whomever she wanted.

And as the past receded we had great joy. Lizzie grew steadily—a year, a year and a half, two years old—and I'd take her riding on my shoulders. Around the block, where we'd look at our neighbors' flowers. Simple things like that. We'd walk down to the river, where we'd feed the ducks, search for turtles sunning on logs, and watch dogs running and playing. Then we'd circle back to the ducks and home again for more flowers in the kind of endless loop that children love.

Or we'd go to the design studio. Lizzie loved that place, which was now in the Peacock family's greenhouse and florist shop. Like Tim, I'd put myself on hiatus from work. I was taking care of family, becoming a stay-at-home dad, and Sheila had taken charge of the business. She'd sold the firm's share in the building downtown, bought the shop from Libby's estate, and shifted our focus from buildings alone to the larger canvas, the full landscape. We were now McBride & Associates. The name left room to bring architecture back into the mix. Someday, maybe I'd be ready.

"You're a good architect," Sheila would say.

I'd pick up a leaf that had fallen from a plant on her desk and I'd twirl it by the stem between my thumb and forefinger.

Sheila would smile hopefully and unroll a set of plans, a not-too-subtle invitation for me to rejoin the practice.

I'd smile back wanly and tuck the leaf into my shirt pocket. Yeah, I know. I'd done that tucking business before. That's where I put another remembrance, the flower from Uncle Hugh's funeral. Seemed like a million years ago.

Now we had Lizzie bouncing around these big open spaces, calling to the birds that still managed to get in and nest near the greenhouse peak, littering the place with her toys, making it hers. Teddy bears in the corner and a jack-in-the-box under a desk weren't quite the same as Tim's antique toy cars, but they were our new direction.

"You're a good dad." Sheila would stare deep into my eyes. "I love you."

That's what I wanted now. To be happily in the present. To share the openness we'd missed that night we'd danced on the porch and avoided each other's unspoken or barely spoken pleas for love. All those other nights when we'd lived parallel lives.

So why couldn't I make it happen?

You could say that my relationship with the world and with the people who mattered was like Lizzie's relationship with Ike. She loved that cat, she wanted to have him around, and for Lizzie's sake, one day I tried to wrestle him into one of those pet carriers. Maybe he'd like the studio, too, I thought. But I tried only once. Ike had no intention of leaving his familiar home, and so he opened his claws and left long scratches on my arm.

Oh, why do those terrifying and tragic yet compelling and wonderful days, those times when we visited the past, still have to interrupt? In my mind, the cat's scratch became the knife cut on Tim's arm, and I fell instantly and deeply into pondering and worrying about the cause and the meaning of all that had happened.

When all went well, I could pretend those events had no meaning. They were like the cat, whose nature it was to scratch and not to think about it, whose actions were neither good nor bad except in our human interpretations. Events in time were just something that happened.

We'd been given a child named Elizabeth. That should have been enough. We'd had and lost our friend Libby; we'd hurt our friend Tim; I'd followed and rejected and sought again my guide, Walter Lee. I'd failed at creating change when I tried to intrude on my family story and I'd failed at creating peace when I brought that story into the present. That should have been enough.

And yet I found myself watching and waiting. I found myself wanting more. Because all wasn't necessarily going well. I found myself chased by the specter of guilt for causing pain and disappearance. Haunted by doubt over what may or may not have happened. Hunting for atonement if need be. And so, very quietly, I began searching for a way into the past again.

Because just as I suspected it would, the day soon came when I realized Tim had been only partially right when he'd accepted what had happened to Libby.

It was a warm and dreamy and cicada-singing day in and around the greenhouse studio, and I guess that had a lot to do with it. Lizzie was waking up from her nap in the little bed we'd set up in what was supposed to be my office. I'd been sitting quietly beside her listening on the radio to the rhythmic chatter of a low-volume baseball game. On a table beside an open window, I'd propped up Tim's old photograph of Babe Ruth and his admiring nurses. It was still in its bashed frame, but it looked just fine. New glass would have been one more thing between me what I needed to see.

"If you're not going to work," called Sheila, "why don't you kids go outside and play?"

That was all it took. A ballgame on the radio, a photograph of my old friend, a nudge toward the door, cicadas singing ever louder, and my attention turned toward leading my child into my old, familiar neighborhood.

Back where I could see the boys playing.

There weren't as many of them as in the years when I was a boy, and they were wearing knee socks with baggy shorts. Neckties for school, loosened but not discarded for playing. It was an innocent, earlier time. No television antennas on the roofs. No enclosed porches and rooms added yet to accommodate growing postwar families. World War II was only a couple of years away, but it hadn't happened yet. No one knew. All so lucky.

Now the boys were chasing a dog with a ball in its mouth, and now a middle-aged woman who'd been watering her garden was turning to watch. She turned and her hose splattered the house's front steps.

It was the kind of scene Tim would have photographed. Houses and gardens neatly and carefully tended, the image populated by the people who did the tending. Except that it was not the brief moment he always captured. The woman stood still, she held her pose for the longest time as if she were being watched as well as watching. The woman did not quickly jump to avoid the boys; she did not turn back to her chore the way most gardeners would have done. She did not correct her mistake, and the water continued to play across the steps. Then up to the porch. She was a fountain, soaking the screen door, leaving droplets clinging in the mesh in a tapestry pattern.

What did change was the direction of her stare. Now she gazed beyond the boys. Now she shifted directly toward me.

Libby was staring at me.

I stared back, open-mouthed with surprise.

Tim had been right about where Libby had landed, but I knew instantly that he'd been wrong about what she was doing. He'd been happy to know that she'd lived, but Libby's survival wasn't all there was to the story. That much was clear.

Libby stared hard at me and I stared hard back, and I could see that I should have been worrying about what was going to happen next. Like I said, Tim was only partially right. Libby was alive, but her life wasn't as simple as living happily ever after.

The day she'd crossed paths with fame and had her photo taken with Babe Ruth, she must have nearly crossed paths with the story she wanted to change. Our city was a single stop on the New Yorkers' barnstorming schedule. But she must not have been sitting on the first-base line. If she had, she'd have been right near Hugh when he caught that foul ball. She'd have recognized him and she could have followed him. She'd have been in the right place and the right time to try again, to chase him down, snuff him out, and end the story.

Either that or she did see him but consciously passed on the opportunity. It could be that she was waiting for something else.

Because as Libby stared at me, she had a go-back-where-you-came-from, leave-me-alone look in her eye. She had the eye of a person with a different plan and the eye of a person with the will to carry it out.

Libby had moved onto our old street. I don't believe either my parents or her parents even lived there yet, but of course, they were coming. We all were coming. Libby was just biding her time. Hell, maybe she regretted her attempts to kill Hugh, maybe not, but now it didn't look like she was doing penance at all.

It was pretty obvious that Libby didn't want to be followed this time, not like when we were children playing and not like when she took me back to our old neighborhood on her return to town. My guess was that she'd elected to stay where she was, deserting her body and the present. That she was happy when her body died. That she'd figured out how to make us quit following her.

What Libby hadn't counted on was Tim's discovering the old photo. She also hadn't counted on my following, regardless of her wishes. Obsessively observing Eddy. It was as Walter Lee said that final day in the garden. My nature had taken over.

And I wondered if it was Libby's nature, whether she'd intended it or not, to take over from the old man, to become another red thread.

It did feel like Libby knew exactly what she was doing in timing her disappearance from the present day. Like she'd known as soon as I'd returned from the past that final time that I'd failed to save Caroline Simms from drowning, that I'd failed to change our sad course of events, and that I was wrung out from trying. As she lay in her hospital bed, still partially in the present but moving steadily toward total immersion in our collective backstory, Libby seemed to know that I'd be too preoccupied with the baby and with building a future to worry about a forty-year-old hit and run. That she'd have free rein.

Hey, proof was right there with me. "Daddy! Daddy!" And then I was back in the present.

There was Lizzie, standing behind me on the sidewalk, pushing with both hands on my butt, trying to get me to do something more than stare at this old neighborhood. I picked up a stone and tossed it onto a hopscotch grid that we'd drawn on the sidewalk the last time she'd come here with me. Some things never change. Libby used to play hopscotch all the time when we were kids, and from her hospital bed, she'd revisited the game when she stepped back in time. My stone bounced on the far square and skidded beyond the chalk lines. Lizzie ran and picked it up. "Again," she said, handing the stone back to me.

My next toss was a little gentler and a lot more accurate, right into the center of the "three" square. Lizzie was delighted, clapping her little hands with her palms open, fingers spread, straight and symmetrical the way children do. I scooped my daughter into my arms and hugged her tight.

Sure, individuals create history. All it took to turn the McBride family on its head was one lie on the witness stand. All Libby had wanted was to save one boy from one speeding car.

But history that matters is created by a community. I smoothed the hair on my daughter's head. Even if it's a community of two. Or, in our case, a community of three. It goes without saying that three is a wonderful number. For many people, it's a lucky number. It had turned into mine. But I couldn't forget that three was also all we had left. Apparently, neither could Libby, trying again to increase the number by adding my brother Stan back in.

As much as I'd grieved for Stan and as much as I understood that most of what had happened over the last few years had been my fault, I couldn't let her do it. After all, the only thing I'd succeeded in changing had been the present. Our daughter was wonderful. But my relationship with Sheila and my relationship with work were still to be determined. My friend was gone, and wherever she was now, she was aiming for the biggest change yet. How cataclysmic would her saving Stan be?

And I realized: the question now wasn't how to save Libby. It was how to stop Libby.

As always, the past lay right in front of me. Every day I heard Caroline Simms's final words drifting across the swollen creek. "We waited too long." I worried that I couldn't arrive quickly enough to do what needed to be done. And so I watched carefully for my chance.

Back at home, I'd find myself staring out that bedroom window. The sun would be sinking behind the trees on the other side of the garden, and the Victorian's porch roof would be stretching out before me. I'd be staring and standing with my hands thrust deep into my pockets, turning over and over between my fingertips the pendant watch Libby had found at the river.

And I'd see two children, my best friend and my brother, whispering to each other on the lawn below me.

Or sometimes I'd see Libby pass by. There'd be laughter and a sailor's accordion music on the porch below, and Libby would pause at the foot of the driveway to listen. She never came in. She seemed to be checking her bearings, verifying that events were progressing on schedule.

It was the phenomenon I'd noticed that day of the hanging. To the people at the party, my father and Libby's father on that first day of their friendship, Great Uncle Hugh trying to remind the other celebrants that the gathering really was about the Confederate veteran's birthday, everyone else diving into their Tom Collins highballs and ignoring the coming war, the party was the center of the universe. Meanwhile, other worlds swirled around them. People were mowing lawns and shopping and making love and fighting.

Libby, she was making her plans.

I knew Libby had a plan because the next time I saw her she was buying baby clothes. I'd taken myself again back to find her and I was walking through old downtown, admiring the postwar cars, the big Hudsons and Kaisers and Buicks that looked like their makers still had tanks in mind, when I saw her through the store's plate-glass window.

The place was filled with reunited, postwar couples, clinging together, beaming and calling each other "darling"—now there's a word lost in time—and Libby was shopping alone. The others seemed to think she was a new grandmother. A few congratulated her as she admired a sky-blue blanket and added it to her stack of purchases.

Libby's shopping seemed innocuous enough. A blanket here, booties there—these could have been gifts. But when she wheeled her selections to the cash register in a baby carriage, she tipped her hand, at least to me. "I need the whole kit," she explained to the cashier. "We're taking a trip."

I recalled a comment Tim had made the day he handed me that photo of the nurses. "Here's what I think," he'd said by way of explaining Libby's presence in the past. "There may be more than one story out there, more than one way to live a life. But even when the details of a life are different, and even when there's more than one life, the essence of the person who lives them is always the same."

That was Libby all right. She'd appeared at the baby store at just about the time Stan was born. Planned that way, I'm sure. I think she was still trying to make up for what she thought was her guilt in my brother's death. Always trying to save little boys the way she'd always insisted she'd saved me from newborn jaundice. I suppose it was a worthy goal, this saving, though what she really needed to do was let go.

But Libby couldn't let go. And when I saw her next, I knew that she was running full steam ahead with her plan and that she was up to no good.

I was at the bus station—who goes there anymore? But that's where I was, by happy or unhappy coincidence, when Libby next appeared.

I'd gone to pick up a set of drawings for Sheila that an out-of-town engineer was shipping for same-day delivery to the firm, and I was almost tasting—my sense of smell was still gone, you know, after that punch Tim threw—I was tasting something oily, either bacon grease oozing out of the café or diesel exhaust fouling the air from the loading bays. Both were distasteful enough to capture my attention. Both were strong enough to bring Libby into full view standing there at the ticket window, though I could hear only one side of the conversation.

"One-way trip? Yes, ma'am," said the agent. "Round trip is cheaper, but if you're sure you're not coming back . . . .

"Ticket for a baby? No, ma'am, not if he sits on your lap . . . .

"Surcharge for a baby carriage? Ma'am, just look around. War's over. These days, we get 'em all the time."

forty-seven

I must have picked up the phone a dozen times. I needed to call the police, but the process was all too unfamiliar and way too awkward. Back where I'd followed Libby, there was no such number as 911. I had to look up the central switchboard in the phone book, and by the time I dialed, I'd either cooled down or I'd become so filled with doubt that I hung up. I never made it beyond the second ring. What was I supposed to say? That a woman from the future had bought a bus ticket?

Sure, Libby had a brand-new baby carriage, a couple of weeks' worth of baby clothes, and a stack of baby toys, but what did that make her? The kidnapper I feared? Or your garden-variety uber-babysitter, your classic Mary Poppins?

But she had that bus ticket, and so I paced the sidewalk. If not an informer, I'd be a stalker.

This could work. I could stay in the past as long as I wanted. In the present I'd be gone only a moment. I'd see all events. And when I returned it would be my daughter who was claiming my attention. From the past, I could imagine the present easily. Once again, Lizzie would be pounding on my butt.

There was nothing illegal about taking a little neighborhood stroll, nothing wrong with keeping an eye on comings and goings. Libby would never go to the police in return. She couldn't risk that. And hell, my parents, who by now had moved in across the street, her parents, now living only a couple of houses away, and all the rest of the neighbors, they might not even see me. I was a watcher, as I'd been on those first visits I'd made back into time. I wasn't a participant.

Correction: I wasn't a participant *yet*.

I wanted to give Libby the benefit of the doubt, but I knew I should have called someone when she started babysitting Stan. Libby would be reading *Make Way for Ducklings* or one of the other classics from the war and postwar era. "Mr. and Mrs. Mallard were looking for a place to live," she'd read and I'd shiver at the idea of Libby taking my brother away to some new home in some other place.

"I've never known a more conscientious sitter," my mother would tell her friends.

My dad would sip from his Tom Collins, then crow: "Not even when you were doing it yourself!"

She'd ignore the insult. "A retired nurse. You can't do better than that." And my mother would steal from Dad's drink.

I couldn't argue. Nothing inappropriate had happened yet.

But when Libby took Stan across to her house, I really should have called. He wasn't even a month old, but everyone was pushing the benefits of fresh air and long walks and it was early summer and the weather was beautiful. Libby and Stan would always wind up at her place before returning to my parents' house. I'd stand on the street and sweat. How long were they going to be in there? What would I do if a taxi pulled up to the curb and Libby stepped onto the porch with Stan and all her baby equipment?

My dilemma was this: I should have called the police, but I didn't want to hurt my friend. On the other hand, maybe calling the police was necessary, if it would keep the both of us, me as well as Libby, from trying again to change history.

Assuming that's what I was doing. Preventing an interloper's act wasn't the same as changing an act by people who belonged there, was it? I have to admit that my ambitions had been growing less, well, ambitious. Either that or I'd just narrowed my focus. I'd moved from trying to change the entire flow of history by altering an event that had already happened, to trying to rescue a single person who had put herself into a time that was not her own, to trying to stop an event that had yet to occur.

And so I stood at the curb. Every so often, Libby would see me and she'd glare from what I imagined was a parlor window, curtains pushed aside the way Walter Lee had pushed his curtains that day I'd walked with Old Jacob. There was a difference, of course. Walter Lee had been guiding me, egging me on. Libby's watching reminded me of the day Tim had followed my yellow tabby, Ike, around my yard with his camera. She didn't like being stalked any more than the cat had.

Libby certainly didn't like it the day I tried a little disruption to her plan. Just to see what would happen, you know. She hadn't done anything yet, but I was feeling brave or confident or cavalier in my actions, and I needed to give my parents a hint that their childcare arrangement wasn't quite what they thought.

Libby'd been sitting with Stan on her front porch, rocking the baby carriage with one hand and reading. It looked like Stan had fallen asleep because she slowly and quietly set down the book, released the baby carriage with care, and went inside the house. Maybe to fetch some toy or get something to eat for herself or the baby; maybe to answer the phone or use the bathroom. No matter. I stepped quickly onto the porch and snatched my brother.

My mother was napping on the living-room sofa. She didn't hear me as I entered or as I crossed to the back of the house or as I laid Stan in his crib. But Stan almost immediately began to cry and when my mother woke she was not the terrified or panic-stricken new mom you might expect. She was just confused. Maybe she was still half-asleep, or maybe partially sedated, but she didn't take the slightest bit of my hint. It didn't occur to her that she should have been caring for her own child. She just took up the baby and walked toward Libby's as if she were following some agreed-upon standard operating procedure.

"Eddy! Eddy!" Libby had been running up and down the sidewalk calling my name. "Eddy, you son of a bitch!" But of course she was the only one who could even guess at what was going on. I hadn't even been born yet. That wouldn't happen for another four years.

But Eddy the man, he was another matter. I stood in the shade of a neighbor's tree and watched, listening to her calling my name. She was up on the porch, then around the side of the house, and when she returned to the front yard, her hair was hanging down limply, her face was red, and she was worried.

That was when Libby finally spotted me. "Eddy!"

I leaned back against the tree. I wasn't exactly victorious. I hadn't accomplished anything with my mother. But at least I'd reminded Libby that I was watching and at least I'd been able to enjoy her frustration. I gave my old friend a little salute of the kind Walter Lee and her father seemed so fond of. She gave me the finger.

And then without hesitation, with a large helping of defiance aimed directly at me, if you want to know the truth, Libby stepped off the curb and met my mother in mid-street, where they completed the handoff of my brother.

———————

The day I broke into Libby's house, it was the Fourth of July. Out on the street, a neighborhood parade was passing and there were firecrackers and

Roman candles and bottle rockets and sparklers. Boys were running wild. Dogs were cowering under porches.

Libby may just as well have been in hiding, too. No one had seen her in about four days and I imagined that my mother must have been about to collapse with fatigue. Stan wasn't a good nighttime sleeper. The day I took him back to our house, my mother looked like she sorely needed that afternoon nap. Probably with a Tom Collins.

Where was that damn babysitter?

It beat me. Could this have been part of Libby's plan? Stan was bigger now. Was he ready to travel? Was she?

Meanwhile, in the street, the parade was on and new moms were pushing baby carriages and waving to their friends on the sidewalk, and dads with cigarettes in their mouths were guiding older brothers and sisters making wobbling progress on bicycles decorated with crepe paper. The colors were basically red and white and blue but with a liberal dose of any other color that happened to be in the house. You know kids. Not always picky, but once they like something, very insistent.

On the sidewalk, a teenage girl was attempting "The Stars and Stripes Forever" on her clarinet. I sighed. There should have been an accordion. But there was no Alvin Peacock to play. Just like I hadn't seen Libby, I hadn't seen my neighbor in days.

A kid on a pogo stick passed, followed by a troop of Boy Scouts bearing flags and marching with as much military precision as they could muster. A dozen or so veterans, happy to be out from under military discipline and back in the civilian world, wore their old uniforms for the occasion but only vaguely attempted a march. They waved and grinned and hollered back to the cheers of their neighbors.

And at the very end of the procession, like Santa Claus in a Christmas parade, came a guy pulling a child's red wagon filled with a case or two of beer buried in about fifteen pounds of ice. He'd hand a can to a spectator, punch a couple of triangular holes using his church-key can opener, receive handshakes from the men or kisses from the women, and move on. This guy was giving Mr. Peacock a run for his money in the friendliness department, but the field was wide open. Where was that former sailor? Then the man walked right by me, as if I weren't there either.

But I was there. I was in the time of my brother's infancy more intimately than many of the other times I'd seen, swallowed for the moment by the impossible youth of all these people, especially by my parents, radiant with their son in spite of their newborn exhaustion—maybe carried by euphoria over and beyond exhaustion—entirely and completely in a state I'd never seen them in before. It was a state I would never see them in again, including after my own birth.

Stan was their first, and everything was all very wonderful. I'd been there with Lizzie and I knew the playfulness and optimism and forward-looking excitement, an excitement made even more intense on the day I was seeing now, this patriotic holiday of lingering postwar euphoria and relief from the world's exhaustion.

It was wonderful, and then it was not.

All at once, I couldn't take it any longer.

Either Libby would steal the baby or he'd later be hit and killed by a car. My parents had no way of knowing, and I couldn't tell them. But I was Eddy. I just had to know.

Now where was that damn babysitter?

Not at home, I'd bet, so it would be safe for me to enter. I didn't know how to stop Libby, but I couldn't wait any longer for opportunities.

I shouldn't have been surprised when I found the back door unlocked. In those days, that's the way people left things. Presumed safe, though I did think about booby traps. When we were kids, Libby and I often plotted to put a bucket of water on top of a slightly ajar door. We must have seen it in a movie or a comic somewhere, and it seemed like it would be a grand trick on whoever pushed open the door. Except we'd never actually done it.

Anyway, that was the old Libby. But I did expect the new Libby somewhere. Waiting to ensnare or confront me.

I was startled one time. There was a rapping at the front door, followed by a tapping at a front window. I imagined Walter Lee peering in.

But it wasn't Walter Lee and it wasn't Libby. It was her landlord, the guy who'd been pulling the wagonload of beer. It seemed I wasn't the only one looking for his tenant. The first of the month, rent day, had come and gone. But Libby wasn't home, and I wasn't about to answer. Eventually he turned away without knocking more and apparently without seeing me. He was descending the porch steps and calling to a friend about wanting or needing or buying more beer. Something about beer. And I could hear more fireworks and more shouting and laughing. Between gaps in the window curtains I could glimpse flashes of children running.

Where was that damn babysitter?

Inside the house, it was so quiet, it was so still, and all the baby things were in their places, not in the original packaging, that's true, but lined up in rows on a table, clothes organized by size and toys standing neatly waiting for their new home.

Libby had been gone for how long? I wandered into the kitchen. The windows were shut tight and the place was beastly hot. I opened the back door and let it stand open. Any food left out on the counters would have gone bad in the July heat. Bananas black, fruit flies buzzing. But there were no full bowls or plates. Nothing in the refrigerator either. It was as if no one had ever been here. Or as if someone were on the verge of leaving.

That seemed very true. Libby's suitcase was spread open on her bed, half-packed. And sticking out from underneath, half-hidden and pinned down by the suitcase's corner as if she'd been afraid it might blow away in the breeze from an open window, was Libby's bus ticket. It was dated July 3. The day before.

I went scrambling for a calendar.

There was a wall calendar laid flat on the kitchen table, next to the toys. I'd missed it once. It hadn't seemed important. Now it looked like Libby had been studying and scheduling. The page was laid open to June.

I flipped back a month. Libby had drawn a red circle around May 12. This was my brother's birthday. Turning pages in the other direction, I passed June, where there were no marks, and I flipped over to July. No marks.

Oh.

There should have been.

In a kitchen drawer, I found the red pen Libby had been using. I unscrewed the cap, drew a little squiggle on a page corner to make sure the pen wasn't dry, and when I knew the ink would flow, I put a big circle around July 1. Libby's birthday.

Visit the past, yes. Touch the past, yes. But you can't live two simultaneous lives. You have only one.

I closed the door quietly as I left the house. With no present day to return to, a present where her body had died, this Libby essence I'd been chasing had taken the only path available. The older Libby lived out her time and handed off to the Libby I knew.

I'd leave the house and the toys for the landlord to clean up. Or my parents. I remembered some of these toys from my own childhood. A cap pistol. A blue stuffed rabbit that by the time I knew it had long since ceased being blue. Stan had loved that thing.

And *Make Way for Ducklings* was always one of my favorite books.

In the evening of the next day, at just about the time the dads of the neighborhood were returning home from work, the kids were outside burning off the last of their energy before coming inside, and the moms were taking a break between dinner preparation and corralling the family to sit together for the meal, a big lumbering Cadillac pulled into the Peacocks' driveway. It wasn't a convertible—that would be a dozen years in the future, as would the tragedy it brought—but the sedan was showy transportation nonetheless. It pulled to a stop with a toot of the horn: shave-and-a-haircut-two-bits.

The scene was still for a moment, as if the people inside were collecting themselves or deciding how they should emerge. Finally, from behind the wheel came Mr. Peacock. He trotted around the car's front end and opened the passenger door. Mrs. Peacock swung both feet onto the driveway but remained seated, awkwardly holding a baby wrapped in a pink blanket. She extended her arms and aimed the child head first at her husband. Mr. Peacock cradled the bundle, but the couple seemed uncertain about how to handle this newness. Once his wife was standing beside him, Mr. Peacock quickly handed the baby back. He reached through to the car's backseat, extracted a suitcase, and slammed the door.

The new threesome proceeded slowly up the front walk, eyes on the baby more than on their progress or destination, but by now the neighbors had seen them and by now they also wanted a part in the homecoming. From next door and across the street, they appeared and they stopped the new family. They ogled the newborn and breathed in her baby smell and waited for a chance to hold her. That honor went to my parents, who'd been the first to arrive.

As my mother held the baby safely in the crook of her elbow, resting her head against upper arm and breast the way mothers know to do, my father reached into their baby carriage and pulled out my brother. He held Stan under the armpits, dangling like a puppet. Or a cat, the way Libby had liked to dangle Ike. "Look what we've got," he announced. "Twins almost!"

And Mr. Peacock replied, in a high-pitched voice: "I'm Mary Elizabeth. Can Stanley come out and play?"

Everyone guffawed, and my mother leaned over toward Mrs. Peacock and said loudly over the racket: "We'll share babysitters after I find a new one."

My father set my brother back in his carriage and clapped Mr. Peacock on the back. I'd seen this guffawing and backslapping before at the porch party where the men had met, and I had to smile at mannerisms and habits repeating themselves.

The new father began handing out cigars. Each had a pink band with a little white stork on it, and all the men respectfully left those in place as they made a big show of taking small bites from one end and striking matches, then an even greater show of big puffing as they lit the things.

When the men were set, Mr. Peacock turned to the assembled children and commenced handing out cigars of pink bubblegum. He began with the girls, who seemed a little perplexed. They rolled the cigars over in their fingers and took small bites as they'd seen their fathers do. Then he turned to the boys: "Here you are, girls!"

The boys bristled and they complained. They stood up straight and looked at each other to see what their pals were going to do. One or two made tentative noises about refusing. But in the end they all took the bubblegum cigars. All took big bites. Some chewed the whole thing.

The boys ignored the girls and the girls ignored them back. The parents gossiped and made plans to get together for barbecues, and they all cooed at the new baby girl, who was sleeping. My baby brother woke and started making peeping sounds. A neighbor kid stuck his face into the carriage, emerged, and shrugged in the direction of his friends. My mother handed the baby girl to one of her friends and took up her boy. Mr. Peacock kissed his sleeping daughter on the forehead. The family turned and resumed its progression toward their house.

And that is where I left them.

EPILOGUE

The child is father to the man.

WILLIAM WORDSWORTH

LIZZIE

The day I came around asking my parents and Tim about what happened back before I was born and when I was a baby, I think they were surprised. They seemed to believe they'd been keeping a secret.

But for as long as I can remember, they'd drink those Tom Collins cocktails, and pieces of their story would come out. I knew all about the baseball. I used to take it down from the mantel and try to read those old timey autographs. I knew about that pendant watch. One time I stole it out of my dad's desk. For a couple of years, I kept it rolled up in a pair of socks in my drawer. Every so often I'd take it out and pin it on my shirt.

I knew that Tim had gone away for a while. He'd been all over the world taking pictures. I'd seen them in magazines and art galleries. He liked people in strange places. Strange, old places.

I knew there'd been another friend who'd also gone away, and that she'd never returned.

Some days when I was younger, I'd climb out my bedroom window and sit on the porch roof, wondering about all of this. Or I'd walk around the yard. I'd check on the garden and check out that dead dog's grave. When Ike died back when I was nine or ten, we buried him next to the dog. I was seeing some kind of pet continuity, but I could never fit the rest of it together.

Now I'm twenty-two. I've graduated from architecture school, I'm about to begin an apprenticeship in my parents' firm, and I feel I'm entitled to know their story. My story, that's different. They don't know what I know. My dad is always talking about the way cicadas are singing and lantana is blooming and rainstorms are coming and, you know, he's right about all that. I feel it, too, though I already know that these don't show only one story. We each have our own story. We each have our own nature. And we each have our own truths.

"So you're okay now?" I ask my dad after he finishes telling his part. I know he feels more than the sweet little scene was suggesting at the end, the one with all those babies and families together on a warm summer evening.

I know because I'm as observant as he is. I'm Daddy's Girl. I've followed him around ever since I was little. Now that I've heard his story about the night I was born, I'll have to get him to walk me from the creek back to the house. Retrace his steps. He'll do it, too. It's not that he's been consciously trying to teach me these things. He was just always overcompensating for not being there at the hospital. But I'd been paying attention and I'd been learning.

Jeez, you know what he used to do? Whenever a big storm came, he'd turn to face the west where the weather came from. He'd silently stare as the sky got darker and darker, until the streetlights came on like it was night. Then he'd get into his old truck and coast down the driveway. He'd try to be quiet so my mom wouldn't hear him, though she probably did. Anyway, when he hit the street he'd pop the clutch and crank the engine and head for the low place in the creek where that man killed himself.

And you know what? When he didn't have anyone to leave me with, he'd take me along. He probably thought I wouldn't notice anything. I was just a baby when he started, but he kept it up for years. He did it even after I'd gone to school and he'd gone back to work. By then I did notice. I noticed a lot.

I noticed when he said one time that he was like Mr. Peacock, that they'd both been hit and hit again, that they'd tried to help and failed, and that they'd failed so badly that everything only became worse.

It made sense. Who else was he going to feel like? His own father, who ran? My dad wasn't crazy. Walter Lee? The guy manipulated my dad and then spat him out when that nutso jumping-in-the-flood plan to save the hanged man didn't work.

I noticed when my dad said he and his neighbor shared survivor's guilt. That was no good. Sucked, actually. All it got them was a place at the fast-running water.

And I noticed all the things he took with him whenever he drove down there. Bent nails from the porch gutter, tucked into his shirt pocket. His sketchbooks. Sometimes that burned-up doll, even though it creeped me out and I asked him not to. Always that old photo of the nurses. He'd put that one carefully on the seat beside him, between him and me, and I'd look at it the whole way out of town.

My dad called these trips his "woolgathering." He'd sit quietly, parked beside the flooding creek. Sometimes he'd stare out the window for the longest time, doing and saying nothing. If the weather had cleared and the water wasn't too high, he might add drawings of cypress knees to his sketchbook full of tomatoes.

One time, when it wasn't raining, he let me get out of the truck to pick flowers. I must have been about seven. I guess he trusted me. But he scared me to death. He made me cry. Because when I returned from the meadow, his truck was sitting out on the flooded road, halfway across, with water swirling around his tires.

He backed out. I climbed in. I asked what he'd been doing. He told me not to worry. He'd done this before when I hadn't been with him. He'd never been hurt. He'd just been waiting.

Waiting for what? Well, now that he and the others have told me their stories, here's what I think.

I think he wanted to hurt himself. I think he wanted to scare himself. I think he'd been watching the water come up the flood gauge and he'd been seeing that dream or whatever it was. The one with the man waving his arms through the window of a floating car. The one where the man stopped and gave him a salute. And then let himself drown.

I think my dad needed to find something from his own lifetime that was strong enough and painful enough to keep him from going back in time. I think he knew he didn't need Walter Lee anymore. He could go muck about in the past any time he wanted. Touring cars and exhibition Yankee baseball games, sailors going off to war and returning, boys with crewcuts and their mock outrage when a neighbor called them girls, these are all very appealing. And a best friend who disappears is very compelling. My dad always said he had no choice but to chase all of those things, all of those pieces of the past. He also knew he shouldn't.

In the end, my dad hadn't needed to stop Libby. She just came full circle, back to her birth. He did need to stop himself.

He did seem to make that work. As far as I know, he never went again. But that was him. I'm me.

"So you're going to the gallery?" I ask them. Tim has another photo show and it's a big deal. We usually all go together, but I'm taking a pass tonight. I need to do some thinking.

I look at Tim and my dad and my mom. "I'm good here," I tell them.

Everyone nods slowly and everyone keeps their eyes on me. Sure, why not, of course. Life has been good since the past went away.

And finally, they're out the door.

"Bye."

Alone now, I toss the baseball a couple of times. I'm thinking I should throw it through the window, just like that sailor with his beer bottle, but I put the ball back on its stand.

In the mirror behind the ball, I see myself. I'm twenty-two. I know I said that, but I'm very aware of my age. I'm about half what my dad was when he first met Walter Lee. And he was half the age of Walter Lee. Is this a coincidence? I'll have to ponder the math and its meaning.

Because there's this boy, and he's sweeping up in a grocery store. He seems like he's nice. I've been seeing him since I was a kid, too, about his same age. He's just doing this little job, listening to the adults, keeping his mouth shut and his head down. It's a long time ago.

Anyway, this boy keeps sweeping and sweeping and the grocer keeps talking to all his buddies and not doing a thing to help. The boy has swept up a big pile of corn silk and husks and a few cherries and other things that have fallen on the floor. He's finished now and the grocer comes over and slaps the boy on the back and gives him some kind of paper.

It doesn't look like much, but now I know that it is. I recognize the grocer as that big guy who ended up in the tree and the boy as my dad's great uncle Hugh who ended up nuts and the paper as a ticket to the hanging that ruined his life. This was the beginning of that long chain of events that killed the boy Stan, who should have been my uncle. The chain their friend Libby was trying to break when she disappeared.

"The boy's a man," said the grocer. I remember that from my dad's story because it sounded so crazy. "It's something he needs to see." I remember that because it was so flat wrong.

Now I do what with this information?

What really?

I'm staring through the window into the night. It was all so long ago. To me, the people I'd heard about over the years were mostly just names. I'd always thought history was history, that it was nothing personal.

But now I'm wondering if I didn't have it exactly wrong. I'm wondering if it's always personal.

And I'm wondering if it's my turn.

All I have to do is listen for the sounds, smell the scents, feel the moving air, and I'll see everything.

Except in my own way, I've already done that, haven't I?

I was right there. In my mom's pregnancy. I was there the whole time.

Which makes me what, our new red thread? It's looking that way. I know that whole long-ago story, like Walter Lee. I know how that story turns out, what it does to our family and friends, like my dad and my mom and Tim.

I know the joys and the knowledge and the obligations. I know the fears and dangers and horrors.

I'm the last of the McBrides, you know.

I could go back and grab the ticket. Stop it all. Save the boy. Maybe some others, too. Yes, I could. I really could.

END

ACKNOWLEDGMENTS

If writing a novel has a red thread other than its author, this project certainly had one in Frank Coffey. My long-time collaborator on nonfiction books and longer-time friend, novelist Frank provided insight and advice that began soon after I started writing and continued to publication.

But a book is a complex fabric. Early, Henry Bloomstein helped define the motivation of characters and the structure of the story. The staff of the Austin History Center helped fill in details with contemporary accounts of long-ago floods, public hangings, and barnstorming New York Yankees baseball.

Readers were generous with specific and general comments: Chris Sneden, who talked with me about science, and Gail Sneden; Bill Forbes, who talked with me about science fiction, and Joan Forbes; Lynda West, who left me an English teacher's margin notes, and Michael West.

At first draft, Susan Wood waded through a too-long manuscript—but found helpful things to say anyway. At next-to-final draft, Holly Webber provided extensive and thoughtful notes—with a valuable copyedit.

My agent, Martha Millard, believed in this book and was professional, smart, tireless, and encouraging in finding it a home.

At Tyrus Books, Publisher Ben LeRoy also believed and turned *One Red Thread* into reality. Editor Ashley Myers spotted opportunities for improvement, and the book is better for her attention.

And always there was family. My late mother, Ruth Wood, a lifelong mystery enthusiast, read my work at age ninety-three and gave it her stamp of approval. My daughter, Emily Wood Jakobeit, survived starts and stops as I changed drafts and my mind, but remained enthusiastic about her old man's scribbling. Her husband, Brandon Jakobeit, also read and provided author photo and website design.

Critical to the entire process, my wife Laura read more pages more times than anyone else. Gently prodding with reminders of what appeals—and doesn't appeal—to readers, she became an indispensable red thread that kept me from losing my way in the past and present worlds I'd created.